THE AZTEC

Bill Vidal was born in Argentina and educated in England. He lived and worked in the USA, Latin America, the Middle East, South-East Asia and Europe before settling with his wife and twin children in East Kent. In recent years he has slowed down his business commitments to devote more time to writing and to his lifelong love for aeroplanes. He is the author of one previous novel, *The Clayton Account*.

Also by Bill Vidal

The Clayton Account

THE AZTEC

BILL VIDAL

arrow books

Published by Arrow Books 2010

1 3 5 7 9 10 8 6 4 2

Copyright © Bill Vidal 2010

First published in Great Britain in 2010 by
Arrow Books
The Random House Group Limited
20 Vauxhall Bridge Road, London, SW1V 2SA
www.rbooks.co.uk

Addresses for companies within The Random House Group Limited can be found at:
www.randomhouse.co.uk/offices.htm

The Random House Group Limited Reg. No. 954009

A CIP catalogue record for this book
is available from the British Library

ISBN 9780099534655

The Random House Group Limited supports The Forest Stewardship Council (FSC), the
leading international forest certification organisation. All our titles that are printed on
Greenpeace approved FSC certified paper carry the FSC logo. Our paper procurement
policy can be found at: www.rbooks.co.uk/environment

Mixed Sources
Product group from well-managed
forests and other controlled sources
www.fsc.org Cert no. TT-COC-2139
© 1996 Forest Stewardship Council

Typeset by Palimpsest Book Production Limited,
Grangemouth, Stirlingshire
Printed and bound in Great Britain by
CPI Cox & Wyman, Reading, RG1 8EX

For William and Victoria

'They will see their gold again like they see their own ears'
Joseph Stalin, December 1936

1936

1

In July 1936 the Spanish Army of Africa, under the command of General Francisco Franco, crossed the Straits of Gibraltar from Morocco to mainland Spain in the opening military operation of the Spanish Civil War.

Between August and October, Nationalist units shattered Republican resistance and reached the outskirts of Madrid. The universal belief that the capital was about to fall was shared by the Spanish government who decreed its own immediate removal to Valencia.

Of paramount consideration were measures to place the nation's gold reserves – then the fourth largest in the world – out of Franco's reach. Several options were contemplated and eventually President Negrín authorised their removal to the safety of loyalist Murcia.

The daunting task of organising this massive movement was given to Bank of Spain Governor Francisco Méndez Aspe, secretly assisted by Alexander Orlov, head of the Soviet NKVD in Spain. Four of the Bank's *claveros* – custodians of the vaults – supervised a hundred carpenters, metalworkers and locksmiths as strongboxes were opened and their contents – almost entirely gold coins – were counted and placed into 10,000 purpose-made wooden boxes.

Working round the clock for several days and nights, the Workers' Socialist Party's Mechanised Brigade, supported by a hundred *carabineros* and militias, drove their trucks from the Banco de España to Madrid's Mediodía Railway Station (now known as Atocha Station) where the boxes were loaded onto a special train bound for the naval city of Cartagena.

On reaching the Mediterranean port the Spanish Navy transferred the boxes to their arsenal at La Algameca fortress from where 2,100 boxes were sent to Paris as payment for assistance and materiel supplied to the Republic by France.

On the twenty-first of October four Russian ships arrived in Cartagena. A Soviet tank brigade quartered in nearby Archena worked for three days and nights loading the cases onto these vessels amid sporadic attacks on the naval base by the Luftwaffe. On the twenty-fifth of October the four freighters sailed for the Ukraine. On board was a consignment of 7,900 boxes of gold coins weighing 510 tons.

Three ships arrived in Odessa on the second of November. The fourth, the *Kursk*, docked eight days later. An armoured train, guarded by a detachment of the 173rd NKVD Rifle Regiment, had been deployed by Stalin to collect the precious cargo.

Thus the bulk of Spain's gold was delivered to Moscow. Stalin promptly added up the entire cost of supporting the Spanish Republic to date and, by applying distorted exchange rates, halved the value of the Spanish peseta against the

Soviet rouble. That measure and a little creative accounting ensured that Spain's bank balance in the USSR had reduced to zero by the summer of 1938.

That same year three significant events concerning the gold took place: Orlov, who had returned to his post in Spain, was recalled to Moscow, but fearing execution defected to the United States. Four Financial Commissars who had counted the gold – Grinko, Krestinski, Margolis and Kagan – were exiled to Siberia. And the Spanish *claveros* – Candela, Padín, Gonzales and Velazco – who had been refused permission to leave the Soviet Union after delivering their treasure, were finally granted exit visas and went off to start new lives in the Americas.

Many Spanish documents that had been kept secret began to surface after Franco's death in 1975. A further twenty years would pass before they could be compared with their Russian counterparts. It emerged that Orlov, while still in Spain, had signed a receipt for 7,900 boxes – which tallied with the number removed from Madrid.

But the consignment note signed by Méndez Aspe in Cartagena was for 7,800 boxes, as was the quantity acknowledged by Orlov – and countersigned by the Commissars – in Odessa.

The hundred missing boxes, if they were found today, would be worth over two hundred million dollars.

1973

2

In pre-Columbian days, before the adventurer Pizarro was blinded by his lust for gold, Inca ruled the high plains of the Cordillera. In Portillo, ten thousand feet up in the Andes range, close to the border between Argentina and Chile, they still tell the legend of the Inca Illi Yunqui's tortured soul.

Just as the twentieth-century elite has gathered in the stunning setting of Portillo for the winter season since the 1950s, so Inca came in summer six hundred years earlier to enjoy his Nascu, a royal mountain banquet where the emperor and his court feasted close to God.

It was during a Nascu that Illi Yunqui's love, Princess Kora-llé, fell down a precipice and lost her life. They say that Inca's grief shook the mountain. No tomb could be constructed within his empire, proclaimed the descendant of the Sun God, which could justly represent the beauty of Kora-llé.

He ordered her body wrapped in the finest linen and, gathering the Imperial Court around a lake, lowered his beloved into its icy waters. As the princess's mortal remains disappeared into the depths, the legend tells us, the water turned an emerald green that exactly matched the colour of Kora-llé's eyes.

Since then, on full-moon nights, it is said that a wailing cry of anguish echoes above Inca Lake, stirring its waters, as Inca's mournful soul voices his eternal lament.

It was that same moon that lit up the road on a cold October night when the dark red Peugeot drove up the mountain. Barely a month had passed since Pinochet had put an end to Chilean democracy.

Some would argue that it was Allende's Marxist regime and its disregard for the nation's institutions that had brought about the catastrophic consequences, but for a whole generation of Chileans this would be their first experience of life under a military regime.

Now, as the army consolidated its position throughout the country, curfews were in force and travel was severely restricted. The road from Santiago to the border crossing was particularly out of bounds.

But the occupants of the Peugeot had no problems getting through roadblocks. Though they wore civilian clothes, their ID cards produced an immediate salute and the barriers were raised to let them pass. As they approached Portillo, the luxury hotel's distinctive blue and yellow façade came into sight. The car was driven by an army sergeant with a major alongside. In the back, a captain from the army nursing corps sat beside two infants.

When the party pulled up at the resort, porters quickly emerged and gathered their luggage. The hotel had been closed to tourists since the September coup. Roads close to the border were restricted to military use.

The nursing officer and her charges disappeared to her room. Her dinner would be ordered from room service. The sergeant decamped to staff quarters and Major Sánchez to his rendezvous in the hotel bar. A log fire projected its warmth from the large stone fireplace that took up most of one wall.

In happier times this room would have been packed with holidaymakers, reliving the day's skiing in a multitude of languages, their faces displaying the outline of UV goggles against the inescapable marks of high-altitude sun.

Tonight the bar was a gloomy place, the staff ill at ease with their unaccustomed clientele, the selection of food and drink on offer noticeably diminished after the recent economic crisis.

Sánchez eased himself into a leather armchair and ordered a glass of wine and a Cohiba. Cuban cigars were one luxury the Allende years had left behind.

An hour and a half later a young couple strode in. They too wore civilian clothes but the man's haircut, like his walk and his shiny shoes, was military.

Sánchez stood up and all three shook hands.

'Sorry we are late.' The female visitor spoke first, 'Roads are still icy on the other side. Everything in order?'

She had blonde hair tied back in a bun. She wore a dark blue ski jacket and smart grey jeans tucked into fleece-lined leather boots. She said her name was Ana Barros – which was almost certainly an alias – and it was clear that she was in charge. Her tall dark-haired companion, dressed in a tweed jacket and cords, was introduced simply as Bandini.

'Of course,' replied the Chilean. 'Things in this country will work properly from now on.'

The Argentines nodded their agreement. It will soon be the same way in our country, they reckoned. This Perón nonsense could only end up depositing the country in the Army's lap. We won't need bullets, they thought, we'll just take over by popular acclaim.

'We should follow your example,' ventured Barros. But they had not crossed the Andes to discuss politics. 'Perhaps we can finalise everything tonight?'

The waiter came over.

'Drinks?' Sánchez offered.

They both shook their heads, 'Later, perhaps.'

'Very well.' Sánchez stood up. 'Shall we go somewhere more private?'

They walked up to the second floor where the Army had reserved a suite. The visitors sat on the sofa and Sánchez placed two red-covered files on the coffee table before easing himself down onto a large armchair opposite. He gestured for the visitors to pick up the files. Each bore the word *Hamelin* on the cover, followed by a four-digit number.

They studied the contents in silence, then swapped dossiers and continued reading. It was all there: dates of birth, medical certificates, blood groups, photographs.

'Orphans?' asked the woman visitor.

Sánchez nodded. They all knew what that meant. Three thousand Chileans had already died in the first month of the revolution. Left-wingers, either by belief or association. Their children would sometimes go to relatives, sometimes to orphanages if they were not claimed.

As in every other country, Chilean social services carried oversubscribed adoption lists. The middle classes liked white babies. Most abandoned babies were half Indian at best. White babies with dead parents were highly desirable.

No comebacks, no consciences in turmoil, no changes of heart to disturb a family's life at a later date.

Tonight's babies were top of the line. A light-skinned blue-eyed girl with a lovely smile and a dark-haired jade-eyed boy. Both of them strong and healthy.

'Are they related?' asked Bandini.

'No,' Sánchez assured him and Bandini nodded approvingly.

'Can we see them now?' Barros asked.

Sánchez nodded, picked up the phone and dialled an internal number. Moments later he stood up and let Nurse Captain Baila in. She carried a baby in each arm.

Barros took the girl first and held her up in front of her with both hands, arms extended. The baby smiled and Barros smiled back, then brought her close and kissed the child affectionately on both cheeks. She repeated the exercise with the boy who looked a little frightened. Barros gave him a maternal hug. She nodded approval and returned the children to the nurse.

As soon as the nurse left the suite they got down to business. Bandini opened his briefcase, took out a bulging envelope and handed it to Sánchez. While the Chilean counted the money the Argentine officer got down to work.

He laid Ana Barros's passport on the table and on the 'children' page he carefully fitted both photographs, taken from Major Sánchez's files.

Their names were inscribed as Juan José and María Luisa Bandini Barros. They were presented as twins and the date of birth they'd been given made them eleven months old.

Bandini then produced a Policía Federal stamp and carefully applied it to the passport page, making sure that it partly covered the photographs. Finally, with another rubber stamp, he added the signature of a Section Chief in the Documentation Department.

His work complete, he passed the document to Barros for approval, then replaced it in his case. Moments later the trio descended to the hotel restaurant. They ate soup, followed by baked cannelloni, and drank a Maipo Valley cabernet.

Sánchez spoke calmly but convincingly about the new Chile that had just been born. The Argentines nodded and suggested that their own country's redemption could not be far away. They had heard rumours within the armed forces.

They never discussed their dastardly business because neither thought of it as dastardly or even as a business. Granted, money had to change hands, but it was an issue of expenses. These operations were not cheap to set up: many people were involved – some of them, admittedly, for purely pecuniary reasons.

But for the likes of Bandini and Barros it was a calling. It was plucking an unfortunate child from a perverted atheist household and giving it a new life in the bosom of an upright Christian family.

Tonight, as soon as dinner was finished, Mr and Mrs Bandini and their two children would drive to Caracoles, a few minutes up the road, and ease their car onto the *lanzadera,* the open-carriage, narrow-gauge train that would take them through the La Cumbre tunnel into Argentina.

In summer they could have avoided the *lanzadera* and driven all the way, crossing the border at 12,600 feet along the Christ the Redeemer Pass. There, on the line that demarcates the two nations' limits, stands the twenty-five-foot-tall statue of Jesus Christ. He holds a thirty-foot cross alongside him and with his raised right hand bestows the love of Christ upon all Andean peoples.

The inscription on the statue's base proclaims that: *'These mountains shall crumble before Argentines and Chileans shall break the peace they swore at the feet of Christ the Redeemer.'*

But on this cold spring night the Bandinis would not see the white-capped mountain summits. They would instead enter Argentina through a dark, dank tunnel. They would arrive in the pretty Norwegian-styled village of Las Cuevas and spend the night there.

The *Gendarmes*, Argentina's border police, would inspect their travel documents perfunctorily – this, after all, was an army family, not a group of Marxist escapees.

In the morning the Bandinis would drive the remaining two hundred kilometres to Plumerillo Air Force base in Mendoza for their flight to the Campo de Mayo military enclave in Buenos Aires. That same day the stolen children would be quietly delivered to their adoptive parents in their respective homes.

But if tonight the eerie calm should be pierced by Inca's wail, perhaps he might be weeping not just for Kora-llé but also for the infamy that was taking place within the southern reaches of his long-lost empire.

2004

3

'Jesús.' Nurse Miriam raised her voice. 'There's someone here to see you.'

The old man looked up from his well-worn wicker chair, uninterested.

'I want a coffee,' he said, ignoring his visitor.

'At eleven,' she replied sternly.

'Bad for me, eh?' He chuckled.

Jack smiled. Jesús was in his eighties, by all accounts.

'Señor Hadley,' she insisted, pronouncing the name 'adlay', '*Profesór* Ad-lay.' She was plump with short spiky hair, and wore a starched white uniform that showed off her smooth ebony skin.

Jesús tilted his head, his eyes focused, appraising the caller. Foreign clothes, he noted at once, taking in the striped cotton shirt, khaki chinos and soft leather moccasins.

'From La Habana?'

'No.' Jack Hadley remained standing, smiling affably at the man he'd finally traced. 'No, from Spain.'

19

'You are not Spanish,' Jesús stated.

'I'm English, Mr Florin, but I've come from Salamanca.'

'So you are a real professor, then?' Jesús's voice was raspy and somewhat short of breath, yet clear and authoritative.

'Yes.'

Jesús tucked in the blanket on his lap and stared out towards the sea.

'I was there,' he reminisced. 'Did you know that?'

Hadley nodded.

'I didn't finish.'

'I know.'

Jesús looked up at the tall green-eyed stranger with new interest. He appeared to be in his thirties and he didn't look English: his skin was too tanned, his unruly hair too dark and he wore no socks. The English always wore socks, even in the tropics.

'Sit here,' he said, pointing at the spare chair. There were only two chairs and a matching coffee table on the veranda. A hundred metres of sandy sun-scorched lawn separated them from a clear emerald ocean where the North Atlantic met the Gulf of Mexico. By the seashore a man folded a net over the side of his boat. The rich aroma of wet tropical vegetation drifted in with the morning breeze as the early showers moved on towards the continent.

'Why are you here?'

'I'm a historian. I'm writing about the war.'

'Which war?'

Hadley had forgotten for a moment. Florin had been in more than one.

'Sorry. The Spanish Civil War, Mr Florin.'

'And what do you know about wars, young man?' Florin fixed his eyes on Hadley's, challenging him.

'I try to learn.'

'What can I tell you that hasn't been written already.'
It wasn't even a question.

'I write about battles, Mr Florin. That's my field.'

'Which one?'

'Madrid.'

'I was there too, at the Casa de Campo.' Jesús nodded.
'Not for long, mind you.'

'Oh?' said Hadley, surprised. 'I understood that the
Eleventh was there . . .'

'I was sent for.' Jesús interrupted. 'Mercer sent for me.'
He frowned. 'And I never went back to the front. Not that
front.'

Hadley remained silent.

Jesús lowered his voice, 'Tell her you want a coffee.'

Hadley walked back into the modest living room and
opened the hallway door. Nurse Miriam had been standing
next to it and winced in surprise.

'A coffee. Now, please,' Hadley asked. She strode off
purposefully.

'Where did you go after Madrid?'

'To Russia,' Jesús said matter-of-factly. 'With the gold.'

Hadley hadn't expected that.

'You went with the Bank of Spain's shipment?'

'Isn't that why you are here?' Jesús looked up, daring
him to deny it.

'No . . .' Hadley hesitated. 'No, not at all . . . It's just
that I'd . . .'

'Well, all the others wanted to know. Even Camilo and
Ché. But there's nothing to know.'

The nurse came in with the coffee and eyed both men
suspiciously.

21

'Do you have a car?' Florin asked his visitor.

'Yes.'

'We will go to lunch, then. Tomorrow. You can pick me up.'

'I'll have to get you permission,' Miriam interjected.

'I have my own Lavrenti Beria to look after me, see?'

'Don't be rude,' she protested.

Florin laughed.

The History Department arranged a small reception to bid Hadley goodbye. Dr Asencio said a few kind words and spoke of his country's growing academic links with her European friends.

'We do, of course, share too much history,' he told the assembled members, 'to presume we can move forward our separate ways. The old continent's history is our history too, and Hispanic history in the New World began right here,' he pointed his index finger at the floor, 'on these very shores.'

Hadley thanked the department head sincerely and joined him in a toast – to Cuba, to Spain and to friendship.

Dr Ascencio steered Hadley towards the oak table that doubled as a bar and poured him a fresh rum.

'Let me introduce you,' he said, extending his left arm towards an approaching figure. He was slightly shorter than Hadley, perhaps in his forties, elegantly dressed in a linen suit which did not conceal an athletic frame. 'Aquiles Sierra, from our Ministry of the Interior.'

'Professor Hadley, we are honoured by your visit, sir.' Sierra shook hands firmly. 'Such tragic times your country is passing through. Your family is all right, we hope?' The voice was warm and mellow but the eyes looked cold. Florin had warned him.

'Yes, thank you,' Hadley replied, taking in the man's tinted glasses and expensive watch. 'I have no family in Spain, Mr Sierra, just me.'

Three days after Hadley had left for Cuba, a train had been blown up by terrorists as it approached Madrid's Atocha Station. Mercedes had been in Madrid – she had driven Jack to Barajas Airport and planned to remain in the capital a few days to shop and visit friends.

When Hadley heard, he'd frantically called her cellphone and every acquaintance who might know her whereabouts until he found her, safely back in Salamanca. 'I left after the bombs,' she said, yawning at three in the morning. 'Between the police sirens and the election crowds, Madrid was unbearable.'

Hadley was sure that Sierra knew all that. Right down to the fact that Jack's estranged wife Jenny lived in London with their children, and that he shared a home with Mercedes in Castile.

'We don't seem to be safe anywhere these days, do we?' Sierra frowned to mark his concern, then shook his head to clear it of disturbing issues.

'So, tell me, Professor,' he asked more light-heartedly. 'Have you enjoyed your visit?'

'Enormously,' replied Hadley sincerely.

'What do you think of our illustrious hero? You met him, I hope?' As if he did not know, thought Jack, starting to feel uncomfortable in Sierra's company.

'Yes. Twice. A lovely man. Truly.'

Sierra tilted his well-groomed head back and let out a roar of contrived laughter.

'I've heard him called many things! But . . . lovely? Oh, you English!' he exclaimed in mock astonishment.

Hadley smiled and shrugged his shoulders.

'We had lunch together. He tells wonderful stories.'

'About our country?'

'Yes, and his life before.'

'Yes.' Sierra's expression turned serious. 'So much life before. I expect we shall never hear all of it.' He stared at Hadley. 'Don't you think?'

'I'm sure you are right,' said Hadley, wanting the conversation to come to an end.

'I'm told it's his time in Spain that interests you.' Sierra's raised eyebrows indicated this was a question.

'Yes.' Hadley felt on safer ground. 'The winter of '36 – the fighting to hold Madrid.'

'And did you get your answers, Professor?'

'Some,' he replied. 'But, like you said, I don't expect we'll ever get to hear the full story.'

'No,' Sierra said with finality. Hadley felt a chill down his spine. 'Will you see him again?'

'Tomorrow,' Hadley admitted. 'I promised to call again before I leave.'

Sierra nodded, lit a cigar and walked away without saying another word.

They had lunched in Varadero. It had been Florin's choice.

'It's where the tourists go,' he'd said louder than necessary, for Nurse Miriam's benefit. '*Food* must be good.'

Hadley drove east in Dr Asencio's Lada and cast Florin a sideways glance. When he had first seen him, the previous day, he'd seemed frail. But today he had walked out of the bungalow on his own, upright, with an unexpected spring in his step. He sported a beige wrap across his shoulders and on his head a black beret, worn straight and casually brimmed in the unassuming manner of a Basque peasant, rather than the arrogant tilt of the revolutionary.

'It's pure vicuña,' Florin said, catching Jack's eye and feeling a corner of the wrap between his thumb and index finger. 'Ménem gave it to me.'

'Ménem?' Hadley was surprised. 'I wouldn't have thought he was your type,' he added jokingly.

'They call this a poncho in Argentina, you know?' Florin ignored the political probe.

'I thought ponchos had a hole in the middle,' said Hadley, playing along.

'They do where I come from.' Florin paused, then said, 'But the same words have different meanings. Even in the same language in the same continent.'

Jack knew Florin was playing no longer.

Florin's story had fascinated Hadley long before they'd met. Jesús María Florin del Valle was a Mexican by birth but very much a Spaniard by heritage. In Mexican terms he was closer to Cortéz than to Moctezuma. He'd been brought up by stern Jesuits in Veracruz and then at the Order's schools in Madrid. Like many a young man of his class he had shunned the privilege of birth and embraced the principles of socialism, but unlike most he had remained a socialist for the rest of his life. When the Spanish Civil War broke out, Florin was a second-year humanities student at Salamanca University and when André Marty organised the International Brigades, Florin joined their officer class. El Azteca, they called him, ironically. They loved names. El Campesino, La Pasionaria, Grishin, Tito, Orlov, Kolya. *Noms de guerre*.

When they reached the restaurant Jesús asked if they could sit outside on the raised lawned terrace, facing

Playa Azul. The beach was already busy with families on a day out. Cars streamed by in both directions. The waiter recognised Florin and made a fuss of him. The proprietor came out of the main dining room to shake hands and was introduced to Profesór Ad-Lay.

They ordered Cristal beers and a plate of shrimps to nibble on while the chef prepared a rice with clams.

'Madrid in '36, eh? It wasn't a proper battle, you know.'

Initially, Franco's troops moved fast. From the *Pronunciamiento* in July, his Army of Africa had raced through Andalucia and Extremadura. By October they had taken Talavera and Toledo and then they reached the edge of Madrid. And there they remained, on the outskirts, along the west bank of the Manzanares for almost three years until the city finally surrendered in March 1939.

'They thought it would be over by Christmas.'

Hadley didn't ask who.

'Everyone thought so.' Florin answered the unasked question. 'The fascists had stormed up.' He waved a hand upwards as if to illustrate Franco's northerly thrust. 'By the autumn of '36, Yagüe's *moros* were knocking on Madrid's doors.'

Hadley nodded silently. Like any good researcher he knew when to remain silent.

'But why do I tell you this, hey?' Florin laughed out loud. He had an infectious laugh that burst out suddenly, in staccato tones, then died just as quickly as it had come. People from other tables heard the laughter and smiled back hesitantly, as if in so doing they shared an intimacy with a living legend. 'You are the historian! You know the facts!'

'Yes,' Jack conceded. 'But what was it really like? I mean for the people involved in the fighting?'

'I told you,' replied Florin, pausing to sip his beer. 'Not at all like a battle. We set up positions along the river, on the Casa's eastern border. Marxist Workers' Party comrades and National Labour trade unionists requisitioned trucks and buses.

'Some covered the northern flank at the University, others went to defend their homes in Carabanchel. We had few uniforms and assorted weapons. In the beginning only our Brigades made an attempt at discipline.

'Some people,' Florin chuckled disdainfully, 'thought you could beat the Legion with the righteousness of our cause.'

The Casa de Campo, purchased by Phillip II in the sixteenth century and turned into a royal hunting ground, had been given to Madrid's people by the Republican government in 1931. Its four thousand acres on the city's western suburbs were planted with oak, ash and the very Spanish *encinas* that covered much of the gently undulating ground.

'You were already with the Brigades?' Hadley asked.

'Yes. The Eleventh and Twelfth were active. But you know how we got to Casa de Campo?'

Hadley shook his head.

'We took a tram! A tram! I almost expected the guard to sell me a ticket! Have you been there?'

'Yes.'

'Well, it wasn't very different then. Without the traders, that's all. Take them away and it's the same place.'

Dirt roads criss-crossed the estate, between the trees, around the hillocks. Where the nobility had hunted and the bourgeoisie had strolled, brother pitched against brother in a skirmishing, sniping war that lasted three years.

'Even our Government was ready to give up the city. They moved to Valencia, in haste.

'There was only one week of hard fighting.' Florin paused as if reminiscing, 'Around the University. Hand-to-hand. Nasty.' He smiled at Hadley. 'My loss of innocence, my virgin-soldier day. But we gave them their first bloody nose and they pulled back.

'Then it all stopped. Franco continued north, and the Madrid front remained static, one long line along the river.'

'With the Casa de Campo in the middle,' added Hadley.

Florin nodded. 'But we fought on all the same. We'd advance a bit, hidden by the trees and the natural contours. Just like the *moros* in Africa. They used the cover of the sand dunes to move in on their enemy. Did you know that? Well, they did the same at the Casa. And so did we. When we saw anyone we shot them, then pulled back and started all over again. I did away with a few of them that way.'

'*Moros?*'

'Fascists. Whatever their race. In between we played cards, sometimes we just walked back towards the *centro*, to a café, for a proper meal.'

Jack had already heard all this, even if it did sound different when the narrative was first-person.

'In the militias' – Florin smiled – 'some went home for the night. In the morning they came back. Most of the time. But, as I said, I didn't stay long.'

'When did you leave?'

'Must have been late October. Antonio came to the front as he did every day, then in the evening he ordered me to go with him.'

They had gone to Antonio Mercer's office at the impro-vised Brigade HQ. The Republican colonel was one of the few trained soldiers defending Madrid. Brought up in Cuba, he had returned to Spain in 1925 where he'd joined the

Communist Party but his revolutionary activities had resulted in exile in 1931. Back in Cuba he'd fought to bring down the Machado government before being spotted by the Soviets and sent to the Frunze military academy in Moscow.

'He told me to report to Barajas in the morning. The government wanted to put its gold reserves out of the fascists' reach. They were sending them to Odessa. I was to join one of the ships at an intermediate stop and travel with the gold.'

'Why you?' Hadley asked cautiously.

Florin shrugged.

'Maybe he liked me. Maybe he trusted me. I asked him later but he never said. We went on to became good friends, though.'

Lifelong friends, in fact. Hadley had done his homework on Florin – before and since Madrid had got involved. The Mexican would serve again under Mercer: at Jarama and Teruel, then at Leningrad, where the Galician reached the rank of general, and they would be reunited yet again in Cuba in 1959.

'I'm impressed by the volume of your work,' Florin said unexpectedly. 'Covadonga, Lepanto, Ayacucho. You seem to know your battles,' he granted. 'Perhaps you even know *something* about war.'

'Thank you.' Hadley could not help feeling flattered but did not wish to change the subject that had been so effortlessly brought to the fore. Neither did he wish to mention his own, albeit brief, experience of war.

'Were you the only *brigadista*?'

'Yes. One or two were regular army, but mostly they were militias,' Florin said. Then, without warning, he looked straight at Hadley, his face expressionless, and spoke in a changed tone of voice. 'But the people who sent you know all this.'

Hadley was briefly reprieved by the waiter's arrival. An iron pan, both handles held with tea towels, was paraded towards their table, steam rising, promising fresh tastes of the sea. Hadley busied himself moving plates and cutlery to make room. He avoided Florin's stare which remained fixed on the Englishman.

The waiter served the rice onto the plates, carefully making sure that most of the clams were dispensed.

'And two more beers,' Florin ordered, offering Hadley some further very temporary relief. The Mexican looked around and smiled at the other tables, acknowledging the quality of the fare. Then, still smiling for the casual onlooker's benefit, he turned back to Jack. 'This is not a game.'

'I . . . I may be slightly out of my depth, Mr Florin.'

The Mexican laughed out loud and once again the patrons shared in their mirth.

'At least you are honest! We have possibilities here!' Before Jack could think of anything to say he added, 'Listen . . .' Then he marked the silence by picking up his fork and selecting a clam which he deftly removed from the shell and brought to his mouth. 'First, you stop calling me Mr Florin.'

'What should I call you?' Hadley smiled.

'You can call me comrade,' he teased, 'or maybe *compañero*. That would be more appropriate.' He guffawed and took a forkful of food.

'If you wish . . .' Hadley decided to play along.

'I don't wish, silly boy! Call me Jesús, like everyone else does!'

'Thank you, I shall. Jesús. Perhaps you could call me Jack.'

'I'll do nothing of the sort. I shall call you Hadley.' He spoke with finality, that matter settled.

For a while they ate without any further allusions to war or gold. Florin spoke of Cuba, of how far the country had come since those early days of revolution, of how they had survived despite America's unrelenting sabotage.

'It's easier now, of course,' he added. Hadley knew that Cuba had many friends now, not just Russia. The Europeans were well disposed towards Cuba too and if this annoyed the Americans it was doubly pleasing to the likes of Florin.

They finished with caramel *flans* and coffee. Florin caught the waiter's attention and signalled for the bill. As he looked around the terrace people smiled back.

'You are clearly popular, Jesús,' Hadley ventured.

'So are you, it seems.' Florin was still smiling but the tone of his voice had become businesslike.

'Can't you see them?' he asked in response to Hadley's puzzled expression. 'The two behind me, out towards the entrance, dark glasses, afraid to smile.' Florin smiled as Hadley looked past him. 'Sierra's men,' he said.

'Sierra?'

'If you haven't met him yet, then you shall.'

'Why?'

'Well,' continued Florin, 'they are not following *me*, are they?' he asked, lowering his voice conspiratorially.

'The other two are harder to spot. The couple there.' He pointed them out with a nod of his head. A man and a woman, their lunch finished, trying not to look in their direction.

'They are not tourists. Not Cubans, either. No, my dear

31

Hadley,' Jesús said mischievously, 'they are yours. It seems as though you did not travel to Cuba on your own!'

At that moment the *patrón* came out of the restaurant shaking his head, arms apart in a theatrically open embrace, proclaiming to all and sundry that there was no bill for Jesús Florin – *mi casa es su casa*, and all that.

'No, no, no.' Jesús spoke jovially, also for all to hear. 'My friend here, he's a wealthy Englishman! He must pay!'

Jesús laughed and the nearby tables joined in as the *patrón*, voicing his protest and concealing his relief, went back in to fetch the bill.

4

The bitterly cold winter of 2004 felt even harsher at Salamanca's eight-hundred metre elevation. As the sun rose on the Castilian plain the deserted rolling hills surrounding the city, clad in the subdued yellows and pale ochre of winter, looked like surreal cornfields spilt from van Gogh's palette.

In the ancient quarter, the imposing edifices of an imperial past cast their day-long shadows upon the cramped medieval streets and sheltered cloisters where January snows would cling to icy stone until early hints of spring announced themselves in March.

Jack woke at six-thirty and rolled towards Mercedes in the dark. The top of her blonde head peeked out from under the duvet. He planted a gentle kiss on it and was rewarded with a muffled grunt.

He was becoming increasingly attached to her. She had appeared unexpectedly, arriving like a whirlwind on a warm summer afternoon and immediately, almost inevitably, storming into Jack's life.

The last thing Jack had sought was involvement. He was still licking the wounds of his failed marriage, but Mercedes was like no one he'd previously encountered: she exuded the magnetic self-assuredness and disarming smile of a contented, fulfilled individual.

Jack had wanted a place in the old quarter, by the University. He had no intention of buying a car, and planned to go everywhere on foot. He'd found rooms in Fonseca College, a Renaissance hall of residence reserved for post-graduate students and academic staff. Then, two semesters later, along came Mercedes, making her dramatic entrance at the wheel of an open-topped silver Boxter impossibly packed with luggage.

She'd pulled up outside the college, right under the sign eloquently depicting – for the benefit of foreign tourists unable to understand *Prohibido Aparcar* – a car being removed by a crane.

'Is this Archbishop Fonseca?' she'd demanded without preamble as Jack fatefully walked past her, trying to catch his breath after climbing San Blas Hill. He found himself staring into a pair of bright blue eyes under a navy cap embroidered in gold with the Royal Yacht Club logo. He nodded.

'And you are?' he asked – a little aggressively, he thought later, perhaps on account of the Porsche, maybe because she sounded so confident.

'Mercedes Vilanova,' she replied, offering her right hand.

'Professor Hadley.' He extended his.

'Ah, right,' she retorted. '*Miss* Vilanova, in that case.'

Jack felt disarmed; she was bloody attractive.

'Sorry,' he said, mellowing. 'Didn't mean to sound stuffy. I live here.' He nodded towards the college. 'Are you moving in?' he asked rhetorically, looking at her cases, and when she replied affirmatively he offered to help with the bags.

They walked through the college entrance into the quadrangle. The lawn looked its best in the early evening sunshine. Mercedes stopped and put her cases down.

'Wow!' she exclaimed, taking in the spacious patio and admiring the two-tiered galleries.

'Have you not been here before?' Hadley asked, surprised.

'No!' she shook her head. 'It's fantastic!'

'What's your room number?'

Under Hadley's gaze Mercedes delved into her oversize handbag. She was tall and svelte enough to wear her jeans fashionably loose. Her white blouse was embossed with a Valentino 'V' that Jack naively took for Vilanova.

She handed him a crumpled letter which he read.

'This way.' He led her. 'Ground floor.'

Mercedes dropped her bags and rapidly looked around the room, opening wardrobes and peering into the bathroom.

'Where's your room?' she asked.

'Upstairs.' Hadley raised an index finger towards the ceiling. 'Three rooms down the hall.'

She reflected for a moment and looked at the small street-level windows.

'Does your room have a balcony?' she asked, recalling how the building looked from outside.

Jack nodded, with a smirk.

'I want one upstairs!' Mercedes demanded.

'*Miss* Vilanova,' Jack laughed, 'there are only forty rooms in the whole of Fonseca. You are very privileged to have a room here at all!'

'We shall see,' she said seriously. 'May I look at yours?'

On the way up, Jack found out that Mercedes came from Valencia and that she'd enrolled for an MA in Latin American Studies. She said she would not 'mess up' her room until she'd spoken to Registration about moving, and Jack's assertion that such an outcome was unlikely led to a wager. Two hours later a knock on Jack's door proclaimed him the loser as she pointed to her first-floor room on the opposite side of the cloisters and demanded the dinner she'd just won.

'Who's the poor devil you got shunted downstairs?' Jack asked later, over dinner.

'Hardly a devil,' she laughed. 'A Peruvian priest! He's not been here before, either – and he's not due in until tomorrow.'

Hadley shook his head in disapproval.

'He'll never know,' Mercedes concluded as an afterthought, hopelessly attempting to look guilty but in reality quite pleased.

By the time Jack's wife had unexpectedly announced that she'd fallen in love with someone else and hoped that Jack would be the one to move out – for the children's sake, was how she'd put it – the marriage was already cold, if friendly. Nevertheless, he had been shaken by the experience.

Spain had been on the cards for some time and when the offer in Salamanca was confirmed it provided Jack with a welcome escape and change of scenery. He would miss the children, but they were young and would soon adjust and, for the moment at least, he seemed to have little choice.

Once in Spain he immersed himself in work, spending

most evenings in his rooms, reading or writing. At times he'd go for walks and admire the city's treasures, but on the personal front he simply did not have a plan.

He had made friends with Jean-Luc Hendaye, a suave French historian who was Jack's age, and with Tatiana, the very pale daughter of a Russian oligarch. She was often seen on Jean-Luc's arm. Jack started spending his weekends in their company and through them started to build up a social life. Tatiana even fixed him up with another Russian blonde conjured out of somewhere, but the relationship, if it could be called that, did not last.

His dinner with Mercedes that first night was Jack's first proper date with a woman since he'd left London. They dined under a starry sky by the archways of the Plaza Mayor and swapped life stories. The impressive three-storey baroque masterpiece was uniformly yet unobtrusively lit along all four sides. At the opposite end of the square someone had strung a thirty-foot banner across the City Hall façade echoing former Rector Unamuno's words to Franco: *You shall conquer because you have the might, but you shall never convince.*

Mercedes spoke of how she had recently returned to Spain after spending four years in Geneva where she had worked for Santander and lived with an American banker.

'What happened there?' Jack asked tentatively.

She shrugged.

'He was recalled to New York. I didn't want to go.' She did not volunteer any more information and Jack did not press her further. But he was surprised to admit to himself that he was glad.

Her family grew oranges in Valencia, Mercedes told him – lots of oranges, Jack would learn later – but at the time he paid little attention and attached no significance to that fact. She spoke very fondly of her parents and told him that she was an only child.

As they sipped after-dinner coffees, the University *Tuna* entered the square. They strolled along in their medieval garb, oversized white collars and cuffs contrasting with black doublets and capes, with just their scholar's sashes adding a little colour. They strummed their guitars and mandolins and banged their tambourines with character-istic joviality, just as poorer students had done to earn their supper in the Middle Ages.

For modern students to be taken into a twenty-first-century *Tuna* required not just musical talent but a good sense of humour – wooden spoons and forks still hung from their belts at the ready for a free meal – popularity and stamina.

They halted not twenty feet from where Jack and Mercedes sat and opened up with a collection of traditional songs to the great joy of locals, students and tourists alike. Exercising the *Tuna*'s right to serenade a lady, they singled out Mercedes and stood her on an empty table before chanting an ode to her beauty. She beamed at the honour and while all twelve musicians focused on her as they sang she stole a glance in Jack's direction and gave him a smile to melt his heart.

Mercedes was walking back towards Jack amidst enthusiastic applause when, spurred by the growing crowd and merry atmosphere, the *Tuna* broke into the first of the *pasodobles* and encouraged bystanders to dance.

'Let's!' exclaimed Mercedes, taking Jack by the hand and pulling him to his feet before he could refuse.

'I don't think I can do this,' he protested as the *Tuna*

rendered an Iberian version of *Adelita*. Mercedes clasped his left hand into her raised right and rested her left wrist on his shoulder.

'Anyone can do a *pasodoble*,' she cajoled. 'Just walk!'

Jack followed as best he could and soon realised that no one was looking at him and there was no need to feel self-conscious.

'It helps if you can walk in tune with the music,' she teased halfway through the second song.

Jack tried harder. He'd been in Salamanca for months and had never danced at midnight in the street.

'It helps even more,' Mercedes continued, looking directly into his eyes, 'if you walk in tune with the music *and* your partner!'

With that in mind she pulled him closer and Jack immersed himself in the spirit of the Salmantine night. She was right. All you had to do was walk in tune with the music and your partner.

That night Mercedes had gone back to Jack's room and spent the night there. It had seemed to him like the most natural thing in the world. Then she'd vanished for three days and he'd felt rejected and despondent. He looked out for her, without being too obvious, but their paths never crossed. On the evening of the fourth day, as he sat reading Salvador de Madariaga, there was a knock on his door and there she was, smiling as usual, as if she'd only been gone ten minutes.

'Remember me, Professor?' she asked, smiling broadly.

'Do I just!' he exclaimed, making no attempt to hide his delight at seeing her.

'Sorry, took me ages to get settled in,' Mercedes offered, feeling that some sort of apology was necessary.

Then she raised her shopping bag to eye level. 'Look what I've got.'

She came into the room and unpacked the contents as Jack looked on: a fresh baguette, a tin of Strasbourg foie gras and the first bottle of Vega Sicilia that Jack had ever seen at close quarters.

'Do you want to drink it now or after?' she asked

'After . . . ?' Jack repeated, half dazed, realising how pleased he was to see her back.

She grinned. It was a special grin, teeth clenched and lips parted in a wide smile. He would get to know that smile in time. Right now all he could do was stand there speechlessly and allow Mercedes to put her arms around his neck and draw him towards her.

5

The long night flight to Madrid was in itself a welcome respite. The safe interlude in the luxury of relative isolation gave Hadley an opportunity to think. The need to take stock was, if anything, highlighted by the unpleasantries he'd experienced on his departure and now expected at his destination.

For the Hispanist in Jack, a trip to Latin America meant more than a long-haul holiday, even without the anticipatory excitement of coming face to face with The Aztec – or the ever-present menace of Captain Pinto.

While in Cuba, Jack had availed himself of every spare minute to explore Havana on his own, to cast his historian's mind upon the island's colonial past. Later, he would realise that wherever he went his every move was being monitored. On his last day in Havana he had packed his belongings and driven to Florin's bungalow. He had been conscious of time running out and of how little he'd accomplished to take back to Pinto.

The flight was not due to leave until ten-thirty. Cuban bureaucracy dictated that he should be at José Martí International at least two hours before that, and he had to return Dr Asencio's car before taking a taxi to the airport.

When Hadley arrived Florin had insisted they went for a stroll along the beach. He wore seersucker shorts under a bright flowery shirt. A white, coarsely woven peaked cap protected his scalp from the midday sun. Had it not been for his black jute-soled espadrilles he might have looked at home on a public golf course in Palm Springs.

They walked straight onto the soft sand from the bungalow's veranda. It was Florin's neighbourhood beach, a place where he could walk undisturbed. Passers-by who knew him waved or nodded as their paths crossed – a brief polite greeting, no more. There were few strangers to be seen.

'I was right, you know?' Florin said, 'They were yours. The couple at the restaurant.'

'How do you know?'

'I do have *some* contacts in this country.' Florin laughed. 'They have real passports with false names.'

Hadley felt silly. If there was an implication he hadn't fathomed it.

'*I* have real passports with false names,' Florin suggested.

'You mean . . . ?'

'I mean they work for *your* government.'

'British?'

Florin's laugh was unleashed again.

'Spain, silly boy. Spain! CNI foot soldiers, any bet you like. I see the hand of Captain Pinto here.'

Jack was unable to conceal his shock. A month earlier CNI would have meant nothing to him. Now he was not just familiar with Spain's intelligence service but he had even met its deputy chief. Florin cast Hadley a sideways glance, perfectly timed to meet the Englishman's alarmed gaze. He started to mumble something but Florin told him to hush. They walked silently for a while until they reached a ramshackle beach bar. Florin ordered two coffees.

'Have you any money?' he asked. Jack quickly pulled out a crumpled note from his pocket and placed it on the counter.

'I mean real money,' Florin clarified, with a satisfied smirk. 'Are you well off?'

'Far from it,' replied Hadley, slightly annoyed by Florin's uncanny knack for wrong-footing him. 'I'm all right,' he added rapidly, defensively even, 'but not what I would call rich.'

Florin seemed to ponder Jack's last statement.

'You are going to need a bit of money,' he said. Then he turned to face Hadley and raised an index finger, holding it motionless in a gesture that demanded silence.

'I shall want you to do a few things for me when you return to Europe. We'll have to find you some expenses for that.'

Jack remained silent. He could not admit that if money was needed Pinto would pay. Florin finished his coffee and suggested that they should move on.

'There's another *rapidito* further along. We'll go and have a coffee there. Now,' he broached the subject as they started walking, 'about this book you are writing . . .'

'*Embattled Madrid*,' Hadley reminded him.

'Yes. Tell me more.'

Florin listened silently as Hadley summarised its contents

before he asked about some other details. When was the manuscript expected? How much more work did it need?

'It's been *almost* finished for some time,' Hadley admitted sheepishly, 'but it's taking me longer than I thought to compile the individual stories . . .'

'Including mine?' Florin stopped and turned to face Hadley.

'Especially yours.' Hadley smiled. 'I was so surprised – and pleased, of course! – when you agreed to see me.'

Florin did not elaborate on that, he just gave Hadley an understanding nod.

'I have an idea,' he said, then resumed his stroll towards the next coffee stop. The mulatto there greeted Florin and poured cups from his thermos flask. Jack paid before anyone had a chance to ask.

'How would you feel about writing my biography?'

'Are you serious?' Jack could not believe what he'd just heard.

'Very serious. Tell me something.' Florin took a sip from his coffee before continuing. 'Why the interest in battles?'

'Battles and history are inseparable,' replied Hadley. 'Besides, for a short while I was in the army myself.'

'Infantry?'

'Yes.'

Florin seemed particularly pleased by the revelation. 'Even better in that case. Battles and my past are also inseparable. Did you ever see action?'

'Only once,' Hadley admitted.

'It's enough,' Florin said, 'I still vividly remember my first, at Seseña, even after all these years.'

'What are these "few things" you'd want me to do in Europe?'

'I'll give you a letter, for your publisher,' Florin continued as though Jack had not spoken. 'And the first instalment of my notes.'

'And then?'

'You'll go to a few places, see some people.'

'I can't leave my job,' Hadley warned.

'I won't ask you to. I know Salamanca's routine. Send me your own timetable. But outside the University's demands, when I say "go there", "do this", "get that", you'll do as I ask. You'll be my eyes and ears. And each time, you will receive another wad of my papers.'

'What sort of things would you want me to do?' Hadley insisted. He expected he would be asked that very question when he got back to Madrid.

Florin did not answer immediately. He appeared pensive and Jack did not want to disturb him. They started to walk back towards the house at a leisurely pace. Children were playing football on the firmer sand, close to the sea. A wild header sent the ball in Jack's direction but just as he started bending down to retrieve it Florin cut in front of him and kicked it back.

'A long time ago, Hadley,' Florin spoke slowly, purposefully, as if for once his words were measured, 'I lost something.' He halted and turned to face him. 'Something of great value,' he added before resuming his walk.

Jack tried to remain calm. Was this the moment that Pinto had predicted would unfold?

'You are going to help me get it back.'

'Why me?' Hadley wanted to know. First the biography – just like that – now this. It didn't make any sense.

'Perhaps . . .' Florin replied after a moment's reflection, 'perhaps you were simply in the right place at the right time.'

When they reached the bungalow they found Nurse Miriam outside, watering the plants. She eyed both of them suspiciously as they walked through the patio doors and into Florin's study.

Florin picked up a manila pocket-file and looked inside. It contained about a hundred handwritten pages. He browsed through them, superficially, as if making sure they were all there rather than checking their contents. Hadley could see that they were penned in different-coloured inks, suggesting they'd been written over a period of time – some passages had been crossed out, others annotated along the margins.

'Why didn't you commission a biography before?' Hadley probed. 'Goodness knows there would have been a queue of eminent biographers vying for the privilege.'

'*And* the money?' A mischievous expression flitted across Florin's face.

'That too,' Hadley conceded.

'Enough has been written about me without my consent. I used to read it all,' Florin reminisced. 'The inaccuracies used to make me angry – when I was younger, that is – then I started getting bored. Same old rubbish quoting from earlier rubbish.'

'Nevertheless, you kept notes.' Hadley glanced at the folder in Florin's hand.

'An old man in retirement likes to make notes. Final stocktake, shall we say? Before closing down the shop.'

'So why commission the work now?'

'Maybe to set the record straight. You might understand one day. This,' Florin said as he handed Hadley the papers, 'is to pay you for what you are about to do for me and to take care of expenses.'

Florin's mood lightened perceptibly. 'I shall use your publisher's fat capitalist chequebook to do the people's work!'

The laughter made the nurse put her head round the door.

'What are you plotting now?' she asked Florin, uncharacteristically good-naturedly, thought Hadley. She glanced at her upside-down nurse's watch. 'Would you like your coffee now?'

'Coffee?' exclaimed Florin in mock astonishment. 'Coffee? You know it's bad for me!'

He turned to Hadley. 'See? She's not content to just imprison me in this house. Now it seems she wants me dead!'

Nurse Miriam's retort as she left the room fell outside Hadley's command of colloquial Spanish.

Florin took a bunch of keys from his desk drawer and walked over to the safe in the wall.

It suddenly struck Hadley that this room, Florin's office, was strangely impersonal: no paintings, no artwork and no mementoes of a rich and varied life. Not even obligatory framed, signed photographs of world leaders such as graced the study walls of lesser men and which Florin, of all people, would have received in abundance.

In fact, Hadley realised, the whole house was like that: comfortable, lacking nothing apart from any evidence that it was someone's home. It was the sterile house of a man who'd shed life's luggage, pointedly avoiding all reminders of a very painful past.

Florin closed the safe and looked at a glittering little object in his hand. He stretched out his hand, palm up and offered it to Hadley.

'For you,' he said. 'A small token. I wouldn't announce it to the world,' he added, grinning, 'but it will serve as an appropriate reminder of how we met.'

Hadley took the gold coin and looked at it. It was about the size of a British fivepenny piece, bore the image of Philip V and was dated 1742.

'Now, Hadley.' Florin sat on his high-backed chair and leaned forward, forearms on his desk. 'I want you to pay attention to what I'm going to say.'

Hadley nodded expectantly and tried to relax, still holding the coin in his hand.

'You are to convey a message from me to Captain Pinto.' Florin raised his left hand, palm forward, in a warning gesture that cut short any retort Hadley might have made.

'There is a large quantity of gold coins hidden away where no one would ever find them. Or so I thought, until very recently. Now there is a serious danger that this treasure will be discovered – accidentally, and by the wrong people.

'When he learns the rest of the details I am certain your Captain Pinto will agree that we must prevent this from happening. We are still in time to beat them to it but, unfortunately, I cannot do this without some help. Are you with me so far?'

Hadley nodded.

'You are to commit this to memory. No notes, not even aides-memoires. Understood?'

'Very clearly.' This was a different Florin addressing him now, Hadley realised, someone who would tolerate no nonsense, more like the man he had envisaged meeting before he'd set out for Cuba.

'Good. Then sit back – and listen carefully.'

6

One thing that most of his contemporaries agreed upon was that if Roberto Pinto had elected to remain in the Navy he would have followed in his grandfather's footsteps and made Admiral.

Pinto had reached the rank of Capitán de Navío by his thirtieth birthday and was destined for the Armada's staff college when, to everyone's surprise, he asked to be placed on the Active Reserve List.

His wife Victoria, younger daughter of a marquess and a socialite at heart, was relieved to be free of the sailor's nomadic existence, having already set up and then dismantled homes in Cádiz, Cartagena and Santa Cruz in a mere six years of keeping up with her husband's vertiginous ascent.

An embassy – perhaps – might have started her packing yet again, but she joyfully embraced the announcement of Roberto's government job in Madrid and the *normal* existence it implied.

'Something to do with foreign policy' was how she explained it to friends and relatives, though her father had gruffly told her: 'Stop being so stupid: he's going to work for my chum Emilio. He'll be a bloody spy.'

Intelligence work was something that Pinto had set his mind on as a young man from that day in 1973 when a Basque terrorist faction had assassinated the Spanish Prime Minister, Admiral Luis Carrero Blanco.

The four-man ETA hit squad had excavated a tunnel under a Madrid street and packed it with a hundred kilogrammes of explosives. As the Admiral, his driver and bodyguard drove away from the church of San Francisco – where the head of Franco's government habitually attended Mass – the charge was detonated with such force that the twisted, smouldering wreckage of the vehicle landed on the second-floor terrace of a building across the street.

At the time Pinto had found it difficult to comprehend how such operations could be mounted under the authorities' very noses, but he realised that Spain was not alone. ETA at home, the IRA in Britain, Palestinian hijackers in the Middle East, Algerian *plastiqueurs* in Paris before them, the trend was already there. The battle against terrorism, Pinto concluded, would be the new front line and he wanted an active role defending it.

But today Captain Pinto had several problems occupying his mind. He walked up to his office window and gently ran his hand through the last remnants of his rapidly thinning fair hair, then stroked his Chaplinesque moustache with his thumb and index finger. As he examined the CNI building's immaculate front lawn, forlorn in the morning drizzle, Pinto yearned for the bridge of his old frigate and the hearty swell of the North Atlantic.

Days earlier, an Al Qaeda-inspired terrorist cell had blown up a rush-hour commuter train as it neared Madrid's Atocha station. Over one hundred and fifty victims were dead thus far and the injured approached two thousand.

The Interior Minister had lambasted Pinto and demanded immediate answers. Later Pinto could not recall exactly what his words had been but he was adamant that they amounted to no more than an off-the-cuff *suggestion* that the atrocity bore all the marks of ETA.

But that was not how it got relayed to Prime Minister Aznar – three days before a General Election which the pundits swore would be bagged by the incumbent – nor the way he in turn put it to the nation: in the immediate aftermath of the atrocity the official finger was unequivocally pointed at ETA.

The intensity of the electorate's anger was matched by angry denials from Basque separatist headquarters. The press soon reasoned that while Basque involvement might increase the Prime Minister's electoral chances, an Islamist attack would favour the Socialist opposition who had been warning about the dire consequences of Spain's involvement in Iraq, and promising withdrawal if elected.

In the end events got the better of such denials as the CNI could offer, and José Luis Rodríguez Zapatero, leader of the Workers' Socialist Party, was elected Prime Minister on the fourteenth of March.

That also meant Pinto would have to sort out another delicate problem. With the previous government's approval, and in exchange for guaranteed oil supplies for Spain, the CNI had covertly backed a plot hatched in South Africa which could soon install Celestino Potro, a political refugee living in Switzerland, as President of his native Equatorial Guinea.

But new masters with different philosophies would now form the majority in the Spanish *Cortes*. Pinto would have to make new friends immediately and draw them to his camp.

Pinto was under no illusions: if his agency's African initiative should end in a debacle, the first neck in line for the political garrotte would be his own.

Perhaps the only positive event he could look forward to on this rainy day in March was Jack Hadley's imminent return from Cuba. Pinto already knew, from his own sources, that his first gambit might, however slightly, have cracked open a door that could lead eventually to the recovery of his country's missing gold.

Like most Spaniards, Pinto had heard of *El Oro de Moscú*, the term by which the massive transfer of Spain's reserves during the Civil War had come to be known.

Initially, Pinto's interest had been that of an avid coin collector. It was well known that pre-Civil War Spain, unlike other countries, had shunned gold ingots and had kept most of its metal reserves in coins.

He had studied the records and was surprised to learn that the bulk of the coins – over two-thirds of them – were British. The rest was made up of Spanish pesetas, Swiss, Austrian, French and Belgian francs, German marks, Italian lire, Portuguese escudos, Russian roubles and Dutch florins as well as Argentine, Mexican and Chilean pesos and a large quantity of American half-eagles.

Pinto pondered the mint dates of the coins. There were huge differences in rarity and hence in resale value between, say, an 1821 George IV sovereign and the identical coin struck in 1824 – a tenfold difference, in fact. Would rare coins have been included with the shipment? Were any of them recognised by connoisseurs, separated and set aside?

In 1985, Pinto changed his naval uniform for dark, understated suits and moved his Moscow Gold files into his new Madrid office. There they languished untouched in a bottom drawer for several years as the new man rose through the intelligence ranks. Pinto assisted the secret service's chief to restructure and reform the organisation, transforming the Cold War CESID into the modern CNI.

Eventually they would move into a new, impressive complex in the city's western suburbs, not far from the vast acreage of the Casa de Campo.

Five years into his new job Pinto came across the Moscow Gold files again and this time he sent one of his staff to gather information from the Central Bank. By then, in democratic Spain, the Franco era of obsessive secrecy was fading into the past and even those documents held back from public scrutiny under the pretext of national security would be accessible to the deputy head of CNI.

The files made amazing reading and contained enough evidence for Pinto to join the ranks of those who believed that the full shipment had never been properly accounted for. The salient facts were clear: even before the Civil War had started, Spain and Russia had considered the idea of depositing the Spanish gold reserves in Moscow – 'a current account in gold' they called it – as collateral for armaments purchases.

With the distinct possibility of an arms embargo against Spain being sanctioned by the western European powers, the Republic needed access to boycott-busting funds.

The first shipment was sent to Paris on the twenty-fourth of July, a week after the Nationalist rebellion, and in September the Council of Ministers authorised the removal of all remaining gold to Moscow.

This final consignment comprised 10,000 wooden crates. The number of crates leaving the bank and arriving in the port of Cartagena tallied. They were said to contain 510 tons of gold. From Cartagena some crates were shipped to Marseille and on to Eurobank in Paris. The remaining gold was loaded onto four Soviet freighters bound for Odessa in the Ukraine.

So far, thought Pinto, no problem. But his research didn't end there.

Francisco Méndez Aspe, Governor of the Bank of Spain, the man in overall charge of the removal operation, attested to the shipment of 7,800 boxes. Weeks later, in Moscow, Director of Foreign Currency O. I. Kagan confirmed the receipt of 7,800 boxes. But Alexander Orlov, head of the NKVD in Spain, personally tasked by Stalin to oversee the movement on behalf of the Soviet Union, had signed a receipt, in Cartagena, for 7,900 boxes. A difference of precisely one hundred boxes containing six and a half tons of fine gold.

Years later, in 1992, Vassily Mitrokhin, the KGB's chief archivist, defected to the West with as many microfiche files as a man could carry. The Americans kept the cream but shared the snippets, accruing goodwill with their allies. Spain received the Moscow Gold files and Pinto had them on his desk on day one. And there it was in black and white: Spanish exit documents stated 7,900 boxes, Soviet entry documents 7,800.

The landing records at the port of Odessa logged the arrival of 5,779 crates on board the vessels *Kine*, *Neva* and *Volgoles* on the second of November 1936 and a further 2,021 crates on board the *Kursk* during the night of the ninth of November. Pinto made a note: where had the *Kursk* been for seven days?

In Moscow, Stalin was quick to claim title to the gold. Supplies to Spain, all of a sudden, became not just a shining example of international socialist solidarity and a boost for the Soviet Union's image of commitment: Spain's treasure also gave Russia an unparalleled business opportunity. Katiuska and Rasante bombers, Chato and Mosca fighters, tanks, armoured cars and artillery pieces by the hundreds, sold at prices dictated by the vendor on the best possible terms: current account, prepaid, in gold.

Pinto had taken the gold files home and had spent the weekend poring over them. Something in what he'd learnt didn't make sense. He had taken out a pad and, reading papers from all sources well into the early hours of Sunday, made up a list of all those key figures who might have known the truth.

Marcelino Pascua, Spanish Ambassador to Moscow and Méndez Aspe. The four *claveros*. On the Soviet side the unquestionable mastermind was Alexander Orlov. Then the four Financial Commissars. None of them would be able to shed any light on the mystery. Pascua had been transferred from Moscow to Paris in 1937 and Méndez Aspe had returned to Spain. Both would later be part of the Republican government in exile. By the late 1970s both were dead and so were the *claveros*. The Financial Commissars, loyal servants of the Soviet State, were banished to the gulag and never seen alive again.

Orlov was the greatest enigma of all. Stalin's telegram giving him the go-ahead for the gold transfer was part of the historical archives, but who was Alexander

Orlov, *really*? A Belorussian Jew named Leiba Lazarevich Felbing for a start. The Russian name was adopted later, when he joined the Cheka, precursor of the NKVD. Yet, even though he had completed the Spanish bullion assignment exactly as ordered and been awarded the Order of Lenin in recognition, Orlov had been certain that his recall to Moscow in 1938 was in order to have him purged.

So he cleared whatever cash was held in the NKVD's Madrid office, gathered enough documents to blackmail Moscow if they tried to follow him, and escaped with his wife and daughter to the USA where he went underground with American protection. He died in 1973.

That left one key player still alive: Antonio Mercer.

He was a hard one to fathom, thought Pinto. The Galician stonemason turned Republican General had certainly travelled a long route. After the war he had returned to Russia and rejoined the Red Army. He fought at Leningrad and made General a second time. Sent off to help Tito in 1946, the Yugoslavs gave him the rank as well. Mercer: three times general.

Mercer, thought Pinto. He had been involved. He and Orlov were close – and they had both been in Madrid when the gold was removed.

In 1976, one year after Franco's death, Antonio Mercer had returned to Spain. He rejoined the Spanish Communist Party, reclaimed his army rank and sued for his full pension.

Then, on a winter morning in 1993, Pinto learnt that Mercer would be attending a funeral in the Valley of the Fallen and he made a point of being there. He recognised the old soldier from photographs. He was eighty-six now and still active in politics.

'General Mercer.' Pinto approached him, hand extended, in the cold and foggy Guadarrama morning.

'Captain Pinto.' Mercer clearly knew who Pinto was.

'Strange, is it not?' Pinto suggested, glancing around the granite mausoleum. 'I mean, meeting here.'

Mercer smiled. The vast monument on the sierras had been built by Franco for himself and Nationalist war heroes, not far from the Escorial palace where Spanish kings were laid to rest. Since the return to democracy the Valley had become open to all war heroes. Today a former Republican combatant was being buried with full honours.

'Stranger things have happened in this country of ours, Captain.'

'Yes.' Pinto decided not to beat around the bush. 'I was wondering if we could have a chat sometime?'

Mercer arched his brows

'About one of those strange things,' Pinto added.

It was Mercer who suggested that now might be a good time. 'At my age,' he joked, '*sometime* could mean *never*.'

Both men walked out together once the eulogies had ended. They pulled up their coat collars and strolled along the basilica's terrace, looking down over the Jarama valley towards Madrid. Mercer took out a cigar case and offered Pinto a Montecristo.

'It's to do with gold.' Pinto puffed on his cigar and went directly to the point.

'That old chestnut again,' Mercer chuckled.

'Well, not quite,' explained Pinto. 'You see, General, I'm a collector.'

Mercer halted and turned to study Pinto's face.

'An important collector,' continued Pinto, 'if I may say so.

Museums aside, I'd say I have the finest seventeenth-century Ibero-American collection in the world.'

'Really? And how do you think *I* can be of help?'

'Missing coins, General. I've studied the records. There is no reference to old coins anywhere. Not in Moscow, not in Madrid. Where did they go?'

'You think the famous missing gold was made up of ancient coinage?' Mercer sounded as if he thought the suggestion was preposterous.

'Is it not a possibility?'

Mercer puffed on his own cigar and started walking again.

'Captain Pinto, let me tell you a few truths.' He linked his arm through Pinto's, whether for support or to make his point more personal the Captain did not know.

'First, there was no missing gold. It is a myth. We were fighting a war and needed every last *duro* for armaments. Many have speculated about this notion but no gold has ever been found. If it existed, do you think it would have remained hidden for more than half a century?

'Besides,' continued Mercer before Pinto could reply, 'I wasn't there. I was in Madrid. The train left Atocha and the gold was gone.

'Alexander Orlov was in charge.' Mercer spat the name. '*He* might have stolen some, given a chance. He was an American agent, did you know?'

Pinto said he didn't. Nor did he believe it. Orlov travelled on American documents at times. He had genuine ones and false ones. He had lived in the United States in the 1920s – on Stalin's orders.

During the gold-removal operation, Orlov had been Mr William Golding of the Bank of America. But that had been his cover. Only the Communists knew that the gold was going to Moscow. If their allies in the Republic – anarchists, socialists, separatists, syndicalists – had got wind of the gold's final destination they would have stopped it leaving the country.

'If there were any old coins,' continued Mercer, 'the *claveros* and Financial Commissars would have extracted them to realise their true value.'

'*Could* Orlov have stolen some of the shipment?' Pinto persisted.

'You still believe the missing-cases nonsense, don't you?' Mercer challenged him.

Pinto waved an open right hand in a non-committal gesture.

'Orlov,' Mercer spoke slowly, 'would not have had the opportunity to separate old coins. Not the way they were packed. He would have had to steal a whole case.

'So, Captain Pinto, here's the way I see it: if there were old coins and these were separated, it would have happened in Moscow. Those coins would have been sold through dealers and would eventually have found their way into collections.'

Mercer stopped walking again and, still holding Pinto's arm, motioned for them to start walking back. In the distance several officials stood outside the monastery, trying to guess what the unlikely couple could be talking about.

'Have you seen them in collections, Captain Pinto?'

The CNI man shook his head.

'No, I didn't think you had,' continued Mercer. 'If, on the other hand, this is not about collecting coins, Captain' – Pinto realised he might have underestimated the old man – 'if this is just yet another attempt by the government to find out if some of their – *our* – precious gold went missing, then let me tell you unequivocally that it did not. What left Cartagena got to Moscow. You can be sure of that.'

'How can you be sure? You said that Orlov *might* have . . .'

'Oh yes, Orlov *would* have, given the chance. But I sent Jesús Florin to keep an eye on him. Now, you tell me, Captain Pinto.' Mercer released Pinto's arm and turned to face him, leaning his hands on the Captain's shoulders. 'Do you think for one instant that Florin would have had any part in the theft of Spain's gold?'

'No, not Florin.' Pinto replied without hesitation.

Not, Pinto told himself, unless Florin had been *ordered* to do just that.

The next time Pinto and Mercer met was two years later, at the end of November 1995. The spy chief was told that the old Republican was ill and had been taken to hospital. Pinto found him quite lucid, if physically diminished and much thinner than he'd been at the Valley of the Fallen. Mercer's son and daughter were also there and the atmosphere in the room suggested last goodbyes.

Mercer looked up from his bed and acknowledged Pinto.

'Did you ever find your gold, Captain?' he asked, managing a trace of sarcasm even in his sorry state.

'No,' Pinto admitted.

Mercer looked away and closed his eyes.

'Ask Florin,' were his last words to the deputy head of CNI.

The following week, on the eighth of December, Antonio Mercer died.

*   *   *

Eight years had passed since that meeting. With Mercer's death Pinto's hopes of learning the truth, let alone finding the gold, had gradually faded. Until now: until Florin himself had, for reasons yet to be fathomed, decided to end thirty years of isolation and Pinto's most dependable source confirmed he might, just *might*, throw the truth about the missing treasure into the bargain. That only left one huge question unanswered: what did the bloody Aztec want in return? For in the intelligence game, Pinto knew for sure, there were no freebies.

Pinto looked up at the cloudy sky and saw a glimmer of sunlight breaking through from the east. Perhaps the rain and gloom would end. Perhaps, after his meetings with Florin, Hadley would bring back the missing clues that might help resolve the puzzle.

Yes, Pinto concluded, let spring's imminent arrival be a symbol of brighter times ahead. He returned to his desk, put away the Moscow files and leaned back on his chair. Any time now, the car bringing Hadley from the airport would be pulling into the CNI forecourt.

7

Friday the thirteenth started like any other day, but that evening, before the last lights went out in Salamanca, it would live up to its ill-starred reputation.

Over a year had passed since Hadley and Mercedes had first met. By spring they had moved out of Fonseca and never looked back. On this cold February morning Jack willed himself out of the warm bed and towards the shower. Two tutorials, a lecture and a visit to the library awaited him, and he needed to spend a couple of hours on his book — *Embattled Madrid: Personal Memories 1936–1939* — before the academic day engulfed him.

Mercedes was working on an essay for her *Poverty and Inequality* module. She would probably spend most of her day in her faculty's library. They were unlikely to see each other until the evening. One of their friends was celebrating his fortieth birthday and they'd arranged to meet for drinks around seven before going to a restaurant.

The book, Jack's fifth, was giving him problems. The

advance had long been spent. Though the university salary came in regularly and relieved some of the financial pressure, he was still paying the mortgage on his former London home.

Jack and his wife – soon to be ex-wife – had remained on good terms, perhaps because of the children. His financial concerns arose from his ambitious claim that *Embattled Madrid* would contain first-hand accounts from former combatants.

Jack had tracked down a good few of this dwindling number, but many Republicans had left Spain after their side's defeat. Most of those approached by Hadley had agreed to tell their story, but now he had to face up to the reality that trips to Uruguay or Nicaragua cost money.

Since Mercedes had come along, she'd paid more than her fair share of their living expenses, especially since she and Jack had set up home together, but a blend of pride and sense of fairness on his part prevented him from taking advantage of his girlfriend's generous allowance as long as he was remitting a substantial portion of his own income to his estranged wife.

Hadley's ace in the hole was Florin, probably the best known ex-combatant still alive – though, admittedly, this fame was probably more because of his subsequent life rather than his role in the battle for Madrid.

Hadley had written to Havana University and the History Chair, Dr Asencio, had replied with the good news: Florin would see him. 'Come over in the spring' was the message. It was well known in press and literary circles that Florin did not give interviews. And whilst Florin had only agreed to discuss Spain, Hadley was hoping that other tales – Russia, Congo, Mozambique – might be forthcoming. So it was decided that as soon as Salamanca broke up in March, Jack would go to Cuba and meet the legendary Aztec.

At ten to eight in the evening, almost an hour later than he'd intended, Jack left the History and Geography building and headed for the General Secretariat where he had to drop off some papers.

He cut across the Minor Schools Patio, taking care not to slip on any ice. Even with the snow pushed to the sides, walking through the cloistered quadrangle that the low winter sun could barely reach could be perilous at times.

He emerged through Schools Yard, where a group of Japanese tourists futilely attempted to spot the Salamanca frog amidst the complex stone carvings of the University's Plateresque façade, and crossed to the administration building opposite the towering mass of Salamanca's twin cathedrals.

Hadley had just spent two hours in the History Department's library in addition to the three he had spent the previous day in that of the Political Science faculty, trying to increase his knowledge of the secretive Jesús Florin. Much of the information available was derived from unauthorised biographies and press cuttings, though there were also copies of papers written by Florin himself and published by Mexico's Autonomous University in the 1950s.

He glanced at his watch and knew he was already running late, but he liked the subject and made no effort to leave. He knew that Mercedes would wait, unconcerned. Besides, their friends and colleagues would be at the restaurant already. She'd be neither bored, alone nor rushed.

'Professor Hadley.' The assistant librarian brought another pile of references to the table. 'I found all these.'

A very young one, Jack thought, perhaps eighteen and wearing a minimalist skirt that even over thick winter tights would, until recently, have been deemed inappropriate for the august rooms of the University of Salamanca. A far cry from that day half a millennium earlier when the first woman had been admitted – and then only because she was Queen Isabella's personal teacher *and* had agreed to dress as a man.

Hadley thanked the young woman as he started reading the pages that she had so diligently earmarked.

On the nineteenth of July 1936, the day following Franco's *Pronunciamiento,* Florin drove five hundred miles from Salamanca to Loyalist La Mancha and joined the International Brigades.

His mastery of modern languages – Florin already spoke English, German and Russian – led him to Emilo Kléber, a Romanian tasked by Moscow to lead the Eleventh. The Brigades were ordered to Madrid and entered the city to a tumultuous welcome. They drove down the Castellana and the Gran Vía aboard requisitioned trucks and sang the *Internationale*.

They were billeted to various quarters – schools, gymnasia, army barracks – while the more fortunate went to the commandeered Ritz Hotel. Florin accompanied Kléber to the hotel's former ballroom on the ground floor and it was there that he first set eyes on Antonio Mercer.

The Coruña-born soldier was twenty-nine years old at the time and already a Colonel. Within weeks he would make General. He was short but sturdy, with a dark complexion, and was smartly dressed in an immaculately pressed uniform. His wavy black hair, a bit too long for a regular army officer, betrayed an air of individuality that would mark much of his future career. He and fellow officers were leaning over maps that were laid open on a large table.

After making the necessary introductions, Mercer set out his plan.

The insurgents had taken up positions west of Madrid after routing the Republican forces holding that flank. Militias had dug defensive trenches but had not counted on confronting Italian tanks. Faced with an armoured attack they had abandoned their positions and run.

Pavel Arman, a young Red Army officer, was given fifteen T-26 tanks with mixed Russian and Spanish crews, supported by the Brigades and Mercer's infantry to lead the counter-attack. The following morning they set off to take Seseña but nothing went as planned.

Arman's tanks charged at full speed and the infantry were unable to keep up. Catching the enemy by surprise, they met with initial success which further emboldened them to drive deeper through the Nationalist lines.

But the professional *regulares,* having had time to regroup, attacked with petrol bombs and destroyed three tanks. As the T-26s began to retreat, the infantry which had been a mile behind when the action started finally arrived as their armour headed home. Met with a fusillade from the enemy, the Brigades started to pull back, but Florin rallied his men and led a surprise charge into Seseña.

The fighting might have lasted ten minutes at most, but ten minutes of close-quarter fighting felt unconnected with time. For many of these first-time combatants it was a dreamlike do-or-die situation where a man lost all sense of reality, survived as if by chance and merely kept on shooting and charging in the irrational belief that by his actions he might break his opponents' resolve.

When the firing ceased and an eerie calm enveloped the

scene of battle, most of Florin's men were still standing while enemy casualties lay scattered along Seseña's eastern edge. Florin had beaten off professional soldiers and it felt good but he had enough sense to realise that a Nationalist commander would rally his troops and come back. The Brigade had two walking wounded to carry and one man down, so badly shot that he would have to be left behind. Florin gave the order and they started to trot back towards the safety of the high ground.

They were hailed as heroes when they returned to their lines. Pavel Arman, despite his attack's failure, was warmly congratulated and shortly thereafter was made a Hero of the Soviet Union in a much-needed propaganda move. Florin, the only infantry officer to lead his troops up to Seseña, was promoted to the rank of Captain.

Mercer spoke to Kléber and the next day Florin was attached to Mercer's staff, a move that would alter the course of Florin's life.

Hadley checked the time again and jumped to his feet. He *was* late. The delay had not been planned. But it would suit those who at that very moment were putting their elaborate scheme into play.

He walked along Libreros Street where, in the Middle Ages, books were made or sold, and turned left past the Law School at San Isidro Square before reaching his destination on the narrow Meléndez Street.

The sound of Friday night was audible long before Jack reached El Patio Chico. A large oak door opened with ease and he pushed aside the heavy curtain that hung behind it to keep the winter out.

Not that it felt like winter inside. Every table along the

narrow room's left-hand wall was oversubscribed, their occupants merging with the crowd that stood four and five deep the length of the bar on the opposite side.

Hadley slowly shouldered his way towards the back, where the room opened up into more sitting areas leading to the main dining room behind a pair of swing doors. He pushed past waiters yelling bar orders in one direction and food orders in another, verbal instructions that somehow registered above the din of conversation and the pitiable efforts of piped music to voice the gentle songs of Joan Manuel Serrat.

A white-clad chef, sweating heavily beside the glowing charcoal, lorded it over the grill beyond the bar. Lamb cutlets, pork ribs, *pinchos* and tortillas accompanied by all manner of salads and the mandatory olives flowed out as fast as the orders were called in. Cigarette and cigar smoke permeated the atmosphere, further diminishing visibility in a less than brightly lit environment.

Hadley spotted Mercedes from afar, her back towards him, the soft golden-blonde hair cut short to the neck unmistakably hers. There were eight people at her table. Sacha Ross, a fellow postgraduate student younger than Mercedes sat next to her. He habitually followed her around like a puppy and, from the way he looked at her, Jack recognised with a well-concealed pang of jealousy that the young man was besotted.

Jaime Torres, a broad-shouldered medievalist whose large head and ginger mop were often the butt of well-intended jokes, and his economist wife Lara sat against the wall. Everyone listened intently to Ramiro de la Serna's impassioned prophecy that the socialists would not be returned to government in the forthcoming elections – nor, at that, in a million years – a contention based less on his political sagacity and more on the wish to hang on to his seven thousand acres of olives around Valladolid.

Torres made a sarcastic remark to that effect and the rest laughed heartily, laughter that only intensified when Ramiro clearly failed to see the humour.

Jack was fond of Ramiro. A corpulent man with a large forehead that looked larger because of his receding hairline, Ramiro was a former Fonseca resident and owned a weekend home half an hour away in Tordecillas. He visited Salamanca regularly, had become great friends with what he called the Fonseca mafia, and today had chosen to spend his birthday with them.

In fact, it had been Ramiro's suggestion that Jack should write to former combatants and subtitle his next book *Personal Memories*.

'You must add the common touch, dear boy,' he'd stated in his aristocratic Castilian intonation. 'Then the magazines will serialise it for the masses,' he continued, eyes open wide as if to illustrate his powers of observation, 'And that's where the real money lies these days!'

Jack hadn't noticed the stranger sitting next to Mercedes, a very attractive dark-haired thirty-something woman, until he reached the table. She was introduced as Ramiro's cousin, Rosa. Jean-Luc, as always casually but fashionably dressed, and Tatiana sat between Ramiro and Lara Torres, completing the group.

Mercedes turned as she noticed the others looking past her and her face lit up as she saw Jack. She quickly shunted chairs to make room for another and slotted Jack between herself and Rosa.

'Good day?' she asked, kissing his cheek as he leaned

towards her. She spoke in a raised voice so as to be heard above the din of the other hundred and fifty people in El Patio. Many were students, finding release after another week of tests, essays and deadlines and looking forward to the weekend.

'We are thinking of going up to the Picos for Easter. What do you say?' Mercedes challenged him, for as far as she was concerned skiing opportunities were never to be missed.

'I thought you found the runs there boring.' Jack knew better than to argue, but the Asturian ski resorts were not Europe's most demanding.

'*The* run, in this case,' Lara joked, emphasising the singular.

'Ah, yes,' Jaime added mysteriously. 'Now tell him the rest,' he urged Mercedes, grinning.

'We are going to the top,' she said, her eyes sparkling in wild anticipation and with a little help from her third glass of cava.

Jack looked at her questioningly.

'By helicopter,' she said excitedly. 'Ramiro's treat.'

'If I'm back,' Jack cautioned.

'Back?' asked Rosa, 'Where are you going—?'

'Cuba,' Mercedes cut in. 'Jack is off to Cuba without me!'

'We'll look after you, Mercedes.' Jean-Luc's Gallic charm came to the rescue.

Food arrived. Four plates of *raciones*, more olives – scrutinised approvingly by Ramiro – bread, *aioli* and two more bottles of cava. Jack asked for another glass and meanwhile shared his girlfriend's.

'Are you at the university?' Jack asked Rosa.

'No.' She smiled a sensual smile. 'Just visiting – staying with Ramiro's family in Valladolid.' By which she meant his mother and sisters: Ramiro was a confirmed bachelor and even casual girlfriends were kept at bay.

'So where's home?' he asked her.

'Madrid.'

'Nice city, I love it there,' Jack said.

Rosa nodded and smiled.

'Yes. But it's nice to get away. Like you going off to Cuba,' she teased, echoing Mercedes's remark.

Rosa's voice was soft and carried somehow without her having to shout. Jack was taken by the intensity of her gaze.

'No. That's work,' he replied in mock seriousness. 'Whatever else this lady might tell you!' He put an arm around Mercedes and pulled her towards him.

The little party walked through the historic city centre and past the mysterious twin doors of the Ursuline Convent, keeping a brisk pace to stay warm. Then they spent the next three hours at Victoriano Salvador's restaurant.

They ate sea wolf with black squid sauce and bluefin tuna steak. Tenderloins in lemon sauce and ribs with prunes. Mercedes and Rosa sat next to each other and Jack could see a rapport developing. Four bottles of Muga *Crianza* and three of Rias Baixas *Albariño* were effortlessly consumed and they rounded up the evening with a Concha y Toro dessert wine to accompany Victoriano's legendary almond-bark pastries.

They were the last remaining diners in the restaurant when Mercedes excused herself and left the table. She returned wielding a guitar, following the chef who carried a small cake with four lit candles. She strummed the first few chords of *Las Mañanitas* and they all sang the Mexican birthday song.

*   *   *

They walked into the apartment at just after three in the morning and feeling a little worse for wear. The two women had linked arms as they walked, propping each other up. Jack brought up the rear. None of them noticed the cold. Nor did they question why Rosa had come with them and had not gone home with Ramiro. When they reached the small block on San Pablo Street, Jack fumbled with the front-door keys and the women giggled.

They staggered up the stone steps, Jack making hushing sounds, vaguely conscious of the sleeping neighbours, the girls barely able to suppress their liquor-induced laughter. It was an old building, once a medieval student lodging and now converted into flats.

Their apartment was on the first floor, at the back, over-looking a small private garden in the shadow of yet another church. It was only a few minutes' walk from the History and Geography building.

Jack opened the door and let the women in, uncon-vincingly demanding that they should keep their voices down.

Mercedes put on some music and Jack went to the bath-room. When he returned the women were dancing together seductively, whether for Jack's benefit or for each other's he could not quite fathom in his own alcoholic haze. He tried to join them but Rosa pushed him away onto the sofa as if daring him to resist, and returned to the beat of Justin Timberlake.

The cold outside was soon forgotten in the overheated flat. Rosa undid her blouse and stared at Jack provocatively as Mercedes smiled her clenched-teeth smile. Staring at her man she deliberately unzipped her trousers. Rosa turned the music louder, picked up her bag from the floor and went to the bathroom. Jack no longer thought about the noise or the neighbours.

Mercedes came over and straddled him on the sofa, then grabbed his face in both hands and kissed him hard and deep on the mouth. They were still kissing when Rosa, minus her skirt, returned to the room. She placed a small plastic bag on the coffee table and shook its contents onto the glass surface. With the long nail of her left little finger she scooped up a few grains of coke and brought them to her nose.

Mercedes moved away from Jack and gripping Rosa's hand – her own nails were too short – she took a pinch and inhaled it. Rosa kissed Mercedes on the lips then took a further nailful and offered it to Jack who shook his head. He was trying to stand up and fetch himself a cognac when he became aware of a persistent distant thumping but was too drunk to understand its implications. Then the apartment door flew open with a loud bang and two uniformed policemen walked in.

8

Havana International Airport was predictably chaotic. The cavernous Terminal 3 might have been up to the task but for the inevitable interference of the state. Interminable and unnecessary queues formed as underemployed officials scrutinised the same travel documents repeatedly. People dozed on the long rows of brightly coloured plastic chairs: some of them had been waiting since the previous day for delayed or cancelled Aeroflot and Cubana flights.

Jack stood patiently in line for forty minutes in order to hand over his only suitcase before moving on to passport control. There were two men inside the immigration kiosk, one in uniform sitting by the slotted window, one in civvies standing silently behind him. As soon as Jack proffered his passport it was passed to the plain-clothes man who signalled Hadley to follow him.

They walked up a flight of stairs to the mezzanine floor. An anxious Hadley was ushered into a small office that contained a desk and two chairs. One glass wall, with privacy curtains pulled open, looked on to a busy open-plan area full of scanning equipment, desks and computers where he could see his suitcase being delivered.

Two men and a woman gathered round as it was placed on a large table. The woman crossed the floor towards Jack.

'The key, please,' she asked, leaning through the open door and putting out her hand. The word 'please' sounded more like an order than a polite request and Jack saw no point in arguing. He looked on while his luggage was opened and his belongings were meticulously removed. The officials examined the bag itself carefully. Hadley glanced at the clock on the wall and wondered when his flight would board.

A fourth man joined the group, was handed Hadley's passport and made his way towards the cubicle. He closed the door, sat at the desk and motioned to Hadley to do the same.

'Mr Hadley,' he said without ceremony, 'may I ask the purpose of your visit to Cuba?'

Interrogation, Pinto's man had said. *They'll start with questions you've answered before. It's to annoy you, wind you up. Then they'll ask you questions you both know the answer to. They'll repeat them again and again. Then new questions before going back to the old stuff. But be careful: now and then they'll sneak one in, something they'd really like to know.*

'To research a book.'

They knew that. The University would have told them – and besides, it was in his visa application.

'Any other reason?' The interrogator glanced at Hadley's briefcase that was lying flat on the desk. He was a small man with thick rimless glasses and curly black hair.

His menacing manner was no different from that of any policeman in a totalitarian state. He wore an open-neck white shirt with a plastic ID badge displaying the name 'Olmos' pinned above its pocket.

'As an historian myself, I spent as much time as possible at Havana University.'

'With Dr Asencio?'

'And other members of his faculty.'

'Who else did you meet?'

'At the University?'

'In Cuba.'

'General Florin.'

'What's your business with Don Jesús?'

'He has helped me with my research on the Spanish Civil War.'

'Did you discuss anything else with General Florin?'

'Ask *him*.' For an instant Hadley felt quite brave. Surely this man had a nerve discussing Florin behind his back.

'Are you a member of the armed forces, Mr Hadley?'

'No.' The minute he denied it Hadley wished he'd been more forceful.

'You are not an officer in your country's army?' There was a sarcastic undertone in Olmos's voice.

'No!'

'Have you ever served in the British army?'

'I held a commission between 1985 and 1991,' Hadley replied truthfully; perhaps this was one of the *'we already know the answer'* questions.

'Did you serve in the Middle East during that period?'

'I have no intention of discussing my service record with you – or anyone else for that matter,' Hadley growled.

'Open that case.' Olmos nodded in the briefcase's direction, reasserting his authority.

Jack released the latches and spun the case round for his inquisitor to look at.

Olmos emptied the briefcase's contents and spread them on the desk. Then he replaced Jack's sunglasses, phone, keyring, pens, camera and notebook computer together with its powerpack and cables in the case and signalled through the glass wall.

'Empty your pockets,' he demanded without looking at Hadley.

The woman who had taken Hadley's keys returned with a hand-held scanner and ran it up and down the length of his body. His watch was also put in the briefcase, which she then carried to one of the X-ray machines. Olmos took her scanner.

Hadley saw a further two suitcases with fresh Iberia tags being delivered to a table in the main area. His pulse quickened as he recognised two familiar faces being escorted to a side office. The door was shut behind them and the curtains drawn. They were the man and woman whom Florin had pointed out in Varadero.

Hadley's interrogator was reading through Florin's notes. He ignored Jack's remark that they were private papers and made his point by closing the file, calling to his colleague to come over and saying simply, 'Photocopy all this.'

'Are you an agent of a foreign government, Mr Hadley? Why are you in Cuba?'

'No!' Hadley protested. 'I told you. I'm a university professor and an author.' He didn't want to add 'and Jesús Florin's biographer' and then he remembered Florin's handwritten letter amongst the papers:

'. . . *Jack Hadley has been commissioned to write my only authorised biography and will have access to all my papers. Jesús Florin, La Habana, 20th March 2004.*'

'We have reason to believe otherwise, Mr Hadley,' Olmos said as if he found the subject tedious. 'We'll be here all night if necessary.'

'My plane leaves in half an hour.' Hadley stated the obvious.

'Your plane leaves when I say it leaves. With or without you. Now, why are you in Cuba?' the interrogator persisted.

As he spoke, Olmos slowly passed the scanner over the rest of Hadley's personal items: sleeveless sweater, paperback novel, notepad, calling cards. When he ran the sensor over Hadley's wallet a light came on and the unit beeped.

'Coins?' asked Olmos.

Hadley nodded.

The interrogator unzipped the little pocket and tipped the contents onto the table. Four euros and sixty-five cents. And one gold coin which he immediately picked up and examined carefully.

'Did you know, Mr Hadley,' he said, with a satisfied smirk, 'that it is illegal to export gold from Cuba?'

'I . . . I had that with me when I came.' Jack wasn't sure why he'd decided to lie.

'Ah.' Olmos put the coin back down on the table and continued to look at it. 'Then you would have declared it?'

'I didn't think one small coin . . . a lucky charm . . .'

Olmos shook his head slowly and tut-tutted.

'It will be confiscated, of course,' he said casually. He shrugged his shoulders, picked up the coin again and told Hadley to remain seated. Then he left the room.

He was walking towards his colleagues by the inspection

tables when something made them all turn towards the entrance. A man in an immaculate olive uniform was just entering the room, removing his cap as he did so but keeping on the dark glasses through which it was impossible to see his eyes. Hadley recognised him immediately: Aquiles Sierra.

The man 'from the Interior Ministry' did not look like a civil servant tonight. He walked up to the group, glanced briefly in Hadley's direction and moved towards a private office, followed by the retinue.

Hadley looked at the clock on the wall once more. It read 22:13. The Iberia flight to Madrid was scheduled to depart in seventeen minutes. Should he try and contact Florin?

Unexpectedly, the various inspectors poured out of Sierra's office and returned to Hadley's luggage. They were carefully repacking all his belongings when Sierra himself emerged and made directly for Hadley. The artificial smile was already on display as he opened the door.

'Professor Hadley.' He greeted him like a long-lost friend. 'A minor problem with gold exports, I understand?'

'A coin, Mr Sierra, one coin. It's worth very little . . .'

'Of course.' Sierra gave a dismissive wave of one hand. 'But you'll understand. We need to have regulations. If we didn't' – he managed a contrived small laugh – 'people might get ideas. Hooligans, economic saboteurs, even common thieves! They'd think they could run away with Cuba's gold!'

Sierra offered the coin back to Hadley. 'And we certainly could not tolerate that, could we?'

The flight took off just after eleven. Hadley declined dinner and accepted a drink instead. He turned on his reading light, adjusted his seat slightly and started reading Florin's notes.

He marvelled at the Aztec's narrative and looked forward eagerly to the rest of the notes that were yet to come. He still could not quite fathom what was going on between Florin and Pinto and inevitably his thoughts wandered back to Friday the thirteenth. Hadley was still trying to understand how he'd allowed himself to be sucked into this strange world of intrigue when, somewhere over the Atlantic, he fell asleep.

The two municipal policemen looked annoyed as they entered the apartment. The older one switched off the music and motioned to his younger partner to follow Rosa who, first to react, had run off towards the bedroom.

'Make yourself decent!' he ordered Mercedes who started buttoning her shirt and trousers. The sudden silence was almost tangible in their alcohol- and drug-induced state. He looked at Jack and Mercedes with evident disgust as the younger man – a hint of a smirk on his lips – escorted Rosa, now fully dressed, back into the room.

'Your ID cards,' he demanded as he put his phone to his ear and spoke to someone.

The older cop ordered Mercedes, Rosa and Jack to sit on the sofa and took the chair opposite. He stared at the drugs on the coffee table. He sent his colleague to search the rest of the apartment and minutes later the younger man returned, holding a clear plastic sachet between his index finger and thumb.

'In the bathroom,' he said, holding up the cocaine.

Jack looked at Rosa but she remained silent, staring straight ahead. They sat there in silence until a third man, smartly dressed, arrived. He took the three ID cards and studied them.

'You are British, Mr Hadley,' he noted, extending a demanding hand as Jack nodded. 'Your passport, please.'

He put the three plastic cards inside Hadley's passport and placed it in his pocket.

'I'm Inspector Rueda,' he said slowly and clearly, as if speaking to a child or someone of diminished mental capacity. 'And this is a very serious matter. Do you understand?'

Even in their befuddled state all three understood well enough to nod.

'We are no longer talking about a disturbance of the peace,' he continued. 'I shall have to refer this to the Guardia Civil.'

The inspector passed a digital camera to the older policeman and told him to photograph the evidence then bag it, ready to take back to the station.

'You have caused enough disturbance in this quarter for one night,' Rueda explained patiently. 'You'll do exactly as I say.'

He told them he would leave now with their documents and the evidence. They were to remain in the apartment and let no one in. A policeman would stand watch outside their door. In the morning, at nine, they were to report to Salamanca Police Headquarters where appropriate charges would be made.

'Any questions?'

'Fuck.' Jack spoke first after the police were gone.

'I'm sorry.' Rosa seemed genuinely repentant.

'We were all in it together, Rosa.' Mercedes took her hand. 'Don't blame yourself.'

'Fuck,' repeated Jack, thinking of the University.

Mercedes stood up and went back to the bedroom.

She returned with a pillow and a spare duvet and put them on the couch. Rosa thanked her.

'We'll all think better in the morning,' suggested Mercedes. 'Let's try and get some sleep. We've only four hours left.'

She kissed Rosa on the cheek, took Jack's hand and led him to bed.

In the morning they were driven to Police Headquarters, near Jesuits' Park. On the way Mercedes suggested that they should get a lawyer.

'Please, let me,' Rosa volunteered. 'I have good contacts in Madrid.'

'Let's hear what Rueda has to say first,' said Hadley.

They reached the large building on Jardines Street and were directed to the second floor. There they sat in a waiting room until ten-thirty. When they were eventually shown into Rueda's office the Inspector was anything but friendly.

'Sorry I'm late,' he said sarcastically. 'I didn't get to bed till five this morning.'

They sat on chairs facing Rueda's desk. The sun streamed in through the tall windows and a fresh breeze brought the scent of acacias from the street. Rosa and Mercedes both wore dark glasses; Jack squinted and wished he'd remembered his.

The Inspector read through two typed documents on his desk. The first one seemed to be three or four pages long.

'If it was up to me,' he said sternly, 'I'd put the three of you behind bars.

'This is a university town,' he continued. 'We expect students to be students. We can accept the odd incident with hashish or marijuana.

'This is also a tourist town!' He slapped his open hand on the table. 'We can expect a little noise from foreigners who cannot hold their drink!'

'But you' – he pointed a finger at Hadley – '*you* are a professor at our great University. You should be ashamed!'

'I'm sorry . . .' Jack started to apologise but Rueda had already turned to Mercedes.

'And what do you think your father will have to say about this, Miss Vilanova?'

'I'm thirty years old, Inspector,' she replied defiantly, to Hadley's consternation.

'As for you, Mrs Uribe . . .' He ignored Mercedes's quip.

Mrs? Jack and Mercedes looked at each other.

'What would your husband have to say? Is he aware of your filthy habits?'

Rosa gave an almost imperceptible shrug but remained silent.

'Unfortunately, however' – Rueda stood up and raised his voice, slapping his desk again as he did so – 'it is *not* up to me!

'It's not even up to the Guardia Civil, they tell me!' He sat down again and took a deep breath.

'It appears,' he continued, 'that at least *one* of you' – he paused and looked at each face in turn – 'has friends in high places. So what's a simple Policía Local Inspector going to do?'

He picked up the second document and read it once again, as if to make sure he'd not misread it the previous dozen times.

'I am to put all papers relating to this case in a bag. Including the evidence and photographs. And then I am to arrange for a car *and* a driver to take the three of you to Madrid.'

'When?' Mercedes still had her wits about her.

'Right now!' roared Rueda, with a final slap on the table. 'Right this very cursed minute!'

They set off in an unmarked police car as the sun reached its winter zenith. Hadley sat in front, next to the driver, the two women in the back. They drove silently in the direction of Avila. In the distance they could see the Sierras they'd be crossing on their way to the capital.

'Where are we going?' Mercedes asked the driver but he acted as though he hadn't heard.

Jack was mulling over the implications of their predicament. A drug-related arrest was enough to get them rusticated with no appeal. Relationships between students and faculty were frowned upon, but given Mercedes's postgraduate status and the fact that she and Jack had become, for all intents and purposes, 'a couple', theirs was marginally acceptable and, thus far, had not been singled out. But with charges of drug possession, disturbing the peace and whatever else the Governing Council might wish to add, Hadley did not think much of his prospects.

The timing could not have been worse. With the job abruptly gone – and consequently no possibility of another position in Spain – finances would be tight. He'd have nowhere to live and the imminent trip to Cuba could be in jeopardy. Hadley felt miserable.

And yet there was something gnawing at the back of his mind, something he could not quite put his finger on but that somehow set off alarm bells inside his head.

The after-effects of the previous night's alcohol coupled with sleep deprivation did not help.

'Please,' Mercedes insisted, 'can you tell us where we are going?'

'I'm sorry, Miss.' The driver sounded genuine. 'I can't say.'

'Are you really married?' She turned to Rosa next.

Rosa looked at her and nodded once. Mercedes shook her head as if asking *what next?* and discerned a hint of a smile on Rosa's face. Hadley appeared to be paying little attention to his girlfriend's questions.

'So who's got friends in high places, anyway?' Mercedes asked.

'Your father?' ventured Hadley, without turning his head.

'*Collons!*' Mercedes exclaimed. She only ever spoke Castilian Spanish, even at home, but turned to earthy Valencian whenever an expletive seemed appropriate.

She pondered the possibility.

'No,' she said on reflection, 'How would he have known, anyway? It only happened hours ago.' She did not have to explain what *it* was.

There they were again, the alarm bells, but still Hadley could not fathom what they meant.

'He's an influential man,' he insisted. 'Someone might have told him.'

'He's just a businessman, Jack,' she protested. 'He couldn't get the Guardia to turn a blind eye.'

Mercedes turned to Rosa. 'What does your husband do?'

'He's a dentist, Mercedes,' she replied. 'No chance.'

They remained largely silent for the next half-hour. Hadley commented on the distance to Madrid as they passed a road sign and Mercedes said she was hungry but neither comment prompted suggestions or sympathy.

The women slept for a while and Jack continued speculating about the possible outcomes of this mess. Soon they crossed the Guadarrama Pass and drove down towards the city.

'Nice evening, though.' Mercedes eventually broke the silence, betraying where her thoughts had been.

Rosa made a snorting sound and Hadley turned round and stared at both women in silent disbelief. He could see that Rosa was trying to suppress an imminent attack of the giggles. Hadley returned his gaze to the road ahead as his girlfriend took Rosa's hand and squeezed it tight. Mercedes, too, felt the giggles about to overtake her.

No one spoke again until they reached their destination in Madrid.

9

Aquiles Sierra sat in his office reading the Aztec's notes long into the night. In terms of the country's internal security, Sierra was a powerful man. On a day-to-day, front-line basis, perhaps the most powerful in Cuba.

But there were certain areas where even Sierra had to be very careful how he trod. Anything that might be perceived as a challenge to the old guard in general and the remaining survivors of the Sierra Maestra in particular was definitely taboo.

And when it came to Old Bolsheviks, Florin was just about the most untouchable of them all. It was, in fact, Florin's money that had bought the *Granma* motor yacht from her American owner in Veracruz.

And it had been Florin's friend and mentor, Antonio Mercer, who had arrived from Moscow with a hundred Spanish-speaking advisers soon after the Revolution's triumph in 1959.

It had also been Florin who'd led the Cuban campaign

throughout Africa and Latin America and paid for it with
the blood of his own children.

Jesús Florin might have been a foreigner but, like
Guevara, he was reckoned to be as Cuban as the Castros,
Matos or Cienfuegos. In modern Cuba the Aztec sat on
the high pedestal of popular lore.

But Fidel himself could not be far from his grave. How
much longer would Cuba's own brand of Communism
endure once the Supreme Commander was dead and
buried?

All Sierra had to do was look at Eastern Europe to realise
that the present system's days were numbered. Whether
for better or worse time would tell, but right now those
in positions of power within the established order were
starting to get ready for life in a new Cuba in which today's
officials would be tomorrow's unemployed and many –
Sierra included – would find themselves the target of pent-
up anger and vindictive retribution from returning exiles.

So Aquiles Sierra lost no sleep over the knowledge that
so many of his own colleagues and the state's ministerial
grandees were lining their pockets, stashing nest eggs out
of reach, forging bonds and soliciting favour with their
foreign counterparts who one day might have the power
to recommend or even approve an immigrant visa or
refugee status for a new wave of Cuban émigrés who would
not become an economic burden to their new adoptive
land.

Ordinarily, if anything unusual involving the old guard
came to Sierra's attention – currency violations, illegal
imports – he would simply note his observations and let
it pass.

In this instance, however, Sierra was certain that the

Aztec was up to something unofficial and perhaps even unacceptable. First there had been that woman from the Spanish Embassy. Her declared role was to do with trade, not an area in which Florin was or had ever been active.

She'd been in and out of Cuba several times in the past but had never attracted Sierra's displeasure or concern. She did, after all, organise many of the exhibitions and congresses that had led to Spanish investment in Cuba.

But when she first made direct and unexpected contact with Sierra there had been a degree of urgency in her voice, a hint of distress perhaps, concealed behind an otherwise perfect picture of composure – but not so perfect that she could avoid Sierra's sixth sense for sniffing out fear or deceit.

Then, a few months later, in rolled this Hadley man, claiming to be an academic from Salamanca. Sierra had him checked out and his story held up. But why would Florin choose an English ex-soldier to write the Aztec's memoirs, if indeed the documents photocopied at the airport were genuine?

And then there was the gold coin. Was Hadley lying? Had he really brought the coin into the country or was it a symbolic signal?

Ten years earlier, Sierra had been young and confident enough to have the Aztec's bungalow bugged. When the devices were found all hell had broken loose but Sierra had been canny enough to deploy only US-made transmitters from his large private collection of similar equipment planted by the CIA and often subsequently discovered by Cuban counter-intelligence within their own foreign legations.

Predictably enough, the US had been at the receiving

end of Cuba's explicit and well-documented accusations at the United Nations.

But Sierra had been taken aback by the sheer vitriol of Raul Castro's reaction – aimed, thankfully, at the Americans. It became evident that Castro regarded any violation of Florin's privacy as a personal attack upon himself and Sierra considered it prudent, in that instance, to destroy all evidence of his unauthorised snooping.

Destroyed or not, however, he had not forgotten the contents, in particular a seemingly jocular conversation between Florin and his former mentor, Mercer, back in 1994. Sierra had not fully comprehended its significance at the time, though he certainly recognised the subject matter.

'General Florin.' Nurse Miriam could not hide the joy in her voice. 'You have a visitor!'

Florin was outside, in the back garden, trying to light the small barbecue in defiance of a gathering September wind.

She had only been with him for two months but the initial shyness – apprehension, even – had evaporated. Now she seemed to genuinely enjoy working for The Aztec.

Back in July, she had been shown into Florin's living room by his orderly, Corporal Truenos.

'And who might you be?' he'd asked, perhaps more gruffly than necessary.

'Miriam Mercado, sir,' she'd answered reverentially in a soft husky voice. 'I am your new nurse.'

'And who says I need a nurse?'

'I . . .' She hesitated. 'I've been sent by Don Raúl, sir. He said . . .'

'Do I look like I need a nurse, Miriam?' Florin stood up and stared at her, arms akimbo.

'Sir, I don't know, Don Raúl said—'

'So how do you know the Second Secretary?' Florin interrupted.

'He's a relative, sir,' she explained. 'My mother's cousin's . . .'

'I see.' Florin was dismissive. 'So, are you a proper nurse?'

She looked to be in her early twenties. She wore a smart polka-dot shirt over light brown trousers and in her right hand she held an official-looking envelope. Her orders, Florin guessed. Her hair was cut short and she wore little make-up. She was, in fact, thought Florin, an extremely attractive girl. What did Raúl Castro think he was doing?

'I am, sir. I'm also a qualified physiotherapist. Don Raúl said your back . . .'

'Ah!' Florin remembered the conversation. He'd complained of recurrent backaches once, when sharing a drink with the armed forces' commander.

'I understand now.' He reached out and took the envelope from her.

She was a Guantanamera, from Baracoa on the south-eastern tip of Cuba. Aged twenty-three and recently qualified at the Havana School of Nursing. Her references included a short handwritten note to Florin referring to her as 'my niece'.

Now she stood on the rear veranda of Florin's bungalow, smartly dressed in her nurse's uniform, exuding the level of confidence that he admiringly approved of in someone so young.

'A visitor, hey? I bet I know who that is!' he replied jovially, raising his voice for anyone inside the house to hear.

'You know who I am, eh, *cabrón?*' The voice thundered from the penumbra of the living room.

Mercer came out through the open patio doors into the garden and the two men embraced. The Spaniard looked tired, haggard even. He had aged considerably since the last time they had met.

'Let me look at you, *pendejo*,' he joked, pushing Florin to arm's length and studying his faded olive fatigues.

'You look good!' Mercer pronounced.

'And you look like shit!' Florin retorted, only half in jest.

Mercer looked round the veranda and sat on one of the new wicker chairs.

'I *feel* like shit, Jesús,' he admitted. 'Not been well lately. I'm eighty-six, you know.'

'You look a hundred and six,' Florin joked.

'Drinks, Miriam,' he ordered, quickly adding, 'Vodka for the General,' before she disappeared into the house.

Mercer did look unwell. Gone was most of his much-photographed mane, and his tanned dark skin had turned a blood-drained grey. He'd never been tall but now he was slightly stooped, adding to an overall impression of fragility.

Florin enquired about Mercer's family, though he knew they were all well – in Spain now, in a socialist, monarchical Spain that neither man here today would have envisaged all those years ago when they had fought so hard for their dreams.

Mercer, like most of Florin's friends, did not ask about the Mexican's personal life.

'What took you so long? You've been in Cuba a week!' Florin chastised him.

'You know what it's like. Spent time with Fidel.' Mercer

lowered his voice and glanced towards the house. 'He *really* looks like shit! And Raúl wanted to take me everywhere. So this is my first free day, and here I am.'

'You *gallegos* like to stick together,' Florin joked. The Castros' parents, like Mercer, had been born in Galicia.

'I don't expect I'll see Cuba again.' Mercer spoke slowly, looking out towards the sea, perhaps recalling his early youth in the Caribbean country where he had discovered both Communism and politics.

Truenos arrived with a tray. He put down a bottle of Stolichnaya on the low table and a bucket of ice which Mercer waved away. The orderly then poured neat vodka into the General's glass and uncapped a beer bottle for Florin.

'Check my fire, Truenos,' he ordered. Then he turned to Mercer. 'You'll lunch with me, yes?'

They drank in memory of old times and absent friends. Mercer stood beside the barbecue while Florin placed the skewered pork over the charcoal. Together they prepared a salad and gossiped about the few old comrades left alive.

'I bumped into Captain Pinto this winter,' Mercer said casually after a break in the conversation.

'Pinto?' Florin seemed unsure of the name.

'Roberto Pinto, the CNI weasel.'

'Ah! *That* Pinto!' Florin's tone suddenly betrayed a degree of interest.

Pinto had worked his way up to the number two job in Spanish Intelligence over the last eight years. Spain was not a problem for Cuba but neither was she Cuba's closest friend. Under Felipe Gonzáles, the Socialist Prime Minister, the two countries had become a lot closer, especially in matters of trade. But the CESID – precursor of the CNI – was full of old-school military operators and neither Florin nor Mercer ever trusted them all the way.

'Yes,' Mercer continued. 'We met at a comrade's funeral. In the Valley.'

'And who might have died that would make both you and Pinto attend?'

'Quite,' agreed Mercer, going off to refill his glass. 'My very thought indeed.'

He poured a second vodka and brought along another Cristal for Florin.

'No, I don't think it was an accidental meeting.'

'So what did Pinto want?'

'He started off with some bullshit about him being a great coin collector.'

'*Gold* coins?' queried Florin sarcastically.

Both men laughed.

'Anyway, he soon admitted that he was after *el oro de Moscú*.

'You sent him packing, I expect?'

'Not at all. Wouldn't waste such a golden opportunity!'

They laughed again at the unintended pun.

'I suggested you might know.'

'Thanks very much!' Florin looked at his former commander quizzically; he was getting an inkling of where this was going.

'So now,' Mercer explained, 'the deputy head of Spain's secret service believes you have something he wants.'

'All I need next,' Florin completed the circle, 'is to find out what *he* might have that *we* want. Right?'

'Exactly right, *pendejo* – we taught you well. But enough of spy games.' Mercer rubbed his hands. 'That pork smells good. Are you going to feed this old man?'

That was the last time they saw each other. Mercer returned to Spain a few days later and the following year, close to Christmas, he died in Madrid, in bed, surrounded by his family.

Several more years would pass before Pinto would have anything that Florin might want to trade. But when he finally did, The Aztec would have to play the most important spy game of his life.

That little, almost forgotten piece of information popped out of Sierra's encyclopaedic memory like a carefully bookmarked page waiting to be referred to.

Pinto was a force to be reckoned with nowadays and he'd once had a bee in his bonnet over the missing gold. The Spanish woman? Was she just Trade, or was that a CNI cover for her dirty work?

And why Hadley? If the presence of that gold coin in the professor's wallet was a simple coincidence my name is not Aquiles Sierra, the Cuban security chief told himself.

Was there a link between Hadley and Pinto? And if there was, did Florin know? Or, even better, was he a co-conspirator?

Sierra had no wish to go to the top of the Cuban command structure with his suspicions. But neither was he about to become a mere spectator and let time prove him right or wrong.

If there was any of that gold still lying around somewhere, some of it would provide the prefect pension should Sierra need to opt for forced retirement in Acapulco or Punta del Este.

But it was not a simple matter of money: Sierra had a personal issue with Florin. It was the man's arrogance that angered him, The Aztec's refusal to defer to the head of Internal Security, the way he always pointedly bypassed Sierra's department and dealt directly with his own contacts across the world – as if Sierra's office and authority did not exist.

Sierra saw that Florin was an internationalist, a man who had adopted Cuba when it suited him. He could be Russian or even Mexican at will and, Sierra believed, had never entirely shaken off his aristocratic roots and airs of superiority even after a lifetime in the bosom of the people's cause.

He'd fought in Spain and Russia just as he had in Africa and Latin America, in pursuit of an impossible utopia that was greater than all nations, a cause never to be questioned, never to be found in the wrong.

After the Revolution he'd come and gone from Cuba at will and though he held no position in the government he enjoyed all the benefits of high office with none of the inherent responsibilities.

Nothing would give Sierra more pleasure than to unmask The Aztec, to find his hidden pot of gold and expose him as a fake, living in make-believe frugality for all to see and admire while at the same time continuing to pull strings across the planet with the independence he'd obtained through his stolen wealth.

After the bugging fiasco, Sierra had taken a close look at Florin's staff. There was some evidence that the nurse, Mercado, might have been expected to report to Castro in the beginning. But he couldn't be sure that was still the case. If anything, she had developed an attachment to Florin over the past decade that Sierra doubted even her uncle would be able to subvert.

Truenos was an army man and Florin was a General. Unless Sierra found something to blackmail the sergeant with there was no way he could be acquired. And the rest of Florin's Cuban friends, by and large, were military, older and suspicious of ambitious younger men.

All the same, reflected Sierra as he lit a cigar, 'unassailable' was not a word in his vocabulary. Knowing what you *cannot* do is already half the battle won. Time to turn to what I *can* do, he concluded.

He had a worldwide covert network at his disposal and he would deploy it to his own advantage. If that Hadley man, the Uribe woman or even Pinto were in cahoots with The Aztec, Sierra intended to find out.

And if any of that gold still existed there was no way that Sierra would let it simply vanish into greedy foreign hands.

10

As he disembarked in Madrid from his flight, Hadley braced himself for another round of questioning, this time from the Spaniards rather than the Cubans but all the same not something he was looking forward to.

He set off along Terminal 4's interminable walkways, wondering whether his new interrogators would meet him at Immigration or outside the Customs hall. He did not have to wait long for an answer.

Ahead, speaking to a uniformed official, the 'Varadero couple' were scrutinising arrivals. Their demeanour was different now that they no longer had to keep a low profile. On their home patch they were manifestly in charge. Florin had been right: Pinto's foot soldiers. Hadley walked straight up to them. Might as well, he thought.

'Will you be taking me to the Captain now or should I go home first?'

They did not seem amused by Hadley's approach but they had their orders. They took his luggage tag and asked him to hand his passport to the border policeman who would see Hadley to a waiting car without further formalities.

The driver was amenable and chatty and seemed to have no idea who Hadley was. He complained about the traffic, the unrelenting rain and Real Madrid's performance until it transpired that Hadley was an Englishman, at which point the subject of the conversation – more like a monologue – switched to David Beckham for whom the club had just paid £25 million.

He was right about the traffic, though: it took over an hour to cover the eighteen miles from Barajas Airport, east of the city, to the CNI headquarters on the western side. Hadley tried to call Mercedes but her phone was switched off. He looked at his watch. Eleven in the morning; she would probably be in the library.

As they pulled into the complex on Padre Ruidobro Avenue, along the sweeping tree-flanked drive, Hadley had a sense of déjà vu, but the modern pink stone building with smoked-glass windows looked more threatening this time. The previous visit had been punctuated by concern but also leavened with curiosity and relief in the knowledge that what was taking place bypassed the Guardia Civil and did not please the Salamanca police. Whatever that first visit held in store, Hadley had speculated at the time, it also implied some form of reprieve. Rueda had said so. '*Friends in high places.*'

Now it seemed hard to believe that only five weeks had elapsed and Hadley was not at all certain that Pinto would be entirely convinced: it had been far too easy. Why would Florin clam up for decades and suddenly start talking? There had to be more to it, concluded Hadley, and he felt certain that would be Pinto's reaction.

In the intervening period Hadley had also started questioning certain aspects of what he had taken for granted thus far, such as who the hell was Rosa Uribe – and why did she have to go about the place carrying industrial quantities of cocaine?

On Saturday the fourteenth, the day after Ramiro's birthday party, Hadley had been delivered by another driver to that same entrance with Mercedes and Rosa. They had stood silently in the winter sunlight, looking for signs of what might be hidden in this modern monolith with neo-cubist sculptures on the front lawn and no discernible corporate identity, just a portico flanked by unusually high, bare flag-poles. The driver had handed over the bag containing the 'evidence and photos' and the porter had signed a receipt.

As they entered the main lobby, they came face to face with the circular blue and white emblem of the Centro Nacional de Inteligencia that covered a good portion of an entire wall. Their silent guide ushered them into a lift and accompanied them to the third floor. They were met there by a second official, a woman this time. She took charge of Mercedes and Rosa and led them away along a corridor to the left. Hadley was escorted in the opposite direction and shown into an elegant, if sterile, room with no windows. He was told to take a seat on a well-upholstered leather armchair and wait.

A few minutes later, a young woman popped her head through the door and asked Hadley if he wanted anything.

'Such as?' What was he supposed to want? A lawyer?

'Something to eat or drink? Captain Pinto will be with you shortly.'

Captain Pinto?

'Just water would be nice, thank you.'

The door was closed again. Was it locked? Was this some form of arrest?

How the hell, thought Hadley, could anything that was said or done last night be of any interest to the CNI? And where were Mercedes and Rosa?

'*Mister* Hadley.' Pinto strode in, all smiles, and used the English prefix. Hadley stood up. It seemed like the right thing to do.

'Coffee? Tea, perhaps?' He couldn't have been more welcoming, like a bank manager greeting a depositor. 'I'm Roberto Pinto.' They shook hands.

'Jack Hadley. I've asked for water, thank you.'

'Now.' Pinto got straight to the point, sitting down on the chair opposite, looking thoroughly relaxed. 'We have a problem, do we not?'

'Mr Pinto, I have no idea why we have been brought here.' Hadley had had some time to think and was not about to be totally subservient, 'Yes, we have a *bit* of a problem.' He pronounced 'bit' dismissively and continued: 'But why have we been dragged to Madrid – and to the CNI, of all places?'

'Mr Hadley,' Pinto leaned forward and spoke in a calm voice, 'a private party involving three consenting adults and a little coke would be *a bit* of a problem.' He paused, but the way he let the words hang suggested he was yet to make his point.

'Raucous debauchery involving a university professor, a student and a high-ranking civil servant, *plus* enough cocaine to satisfy the needs of a Hollywood premiere party is, to put it mildly, a very serious problem indeed. And that's *before* the press get hold of it!

'So.' The smile returned. 'Let us agree we are both on

the same side and see how we can best deal with this. Shall we?'

'Why?' Hadley had to ask.

'All in good time.' Pinto raised an admonitory hand. 'All in good time. Now, tell me, where did the cocaine come from?'

'I don't know.'

'So you didn't supply it?'

'No.'

'Not very chivalrous,' Pinto said, with a smirk, looking at the ceiling, addressing no one in particular.

'Should I not have a lawyer with me?'

'God forbid!' Pinto looked horrified.

'So can you tell me what the hell is going on, then?'

'Do you believe in fate, Mr Hadley?'

'Sometimes.'

'Well, *I* do!' Pinto said with conviction. He stood up and walked to a telephone on a side cabinet. 'Have you eaten anything today?' he asked, seemingly concerned.

'No.' Suddenly Hadley felt hungry.

'Then we will talk over lunch.'

'What about the girls?' He suddenly remembered Mercedes's complaint about being hungry.

'They are being well looked after,' Pinto replied dismissively. He ordered food over the phone and returned to his chair.

'Fate, Mr Hadley,' continued Pinto, 'that's what this is about. An extraordinary coincidence of events which led me to look in your direction at precisely the very moment that you happened to need a helping hand.'

'Why? Why did you look at me?'

'The common link, Mr Hadley, is found in a name: Jesús María Florin del Valle.'

'Jesús Florin? I haven't even met him yet.' Hadley remained puzzled even after Pinto's revelation.

'*Yet,*' Pinto was quick to point out. 'But, as we both know, you are about to. So here's how fate intervened:

'First,' Pinto pressed his extended left index finger with his right, 'Spain has been interested in The Aztec for a very long time. Nothing nasty, let me add, just a few questions that . . .' he paused as if looking for the right words '. . . it would be most helpful to have answered. But, again as you know, Florin is a bit of a recluse. No interviews, et cetera.

'Secondly,' the right index finger moved to the left middle one, 'my sources tell me that an English visiting professor in Salamanca has managed to secure a meeting with The Aztec. "Who is this man?" I ask myself. Naturally, I get my people to find out, right?'

Before Hadley could reply there was a knock on the door and a waiter came in. He wheeled in a small trolley and laid a white cloth on the coffee table. There was a selection of drinks on offer but both men took only water. A basket of bread rolls was put on the table as well as a platter with cold meats and cheeses and a fresh-fruit bowl. Lastly the waiter placed a bright metal thermos coffee jug and small cups on the sideboard. Pinto thanked him and waited until he had left the room.

'Finally,' he moved to the ring finger and continued his analysis, 'just as I am starting to envisage a way forward, an arrangement whereby your forthcoming visit to Cuba can be beneficial – to you, naturally, but also to your host nation, to Spain – my sources, God bless their diligence, inform me that you have got yourself into one big mess and that unless we do something very, very quickly, this once-in-a-lifetime opportunity will almost certainly leap away from our grasp.'

Pinto leaned back, an enquiring look on his face inviting Hadley to confirm that he followed the reasoning.

'So I had to intervene,' concluded Pinto. 'Not at all easy, I must say. I had to get the Minister himself to sanction this, but here we are. So, you see now, Mr Hadley? Do you understand why you are here?'

'I'm starting to. But what on earth do you think I'd be able to do for you in Cuba? All I have is an invitation – and even that is through Havana University – to meet with Florin and ask him to reminisce about Madrid in the autumn of 1936.'

'Yes, we are aware,' confided Pinto and Hadley could not hide his surprise. 'We have sources in Cuba as well, as you'd expect.'

'Let me get this straight, Mr Pinto: are you saying that if I help you out with whatever it is with The Aztec that you want to know, my problem in Salamanca disappears?'

'That would be the intention.'

'And Miss Vilanova? Mrs Uribe? What will happen to them?'

'How well do you know Mrs Uribe?'

'I don't. I met her yesterday. She's a close friend's cousin.'

Pinto made a disapproving face. For a man involved with the dirty side of life he seemed a little quick to judge, thought Hadley.

'Well, allow me to enlighten you. Mrs Uribe works for the State Commerce Secretariat, Foreign Trade Section.'

'What does that mean?' Hadley wasn't sure whether this was leading anywhere.

'For a division called ICEX, to be precise. Do you know what that is?'

'No.' He did not.

'Let us just say that wherever in the world a business opportunity arises that might be of interest to Spain – from Afghanistan to Zimbabwe – ICEX will poke its nose. And if that opportunity arises anywhere within Latin America, then the person at the forefront of Spain's thrust would be Rosa Uribe.'

'I see.'

'She's the face of Spanish trade in an entire subcontinent. So, to answer your previous question, Mr Hadley, we have a second and, if I may say so, even more compelling reason to protect Mrs Uribe.'

'And Mercedes?'

'Miss Vilanova is of little interest to us either way. Her father, of course, is well known in business circles. He would not be amused to see his daughter on the front page of Valencia's papers and we certainly could not prevent that if the story got out. But it won't, of course, because we are not about to let that happen, are we?'

'I get the message.'

'Good, I knew you would. I hear you were once a soldier?'

'That was a long time ago,' replied Hadley dismissively.

'Well, I was once a sailor, see? We are both plain-talking men, Mr Hadley, no need to go round in circles: we need your help and you could do with ours. Serve us this once – and learn your lesson, of course – and the last twenty-four hours never happened. You have my word.'

Pinto stood up, as if to signify that the meeting was ended.

'So that's it?' asked Hadley, incredulously. 'We are free to go?'

'You are and so is Miss Vilanova. You will, of course, come back for briefing before you go to Cuba.'

'And Rosa?'

'Mrs Uribe is a different matter. She's a government employee, highly exposed to foreign influences. Any suggestion of a drug habit would need to be investigated. As I said,' Pinto added patronisingly, 'we must be sure to protect her.'

11

Rosa Uribe opened her eyes just wide enough to read the digital display on the bedside clock. She smiled a sleepy smile: 06:35. Just as she had done on three successive mornings, she forced herself out of bed and quickly made for the hanging cords that would pull back the curtains of the triple window of her east-facing hotel room.

She drew the curtains wide with one swift motion and dashed back into bed. She puffed up three pillows, piled them against the centre of the headboard and propped herself up into a comfortable position, pulling the bedcovers up to her chin. Then she peered out into the last moments of darkness as she awaited the start of nature's show.

Through the windows she could see lights coming on in some of the high-rise buildings in the elegant eastern suburb of Las Condes. Slowly, the distant outline of the mountains beyond began to take shape against the gentle pink of early dawn. Their sheer magnitude made them look deceptively close. She held her breath in anticipation of the pink turning briefly into red before the sun leapt out from its hiding place behind the Andes and delivered its morning brilliance on the city of Santiago.

It was, thought Rosa, the best hotel window in the world. She did not feel like going down to the gymnasium that morning, she had worked out hard enough the previous day. She had, in fact, felt so healthy throughout this trip that she'd been able to cut down on her normal level of medication. She was under no illusions, of course, but for the moment at least she could pretend that life would go on.

Today she would treat herself to breakfast in bed, followed by a leisurely bath. She would then get her hair done in the hotel's salon and make it to the embassy in plenty of time for her appointment at ten-thirty. She loved the Chilean capital, even if this particular visit was inevitably marred by the very nature of her unpalatable assignment.

'It's a bit political this time, Rosa,' Pinto had said over lunch in the CNI canteen.

'Oh. When isn't it political, Roberto?' she'd challenged.

'I should have said more political than usual,' Pinto humoured her, 'in that there's not a real national security element involved.'

It was, in fact, more akin to the proverbial hot potato. Pinto could not entirely figure out Judge Pinzón. The judge had got it into his head that he would prosecute the perpetrators of atrocities that had taken place in the Americas twenty and thirty years earlier, in the bloody 1970s and 1980s. He had cast his net wide: Argentina, Chile, Uruguay, Guatemala, Nicaragua, Ecuador, El Salvador. At first Pinzón had claimed jurisdiction on the grounds that the victims were Spanish citizens, a contention that was accurate, if only up to a point: huge numbers of Spanish immigrants who had settled permanently in Latin America retained their nationality of birth and were thus able to pass it to their children and grandchildren.

Though the laws of most countries in the region declared anyone born within its territory a citizen, they also recognised dual nationalities through bilateral agreements with selected European nations. Thus a great many second- and third-generation South Americans were Spanish, French or Italian citizens even if, for the most part, they had never set foot in Europe.

Later on, Judge Pinzón appended a corollary to his argument by concluding that as Spain was part of the European Union, his Madrid Court was entitled to seek justice for any EU national whose fundamental rights might have been abused. Eventually, he had reasoned further that he had a duty to bring to justice any perpetrators of crimes against humanity committed anywhere in Hispanic America against anyone at all.

The judge was a direct descendant of Vicente Pinzón – commander of the caravel *La Niña*, which had sailed alongside Columbus's *Santa Maria* on the voyage that would stumble upon America – leading some commentators to suggest that Judge Pinzón was suffering from delusions of empire.

But, whatever might have been said behind his back, few politicians saw any gain in publicly denouncing the judge's motives or contentions and risking falling into the trap of having to defend their own stance on human rights.

Pinzón's determination represented a more irksome nuisance for Ministers, because he used his senior position within the judiciary to approach them directly with specific requests for extradition orders against an extensive list of people – from former presidents and military commanders to bottom-rung policemen singled out by 'witness declarations' – so that they might be examined in his Madrid Court.

With no one in power wishing to be the unfortunate subject of Pinzón's next weekly press conference, Ministers and Secretaries of State found it easier to acquiesce than to argue against the validity of the judge's requests.

'Pinzón accosted key Cabinet members – Interior, Foreign Affairs, Defence – who in turn made all the noises the judge wanted to hear,' Pinto explained, 'and formulated a common strategy: they dumped his demands in my lap!'

Rosa smiled knowingly and challenged Pinto, 'And now you want to dump them in mine?'

'I've asked our people on the ground to gather evidence,' he continued, undeterred. 'But we are going to have to do some sifting. All I'm asking is that you go over there, take a look, a country at a time, when you can, alongside your work for Commerce. Study their findings, reject the vendettas. Bring back a few with potential. No rush. I'll report we are working on it and give them something to keep the Judge at bay.'

'Anywhere in particular you want me to start?'

'Actually, yes.' Rosa thought she detected a slight blush on Pinto's face. 'He's got his claws into Chile at the moment. He's ranting that Pinochet escaped us once – you remember his arrest in England, don't you? – and figures in a minute the General's going to drop dead and that'll be that.'

'He's not seriously expecting to get Pinochet here?'

'No. But I think he wants to get at his cronies while "Pinnochio" is still alive.'

'I've no more ICEX trips to Chile scheduled for this year.'

'We'll take care of this one. Go get pampered for a few days at that lovely Grand Hyatt in Santiago and come back to me with what you can.'

But Rosa had not gone to Chile straight away. Her work at ICEX took precedence and had taken her to El Salvador and Argentina first where the local CNI operatives had been gathering names and evidence for some time and handed her a number of case files.

She had expected them to make sad reading but had been unprepared for the revelations of the intense nature of the violent internal conflicts, when both factions knew each other intimately enough to personalise their hatred.

Looking at the beautiful countries in which these events had taken place and recalling the friendliness she had always encountered in their people it defied belief that such brutal deeds could have taken place. Worse still, she felt, the majority of the perpetrators still roamed freely, and more often than not were leading comfortable lives.

But it was the atrocities against children that finally got to Rosa so that during two months spent gathering information for Pinto's 'political' she started questioning her own *raison d'être* and the allure of foreign trade successes began to lose its shine. And it was in that frame of mind that she arrived in Chile that fateful December of 2003.

Rosa's office in Santiago was on the eighth floor of a block in the Providencia district. As an integral part of the Spanish Embassy it enjoyed full diplomatic status, though its official designation was *Oficina Comercial*.

Luis Bianchi sat opposite Rosa at her large desk, silently browsing through the previous day's Madrid newspapers as she read the documents he had just delivered. He was a handsome man in his mid-forties, a father of six and a partner in a small law firm based in the port city of Valparaíso. He was also a human-rights activist and for the past three years he had assisted Spain in its search for murderers on the run.

Rosa had never heard of Osvaldo Ortiz but she felt a chill as she studied his file. It soon became clear that – whatever Judge Pinzón's true motives – bringing this scum to justice would be a pleasure.

Ortiz had been born in the southern Chilean city of Valdivia where his father was a tailor and his mother a seamstress. Though the Ortizes, by and large, could rightly claim Iberian lineage, Osvaldo's mother was half Mapuche Indian and from her he had inherited skin that was a shade of olive, jet-black hair and narrow eyes. As a boy he excelled at school and enjoyed a happy childhood. When a massive earthquake tore Valdivia apart one tragic autumn afternoon in 1960, Osvaldo's father, elder brother and his only sister were among the five thousand who died. With two million left homeless and overstretched charities being the sole remaining resource, Ortiz's distraught mother decided to take the boy north to Valparaíso where her sister and her police-officer husband lived simply but comfortably.

Osvaldo went on to complete his baccalaureate with top honours. But without funding for a university education he opted for a military career and in March of 1967 was admitted to the Bernardo O'Higgins Military Academy in Las Condes.

He was a twenty-one-year-old sub lieutenant in 1970 when socialist Salvador Allende was elected President, and that same year Ortiz went to work for Army Intelligence. In the three years of economic and political turmoil that followed, Ortiz increasingly became allied to reactionary factions within the armed forces that viewed Allende's ever closer association with the Soviet Union and its Cuban puppets with disgust.

The profound crisis that ensued as a consequence of failed Marxist economics made life extremely harsh for Ortiz's mother, who through great effort and long hours had managed to rent a modest place in Valparaíso and just about make ends meet. Hyperinflation also shattered any hopes of middle-class living standards for salaried people, including the military-officer class.

In his role within the intelligence community, Ortiz became aware of the extent of foreign interests: signal and diplomatic intercepts revealed the degree of Soviet and Cuban involvement, right down to individual cash payments and secret bank accounts – information that was sometimes unearthed by the Chileans themselves, at other times through tips or timely information passed on by the CIA.

By 1973, freshly promoted to Captain and assigned to counter-intelligence, Ortiz would be at the cutting edge of the brutal repression that would follow in the days immediately after the military coup of the eleventh of September.

While the presidential Moneda Palace was still smouldering and the tanks were rumbling through Santiago's streets, Ortiz and his team were already rounding up pre-selected people whose activities and whereabouts had been tracked for months. At first, these were driven en masse to the city's football stadium to pre-empt any escape attempts. Then they were assigned individually or in small groups to specific interrogation and torture units in pre-assigned locations.

Ortiz's name appeared repeatedly in testimony extracted

both from former inmates and indicted staff of the notorious illegal detention centres of Villa Grimaldi, the Tacna Regiment and the Air Warfare Academy. A total of 119 murders were attributed to Ortiz in the documents delivered to Rosa Uribe by Bianchi.

'It seems extraordinary that this could have happened in Chile,' she said, putting down the papers.

Bianchi nodded.

'It's been thirty years,' Rosa ventured, 'but I expect it's neither forgotten nor forgiven, right?'

'There's still considerable resentment. On both sides.'

It was Rosa's turn to nod in agreement. Then, as if she'd only just realised what she had read, she picked up the list again. Two names stood out. How could she have missed them before?

Florin del Valle, Lucía Irene, 34
Florin del Valle, María Luz, 11 months

'Are these . . .' She hesitated, turning the page for Bianchi to see, her finger poised against the names. 'Are these members of Jesús Florin's family?'

'Yes,' he replied without having to look.

'Goodness. This could have all sorts of implications.'

'I know.' Bianchi lit a cigarette.

'Mrs Uribe . . .'

'Rosa.'

'Rosa, thank you. Rosa, there is something I would like to show you. Are you very busy today?'

'Well, not exactly busy.' She was non-committal. 'What did you have in mind?'

'It's one hundred and twenty kilometres away. We could be there for lunch. I assure you it will be worthwhile.'

* * *

114

They drove north-west on Highway 68 towards Valparaíso as the summer sun reached its zenith. Bianchi turned the air conditioning high and they spoke about life, politics and Rosa's work in commerce. Bianchi did not touch upon the purpose of this outing and Rosa did not ask. So far he had impressed her as a sensible and rational man.

They reached Viña del Mar two hours later and Bianchi went directly to the seafront before continuing north along the coastline. It was Rosa's first visit to the seaside resort that was now in full swing at the start of its season. Bianchi drove slowly, restricted by holidaymakers and traffic, and she was able to appreciate endless white-sand beaches caressed by a light oceanic breeze and bordered by radiant, brightly coloured flower beds. Everywhere people in bathing suits or scanty clothing flitted between beach umbrellas and seaside eateries, temporarily escaping the sun's punishment.

The crowd thinned gradually as they left the resort's centre and continued along Avenida Borgoño. To their left the beaches gave way to rocky promontories and on the right expensive-looking villas and high-rise apartments with adjoining golf and tennis clubs were evidence of some very recent developments.

Where the road briefly turned east, past a newly created yacht marina, a clutch of houses stood in a privileged position, between the road and the Pacific Ocean. All bar one looked new and Bianchi drove his car up to the incongruous single-storey timber chalet that had evidently fallen into a state of considerable disrepair. He opened the car door and invited Rosa to follow him.

They walked along an uneven stone path along the left side of the house towards what would have been a front garden, stretching fifty metres or so to a low wooden palisade on the cliff's edge. The north-west-facing house frontage had a full-length covered veranda raised a few feet from the ground and now devoid of any furnishings. Double French windows, firmly closed and padlocked, could not entirely keep the house from the elements as the peeling wooden frame rotted and glass panes dropped out.

'Florin's house,' Bianchi said in response to Rosa's puzzled expression.

'Dear God.' She had an inkling that the visit would have something to do with Ortiz.

'Strictly speaking,' Bianchi observed, 'it's still his.'

'Oh?' Rosa looked at him questioningly.

'The deeds were registered to Lucía Florin. After she "vanished" it was left empty for a while, then in 1974 or '75 some Navy people moved in here but only stayed a couple of years. Everyone knew it was Florin's house and as fear of the military began to wane, the occupiers started getting angry stares and a fair share of abuse.'

'But with Lucía and her daughter dead the house would have passed to Jesús. They could have confiscated it. Proscribed foreign terrorist and so forth,' Rosa reasoned.

'Trouble was, Lucía was not officially dead – to this day her body hasn't been found.'

'Of course.' Rosa nodded in agreement. 'He could come back now, if he wanted.'

'He never has.'

'Municipal taxes . . .' she started to say before Bianchi interrupted.

'All paid. No. He knows it's here. And we suspect this is precisely how it will stay until The Aztec dies.'

'He is a puzzle, isn't he? The Aztec.'

'He's more than that. I don't think he's ever forgiven us Chileans. I think he leaves it untouched to remind us, right here, where the rich and famous come to play, of what we did to him and his family.'

'I think I've lost my appetite.' Rosa winced.

'Nonsense!' Bianchi chided her. 'It was just something I wanted you to see. When we get back to Santiago you will understand why, but in our line of business it pays to keep in touch with reality.'

Rosa smiled. She knew he was referring neither to Trade nor the Law.

'All the same, you cannot come to the coast without sampling our king crabs.'

Bianchi drove back through Viña and across Puente Casino into Valparaíso. He took Rosa to the *Bote Salvavidas*, the lifeboat station on the ocean front with its restaurant perched on top. Once a staff canteen, the restaurant now earned enough to fund the lifeboat and served the finest seafood on the South Pacific coast.

'Luisito!' The *Bote*'s manager, Gabriel, beamed as he saw them enter and gave Bianchi a warm embrace. In turn he introduced Rosa as 'a very important lady from Madrid'.

'This big-guns lawyer,' Gabriel told Rosa while keeping an affectionate arm around Bianchi's shoulders, 'used to wash dishes in here when he was an innocent boy.'

'Must have been a long time ago, Gabi,' Bianchi jested as Rosa watched in surprised amusement.

It was too hot to sit outside but they were taken to a window table with stunning views over the harbour.

'Did you really?' Rosa asked once they sat down.

Bianchi smiled and nodded. 'Lived off tips and dreamed of putting the world right.'

'Have you stopped dreaming, Luis?' She surprised herself asking the question.

'No,' he said with little hesitation

'Neither have I.'

Over lunch they talked at length about Jesús Florin. Bianchi seemed to know a lot about him though he would have been a teenager in The Aztec's Chilean days. When Rosa asked him whether he had ever met Florin, Bianchi spread his hands like a laid-back priest about to bless the congregation and shrugged his shoulders in a manner that could have meant yes or no. She did not press him. But in that instant she noticed that the signet ring on Bianchi's little finger had a small gold coin as its centrepiece.

They got back to Santiago at six-thirty. As they pulled up outside the Hyatt Hotel, the doorman opened Rosa's door and Bianchi walked round to the car's boot. He took out a large white envelope that was sealed and tied up with green string.

'I want you to have this, Rosa,' he said, his voice betraying a degree of nervousness that she did not fail to detect. 'I don't know what to do with it. Perhaps – at least, I hope – you might.'

She took the envelope, thanked Bianchi for the day out and walked into the air-conditioned atrium. From her right the gentle melodies of a guitar and *quena* drifted through the open doors of Duke's Bar. Rosa went in, ordered a pisco sour and listened to a folk trio for half an hour while reflecting on her strange day with Bianchi.

And then, as always when she was alone and melancholy, she faced the harsh reality of the illness that had come back to haunt her ten years after she thought she had beaten it. Sometimes she would cry for ages and be consumed by rage and frustration. On other occasions she would lose herself in Max's embrace and sob silently, finding solace in his love.

'It's life's lottery, my love,' he would say, stroking her hair and holding her tight. And they always agreed in the end that life would go on, for as long or as short a time as it lasted, to the full and as normally as possible.

At seven Rosa went up to her room, tossed the envelope on her bed, took off her clothes and put on a bathrobe. She poured herself a glass of cold fizzy water and placed it on her writing desk before walking up to the large wardrobe and retrieving her little computer from the safe.

Usually she took advantage of the hotel's Wi-Fi system but not tonight, opting instead for the security of a hard-wire connection and logging into the CNI archives in Madrid.

Predictably, there were files galore on Jesús Florin going all the way back to the Civil War years. His time in Russia, his marriage to Natalia and the personal tragedies that followed. Friends, enemies, all were covered in the summary and cross-referenced to in-depth documents, half of which Rosa had no access to without additional clearance from above. Very little had been added since 1979, perhaps because by then Florin had ceased to be perceived as a major player.

She read what she could on the Allende years, found three entries for Lucía Florin (née Bamberg), 1939–1973, and just two lines for María Luz Florin, 1972–1973. She also discovered that Lucia's mother, Eva Bamberg, was listed as missing, presumed dead.

There was not a great deal on Osvaldo Ortiz – just a

passing, unrevealing mention that was not a patch on what Bianchi had dug up. Rosa switched off her computer and returned it to the safe. She took Bianchi's envelope and sat on the sofa facing her windows on the world. The sun was behind the hotel now and her private mountains had turned to myriad shades of gold and copper.

There was a single file in the envelope. It had red cardboard covers simply marked *Operación Hamelín* and amounted to twenty-six pages, including appended documents. By the time Rosa had finished reading and rereading it, tears were running down her face and her mountain was submerged in darkness.

She lay on her bed for a while, then reached for the phone and called her husband.

'I miss you, Max,' she said.

'Are you all right?'

'Yes, I'm fine.'

'You don't sound it, darling.'

'I'm sorry. I'm just tired. This trip has worn me out.'

'Has that prick Pinto been upsetting you?'

'No.' Rosa smiled. 'I'll be all right. Just now, I miss you.'

'Come home, then.'

'I will. I leave tomorrow. I'm done here.'

'I love you,' Max said tenderly.

'I love you too,' she replied. Then she hung up.

Rosa remained on the bed, trying to comprehend and accepting that she probably never would.

Hamelin was not life's lottery. It was man-made. It was up to man to put things right.

With her mind made up, Rosa dialled the hotel's operator and asked to be put through to the travel desk. She changed her flight reservations and then went methodically around the room, packing her belongings. She had a leisurely bath and fell asleep by nine.

In the morning she rose early but did not bother to draw the curtains. After settling her account she penned a short note to the Spanish Ambassador – thanking him for his hospitality and apologising for her unavoidably sudden departure – and asked the concierge to have it delivered on her behalf.

Rosa then took a taxi to Pudahuel Airport and at 08:30 boarded flight LAN584 to Havana.

12

The driver opened the car door for Hadley and let him walk into the CNI's Estrella wing unaccompanied. He gave his name to the receptionist who in turn announced him over the phone. An instant later the same secretary who'd escorted Mercedes and Rosa on their previous visit emerged from the lift.

This time she took him to Pinto's office on the fifth floor. It was large and welcoming and bathed in natural light even on a rainy March morning. The Captain looked up from the papers that he was perusing and smiled at Hadley, waving his hand towards one of two matching leather-backed oak chairs on the other side of his desk.

'Our traveller returns!' Pinto sounded as though he wanted to make light of it, but he looked tired, even stressed, thought Hadley. This was not entirely unexpected, what with the election, the bombings and all that.

'Not too tired, I hope?'

'Well, I *am* tired, as a matter of fact, Captain Pinto.'

Hadley had rehearsed this meeting many times over in his mind. 'But the sooner we can get this over with, the sooner I can go back to my life.'

'Coffee?' Pinto pressed a buzzer and within seconds a waiter – he must have been standing outside the office door – looked in. Pinto nodded in his direction and the door was closed.

'Very well. Suppose you tell me all about it and we'll see where we go from there.'

So Hadley told him, from the very beginning at the bungalow, and how he'd been unnerved by The Aztec's early reference to the gold.

'As if he *wanted* to talk about it,' Hadley said.

Pinto nodded as the waiter arrived, deposited a silver tray with two cups and a pot on Pinto's desk, and departed silently.

'During lunch, in Varadero,' Hadley continued, 'he even mentioned you by name.'

Pinto seemed neither surprised nor bothered by the revelation. He just smiled.

Then came the difficult bit: the third meeting – the suggestion that Hadley should write Florin's memoirs and the parting gift of the gold coin. That made Pinto sit up.

'You have it with you, I hope?'

'The manuscript?'

'The coin!'

Hadley fiddled with his wallet as Pinto held out his hand impatiently. Hadley did not mention his difficulty at Havana airport.

'Marvellous!' Pinto exclaimed, feeling the coin between his thumb and forefinger. Then he walked over to the large window to have a look at it in a better light.

'Absolutely marvellous,' he repeated. 'A half-escudo, Madrid Mint, 1742. Well done, Professor.' Hadley was surprised by the sudden acknowledgement of his status. 'I think our man wants to play.'

'There's a message to go with it,' Hadley added tentatively.

'Go on,' Pinto encouraged him.

So Hadley told him about the hidden treasure, the imminent possibility that it might be lost to an unacceptable sovereign party and The Aztec's request for help in retrieving it.

'Ha!' Pinto shouted and threw his head back dismissively, 'Does he expect me to accept that at face value? Is this it?' He pointed at the coin and the manuscript. 'Is this the sum total of The Aztec's proof?'

'I haven't finished,' retorted Hadley.

'Sorry,' Pinto apologised. 'My fault entirely. Please carry on. I shan't interrupt.'

'He said that if you agree in principle he will offer you all the proof you need before mounting the operation.'

'And were I to agree' — Pinto seemed to be questioning Hadley as though the Englishman was Florin himself rather than his messenger — 'did The Aztec say *who* gets to keep what is undoubtedly Spain's property?'

'Yes,' replied Hadley though he wasn't sure how this would sound. 'He proposes that what remains of the gold is shared between Spain and Cuba.'

'*What?*' This time the volume of Pinto's voice went up a few decibels. 'Is this man out of his mind? Does he seriously believe that Spain can agree to let him keep what has been stolen from the nation?'

'Captain Pinto,' Hadley continued with Florin's well-rehearsed arguments, 'Jesús Florin said that the gold belonged to the Spanish Republic on whose orders it left Spain and on whose behalf what remains is held . . .'

Pinto grunted and made a dismissive gesture with his hand. He seemed to be thinking now rather than listening.

'He also asked me to tell you that there's a mix of old and new coins . . .'

Pinto suddenly perked up.

'That the majority of the coins are new – nineteenth century, he said – but that the old coins, though few, are worth as much or more than the new ones.

'He suggests' – Hadley was glad the message was coming to an end – 'that Spain keeps the ancient coins and Cuba the new ones.'

Pinto had calmed down. When he spoke again he had fully regained his composure, but it had been clear to Hadley that The Aztec knew how to touch a nerve when necessary.

'And how am I to reply to this proposal?'

Hadley explained about the errands that he would be asked to run in return for the biographical material.

'Show me,' demanded Pinto.

He pressed his buzzer again as he flicked through the first few pages and presently a secretary walked in. Hadley realised that the desktop console had three buttons. Black, green, red. Waiter, secretary and what? The heavies?

'Photocopy all this, please. In duplicate,' he said. Then he turned back to Hadley.

'What's the connection between your "errands" and the gold?'

'He said the first errand would establish his credibility. And that he would give me something to bring back.'

'Did he say where he wants you to go?'

'No.'

'When?'

'No.'

'Interesting,' commented Pinto.

'Why?'

Pinto did not reply. He stood up and paced the room pensively as though his visitor was not there. Hadley in turn decided to peruse the walls of Pinto's office and look for clues about the man: photographs abounded, some of ships, while others showed groups of smiling naval officers. On a shelf, halfway up a floor-to-ceiling bookcase, were scale models of a modern F-100 frigate and an ancient three-masted galleass.

The one painting, given pride of place behind Pinto's desk, looked like an original and depicted the Marquess of Santa Cruz.

'You know who that is?' Pinto caught Hadley's studious look.

'Don Álvaro de Bazán, first Marquess?'

'Spot on,' Pinto enthused, promptly adding, 'But of course, I should have known. Just your field, is it not?'

'Yes. Painted just after Lepanto?'

'Indeed – 1571.' Pinto gazed at the painting for a while himself. The admiral had been forty-five when he'd commanded the naval division that defeated the Ottoman Empire in a massive 600-ship engagement.

'Different times,' Pinto said, almost nostalgically. 'Sadly, there's little time to dwell upon the past these days. The harsh realities of modern life are too demanding.'

'Yes – in my present predicament I'd agree with that.'

'You can go home now,' Pinto said, laughing.

'Are we done?'

'We are.' He made it sound as though it went without saying. 'After debriefing, of course. You can go downstairs now, or, if you are tired, stay the night in Madrid as our guest and we'll do it tomorrow.'

'And then?'

'Then we shall see.'

'You gave me your word, Captain Pinto. Serve this once, you said, and the slate is wiped clean.'

'Yes, and I stand by my word. You can go and write The Aztec's memoirs. You can even' – he pushed the gold coin lying on his desk towards Hadley – 'keep the coin.'

Hadley raised an eyebrow in surprise but Pinto showed no interest.

'It's not uncommon. Valuable, all the same. Around three hundred euros. I have my generous side. However,' Pinto cautioned, 'the minute Florin wants you for one of his "errands" we shall want to know about it.'

'I thought as much.'

'*And* we shall be with you along the way.'

'Yes, and now that you mention it,' Hadley had waited for an opportunity to say this, 'perhaps you could get someone smarter than the pair of monkeys you had follow me to Cuba!'

'Oh?'

'Florin rumbled them from the outset. Right down to their phoney passports.'

'Did that upset you, Mr Hadley?'

'Yes, quite frankly, it did.'

'Perhaps they were decoys,' Pinto said, his tone slightly mocking.

'What do you mean?'

'Perhaps they were *meant* to be noticed. A warning shot

across the bows. We know and we know you know, sort of thing.'

'It's all a bloody game to you people, isn't it?'

'Far from it, Mr Hadley.' Pinto stood up and pressed the red button once, 'This is very serious. But let me assure you that you had a proper guardian angel. One that neither you nor Sierra's thugs would have *rumbled*, as you put it, in a million years.'

A burly man in a tailored leather jacket arrived just as Pinto walked Hadley to the door.

'Minguez here will take you downstairs. It won't take long. Minguez's team are good at this. Just tell them all you know.'

Pinto watched them walk towards the lift, closed his door and walked back to the window. It was getting a little brighter. Perhaps the rain might stop.

He admitted to himself that he quite liked Hadley. He would have liked to have him stay and chat about battles. Pinto had only just learned about Hadley's book on the battle of Lepanto. It was currently available only in English but he had asked his secretary to order him a copy anyway. But social chit-chat right now would have been inappropriate. Hadley still had a lot of work to do for CNI.

Phase one had gone well, exactly as predicted by the most visible yet invisible of Pinto's agents. She was special. Pinto had recruited her shortly after meeting her at an embassy reception in Lima. She had been in Peru escorting a trade mission while Pinto was also in that country, though admittedly on less salubrious business. The incumbent Spanish ambassador was a retired Rear Admiral and he'd invited Pinto to the mission's farewell cocktail party. The embassy's ballroom was packed: waiters milled between the elegantly attired ladies and the men in dinner jackets, dispensing canapés and champagne.

When Pinto first set eyes on her she had been chatting with a prominent local businessman whom the ambassador thought that Pinto should meet; he was a well-known collector of Hispano-American coins. He and Pinto knew each other's names but they had never met. The two men shook hands.

'Have you met Captain Pinto?' the ambassador asked the very attractive dark-haired woman. She wore an unquestionably expensive pale cream dress under a burgundy bolero jacket simply adorned with a beautifully crafted gold and ruby brooch.

'I don't think I've had the pleasure.' She smiled an electric smile.

'Mrs Uribe,' the diplomat introduced her. 'From our Commerce Secretariat.'

'Rosa,' she said, extending her right hand. 'And you, Captain? Are you an attaché?'

'No, not at all.' Pinto smiled. 'More of a liaison visit – I'm Madrid-based.'

The two men talked about coins and Pinto accepted an invitation to look at some rare Potosí Mint examples in the morning.

Rosa listened attentively. She acknowledged that she knew little about coins but could understand the fascination they held. They made small talk for a while longer and then she excused herself and moved on to circulate amongst the many guests.

Pinto stole a glance in Rosa's direction a few times during the evening, admiring the way she worked the room. Then he said farewell to the ambassador and returned to his hotel.

She could be useful, he thought as he showered before bed. If she worked for the government she'd have a file. He would make a point of looking it up once he was back in Madrid.

When he did, she lived up to everything he had expected: a high achiever from the word go. Madrid-born into a solid middle-class family, top grades at a fashionable convent school and third in her Economics class at Madrid University. An INSEAD MBA followed and on her return to Spain she made the top five per cent in her Civil Service *Oposiciones*.

But her current job, with ICEX, was the icing on the cake as far as Pinto was concerned. No need to devise a cover. Rosa Uribe's job *was* the perfect cover: travelling the entire Spanish-speaking world with quasi-diplomatic status, going in and out of embassies at will with access to top people at every destination. Politically neutral, perhaps, but by background surely leaning towards conservative.

Her husband, Máximo Uribe, was a Basque so Pinto flagged a little caution – he would have him thoroughly vetted – but he was Madrid's best-known dental surgeon and was believed to be politically inactive. There were no children.

Was Rosa Uribe patriotic? Her job implied that at least on the economic front she cared. In recent years, Spain's expansion into Latin America had been astounding. What had once been taken by the sword and subsequently lost to the sword was being regained with the chequebook. Telefónica, Ferrovial, Santander, BBV were now as well known in South America as in the Peninsula itself. Airlines, utilities, energy companies, banks – one by one prime trophies were taken. A twentieth-century *Reconquista*. Rosa

Uribe was in the thick of it – and she was only thirty-six. Pinto concluded that she was definitely worth approaching. And it had paid off.

She had proved a most sagacious and dependable source. She and Pinto had established a good working relationship and he was her direct control – she had made it a condition.

Each time she was given an assignment she delivered. She moved freely throughout Latin America without attracting undue attention – Spanish embassies and chambers of commerce were her offices and her covertness lay in her high visibility.

The only time Pinto and Rosa had discussed Moscow's gold had been over a lunch and had not been intended as a prelude to an operational decision. She had merely enquired about his coin collection, recalling the conversation in Peru, and Pinto had eventually got around to his belief that the missing gold of the Republic probably contained the best pieces from the Bank of Spain's vaults.

'Can it be true?' she asked, at the time more from amusement than interest.

'I am convinced it's true,' said Pinto unequivocally.

'Surely, if it is true, *someone* must know,' she reasoned.

'They are all dead, Rosa. All but one.'

'Who?'

'Jesús Florin.'

'You must be joking!'

'I'm not.'

Rosa went silent for a while. Pinto let her do her thinking.

'Of course, he was well involved with the Republic,' she reflected.

'Have you met him?' asked Pinto.

'Yes,' she recalled. 'At a function in Havana. We were introduced, but I don't remember him having a lot to say.'

'No, that's the problem. He's not very fond of talking.'

That had been the full extent of the conversation. Until January of this year. Rosa had asked to see Pinto to give him a snippet of information that might be useful to him. Her cousin Ramiro had been bragging about this great idea of his. He'd prevailed upon a friend, an English visiting professor at Salamanca, to write to Spanish Civil War veterans and ask for interviews. For a book he was writing, she explained.

'Unbelievably,' she said, 'he has secured an interview with The Aztec.'

For two weeks Pinto's men in Spain and England dug up all they could on Jack Hadley but were unable to come up with anything that stood out. All Pinto needed was a handle, a lever, a hook that he could use to his advantage. They learned that Hadley was separated from his wife with whom he had two children and that he lived in Salamanca with a Spanish woman. Pinto also ran checks on her: her family background was interesting, but nothing that could be of use to him right now. And time was running out.

Pinto needed Hadley unquestionably on board before he left for Cuba. It had to be a solid bond. Pinto could not run the risk of Hadley – an English *academic*, for God's sake, pinko suspect from the outset! – being more sympathetic to the wily Aztec than to the Spanish cause. On the positive side, he had been an army officer – but why had he quit? No answer there.

Payment was an option but Rosa had a much better suggestion and Pinto had to agree that it was workable even if it surprised him to hear it from her. His first reaction was to use a trained field agent but he realised that Rosa was right: she was ideally positioned to execute it herself.

Pinto had already observed the seemingly paradoxical character trait. He knew Rosa to be genuinely gentle and compassionate – the virtues oozed from her actions and reports. But she was also capable of chillingly cold-blooded manoeuvring in pursuit of what she considered a just cause.

'Get me a hundred grams of pure cocaine,' she asked Pinto. 'Then be ready to move the moment I send word. I'll deliver your man Hadley to you on a platter.'

On the evening of the thirteenth of February, Pinto had received her message: *It's on tonight*. In the early hours of the fourteenth of February a coded text had been sent from her mobile phone giving the signal to go immediately. Within seconds several CNI staff took turns phoning the Salamanca police complaining about noise from a city-centre apartment – loud music keeping the old town awake, wild partying causing a disturbance.

Within minutes the Policía Local had identified the source of the annoyance and the CNI observer – and fall-back, if need be – outside Hadley's flat confirmed that two policemen had arrived, giving Pinto his hold over Hadley. He had already secured the authority to override the police as he saw fit.

True to her word, as ever, Rosa Uribe had delivered.

13

Not long after Hadley's return from Cuba, Florin sent him on his first 'errand'. During the last week in March, Jack had heard from his agent in London: the publisher's under-standable initial displeasure over *Embattled Madrid*'s delay had been replaced by a level of excitement that went beyond his own firm and set tongues a-wagging among London's literati.

In publishing terms it was a coup, and the offer of world rights in the first and – in view of the subject's age – prob-ably the only official biography of The Aztec did produce the anticipated large advance against what was undoubt-edly destined to become a global best-seller. With the first cheque in the agent's hands and net proceeds shortly on their way to Jack's account, he looked forward to a care-free Easter break.

On Thursday, the eighth of April, Hadley slid into the passenger seat of Mercedes's little sports car for the short drive to Valladolid. They had agreed to spend the holiday with her parents and Jack had prevailed upon Mercedes that they should fly rather than endure the anxieties of six hundred kilometres each way while she gave her Porsche 'a proper run'.

The little Air Nostrum jet took them to Barcelona in an hour for a quick connection to Valencia. During the flight, Mercedes quizzed Jack again about Jesús Florin. On Jack's return from Cuba he had recounted every detail of his visit, right down to his difficulties at the airport and the gift of the gold coin.

'Do you think the gold really exists?' She had been sceptical from the outset.

'I'm not sure. There must be something, otherwise why the hell would Pinto go through all this trouble.'

'Something, yes,' she agreed. 'But maybe it's something else, not just the gold. Pinto may be using us. It's what they do, his sort of people . . .'

'I'll tell you what I can't work out,' confided Hadley. 'How the hell did Pinto get to us so fast?'

'What do you mean?'

'I mean we get busted by the cops on a Friday night and by crack of sparrow's on a bloody Saturday the Locals and the Guardias have been taken out of the equation.'

'*Merda!*'

'And where's Rosa? What sort of deal have they done with her?'

'I've called her many times and left messages. Ramiro said she was abroad. She's something in the government, to do with trade missions.'

'Well, like I said, there's more to this than meets the eye. Meanwhile we have to please Pinto. Basically, we're screwed.'

'And the gold?' Mercedes asked.

Jack did not know what to think. But there had been far too many references to gold. There had to be a connection.

'I'm not sure about that, either. But I've a hunch it's for real.'

After days spent speculating, Mercedes's interest had turned to Florin.

'What was he like?' she wanted to know.

Like most people, she had only read about The Aztec. His role in Latin American politics was touched upon in the course of her current studies. His past exploits, like Guevara's, made good reading in the press from time to time, but to Mercedes he was a minor, albeit colourful character in the web of twentieth-century liberation movements.

His academic legacy from 1950s Mexico was of little consequence and his achievements in the field of battle, though not to be belittled in human terms, were perceived as those of a straightforward participant rather than a visionary leader.

The personal side of Florin's life was also a favourite of Sunday supplements and feature magazines. Much had been written, often based on myth and hearsay, about the tragic life of a veteran warrior who had survived a score of battles and outlived three children and two wives.

So, when Hadley had come home with a commission from The Aztec and reams of hitherto undisclosed first-hand material, Mercedes had laid first claim to it and sat up reading the notes long into the night.

'I mean, as a person. Was he easy to talk to?'

'I quite liked him,' Jack admitted. 'Sometimes I even stopped worrying about Pinto.'

'He is very old, isn't he?'

'Yes. But surprisingly fit.'

'Does he sound Mexican?'

'Not to me. More like Cuban, really. To be expected, I guess, after living in the country for thirty years!'

'Thirty years can mean nothing,' she laughed. 'Wait till you meet my mum.'

The very notion of meeting Mercedes's parents after a year of living with their daughter seemed strange. The apparent permanence of Jack and Mercedes's relationship had developed naturally and had never been consciously planned. From the outset she had known that Jack was still married and during school breaks, Christmas in particular, they had gone their separate ways. Neither had asked for or sought anything other than a comfortable and happy life together while at Salamanca. However, as time passed the bond had grown stronger and, though they had not said it in as many words, neither Jack nor Mercedes any longer contemplated life without the other at their side.

As spring approached, Jack's divorce was finalised and plans were made for his children to visit him in Spain during the coming summer. His existence was no secret in the Vilanova camp either, so Easter seemed like an appropriate time to pay a visit to Valencia.

Mercedes's mother had come to fetch them from Manises Airport – despite Jack's protestations that he would hire a car – and drove them south along the coast to Sant Feliu, the Vilanova estate in Xátiva. On the way they passed through the county capital, Alzira, and, on its outskirts, the vast packaging and shipping complex of Vilanova Taronger, with dozens of orange-coloured rigs and trailers lined up on the loading bays.

'That's my father's office,' Mercedes said, as if describing the landscape without wishing to dwell too much on any one feature.

'We are now the biggest in Spain,' Susana Vilanova volunteered proudly. Hadley was amused by her pure *porteño* accent and recalled his girlfriend's warning, with a smile. She was shorter than Mercedes and her youthful modern haircut was not unlike her daughter's – even if its colouring, though similar, was undoubtedly artificially enhanced.

'You are from Argentina, I believe, Mrs Vilanova,' he observed politely.

'Please call me Susana,' she said affably. 'Yes, I am.'

'Mum refuses to learn Valencian,' Mercedes teased. 'She calls it a dialect.'

'Well, there's nothing wrong with the language of Cervantes,' Susana said, defending herself.

They laughed. But Jack wondered how she managed to integrate in a region that wholeheartedly embraced its own language and culture.

'I can't argue with that,' Hadley agreed. His Spanish, though accented, was grammatically flawless and Susana Vilanova made a flattering comment.

They skirted the ancient town of Xátiva itself and Mercedes promised to show Hadley around it during their stay. Its history predated Roman times when it lay just off their Via Augusta, and it contained enough medieval churches, monasteries and hospices to keep the casual visitor interested for days.

The entrance to Sant Feliu, overlooked by the Iberian-Roman castle on Mont Sant, was just south of Xátiva. Two white stone pillars stood like sturdy sentries either side of open gates marking the start of the mile-long elm-lined driveway that curved along the gentle slopes of Sierra del Castillo. Where the road straightened, the trees gave way to flower beds and lawns and beyond them stood a large single-storey red-tiled house, built on several stepped levels to fit into the lightly sloping ground. Along much of the house's front, garden furniture and potted plants were methodically placed on the tiled surface of a large terrace raised two steps above the lawn.

Hadley assumed that the dapper smiling man emerging from the house at the sound of the approaching car was Mercedes's father – even before she said, 'There's Daddy.'

Luis Vilanova appeared younger than his sixty-three years. He was surprisingly tanned this early in the year and looked remarkably fit, like one who made a point of exercising and caring for his physical appearance. His salt-and-pepper hair was immaculately groomed and his casual weekend attire suggested expensive labels. As he walked down the stone steps towards the parking area his smile was for all to see, but there was little doubt that he had eyes mainly for Mercedes and that the effusiveness of the hug she gave him in return indicated a reciprocal feeling.

'Jack, welcome to Sant Feliu. We've heard so much about you.'

There was something very commanding about Luis Vilanova – he had the relaxed assertive manner of one accustomed to take charge. He led them into the house and gestured at servants to deal with the luggage.

'You two may want to freshen up after your journey.' When Vilanova spoke his words sounded more like a polite order than a suggestion. 'Then we shall have the *aperitivo*.'

Moments later they gathered around the drawing room's bar and made small talk about Jack's work at the

University, his writing and the latest development: Jesús Florin's biography.

'Apparently,' Mercedes volunteered, 'he's quite a pleasant man.'

'Is he, darling?' asked her mother. 'Who is he?'

'Jesús Florin,' explained Hadley. 'He's a Mexican old-timer, former soldier, *guerrillero*, political philosopher, darling of the left once upon a time.'

'Oh, I don't think we were too fond of *guerrilleros* in this house!' Susana remarked, betraying a twinge of alarm and looking at her husband.

'Don't worry, Mum,' Mercedes laughed. 'It was a long time ago. It's just his biography that Jack is working on.'

'Quite pleasant, is he?' Vilanova's tone was quite icy as he said it.

'Well, with me he was.' Jack tried to sound apologetic.

'It will be interesting to see how you perceive him once you've done your research. He seemed to have a penchant for getting involved in other people's wars.'

'Well, he fought against Franco and Hitler . . .' Jack assumed that, as a Valencian, Vilanova would at least object to Franco.

'Yes,' Vilanova laughed. 'And in support of Stalin!'

'Point taken,' Jack had to concede.

'And was rewarded with banishment to Siberia, if I'm not mistaken.' Vilanova shook his head. 'Anyway,' the smile was back, 'let us not get into politics. Let's have lunch and then we can show Jack around Sant Feliu. How does that sound?'

Lunch was served by a neatly attired maid and the conversation was kept light. Business, Vilanova explained, had never been better and his company was opening its own distribution depots in both England and Germany.

Customers in northern Europe, he asserted, could be eating VT oranges within forty-eight hours of them being picked.

Mercedes said that was enough about oranges and Susana took the hint. The Vilanovas, it transpired, had been in the area since Peter IV had made Játiva a city in the fourteenth century.

'We were *villanos*, of course,' Mercedes clarified. 'Landed *peasants*,' she added just to tease her mother.

Over coffee Vilanova complimented Hadley on his books. He had finished the one on the battle of Ayacucho and had started reading Covadonga.

As the men discussed the intricacies of warfare, the women seemed at least relieved that the first round appeared to be progressing well.

After lunch Mercedes and Susana went out on the terrace to enjoy the spring sunshine and Vilanova invited Jack to join him in an open Suzuki for a drive around Sant Feliu.

'We grow all native types here, Jack,' he explained as they crept between endless rows of orange trees. 'Clementinas, Clemenvillas, Hernandinas, Nevelinas. The lot.'

'It's amazing. This is huge.'

'Yes. Right now we are harvesting Navelates and will continue until May. Then we are finished till October.'

They reached higher ground on the lower slopes of the rugged Sierra and Vilanova stopped the engine. At their feet, in the ensuing silence, a green and orange blanket seemed to stretch as far as the eye could see.

'Three thousand hectares,' Vilanova stated, guessing Jack's thoughts.

'Was this your family's land?'

'No.' Vilanova seemed to be choosing his words carefully.

'My family lived in Xátiva and they farmed a little land. But this,' he surveyed the expansive groves, 'this is all down to me.'

'Mercedes tells me that you spent some time in Argentina.'

'In the 1930s, after the carnage of the Civil War,' Vilanova said, 'my parents went there. Argentina offered lots of promise then.'

'Before you were born,' observed Hadley.

'Yes. I was born in Buenos Aires,' explained Vilanova. 'So was Mercedes. Susana is pure Argentine, of course.' He laughed, meaning perhaps that she was Argentine not just by birth but in her entire attitude and mannerisms. 'She is from Trelew, in Patagonia.

'But things didn't go that well for my parents down there. Bad times marked by political and economic turmoil. They returned home thirty-five years ago and eventually we followed.'

'Did you farm in Argentina?'

'No, not at all. My parents did, for a while.' Vilanova turned to look Jack in the face. 'I was in the army.'

'Then I'm doubly flattered that you enjoyed my writing!' Jack looked at Vilanova and smiled.

'I look forward to reading the next one.'

Hadley remained silent for a while, then felt he had to mention it. 'I was in the army, too – did Mercedes tell you?'

'No.' Vilanova looked surprised, though not unhappy with the revelation.

'Well, I was,' Jack smiled sheepishly. 'When I left school. I was eighteen and had no idea what I wanted to do with my life.'

'Was your father in the army?'

'No, this was my choice, if anything. It came out of the blue.' Hadley smiled, reminiscing. 'I think my parents were far from pleased. But I served six years and I don't regret it.'

'How long ago was that?'

'1985 to '91.'

'Gulf War?'

'Yes.'

Vilanova knew better than to ask but Hadley felt it.

'I really didn't mind the fighting. It was what we trained for. *And* we believed we were on the side of virtue.' He glanced at Vilanova, hoping his last remark would not be taken as criticism of the older man's type of soldiering.

'But we never finished the job. I left the army after that.'

'Because the job was unfinished?'

'Maybe. I'm not sure,' Hadley confided. 'I was short-service, six years, so I simply elected not to stay on. Plus, I had a university place waiting,' he added, with a genuine smile. 'Never looked back, really, no regrets.'

They set off down the gentle incline between two rows of squat orange trees. The soil underfoot felt rich and, like the trees, well cared for. A sweet citric aroma hung in the air as though there was no breeze.

'I understand you have been married, Jack.'

'Yes.'

'All over now?'

'Yes. I have two children as well. Their mother has custody.'

'Mercedes mentioned them.' Vilanova looked directly at Hadley. 'I believe she's rather fond of you.'

'I hope so. I'm certainly fond of her.'

'Mercedes, as you may have learned, is very much her own person.'

'Yes, that was evident from the very start.' Both men smiled. Jack told the story of how she'd moved into Fonseca, which made her father laugh.

'Selects my wardrobe too,' he continued jocularly, recalling how after a few months together she had taken Jack shopping and demanded he threw away half his clothes. Rolled-up sleeves and beige jeans are not a substitute for summer clothing, she'd stated, before threatening to confiscate all his socks if he wore any between June and September.

'Be careful with Florin, Jack. I know his kind.'

Vilanova's admonition took Hadley by surprise.

'I . . . I'm not planning to get involved with him, Mr Vilanova.' But even as he said it Hadley knew that wasn't entirely true. 'Except to the degree that my research . . .'

'You are a grown man, Jack. Just be aware: Florin is and always was a ruthless, fanatical Marxist. Don't be deceived by his age.'

They turned back towards the car. For the moment, at least, the subject appeared closed.

'Luis, by the way,' Vilanova said suddenly. 'Luis is my first name.'

But Hadley was thinking. If Luis Vilanova had been in the Argentine army in the 1970s he would have served through the nasty times. He was bound to know a lot about Florin. As they drove back towards the house, Hadley started to wonder how Vilanova had managed to amass the serious wealth represented by Vilanova-Taronger.

On Saturday morning Mercedes saddled two horses and took Jack on a ride close to the Sierras. The sun shone the bright yellow of spring and a light breeze blew in from the Mediterranean.

'What will happen to all this?' he asked her as they rested under a row of chestnuts and surveyed Sant Feliu at their feet. 'I mean, when your father retires. Have you thought of coming back to run the company?'

'No. I thought about it, but I don't think it is for me.'

'Who, then?'

'Oh, the company has good managers, Jack. It will function without Dad. The land,' she nodded towards Sant Feliu, 'goes with the company. The house will one day be mine. But that's a long way away, I hope, and I shall never sell it.'

'Did your parents ever wish they'd had more children?'

'Mum couldn't have any more after I was born.' Mercedes sounded a bit melancholy. 'But I think Dad would have liked a son or two to continue with the business.'

'I guess,' said Hadley. Then he added in an upbeat tone: 'If you ever change your mind, I'll come back and work for you. This is paradise!'

She rewarded him with a long kiss.

They returned to the house by noon in plenty of time for the traditional *aperitivo*, which was followed by a light lunch and a rest. In the afternoon Hadley accompanied Mercedes and her mother into Xátiva.

While the women shopped, Hadley visited the Royal Monastery of Santa Clara and the Almodí Municipal Museum. In the museum's fine arts section he paused and smiled at the sight of Philip V's portrait, the very same monarch whose face was stamped on the gold coin that Florin had given him.

In the early 1700s there had been a war of succession between the Hapsburg and Borbón dynasties. Xátiva had supported the Borbóns and in reprisal the victors had burned down much of the city. Later on and to this day, the Xátiva Arts Museum expressed its sentiments towards the Hapsburg king by hanging his portrait upside down.

In the evening, dinner at Sant Feliu was a grand affair with a score of local notables in attendance. The women gossiped over Mercedes's latest foreign boyfriend while the men flirted with her, secretly wondering why she'd walked away from a fast-track job with Santander and openly praising her academic achievements.

On Easter Sunday, Luis Vilanova led his family – with Hadley appended to it – to *La Seu*, Xátiva's basilica. After Mass they milled around with other parishioners as Luis and Susana endlessly kissed cheeks and shook hands.

Once the senior Vilanovas finished wishing everyone a happy Easter, they returned to Sant Feliu. Jack and Mercedes chose to remain in town a little longer and Luis suggested that they should phone when they wanted the car to pick them up.

They strolled under the arches towards Plaça del Mercat and Hadley admired the local architecture. Luckily, he observed, the old town at least had been sympathetically spared the vandalism of 1950s modernity. The houses, two and three storeys high, some in gentle pastel colours, seemed to Hadley more reminiscent of Italy than Spain. But then, in its heyday Xátiva would have had influences from the whole Mediterranean.

They found a café with outside tables overlooking a quaint little square and sat down with the Sunday papers and a couple of cold beers. From time to time they looked up from their reading as families in their smartest clothes dashed to and from one or another Easter event or procession.

They did not see the man approach and even though

they heard his scooter it was not a noteworthy sound in any Spanish town. He pulled up across the square from the café and from the large box mounted behind the pillion seat he extracted a fat padded envelope. Then he walked purposefully to where Jack and Mercedes were sitting.

'Jack, Mercedes, good morning.' He extended his gloved hand, which they both shook in turn, with puzzled expressions and the embarrassed smiles of those unable to place someone they felt they should know.

'May I?' he asked politely. Despite his civil manner, he pulled over a spare chair without waiting for an answer.

He was middle-aged, dressed in dark trousers and a beige windcheater. He wore a black beret, dark glasses and black woollen gloves, not unusual apparel for a scooter rider.

'Jesús Florin sends his best wishes,' he said, leaning towards the couple and lowering his voice, 'and asks me to deliver this.' He pushed the envelope towards Jack.

'Is that it?' Hadley asked. 'No message or anything?'

'Well, it's all in there.' The man tapped a gloved finger on the parcel. 'But I think you'd better read it soon. There's not much time.'

With that he stood up and shook hands again. He wished them a very happy Easter and then crossed the little square, back to his scooter. He disappeared around the first corner with the same putt-putt that had preceded his arrival. Jack and Mercedes listened silently until the sound had faded.

The bulk of the package was made up of another instalment of The Aztec's material, covering the next twenty years of his life. There was also a smaller envelope with Jack's name handwritten on it.

'This takes us to the end of the Civil War,' Jack exclaimed, having looked at the first and last pages.

'I see that.' Mercedes replied, edging her chair closer to Jack's.

'It must contain what Pinto wants.'

'If he hasn't held back,' she cautioned, now searching the pages for clues.

Jack opened the smaller envelope and read Florin's short note.

> *Take a holiday. Fly to Tivat and go to Budva, this Tuesday, April 13th. A room has been reserved for you at the Villa Montenegro. Behave like tourists, enjoy the Adriatic Riviera. A man called Klejevic will contact you. Trust him.*

Jack and Mercedes looked at each other questioningly but knew they would do exactly as The Aztec asked.

'*Martes trece*,' Mercedes read the date out loud. Tuesday Thirteenth.

A bad omen in Spanish lore.

14

Rosa paid for her taxi and entered the lobby of the Meliá Cohiba while porters took charge of her luggage. The hotel's General Manager raised his eyebrows in alarm on seeing her and wondered why he hadn't been made aware of her impending arrival.

'Mrs Uribe.' His professional smile instantly appeared. 'How wonderful to have you back with us.'

'My apologies for not warning you, Ramón.' She relieved him of his anxiety. 'Last-minute arrangement, hardly knew about it myself.'

Back in control, the manager immediately and imperceptibly organised the valued guest's arrival. No check-in formalities were necessary; he merely whispered a room number and the wheels were set in motion.

'Please allow me to accompany you, Mrs Uribe.'

They took the lift to the Royal Service floors. By the time they reached the Private Reception the electronic keys had been prepared and a maid was rushing ahead to place fresh flowers in Mrs Uribe's rooms. It was a corner suite facing north and west with clear views over Boca Chorrera and Saint Dorothea's Castle.

She declined the manager's offer to have a butler unpack for her and as soon as she was alone she went directly to the telephone. She had no idea how to make contact without raising questions at the embassy so, flinging protocol out the window, she called the Interior Ministry and left a message for Colonel Aquiles Sierra. An hour later Sierra was knocking on her door.

He was dressed in civilian clothes and had not bothered to stop at reception. To the many tourists and business visitors he would have been just another executive in a suit. But to many Cubans his was a familiar face. He moved around Havana unchallenged, whether in or out of uniform.

Rosa invited him in and immediately turned to the purpose of her visit.

'I need an immediate and very discreet meeting with General Florin. Could you arrange that?' She spoke assertively, holding Sierra's cold stare as they sat facing each other on armchairs a few metres apart.

'And the purpose of this meeting?' Sierra was equally blunt.

'It is personal. For the General's ears only.'

Sierra nodded, slowly. Rosa had expected this. Intelligence people didn't dispense favours without a trade-off. If there was good material here he would want it for himself.

'General Florin does not receive visitors, Mrs Uribe. If I am to disturb his self-imposed isolation I would need to have—'

'Colonel Sierra,' she interrupted, 'I came to you to gain time, not to waste it. Please hear me out,' she added firmly.

Not a man over-endowed with patience, she surmised.

'I repeat: it's personal. It is either delivered by me, verbally and in private, to the General himself or it is not delivered at all.'

Sierra started to ask whether this was an official overture from Spain or her own private initiative but Rosa cut him short again.

'I haven't much time, Colonel.' She stood up to signify the meeting's end. 'Today would be ideal, tomorrow possible, but after that I return to Madrid.'

Later that evening Rosa sat on a wicker chair on Florin's veranda. Sierra himself had driven her to the beachside bungalow but had not been invited in. There appeared to be little love lost between the two men. She sat silently, sipping the rum punch that Miriam had prepared for her and watching the wide silver band cast by moonlight on a dead-calm sea. She was aware of Florin's breathing as he read the two files, and she prayed to God that she was doing the right thing. Jesús put both folders down on the coffee table and remained silent for a while.

'Thank you.'

The way he said it lifted Rosa's heart.

'I presume you are married, Mrs Uribe?'

'Yes.'

'Do you have children?'

'No.'

'Have you ever wished you had some?'

'Yes.'

'Me too.' Florin looked at her and smiled a tender smile.

'Does your employer know you are here?' He asked the question kindly, not Sierra's way.

'ICEX?'

Jesús laughed. It was the first time she had encountered his infectious laughter.

'No,' Rosa replied, smiling.

'May I ask how you came to possess these papers?'

'I've just come from Chile,' she explained. 'From a source there. A lawyer in Valparaíso.'

'My wife was a lawyer. From Valparaíso.'

'I know. The Ortiz file we had asked for,' Rosa volunteered. 'The other one came from him. Unsolicited. To be dealt with it as we saw fit.'

'And so you are here.'

'Yes.'

'On your own initiative?'

'Yes.'

'In our business,' Florin said, 'we are always asking questions. But we seldom trust the answers we get.'

Rosa nodded her agreement.

'But today I feel at ease with you.'

'Thank you.'

'It is I who must thank you.' He said it this time as if he had forgotten she was there. Rosa could tell that his thoughts had carried him to distant places.

'I used to torture myself.' He spoke candidly when he returned from wherever he had been, like a man treading on uncharted ground.

'*Why?* I would demand at first. When my heart stopped bleeding it became: *Who?*

'Eventually I got the name: Osvaldo Ortiz. But the trail was cold. We lost him. As the years passed my friends begged me to let sleeping dogs lie.'

'Perhaps I shouldn't have . . .'

'No,' Florin replied quickly, almost as if he feared that

what had been so generously given to him might be taken away.

A passing cloud temporarily obscured the moon and Rosa rubbed her hands along her forearms. The sudden chill that she felt was not entirely on account of the cool December night.

'Let's sit inside.' Florin had noticed.

He stood up, picking up their empty glasses and calling Miriam as he did so. Rosa led the way into the living room. A small fire burned at one end and they sat close to it. Minutes later Miriam returned with fresh drinks.

'Even now,' he said when the nurse had gone, 'I might have let it go.'

'Perhaps even now it might be for the best,' she suggested. 'It won't bring Lucía back.'

Rosa felt uncomfortable, an intruder in an old man's buried past, a sensation only heightened by the undisguised emotion in Florin's voice.

'It would reopen old wounds. Am I up to it?' He looked up at her, smiling inquisitively.

'But then there's this,' he continued, picking up the unopened Hamelin file, holding it in both hands, staring at it, 'and it seems I have no choice.'

He put the file back on the table and sipped his drink.

'You still have a choice, Mr Florin,' Rosa suggested. But her tone betrayed what she herself might choose, given the same predicament.

'I need to think,' he said. 'May I see you tomorrow?'

'Of course. But tomorrow night I must go home.'

Florin's orderly accompanied her out. Miriam smiled as she walked past. Jesús seldom had lady visitors any more. Miriam missed that.

Colonel Sierra drove her back to Havana. He had obviously been told to wait outside. Rosa did not think that too many people in Cuba could give orders to Aquiles Sierra, but it would seem as if Jesús Florin was among the few who could. This time Sierra did not try to engage her in conversation and Rosa was happy to leave it at that.

Back at her room she called Max and told him she was spending the night in Havana.

'You sound happier,' he said.

'Yes,' she agreed. 'But I still miss you.'

'Come back.'

'I'm leaving tomorrow night, without fail.'

Rosa went to bed sometime after midnight, her head still spinning as she considered the implications of what she had done. How much would she have to tell Pinto? What devious scheme would he want to put in place to gain favour from the Cubans? Indeed, would the Cubans be involved at all or would Florin keep this to himself? She had little doubt that he would want to get to Ortiz and even less that, sooner rather than later, Florin would show up in Spain.

She eventually closed her eyes, having concluded that the next move was up to The Aztec. She could only decide how far she was prepared to go once she learned what he had in mind.

In the morning Rosa called briefly at the embassy before returning to Florin as agreed, but this time she took a taxi rather than risk another ride with Sierra. In Havana everyone had spies.

If Florin had been badly shaken by the information she

had delivered the previous evening, he did not show it today. He had opened the front door for her in person and greeted her with a smile. He was in one of his shorts-and-flowery-shirt ensembles and on the surface appeared unburdened by either age or pain.

But Rosa reminded herself that this man had known strife and pain at a level that most could only imagine. Even after the inevitable erosion of his faculties brought about by age, she could not assume that Florin could no longer muster inner strength from somewhere and push on to fight another day.

It was already ten-thirty when she arrived at the beach house and the temperature was rising rapidly after a relatively cool night. It would soon reach the moisture-saturated high twenties and remain at that level all day.

Florin kissed her paternally on both cheeks while smiling and holding both her hands. She did not try to stop him.

'We can sit outside for a bit, Rosa. May I call you Rosa?' he asked. 'If it gets too muggy we can always come back indoors.'

'It's fine by me either way.'

'Visitors from Europe sometimes find the humidity too much.' He appraised her choice of clothing and nodded approvingly.

'I'm fine,' she reassured him. 'Really.' So they took their seats on the veranda.

'I've been asking questions.' Florin started the conversation. Rosa gave him a quizzical look that held an element of surprise which he picked up on.

'I'm not without friends in Africa, you know?' he added, betraying a degree of pride, 'Nor, for that matter,' he continued, 'in Spain or South America. All of whom' – he stared Rosa directly in the eye to gauge her reaction – 'I shall need to call upon if I am to act on this information which you have so kindly brought to my attention.'

'I see.' She was non-committal.

'Our friend in Africa' – he said the word in such way that it could mean anything but friendship – 'has quite a reputation. He is powerful, influential, even wealthy, I believe,' he said disdainfully.

'I know, it's in the file.'

'Sorry, of course.'

'It should not be very difficult, in your position, to . . . to find a just solution,' Rosa hinted.

'No.' Florin seemed amused by her choice of words. 'No. I could find a permanent solution this very day, if that was what I wanted.'

His eyes hardened and Rosa knew he meant it. Florin had fought in the Congo and in Mozambique. He had lost a son in Angola. Nothing could keep Ortiz alive, however exalted his position, if Florin called upon his African brothers to settle the score.

'But the reckoning will have to be on my terms.'

'You can't go there yourself, Mr Florin,' she said, concerned. 'You'll be no match for him. He will kill you.'

'I've no intention of setting foot in his country.'

'You'll find it just as hard to make him step outside it.'

'I've had some thoughts,' Florin continued. 'Details still to be worked out, but nevertheless a workable plan.'

'Why tell me that, Mr Florin?'

'You could help to make it happen.'

'I'll do nothing that might go against my country's interests.'

'I would not expect you to,' he assured her, 'on the contrary: I'll give you something to take back.'

'I'm listening.' Suddenly this was taking an unexpected turn.

'Your chief – Pinto. I understand that he collects coins.'

Rosa laughed. Did the world's entire intelligence community know about Roberto's obsession with gold coins?

'Do you propose buying me with thirty pieces?'

'I'm not talking silver here. I mean gold.'

'I don't think I'm entirely with you.' She knew she was lying as she said it. She recalled her conversation with Pinto years ago. Gold would get her chief's undivided attention.

Florin let out another of his laughs.

'This man Hadley, in Salamanca,' he asked, 'Do you know him?'

'No. Never even heard of him until I read the Chilean files.'

'But you could find out. If you wanted to, that is.'

Rosa smiled and nodded. 'I'm not without friends in Salamanca, you know.'

That made Florin laugh.

'Together we could create a friendly spy,' Florin continued. 'Friendly to us, friendly to you. Trusted by us, controlled by you, and too much of an amateur to deceive either.'

'Is that the only reason?'

'Well, I'd like to see what mettle the man is made of,' Florin reasoned, 'and by using him – an Englishman – we can relax a little about Cuba versus Spain.'

'What would you expect from me?'

'You can be my secret voice in Spain. My own *Malinche*.'

He took the name from the Nahua Indian interpreter, companion and confidant always at the side of Hernán Cortés as he and his three-hundred conquered the Aztec empire.

'*Malinche* was a Mexican serving a Spaniard,' Rosa countered.

'This time it could be the other way round.'

'She was also his lover.'

'If only I was a younger man!'

Rosa laughed at the flirty remark and then spoke seriously.

'Mr Florin, I came here on a moral issue. I came to you because I believed then – as I continue to believe – that it was the right thing to do.'

'For which, once again, I thank you.'

Rosa's tone of voice did not change nor did she acknowledge Florin's gratitude.

'We both know we can play with my superior's interest in the – probably mythical – missing gold.'

Florin did not argue the implication one way or the other.

'And even if the end result is gold doubloons by the bucketful, which is seriously doubtful, I'm not in the business of assisting foreign interests, however deserving, for a fee.'

'What would satisfy you?'

'I accepted this job in order to serve Spain, Mr Florin.' Rosa looked pensively towards the ocean as she chose her words, 'It may be old-fashioned, but that's me.' She turned to face Florin. 'I don't need a career and I certainly do not need to put my country's interests at risk. You want me to recruit this Jack Hadley? For our mutual benefit, you say. But what exactly *is* that benefit? If you expect me to draw on Captain Pinto's numismatic passion you will have to answer this: what exactly is in it for Spain?'

'Very well, Rosa.' Florin was suddenly businesslike himself. 'Please sit down and I'll give you something.

'Does the name Celestino Potro mean anything to you?'

'An African exile' – Rosa hesitated, trying to place him – 'he used to live in Spain.'

'Your Captain Pinto,' Florin continued, 'is secretly backing Mr Potro as the next president of Equatorial Guinea. There will be a coup in a few months' time, carried out by foreign mercenaries. Financed in Spain and South Africa, launched from Zambia and aimed at securing Guinea's oil.'

Rosa did not interrupt him. She would follow up on this in Madrid. It could be possible.

'But the plot will fail, Mrs Uribe.' She did not fail to notice the form of address. 'Your country will end up on the wrong side of the fence and minus a secure source of oil – now that your Mr Aznar has decided to join Bush and Blair and meddle in Iraq's affairs.'

'So what exactly are you offering?'

'You find a way to bring that Jack Hadley to me with your boss's blessing and I'll help Spain be on the winning side in Equatorial Guinea.'

'Is that what I am to tell Captain Pinto?'

'No.' Florin shook his head. 'That's what Hadley will tell Pinto when we are ready. That will be the settlement of my debt to you.' He nodded towards the files that Rosa had brought him.

'No, you tell Captain Pinto that you heard a whisper from your sources, in Chile, if you like, that Jesús Florin wants to break his silence about the Civil War – missing gold included – and has singled out an Englishman to hand his papers to. A professor at Florin's *alma mater*, Salamanca.'

'I see.'

'I will do the rest after that.'

'So I need to trust you?'

'Yes.' Florin held her deep stare.

'Somehow I do, Mr Florin. But please remember what I've said. I serve only Spain.'

'I won't forget it. Now, without trying to teach you your craft—'

'My craft is commerce, Mr Florin.' She smiled as she interrupted him. 'I'm an amateur in the field of state-sponsored deviousness.'

'How would you account for this trip to Cuba?'

'Checking up on the Chilean whispers?'

'Good. Then perhaps I can explain to you what I have in mind.'

They spoke for another hour, this time like two professionals with a common objective in mind. Around noon Miriam served sandwiches and fruit juices in the dining room. When they had finished eating Florin escorted Rosa to a waiting taxi.

'Just one question,' she asked as they reached the kerb, 'if I may?'

'Go ahead.'

'The missing gold: did it exist?'

'Yes.' Florin did not hesitate.

'So it's really still around?'

'That's two questions.' Florin laughed and held the taxi door open for her.

15

Mercedes put a pillow on Hadley's shoulder and rested her head against it in an attempt to get some sleep. Hadley looked out of the window at the dark star-studded sky and tried to guess what lay ahead. He and Mercedes had been through a hectic few days since they'd first set off for a leisurely Easter weekend in Valencia.

On Sunday evening, over supper, they had announced, much to Susana Vilanova's disappointment, that they would have to leave the following morning – something urgent had come up in connection with Jack's writing commitments, they explained, and he had to meet with people in Montenegro.

Hadley had caught a quick flash of alarm in Vilanova's eyes but the orange-grower made no comment other than a polite expression of regret to see them go.

On Monday morning the couple flew back to Valladolid and as they left the Castilian airport Mercedes decided to phone Ramiro and ask how he was getting on heli-skiing in the Picos de Europa.

'I'm back home, old bean,' he lamented. 'Piss-poor snow, not worth hanging about for.'

She felt guilty about having had to opt out from his long-standing invitation but other factors which she was not about to air in public had come into play. In any case, she had heard that the Torreses, Jean-Luc, Tatiana and the ubiquitous spare Russian had set off for the mountains on Good Friday.

On learning that his friends were in Valladolid and on the way to Salamanca, Ramiro insisted that they should call in at his place in Tordesillas – 'a five-minute detour' – and join him in an Easter Monday drink.

'I've tried to call Rosa a zillion times,' Mercedes moaned later, licking from her lips the sugar from Ramiro's Easter cake, 'but she does not return the calls.'

'She's been away somewhere,' Ramiro explained. 'Santo Domingo, I think. Or perhaps Costa Rica. With a bunch of hoteliers, Max told me. Flogging Spain as usual, my high-powered little cousin.'

'Is Max her husband?' asked Hadley.

'Yes – Máximo Uribe. You haven't heard of him, obviously. 'Course you wouldn't have.'

'I thought he was a dentist,' suggested Mercedes.

'He *is*, darling,' said Ramiro, smirking. 'Dental surgeon to celebrities. *Todo Madrid* lines up to see him. Royalty, politicians, movie stars.'

'No children?' asked Mercedes.

'No.' Ramiro lowered his voice, looking round as if to spare the servants' sensitivity. 'No, it was all very sad.'

Rosa had become pregnant with twins in the first year

of her marriage but six months into her pregnancy one of the unborn babies had died.

'Agonising experience,' continued Ramiro. 'Rushed to hospital for surgery, second baby – a little girl – never had a chance. Lived three days in an incubator. That was it.'

Hadley and Mercedes listened in shocked silence.

'Gets worse. Shan't bother you with details, old bean. Hysterectomy and all that.' He shook his head in horror. 'You get the idea.'

For a while they spoke of Rosa, her career with the government, her closeness to Max. Hadley conjured up a vision of a wild Rosa on Ramiro's birthday night but said nothing. Increasingly, he'd felt he had some sort of score to settle with Ramiro's cousin.

'She was very helpful, you know? Your letters to old Reds,' Ramiro said.

'What do you mean?' Hadley asked, surprised.

'Remember when I suggested you should write to ex-combatants? *Embattled Madrid*?'

'Yes, of course. You did say you had a cousin . . .'

'Exactly. Rosa. She got us the list. Addresses, whereabouts. From her Ministry. Useful contact, cousin Rosa.'

'I never thanked her properly, now that you mention it,' Hadley said reflectively. Nor had she commented, he thought, when they had first met and he'd told her he was going to Cuba.

'I'm sure there will be another opportunity,' Ramiro assured him. 'She called the night after my birthday. She was back in Madrid. Said how much she'd enjoyed meeting you both.'

'I'm glad to hear it,' Mercedes said, smiling.

And that she said no more than that, thought Hadley.

* * *

When they got home that afternoon Hadley telephoned Pinto. The spy chief had given him a cellphone number to be used if Florin got in touch. 'Call me anytime, day or night,' he had demanded.

On Easter Monday, Pinto was attending a buffet lunch in Aranjuez at the home of his newly appointed Minister. He moved from room to room, trying to look attentive as politicians and their hangers-on accosted him to offer their advice on how to hunt down Al Qaeda murderers or how to filter the rush of citizens from seven eastern European states claiming their right to settle in Spain following their countries' admission to the EU a week earlier.

So when Hadley telephoned, Pinto welcomed the interruption and on hearing the news ordered him – making sure he was in his superior's hearing – to meet him at CNI headquarters early in the morning and be sure to have his luggage with him. Explaining with a pained expression that something urgent required his attention, Pinto offered his apologies and left the party.

Hadley decided to take Mercedes along whether or not Pinto approved. As it happened it turned out to be a good move since Pinto, already endowed with a naturally pleasant temperament, was charm personified in her presence. He read through the second instalment of Florin's notes while his guests – that was what he'd called them – enjoyed their morning coffee.

'Interesting character, don't you think?' he asked, as though he had been reading a novel. Pinto pressed his buzzer and asked the secretary who instantly materialised to make two copies of The Aztec's notes.

'So,' Pinto leaned back on his chair, 'if we go by what's

in there,' he nodded towards the closing door, from which Hadley concluded that he was referring to Florin's papers, 'at some point, at least, our missing treasure was tucked away in Yugoslavia – wouldn't you say?'

The others both nodded, confirming to Pinto that Mercedes was privy to developments thus far.

'Which is not altogether outlandish,' he observed.

Tito was not in charge of Yugoslavia yet, but he led her underground Communist movement and commanded a huge following across the entire country. And he was Mercer's close friend. The *Kursk* could have easily detoured up the Adriatic – which would account for her late arrival in Odessa. Orlov was unquestionably involved and Florin's claim that he too had been there tallied with information that Pinto had gleaned from other sources.

But equally – Pinto hedged his bet – if this *was* a carefully contrived fantasy, its creators would have made sure it fitted in with known facts *and* deployed the confirmatory 'other sources'.

Pinto had to let it play out. But he would keep an open mind, at least until Florin showed his hand, because at that juncture Pinto was far from certain that he understood the exact nature and objectives of The Aztec's game.

'I take it you are both planning to enjoy the charms of Montenegrin hospitality?'

'We are.' They replied almost in unison.

'Well, let's hope you come back with some answers. Because the one thing I'm willing to bet on is that wherever that gold may be, you won't find it in Montenegro.'

'So what's the point of going there?' Mercedes wanted to know.

'That's what we shall have to ask Mr Florin in due course.'

Pinto made light of it. 'Meanwhile I'm sure Mr Hadley will collect further biographical material.'

'I intend to.' Hadley was not about to apologise.

'At the government's expense,' Pinto said, with a grimace. Then he turned to Mercedes. 'Of course CNI can only pay for Mr Hadley.'

That proved a little contentious, but in the end it was agreed that the hotel room cost the same whether it was occupied by one or by two people, sustenance would be on a per diem basis which could easily feed both, and Miss Vilanova's ticket could be bought by CNI by way of a *loan*.

And if Pinto's agreeable disposition towards his 'guests' needed reaffirming, he certainly did this by inviting them both to lunch while travel arrangements were made by CNI's VIP travel department.

Jack and Mercedes reached their hotel just after midnight and went straight to bed without even pausing to close the blinds. Hadley's sleep, though deep, was visited by incomprehensible dreams in which Pinto threateningly demanded gold, and a larger-than-life Florin laughed out loud and smiled knowingly at Mercedes. Yet he was sufficiently exhausted not to wake up until the serene light of early dawn tiptoed softly into the room and underscored the beauty of his surroundings. He slipped out of bed and ambled up to the double French windows that opened onto his room's private terrace.

For a moment, as he walked out into the Adriatic morning, he could not recall where he was, until he saw Villa Montenegro's smart logo embossed on the outdoor chairs and looked down past the far edge of the infinity pool that blended into the aquamarine sea a few hundred feet below.

Hadley walked back into the room, ordered breakfast

from room service and crawled back into bed, from Mercedes's side this time, pressing himself hard against her, hugging her and catching a glimpse of her sleepy smile as he kissed the side of her neck.

'Are we here?' she asked jokingly, then rolled over to face him and kissed him long and softly in the mouth.

'No idea where I am,' he mumbled. 'Feels like paradise.'

'Feels like something else to me,' she teased. 'If you were feeling like this, why did you order breakfast?'

'We can ignore them,' he persisted.

'They'll let themselves in,' Mercedes countered.

Hadley broke free from her, ran across the room and locked the door. Ten minutes later the maid knocked, called out politely and tried in vain to let herself in. They ignored her.

Later, Hadley retrieved the breakfast tray from the floor outside their room. He drank the fruit juice and ate the brioches while Mercedes tucked into the fruit and sipped a tepid coffee.

At noon they took a walk around the hotel's grounds – with Hadley carefully scanning every face in sight, however innocent they might appear, for a telltale sign that might reveal The Aztec's latest emissary.

Encouraged by the spring weather, the local population's open friendliness and the instructions that they should behave like ordinary tourists, Jack and Mercedes walked down the hill and across the narrow isthmus into tiny Saint Steven Island where a quaint cluster of traditional houses bunched up around a maze of narrow streets. Mercedes took photographs while Hadley continued to look over his shoulder before they decided to explore further afield and took a taxi to nearby Budva.

Budva Old Town stands on a little peninsula in the city's western flank, thrust into the sea next to the yacht marina. Though Budva's heyday was in Venetian times, the charming architecture that Mercedes and Hadley were admiring was very recent – a meticulously sympathetic reconstruction of an ancient town that had survived wars, sieges and Nazi occupation but had eventually capitulated to the forces of nature when an earthquake razed it to the ground in 1979.

On this sunny morning of spring the tourist hordes had not yet descended upon Budva and, for the moment at least, it was simply another Slavic town going about its daily business. Jack and Mercedes, clearly foreign to the local eye, chose a café by the marina and sat offering themselves in full view to whoever The Aztec's messenger might turn out to be.

'You think we are being watched?' Mercedes asked, though nothing in her tone betrayed concern. In fact, thought Hadley, she was, if anything, enjoying the experience.

'I'm certain we are!' he replied, perhaps a little impatiently.

'Jack?' Her tone suggested she might have read his mind.

'What?' He looked at her, unable to conceal his own anxiety.

'You know what Dad said, about Florin?'

'What?'

'About him being a terrorist.'

'What about it?'

'Do you think we are being stupid, getting mixed up with all this?'

'What choice do we have?'

'I haven't said anything to Dad,' she said guardedly,

'but I think he might know how to handle this sort of situation.'

Hadley thought about her suggestion for a while and Mercedes did not disturb his silence. Overhead, a trio of inquisitive seagulls vied for a vantage point over the harbour. An old man rested his arm along a young boy's shoulder while the child threw morsels of bread into the water. Perhaps the seagulls were waiting for that elusive opening when they could outsmart the fish.

'Your dad told me he'd been in the army,' said Jack, and Mercedes turned to look at him, evidently surprised. 'In Argentina,' he added.

'He must like you,' she said. 'He doesn't often speak about those days.'

'He also warned me about Florin.'

'What did he say?'

'He told me to be careful. He said that Florin was a ruthless fanatic.'

'He knows about political intrigue and secretive shenanigans, Jack,' Mercedes replied after a moment's reflection. 'I think, if it's OK with you, I might tell Dad about Pinto, Florin and the gold and ask for his advice.'

'What? Tell him everything?'

'Well,' she smiled at last, 'not *quite* everything! I can talk to him, but he's still my dad.'

They ate a plate of fresh grilled squid and drank a small jug of local wine while still examining every approaching figure in anticipation of some sort of contact. But none came. In the mid-afternoon they set off at a leisurely pace towards Villa Montenegro but after two miles had had enough of the hilly road and its unruly traffic and flagged down a bus.

As Hadley stood just inside its door trying to explain to the driver that he could only pay in euros, he caught sight of an overtaking car.

He had seen it earlier: a pale green people-carrier of some sort. It had been parked outside the hotel and also at the Budva marina but he'd thought nothing of it at the time. Now Hadley paid more attention as the vehicle drove past. There were three male occupants and they stared into the bus as they passed.

Hadley took a seat alongside Mercedes who had not failed to notice where his gaze had been directed. Three miles further along the coast they got off the bus at Saint Steven and continued on foot. The green car was in the hotel compound once again when they arrived but there was no sign of its occupants.

Hadley enquired about messages in reception but there were none, so they climbed the stairs to their first-floor room.

'Do you think they were looking at us?' Mercedes pulled up a chair and sat by the French windows.

'I'm sure of it,' he replied.

'What did they look like? Did you see their faces?'

'Not that well. The one in the front, next to the driver, had a stern expression on his face.'

There was a knock at the door and Jack and Mercedes stiffened. Jack hooked on the safety chain and cracked the door open.

'Jack Hadley?' It was the stern-faced man, but he appeared to be alone, and smiling.

'Yes?'

'Klejevic,' he said, still smiling, hands hanging limply by his sides, perhaps intentionally in full view. 'Ivo Klejevic?'

'Of course.' Hadley pushed the door shut and released the chain before opening it again. 'Please come in.'

Klejevic entered the room and Hadley checked there was no one else lurking along the corridor before closing the door again.

Klejevic bowed politely. 'You must be Mercedes.'

He was broad-shouldered, stocky, a few years older than Hadley perhaps, but younger than his full grey mane suggested. He had the lined weather-beaten face of one who spent much of his life outdoors and the rod-straight spine of a man whose lifestyle demanded fitness.

'I think you saw me, on the road,' Klejevic said, smiling sheepishly.

'Yes.'

'I didn't mean to alarm you.'

'It's OK.' Hadley waved him towards a chair and all three sat close together.

'I was checking,' Klejevic offered by way of explanation. 'Jesús said I am responsible for you while you are here.'

'Checking what?'

'If anyone else was watching you,' he said casually.

'Why should anyone be watching us?' demanded Hadley.

'People can't seem to stop poking their noses into The Aztec's affairs.' Klejevic was not apologetic.

'Is anyone watching us, Ivo?' asked Mercedes.

'I haven't seen anyone. But I won't stop looking.'

'Do you know Jesús Florin?' Hadley asked.

'I have met him.' Klejevic betrayed a touch of pride when he said it. 'He and my father were close friends. They served together in Leningrad.'

'With Mercer too?' Antonio Mercer's name kept cropping up in The Aztec's notes.

'Oh yes.' Klejevic beamed. 'All three were friends. General Mercer was here many times. Did you know him?'

Hadley shook his head.

'So, where do we go from here?' he wanted to know.

'Tomorrow,' Klejevic explained, 'my friends and I will come and fetch you. In the morning, maybe eight o'clock if that's all right for you?' He waited for Hadley's assent before continuing. 'We'll drive to the interior.'

'Where are we going?'

'Moraca River Canyon. It's a very beautiful place,' he said.

'Why are we going there?'

'I will show you.'

'Is it far?'

'No. You will see tomorrow.' Klejevic looked at Mercedes and back to Hadley. 'It's countryside, rough ground. Best to wear comfortable shoes.'

'We'll be fine,' Mercedes assured him.

Klejevic stood up and extended his hand to each in turn.

'It is my honour to look after The Aztec's friends,' he said in earnest, while silently hoping that the fish would take the bait.

16

They met under bright chandeliers at a Mexican Embassy reception in November 1970 – the month that Salvador Allende assumed the presidency of Chile.

Since Castro's 1959 victory, Cuba had been a political pariah cut off from the rest of the American continent. When Florin arrived in Chile in the spring of 1970 to advise the Left on electoral tactics, only Mexico and Canada – ironically, the United States' closest neighbours – had defied the Washington-led pan-American boycott and maintained diplomatic relations with communist Cuba.

Florin had therefore come to Chile as a Mexican, bringing with him large sums of money to help Allende's campaign and, on this day of electoral triumph, he savoured the taste of victory at his native country's diplomatic legation in Santiago.

Lucía was there too, enjoying the heady moment that none had thought possible: the democratic election of an openly socialist government in Latin America. And while no one was naive enough to believe that the campaigning had been clean and above board, the votes had been freely cast and honestly counted.

Florin would later admit that it had been Lucía's looks that immediately attracted him. She was tall and had a natural presence that made her stand out in any crowd. Her deep suntan contrasted with her cropped fair hair, which after a summer spent rallying and advising peasant communities had been naturally bleached by the sun into a shade just short of platinum.

She was already a renowned political activist and a cause célèbre in legal circles. Under the previous government much of Chile's land had been taken into state ownership and redistributed, but Lucía had been assisting Allende to draw up a plan that would put all productive farms over eighty hectares in the hands of those who worked on them.

Like the new president, she came from Valparaíso and was a graduate of the State University – Allende was a doctor, she a lawyer – and like the president before her she too had already made her mark by the age of thirty-two.

'General Florin.' She held out her hand. She was chatting with fellow activist Gladys Marin as he approached her. Jesús Florin's presence in Chile as an unofficial Castro emissary was an open secret.

From the day Allende took office, Florin had become part of the team in the Moneda Palace, much to the horror of the defeated conservatives who had warned that electing Allende was tantamount to inviting Havana and Moscow to the ball.

'I'm Lucía Bamberg,' she said, with that broad smile of hers that would soon enchant him. He noticed that her eyes were the palest aquamarine and the grip of her hand was firm and sensual. From the very instant he took her hand, Jesús Florin did not want to let her go.

'Would it be considered chauvinistic, Dr Bamberg, if I said you have the most beautiful smile?'

She laughed a crystalline laugh.

'Oh it would, it most definitely would if you were Chilean, General Florin, but you are Mexican. We know you can't help it.'

They talked about Chile, the future and Allende, and a little about themselves. Several times they were parted by well-wishers who needed him or her to meet the chair of this or the leader of that, but even while apart they sought out each other with their eyes and when they could escape for a short time they would continue their conversation.

They had agreed to meet again but to Florin even a day had seemed too long. His own time was mostly spent in the capital whereas Lucía's practice was based on the coast, but they both soon found excuses to visit their respective cities. Their first outing alone together had been in Valparaíso. Lucía had taken Florin to her favourite eating place, the cooperative restaurant perched atop the lifeboat station where they ate fish soup and watched the sun sink into the Pacific. It was to become a regular spot for their nights out during their fatefully short time together.

They talked politics and dreamed of a fairer world but both were realistic enough to know it would take guile, determination and powerful friends just to hang on to what had already been achieved. Over the next two years the Soviet and Cuban embassies in Chile would expand beyond measure. Where two dozen staff might normally be expected, Castro fielded two hundred, causing alarm in adjoining countries that in turn sought aid from Washington.

The same domino theories that had justified the war in Vietnam were now expounded in Latin America; the economic dirty war would soon commence.

During the Allende years, Lucía continued to develop People's Committees and to rally peasants into ownership of land. Florin's work, conversely, was covert in nature and he gradually built up a powerful network of committed agents the length and breadth of Chile, a military and security arm of the communist party modelled on the Soviet Cheka that would not simply confine itself to Chile but would start supporting subversive movements throughout the region.

Thus the scene was set for confrontation, and the economic disaster that would result from Allende's reckless Marxist doctrine would start a chain reaction that would unleash right-wing military dictatorships throughout the subcontinent for almost a decade.

But neither Jesús nor Lucía envisaged such an outcome in 1970. The following summer they married in a quiet private ceremony in Valparaíso's Civil Register and set up home in Viña del Mar.

'I'm glad she's a girl,' Lucía said, lying in Florin's arms in the quiet of a Viña Sunday afternoon. A few feet away María Luz slept in her cot while the Pacific Ocean swayed gently past the garden and the cliff, as though mindful not to disturb such peace.

'I shall always know how to bring up a girl on my own when you feel the urge to go warring off in distant places.'

'It's an urge I haven't had of late,' Florin responded, his eyes half-closed. They lay on the bed with the air conditioning turned off. They both preferred the open garden window and half-closed blinds, even if the heat was at times uncomfortable.

'Long may it last.' She raised her face and kissed his cheek. 'But somehow I doubt it.'

'I mean it. Everything I want is right here. I've given my best.' He lightened up a little. 'Besides, I'm getting too old for all that rough stuff.'

'I agree.' Lucía poked at his ribcage. 'Definitely too old. I must write to Fidel and warn him, lest he has other ideas.'

He could feel her face smiling against his chest.

'He's never asked me to do anything, you know?'

'All that time in Africa was your own initiative?'

'Yes.' He spoke sincerely, remembering. The mention of Africa was always accompanied by enduring pain.

'Ernesto's idea in the first place,' Florin admitted, 'but I did not take too much persuading.'

'Do you miss him?' Lucía asked and instantly regretted her words. She meant Ché, but for one unforgivable second she'd overlooked the fact that Guevara had not died alone.

'I miss all of them.' He'd sensed her realisation. 'Every day.'

'I'm sorry.' She tightened her arm around his chest and looked towards the cot. Perhaps it would mark a new beginning.

A more unlikely pair was hard to imagine. Where Guevara was introverted and serious, as if forever carrying with him the burdens of the world, Florin's exuberant, jovial personality made him appear as if he didn't have a care in the world.

Eleven years had passed since the horror of the Gulag when Guevara and Florin went to the Congo with the Cuban advance party. And another five since Ché's death in Bolivia in 1967. Yet Florin could recall every minute of his time in Africa as if it had happened only yesterday.

They lay around in a circle, tired, covered in dust, yet content and even joyful in spite of their painful losses. The jungle was alive in the way that only the tropical rainforest untouched by human ignorance can be, full of sounds that to Jesús and Ché were as alien as the inhabitants of the thousand galaxies that canopied the African sky. But they were joyful sounds nevertheless.

The young men, all nineteen survivors, displayed the paradoxical expressions of the African boy-soldier who can at once be grateful that he has survived, in pain because his brother didn't and, forgetting both, opening his eyes wide in disingenuous astonishment at the sound of a pocket-sized transistor radio.

They had names like Bienheuré, Jean-Baptiste and Peregrin, indicating that they had once been Belgian subjects even if no one had bothered telling them. But they had seen Laurent Kabila embrace these two white men and pronounce them true lieutenants of the murdered Patrice Lumumba, so they followed them and the other Cubans into battle without reservation.

They were confident enough about the day's achievements to light a campfire at night. For the Congolese youngsters the forest's night-time smell was part of their God-given environment; but for Jesús and Ché it was an intoxicating experience.

'You are fucking crazy, Jesús,' Guevara said half in jest, laying his weapon down beside him as he rested against a tree.

'We won the day, didn't we, *mano*?' Jesús challenged him with a broad smile as the boys looked on.

'All luck, man. We could have been wiped out.'

'That's the problem with you southern pussies,' Florin laughed. 'No balls,' he said, exaggeratedly grabbing his testicles and tilting his head in Guevara's direction as he added '*Il n'a pas les couilles*' for the benefit of the boys.

They all laughed and imitated the gesture.

'We could have got our heads blown off, you reckless fuck!' Guevara spoke in Spanish but the boys could already swear in half a dozen languages. Foul language, angry foul language in particular, made them guffaw.

They had been outnumbered three to one and still Florin had gone ahead with the attack. They'd had the advantage of surprise but Guevara still thought they'd just been lucky.

That night they ate and slept with their guns by their side, each ready to jump up and defend his brother if the need arose and in the morning they would go seeking a new fight. Jesús and Ché knew that their young tigers would become tragic pawns on a chessboard of brutality and that most of them would be dead before their twentieth birthday, but nevertheless the fight had to, and would, go on.

Later, as the boys slept, their leaders shared a drink and a cigar. It was then that Guevara spoke the words that Florin would never forget.

'I'm going back to Cuba soon,' he said.

'What's happening?' Florin was surprised; there was still so much to do in Africa.

'We've been talking,' Guevara confessed, 'with Fidel. This' – he waved his arm around him, whether at the forest or at the sleeping boys wasn't clear – 'must continue, of course. But I'm not getting any younger and I want to take the fight home.'

'To Argentina?' Florin had not expected that.

'Eventually.' Guevara nodded. 'But not yet. Right now, in Argentina, we'd lose. We are going to start with the poorer nations. Fidel has said yes to Bolivia. I expect that means Moscow approves.'

'When?'

'Next month . . .' Guevara sounded uncomfortable with the conversation. 'There's something else: Yuri wants to come with me. He's already asked his Comandante, and he begged me to ask you.'

'Yuri? He's eighteen . . .' Florin stood up and paced around the small encampment. Yuri. He was a soldier; he'd graduated from the Academy four months ago and was eager to prove himself. His older brother Leonid was already with a regiment and had accompanied Cuban advisers on an Angolan tour.

Florin tried to see the stars through the jungle's canopy and thought of Natalia. Ten years had passed since he'd held her dying body close to him on a dark Siberian night as a pair of confused little boys looked on. *I'm still fighting, my darling, and leading these African children. Where's the honesty if I say no to our boys?*

He walked back to where Guevara stood quietly, leaning against a tree. He embraced him briefly and said simply, 'You take care.'

That had been five years ago. Two years later, Guevara, Yuri and their entire unit would lie dead in the Bolivian jungle. The following year the last of Natalia's bloodline would perish as Leonid's MPLA detachment fell victim to a deadly ambush near Luanda.

Florin returned to Cuba, his will sapped, his vision of the future clouded. But time heals and human passions rekindle and when the opportunity came along to pursue his dream without guns and on his own continent, it was Florin who asked to be sent to Chile and Castro had gladly acquiesced.

Now the Chilean dream was falling apart. A massive middle-class revolt emulated the workers' marches of bygone days. Women beat their empty saucepans in seemingly endless demonstrations as they marched through Santiago's streets, exposing the total failure of Soviet-sponsored agrarian reforms that had left the nation without food.

Collapsing copper prices in world markets were depriving the regime of its major source of income, turning the recently nationalised mining industry into a labour liability. Day by day the nation's enchantment with Allende was drawing to a close. Once again it looked as though lines were being drawn for the differences to be settled in blood.

'How long will you be gone?' Lucía asked.

They had lunched at the *Bote Salvavidas* where the waiters too lamented the shortage of fine produce – even the vineyards seemed to be run-down.

María Luz sat on a high chair and banged a spoon on its tray as the young busboy fussed over her. He had taken a shine to the Florin baby from the first time she'd been brought round in her carrycot and now regarded serving her as his exclusive right. He planted a kiss on the child's cheek and went off in the direction of the kitchen to bring her a 'special treat'.

'Not long,' Florin assured Lucía, 'maybe a couple of weeks. There are people flying in from Moscow, too.'

'This is a mess,' she lamented when no one was listening.

'I know. And asking the Russians how to deal with the

economy is a joke. They'll quote the usual lines from the ideologues.' Florin did not try to hide the disdain he felt for Moscow's theorists.

'They'll have to change tack,' Lucía continued, 'or Chile will grind to a halt.'

'Yes, and they'll also have to get tougher with foreign-funded disruptions.'

That made Lucía smile.

'My unwavering Jesús,' she teased him. 'Unquestioningly loyal to the end.'

The boy came back into the dining room. He carried a shiny metal bowl full of pink ice cream into which three cats' tongues were embedded.

'*Para mi novia*,' he said – 'for my girlfriend' – placing the bowl on María Luz's tray.

'Well? Have you thought about our last conversation?' Florin asked him as the lad spoon-fed María Luz the ice cream.

'Yes, sir,' he replied immediately. 'I'm going to be a lawyer.'

Florin and his wife exchanged glances and smiled.

'What happened to the fisherman idea?' Lucía asked.

'I told my teacher I knew you and that you are a lawyer and she said that I was bright enough and if I worked hard there was no reason why I could not go to university.'

María Luz cried out, demanding another spoonful.

'How old are you?' Florin asked.

'Thirteen, sir.'

'So you'll be going to university in five years.'

'Yes, sir.'

'You'll need to start saving. If you want to be a lawyer you'll be a poor student for five years.'

'I can still work here. I can be a proper waiter then.'
He appeared undeterred.

'I'll tell you what I'll do for you, Luisito,' said Florin,
taking out his wallet and extracting a small coin.

'I'll give you this to start a fund towards your education,'
he said, handing the coin to the boy, 'but you must not
sell it until the day you start your university.'

Luisito looked at the glimmering coin, mesmerised
by it.

'Is it gold?' he asked

'It is,' Florin assured him, 'and if you continue to do
well at school I shall give you another for each birthday
and one each Christmas. Then you will have ten to sell to
help pay for your upkeep as a student.'

'Eleven!' the boy corrected him, holding out his new
coin. 'And when I'm a lawyer,' he said excitedly, 'I will
marry María Luz!'

They all laughed and Luisito went away to show off his
gold coin in the kitchen.

But it was not to be. This would be last time Luisito
would see the Florins, and the half-sovereign he was so
excited about would be the only gold coin he would be
given in his life.

17

They set off at eight as planned. Klejevic had brought two younger men along whom he introduced as Brako and Goran. Trim and clean-faced with close-cropped hair, they might have been soldiers out of uniform.

The car was a seven-seat Fiat and Hadley sat next to Klejevic in the front. Mercedes was given the entire middle row and the two youths slid onto the rear bench.

Hadley noticed Klejevic scanning the large wing mirrors every few seconds as they set off along Highway 65 in the general direction of Podgorica.

'Spotted anyone yet?' he asked with an unwarranted touch of sarcasm which he immediately regretted in his voice.

'Not sure,' the driver replied seriously, which made Hadley sit up and turn to look at Mercedes. He saw Brako sitting sideways, his right arm over the rear seat's backrest, maintaining a constant lookout.

'Who are we looking for, anyway?' Hadley asked.

Klejevic shrugged.

'Many people would like to know what you are doing here.'

Ten miles north-east of Saint Steven they came to the long causeway across Lake Skadar. Mercedes drew a deep breath on seeing that vast expanse of water surrounded by hills.

On reaching the northern shore Klejevic pulled up on the hard shoulder and jumped out of the car, wielding a pair of binoculars. From this spot he had miles of clear view across the causeway, including the lake's southern approach. Brako spoke quietly to Goran and they both looked searchingly in all directions.

Once satisfied, Klejevic nodded approval and their journey resumed. A few miles further along they turned off the main highway along a minor road that roughly followed the course of the Moraca River as it gradually cut its way into the rising ground to form a steep canyon.

Twenty minutes later they turned again and continued along a rough unpaved road flanked by rocky boulders until they reached a wide opening occupied by a large stone farmhouse surrounded by crumbling outbuildings.

A pick-up truck and a vintage Russian tractor outside the house looked as though they'd been abandoned. Klejevic parked next to them as two men in peasants' clothes and a woman wearing a brightly coloured headscarf emerged through the front door. Hadley and Mercedes were asked to remain in the car while the others went to the house.

They seemed to know each other well, judging by the amount of kissing and back-slapping. Hadley could not hear their conversation — nor would he have understood the language if he had — but there was much gesticulating as they pointed at the hills and rocky escarpments, concerned looks in their faces.

Goran walked back to the car and opened up the tailgate, then lifted a panel on the boot's floor and removed a pair of Uzi sub-machine guns. He smiled reassuringly at Mercedes, making no attempt to conceal the weapons, and returned to the little group by the farmhouse door where he handed one of the guns to Brako. After a moment's further deliberation Klejevic returned to the car.

'OK, we go now,' he said, opening the door for Mercedes.

'Where to?' Hadley asked, not expecting an answer.

Klejevic slung a canvas rucksack over his shoulder and led the way around the main farmhouse and along a rough lane that split the rock face beyond it. Hadley and Mercedes fell in step behind him, as did one of the men from the farm, his right arm casually resting on a gun suspended from a sling over his shoulder. The remaining couple went back inside the house as the two young men took up positions in the derelict buildings to guard the approach road.

Their narrow path was strewn with rocks and heavy boulders, making rapid progress difficult. It was bordered by steep granite sides and it looked as though much of the debris on the ground had dropped off in recent times.

'Be careful where you step,' Klejevic warned. 'You can easily get hurt here.'

They moved on in relative silence, jumping over the smaller rocks, squeezing between the larger boulders and the rock face where appropriate. After a good half-hour of unsteady progress Klejevic halted before a narrow cavernous opening. A large stone slab stood next to it. Hadley guessed it would easily hide the entrance if it was moved a mere two feet.

Klejevic put down his rucksack and pulled out two kerosene lanterns, handing one to his nameless colleague. The foursome entered the narrow dark passage in single file, Klejevic leading the way and Hadley following Mercedes.

'This was much wider before,' explained Klejevic, the faint echoing of his words suggesting they were heading towards a larger cavern. 'It was almost sealed off by the earthquake. You heard about it?'

Hadley vaguely remembered the news item and said so.

'1979,' continued Klejevic. 'Many people died.'

Gradually the passage widened and the ceiling rose. They came to a large chamber, perhaps fifty foot square and with a high vaulted ceiling, and even in the feeble light provided by the lanterns Hadley could see that at some point it had been visited by man.

'Well, here we are, Jack Hadley,' Klejevic said. 'He said I should bring you here, and I have.'

'What is this?' Hadley tried to make sense of the few clues: remains of old pallets, bits of broken timber, half-decomposed canvas bags, dark green tubular-framed campsite bunks.

'This,' explained Klejevic, 'is the answer to the question of where the *Kursk* disappeared to for seven days.'

Klejevic and his companion perched their lanterns on a flat rock and turned the wicks up. In the ensuing brightness, he singled out a piece of debris that might have once been part of a wooden box – two portions of adjoining sides held together by an angled metal strip – and dragged it closer to the light. He picked up an old rag and dusted the faded markings on the timber. There was no mistaking the stencilled markings: *SS Kursk, Odessa*.

The second man tapped Hadley on the shoulder. He handed

him a torn canvas bag with part of its leather trim and its brass lock still attached. That too was easily identifiable by the unmistakable logo of the Banco de España.

'So it's true, then?' Mercedes took the bag from Hadley and examined it carefully.

'What is true?'

'About the gold: the missing gold of Spain. It was brought here?'

'My father and Jesús Florin brought it here in 1936. It was before my time,' Klejevic explained, 'but I've known about this place since childhood.

'Anyone else?' Jack asked tentatively.

'Orlov,' Klejevic spat on the ground. 'The American spy Orlov. He was here as well.'

'Why here?' Jack asked. 'Why did they take it off the *Kursk*?'

'On orders from General Mercer,' explained Klejevic.

'But why?' Jack was still not convinced by the answers. 'Surely they weren't stealing it?'

'No!' Klejevic shook his head, smiling. 'It was like insurance,' he explained, 'in case the Republic lost the war. To fund the fight that would continue if Franco took over the country.'

'What happened next?'

'Jesús came back. In 1939. Mercer sent him, after the spy Orlov defected to America. Florin and my father opened the boxes and removed the bags inside them. Back to the coast again, loaded onto a Spanish Navy fast boat.'

'Are you sure?' Was this a message from Florin to Pinto, wondered Hadley. Was it saying that the gold had come to Montenegro on board the *Kursk* and gone out again on some sort of gunboat?

'I am sure that's what my father told me,' Klejevic assured him, 'and I am sure that anything he ever told me was true. But you will see the photos. Judge for yourself.'

'This place was never used again?' Hadley looked at the bunks and other telltale signs of human habitation.

'The partisans, Tito's people, used it during the German occupation. Others too, after the war. Smugglers, even. Since the earthquake it was not so easy.'

Perhaps, thought Hadley, even more recently, as Yugoslavia broke up viciously. But that was not his business. In fact, nothing about this place was his business. Suddenly he just wanted to go home.

'Mercedes,' Klejevic invited her, 'you take your photos now, please. But no faces.'

As she went about documenting the cave's contents, Hadley examined the canvas bag again.

'May I take this?' he asked

'Sure.' Klejevic shrugged. Anything he wants, The Aztec had said. 'Please take it.'

That might be the clincher with Pinto, thought Hadley. Give him the bag, tell him his bloody gold had been there, then got loaded on a Spanish boat and taken God knew where. Back to Spain if you like, maybe even to the Nationalist side. Who knows?

Florin was keeping that card close to his chest and would probably be inflexible until Pinto agreed to help with the recovery.

They returned the same way they had come. As they approached the farm again Goran waved an all-clear but still kept a watchful eye on the high ground. Neither he nor Brako joined the party in the traditional round of slivovitz, kissing and handshaking before they boarded the car for the drive back to Saint Steven.

This time Hadley sat next to Mercedes and placed his arm round her shoulder. The two young men kept gazing round.

There was nothing of value in that cave, Hadley was thinking – what the hell was all the fuss about? And who cared so much that guns and subterfuge were necessary? They'd come all the way to Montenegro to take a few photos for Pinto and bring back a piece of Bank of Spain canvas. None of it made sense. What was Florin's game? If it was purely to prove that the gold had been there, then the evidence offered could just as easily have been faked.

Back at the hotel, Klejevic walked in with Hadley and Mercedes. He carried a small satchel with him.

'I have something for you,' said Klejevic, raising the satchel for Hadley to see.

'From Jesús Florin, I take it?'

'Yes.'

'Let's find somewhere quiet.' Hadley led the way.

'I'm going to buy some bubbles from the shop, if you don't mind,' Mercedes said, excusing herself. 'Then I'll go back to the room and relax for a while in the jacuzzi.'

The two men found the television room empty and sat on the soft sofas. Klejevic opened his bag and took out the now familiar large envelope. In addition to the notes there were two old photographs. They'd been taken in daylight under a menacingly overcast sky and showed a dark-coloured vessel – sprouting many antennae – that was tied alongside a makeshift dock.

'Is this here?' Hadley tilted the top photograph towards Klejevic.

'Budva,' he confirmed.

There were half a dozen smiling men next to what appeared to be an open-deck torpedo boat.

'That's my father.' Klejevic pointed at a figure in the centre of the group. 'Stefan.'

Hadley nodded in acknowledgement, but he was looking at the tall thin person on the far right in both pictures. He wore a long black leather coat and a beret with a military badge on it. Sixty years might have passed but time could not disguise the mischievous expression or the wandering eyes: Hadley was looking at a young Jesús Florin.

He was about to peruse The Aztec's notes when a distraught and clearly alarmed Mercedes came running down the stairs, shouting Jack's name.

'There was a man in the room!' she yelled, as she reached the bottom of the staircase, 'He jumped out, over the balcony!' Mercedes waved her hand towards the front of the hotel.

Klejevic swore loudly and drew a handgun from his waistband. Hadley moved protectively towards Mercedes as Klejevic made for the front doors, calling out to Goran and Brako.

The man and woman in reception stared in stunned disbelief but did not intervene. There were not many people about that afternoon.

'Did he attack you?' Hadley asked.

'No.' Mercedes shook her head, her composure returning. 'I think he was as shocked as me when I burst in on him. He just dropped everything and escaped through the terrace door.'

'Dropped what?'

'I don't know. He was searching the dresser's drawers – whatever he had in his hands.'

They heard the screech of tyres and the crunch of flying gravel as Klejevic's Fiat shot off towards the car park exit.

'Did you get a look at him?'

'Yes.' Mercedes had no doubts. 'Our age, slim, dark hair, and a goatee beard.'

'Clothes?'

'Dark jeans and a green T-shirt.'

Jack took Mercedes by the hand and walked her out towards the car park. He did not wish to leave her alone but neither did he want to ignore what was happening outside.

There was another screech of tyres, this time coming from behind the hotel's perimeter wall, further downhill, followed by loud shouts – like orders or warnings – in two languages. Then the unmistakable crack of a single gunshot, followed seconds later by a short burst of automatic fire. Hadley recognised the Uzi's sound.

Moments later the Fiat returned. Klejevic was on his own as he strode back to the hotel. He shouted something at the reception staff and they immediately moved to close the front doors.

Hadley and Mercedes followed Klejevic upstairs to their room. It looked a mess. Clearly the intruder had been in a hurry. Every drawer and cupboard had been opened and the contents carelessly turned out. Clothes, papers, toiletries and other personal belongings had been removed and dropped.

They became aware of Klejevic frantically talking into his phone. He too noticed both Mercedes's evident concern and Hadley's mounting anger.

So far Klejevic had failed to explain the gunshots.

'We go now!' Klejevic ordered. 'Get your things together and make it fast.'

He moved to the balcony and scanned the grounds. He dialled again, and spoke to Goran in short sharp sentences as Hadley and Mercedes hurriedly crammed their possessions into their two bags.

They walked back down to the car park where a panting Goran was waiting. There was no sign of Brako. Klejevic spoke to the couple on the front desk as they silently observed two of his guests walking out with their luggage, bills unpaid, and again said something in Serbian which appeared to be accepted without argument.

Klejevic had to be something official in this country, Hadley concluded. That would explain why his men could carry weapons in their car and appear unconcerned.

A little way down the hill towards Saint Steven they saw Brako. He was standing on the sidewalk, an Uzi in his hand, next to the prostrate body of a man in dark jeans and a green T-shirt. There was a handgun on the pavement. Brako wore a large ID badge suspended from a lanyard round his neck. The few bystanders who had gathered kept themselves at a prudent distance.

Mercedes brought her hand up to her mouth to suppress an anguished cry. Goran, now driving, did not stop.

'Who was he, Ivo?' Jack asked.

'We don't know yet.' The reply was non-committal.

'Didn't he have any identification on him?' Hadley persisted. If someone was out to harm him or Mercedes he was damned if he was going to let it pass without even asking who the hell the man was.

'Yes. He is a foreigner.'

'So?' Jack was puzzled.

'He had a Mexican passport in his pocket. If the passport is real, we have a name. No address, no occupation, no explanation for him being here – in Montenegro or in your room – and no idea who sent him or why. But,' Klejevic said all this while glancing at the rear-view mirror, 'I assure you we shall find out.'

'Why did you have to shoot him?' Mercedes wanted to know.

Klejevic was silent for a moment before turning slowly to face his passengers.

'He was ordered to stop and he kept running.' Klejevic's measured tone of voice suggested that he was only going to say this once, to humour his guests because they were The Aztec's friends and for no other reason.

'He was warned again but he fired his gun at Brako in reply. So we stopped him.'

Klejevic slowly turned back to face the road ahead. 'It is unfortunate that he died,' he added.

But Hadley was not totally convinced by the sincerity of that last remark.

By then they were travelling at speed on the road to Tivat Airport. But before reaching it they turned onto the motorway leading to the Croatian border. Klejevic saw his passengers' questioning looks.

'There's no flight from Tivat straight away. It's best you get away from Serbia and Montenegro.'

They drove across the border without hindrance and their vehicle was not searched. Klejevic spoke authoritatively and a uniformed official waved him on.

At Dubrovnik airport Goran remained with the car and Klejevic led his charges into the passenger terminal. There were no direct flights to Spain that evening but a flight to Vienna would depart in forty minutes and they could make a connection to Madrid. Hadley paid for the tickets and Klejevic escorted them past Customs and Immigration.

'Will we find out?' Hadley asked before they parted. 'Who the man was, I mean.'

'I'll tell Jesús,' Klejevic assured them, but Hadley could tell that something was troubling him.

'You know, Mercedes' – perhaps he addressed her because he had been so brusque when she'd questioned the necessity to kill the Mexican – 'these are not easy times for Montenegrins. There are many people who would do us harm. But independence is not far away, and unlike some of our neighbours we shall gain ours peacefully.

'Meanwhile we will not tolerate the slightest attempt to derail our progress.'

Klejevic did not, however, reveal the rest of what he knew: that the Mexican passport was phoney and that the dead man was Cuban. Neither did he tell them that he, Klejevic, had started to worry that his security measures had been too good and they'd managed to lose the Cuban on the way to the farmhouse where they had planned to confront him in the first place.

And he certainly did not repeat Florin's very specific instructions that the Cuban agent should be taken alive and then beaten, tortured or whatever it took to get a quick admission that he was on Sierra's payroll so that Serbia and Montenegro could protest to Cuba. Nor did Ivo Klejevic admit that no one had counted on the man's stupidity in taking on with a handgun two guys armed with Uzis!

The three of them shook hands politely if not warmly as the flight was called and soon Jack and Mercedes were on their way to Vienna. They held hands and looked out over the puffy white clouds.

'I'm sick of this entire business now,' he told her. 'As soon as we get home I'm going to tell Pinto to get lost.'

'Yes, please!' Mercedes smiled but Jack could see that she was still in shock from the killing, 'And even if he makes good his threat we'll overcome it.'

'I'll still have to talk to Florin, though.' Jack saw the concern on her face as he said it. 'I have to get the rest of the material. Now more than ever I want to write his full story.'

'You won't tell Pinto that, will you?'

'No. Stuff Pinto. We owe him nothing.'

'Do you think the Mexican had something to do with Florin?'

Hadley thought about it.

'I don't know. But maybe someone else in Cuba might be interested in that bloody gold.'

Like Aquiles Sierra.

They changed planes in Vienna quite effortlessly and settled down with a drink on their way to Madrid. Then Hadley opened Florin's envelope again and they both started reading.

18

Jack and Mercedes decided to stay the night in Madrid. During the flight from Vienna they discussed at length the difficult situation they were in. Their initial relief at Pinto's intervention after the drugs bust had been followed by Jack's excitement over his first meeting with The Aztec and – Mercedes was the first to admit – a definite buzz over the prospect of an inside track to the elusive Republican gold.

But their Yugoslav experience, culminating in the shooting, had brought them face to face with the covert world's harsh reality. Now they had made up their minds to extricate themselves from Pinto's world as soon as they returned to Spain.

They would call on him in the morning, hand over what they'd brought back from Montenegro and go home. With luck, if their conclusions were correct it would be their last-ever visit to CNI. But there remained one issue to clear before they met with the Captain.

Mercedes phoned Ramiro de la Serna who jumped with delight on hearing her voice. She and Jack had correctly assumed that since it was Thursday he would still be in town rather than in Tordecillas. It was almost ten in the evening – early by *madrileño* standards – and Ramiro confessed that he had been debating whether to eat in or out. Mercedes's unexpected call had settled his dilemma.

'Come directly to *El Espejo*,' he said enthusiastically, 'and I'll hear nothing about where you two are staying tonight.'

They retrieved Mercedes's car from the airport car park and got to the restaurant on Recoletos by eleven. Ramiro was already at the table, sipping an Oban malt and holding court over three waiters as he passed judgement on their olives. He beamed and raised his non-olive-eating arm as he spotted them alighting from the poorly parked Porsche. He had chosen a secluded table in the pavilion, where he could smoke to his heart's content.

'And where the devil have you two been this time?' he enquired – he'd seen them five days earlier on their return from Valencia. They had avoided mentioning their impending trip at the time.

'It's a long story.' Hadley made light of it. 'But, if you must know, Montenegro.'

'Montenegro?'

'Yes.' Mercedes too laughed it off.

'Well.' Ramiro feigned a lack of interest. 'Shan't be asking why anyone would need to go gallivanting off to Montenegro at short notice, dear boy, but if you ask me . . .'

'We shan't be asking you, Ramiro,' Mercedes said teasingly.

'Shan't be telling you who was in Valladolid on Easter Monday, in that case,' Ramiro riposted, getting his own back.

The waiter came over and Ramiro ordered a 1970 Navarrese *Chivite*, another plate of olives and a *ración* of Manchego cheese.

'Let me guess,' ventured Hadley. 'Cousin Rosa?'

'Spot on. Sends her love to you both. But I must say, she *did* look rather tired: dark circles, not her usual sparkle. She really should slow down, I reckon. Still, Max was in fine fettle, I'm happy to report. Told them I'd seen you that very morning. Now, what shall we eat?'

Hadley wondered whether Rosa's visit had been a coincidence. Had she somehow learned that Jack and Mercedes had been in Tordecillas?

'The onion soup is to die for in this place,' Ramiro suggested without taking his eyes off the menu, 'and you couldn't improve on a salt-baked sea bass after that.'

They were too tired to argue and in any event Ramiro's choice was usually good.

'Was it a family occasion?' Hadley asked once the wine had arrived and the waiter had taken their order.

'No. Out of the blue. They called my mother, invited themselves to tea and she in turn informed them of my presence.' Ramiro never had a problem in proclaiming his importance.

'Let's eat,' proposed Mercedes, winking at Hadley.

Ramiro took one spoonful of soup and then put the spoon down.

'All right, I give up,' he conceded. 'Why *were* you in Montenegro?'

They laughed. They knew their friend's infatuation with gossip. A secret kept secret was beyond his comprehension. Hadley leaned forward before lowering his voice.

'It's to do with Jesús Florin. Juicy facts about his time there; people who knew him.'

'When was he in Serbia?'

'1930s, more than once,' Hadley told him. 'Yugoslavia, as it was then. Even met Marshal Tito, and General Mercer.'

Ramiro went back to his soup. He looked pensive.

'All those bloody Reds together. They should have stayed in Yugoslavia, right?'

'Let's not knock him too much,' Mercedes said, steering the conversation back to where they wanted it. 'Jack is getting paid a lot of money to write Florin's biography.'

'Thanks to you,' Hadley added.

'Well, not quite . . .' Ramiro seemed slightly embarrassed by the suggestion.

'Oh, I know, you told me Rosa provided the list of names for *Embattled Madrid*.' Hadley hoped he sounded casual in his recollection. 'But wasn't it your idea in the first place?'

'Perhaps,' Ramiro admitted awkwardly. 'I mean . . . she came to Valladolid one weekend. Said she'd been to Cuba and had heard a whisper that this Florin fellow had read some of your stuff – all those battles you write about. Asked if I knew you.'

Someone is lying, thought Hadley. *'What do you know about wars, young man?'* had been Florin's initial comment. He remembered it distinctly. It was only on a second meeting that he had acknowledged Hadley's work.

'Rosa met Florin?' Mercedes asked.

'Rosa's met everyone, darling,' Ramiro said in earnest. 'She's always attending these embassy do's where all whispers are first uttered.'

Their sea bass arrived. The waiter presented the salt-encrusted dish for their inspection, then moved to a side table to detach the fish before serving it.

'Then I'll really need to thank her, Ramiro,' said Hadley. 'You must bring her to Salamanca again.'

'Love to do that, dear boy – like I said, she's always asking after you both.'

'So did she offer you the list of names, Ramiro?' Mercedes made the question sound innocuous.

'Actually' – Ramiro suddenly perked up, relieved that he had something positive he could say – 'that was *my* idea. Yes. When she asked me to find out if you'd fancy a few interviews with ex-combatants, *I* suggested that she – since she's so well placed – might conjure up the list of those to write to! And here we are now. Let's drink to that.'

Hadley met his girlfriend's eyes as they raised their glasses: neither had missed the significance of what had been said. Ramiro, unaware of his friends' unspoken words and pleased to have got any misunderstandings off his chest, drained his glass in one gulp and simultaneously signalled for another bottle.

In the morning Jack and Mercedes went directly to CNI headquarters. They had stayed up late, humouring Ramiro as he enjoyed his nightcap cognac and prising out from him what they could about Rosa.

They were now certain that Rosa worked for Pinto. It would explain how he'd been able to get involved so soon after the drug raid: Pinto would have known in advance that it was going to take place. It also pained them – Mercedes in particular – to discover that *dear cousin Rosa* was not the lovely person she was made out to be.

She remained the focus of their conversation as Mercedes followed the satnav instructions to Padre Ruidobro Street.

'How could she, Jack?' Mercedes could not hide her disappointment.

'Don't beat yourself up about it.' He tried to comfort her but was at a loss himself. 'They inhabit a foul world.'

'Remember that night in El Patio Chico?'

'Do I, indeed!'

'No.' She nudged him with her elbow. 'I mean in the Patio. When we said you were going to Cuba. She feigned surprise.'

'You are right.'

'Bitch!'

'I meant it, you know? About Ramiro bringing her to Salamanca.'

'She won't come. She's been dodging us ever since that night.'

'You may be right. Now . . .' Hadley changed the subject. 'About Pinto.'

'You are not having second thoughts?'

'No way!' Hadley could not repress a smile at the horrified look on Mercedes's face. 'No chance of that. But he will come up with reasons why we can't quit.'

'So? We are still quitting, right?'

'Absolutely.' Hadley meant it. 'But be prepared for more dirty tricks.'

Their bag containing the Montenegro items was put through a scanner and they were then shown directly to the fifth floor even though they had no pre-arranged appointment. Perhaps, thought Hadley, they had been watched from the moment they'd landed.

Their escort knocked on Pinto's door and cracked it open. Pinto was talking on the telephone but he waved them in and pointed a finger towards a door at the far right of the room. The secretary beckoned the visitors to follow her through it.

It led into a conference room that had a large circular table in the centre and a dozen chairs around it. One side of the room was hung with curtain wallings identical to those in Pinto's office. The wall opposite was almost entirely covered by three maps: Spain, the world and Europe, in that order. A second door, opening to the fifth-floor corridor, spanned much of the map of Southern Africa and at the far end a sideboard looked as though it could contain a cocktail cabinet.

Hadley and Mercedes chose seats next to each other and put their trophies on the table. They waited anxiously for Pinto to come in.

When he finally joined them he did not look his usual self. He had loosened his tie and there were shadows under his eyes, which looked like those of a man who had not seen a bed the previous night.

Hadley assumed that his haggard appearance was not just on account of Moscow's gold, though he did not know the full extent of Pinto's worries.

A few days earlier four of the Atocha atrocity perpetrators, cornered in their Madrid flat by the authorities, elected to blow themselves up rather than be captured. They took one policeman with them and injured another eleven.

And CNI's Malabo initiative sat on a knife edge. 'Have you considered the alternative option?' the Minister had enquired. 'Warning Penang of the impending coup and letting him show his gratitude with fresh oil contracts?'

It was a way of saying that Pinto had two choices: back the coup and pocket Potro or sell Potro to Penang and back the President. Get it right and Pinto would receive a quiet pat on the back while the Minister hijacked the credit. Get it wrong and expect the traditional *'I did warn you'* and early retirement.

'I trust that you are both well,' Pinto offered by way of greeting. The way he emphasised the pronoun implied that others – himself included, perhaps – were not.

'Not really.' Hadley thought he might as well be upfront. 'But we'll come to that.'

There was a knock on the 'African' door and the woman who let herself in was introduced as Irma Diaz from the Research Section. Pinto drew her attention to the objects on the table.

'Irma has been studying the 1936 shipping documents,' he told Hadley. 'Perhaps you can tell us how you came to have these items?'

As Irma busied herself with the Bank of Spain's money bag and packing remnants, Hadley told Pinto everything, from their arrival in Montenegro and even doing the tourist bit to their first meeting with Ivo Klejevic and the trip to the canyon the following day.

'Did you take photographs?' Pinto interrupted.

Mercedes explained they were all in her camera and Pinto's suggestion that the camera should be held by CNI led to some disagreement.

'It contains my own private photos as well,' she said.

Eventually Diaz left the room with the camera and returned twenty minutes later, having made copies of the Montenegro shots. During her absence Hadley finished recounting the previous day's events, culminating in the shooting of the Mexican, an unexpected event that produced a poorly disguised alarmed expression from Pinto.

'What do you think, Irma?' Pinto asked, pointing at the items on the table.

'They look real enough,' she said. 'We'll need a little longer to be sure.'

Pinto nodded and Diaz collected the rest of the material, along with the latest instalment of The Aztec's notes to photocopy, before excusing herself.

'You had something else to tell me, I believe,' Pinto challenged Hadley.

'I have. *We* have, rather,' he added, looking at Mercedes. 'To put it bluntly, we've had enough.'

Pinto frowned questioningly.

'It's not that simple,' he explained after a pause that, if it had been intended to make Hadley explain himself, had not worked. 'We still have a job to finish.'

'I am sorry, Captain Pinto, we are going to have to be firm here: *you* may well have a job to finish, but *we* do not. We are not about to risk our lives playing your cloak-and-dagger games. In fact, we now regret having gone along with you in the first place. Still, there's nothing we can do about that now.'

'As I recall,' Pinto let a hint of sarcasm drift into his speech, 'you had little choice at the time.'

'On the contrary,' Hadley said, 'as I recall, I suggested calling a solicitor and your reply was, "God forbid".'

Pinto drummed his right hand's fingertips on the table. The corners of his mouth turned down in displeasure.

'You are our conduit to Florin, Mr Hadley. I will not sever that link at this juncture. I'm simply not in a position to do so.'

'Then find another conduit.' Hadley held his ground.

'I don't suppose for one moment' – Pinto ignored

Hadley's last comment – 'that you've considered there might be issues at stake which transcend the simple matter of finding Moscow's gold.'

'That's your problem, Captain Pinto. I don't have a crystal ball. Mercedes and I have made up our minds and that's final. We've helped you enough.'

'Whatever the consequences?' For an instant the usually civil Pinto sounded menacing.

'Whatever the consequences.'

'Does that go for you as well, Miss Vilanova?'

'It does,' Mercedes did not hesitate. 'I've nothing to be concerned about.'

'Do you think your parents would feel the same way?'

'What the hell is that supposed to mean?' Hadley could not mask his anger. Was this devious character now trying to intimidate Mercedes?

'I was not addressing you.' Pinto was still staring at Mercedes. 'I suggest you discuss this at home before rushing into actions you may later regret.'

'Well, then, since you choose to be unpleasant, let me spell it out for you, Pinto: I *am* going to a see a lawyer and I *am* going to tell him what I think.

'And that includes my belief,' Hadley continued, barely containing his anger, 'that this entire drugs bust was a load of bullshit, that you set this up so that you could get to Florin.'

'Now *that* is utter nonsense,' Pinto retorted equally forcefully. 'You know you sought out Florin of your own accord and made contact with him long before we met.'

'No.' Hadley stared at Pinto, calling the man's bluff. 'That's just it. That was just the way it was supposed to look.'

'I should be very careful with that line of reasoning, Mr Hadley . . .'

206

'You bastard.' Mercedes was unable to contain herself. 'You've been playing with our lives for your fucking bits of gold.'

'Miss Vilanova, don't make me exercise the full extent of my powers . . .'

'We know for a fact that it was Rosa who planted the Florin idea in her cousin's mind—'

'Listen to me, Pinto.' Hadley squeezed Mercedes's forearm. He could sense her becoming too emotional in her anger. 'We are going to walk out of here and you, your bloody gold and whatever your Machiavellian schemes may amount to can go to hell for all we care.'

Pinto was still holding Hadley's stare but there seemed to be something else distracting him – it was almost as if Hadley could actually see the man scheming.

Unexpectedly, Pinto stood up.

'I see no point in continuing with this meeting,' he announced.

'Suits us,' replied Hadley, rising too and taking Mercedes by the hand.

'I shall be in touch, very shortly, and I advise you to reflect on what has been said here today.' Pinto made a point of looking at Mercedes as he finished his sentence. 'And do not even dream of interfering, nor of divulging, or even discussing what you've learned—'

'No more threats, Pinto!' Hadley had had enough.

'Because if you do,' Pinto continued, undeterred, 'you will make my job very easy: I shall simply have you both arrested. You, a foreigner,' he pointed a finger at Hadley, 'on espionage charges and you,' he turned and glared at Mercedes, 'on a simple charge of treason!'

'Fine,' retorted Hadley. 'But I have signed a contract to

write Jesús Florin's biography and I intend to continue doing so. Which reminds me – I want the notes I just *loaned* to Miss Diaz returned to me before we go.'

'They will be waiting for you in reception. I bid you both good day. And I suggest you heed my warnings. You'll be hearing from me.'

With that he saw them out through Africa, beyond which a secretary awaited.

19

Pinto slammed the conference-room door and returned to his office. He read what he'd noted down during the meeting. Could there be any misunderstanding? He would send for the tapes in a moment but he was sure that those had been Mercedes's words.

'*We know for a fact that it was Rosa who planted the Florin idea in her cousin's mind.*'

There had to be a mistake here. He would dig up the tapes of his chat with Rosa Uribe back in January. But he was certain she had told him that Jack Hadley *had secured an interview with The Aztec.*

If Mercedes was right, then Pinto had a serious problem on his hands. Could Rosa have an agenda of her own? Could she be working for someone else? Why? Who? None of it made sense and yet the two statements were in conflict.

Pinto considered the implications. Suppose for a moment that Rosa was a double. Was this about the gold or was there something else? Something in Latin America? Africa?

What could Rosa possibly have access to that might make her valuable to the Cubans? And where did the dead Mexican fit in with all of this? Pinto had a good relationship with his opposite number in Mexico City. He would make a call.

He took a cigar from a leather-covered humidor and rolled it between his thumb and fingers. He leaned back on his chair and lit up, watching the curls of smoke rise towards the ceiling extractors. Double agents, Pinto reflected, could be lethal, the most cruel of knives straight into your back. Undetected double agents, that was. Once you knew their game it was a different story, an asset even.

It was time he took a closer look at Rosa Uribe and, if his suspicions turned out to be true, play her double-dealing as his trump card.

Pinto jumped as his direct line rang.

'Pinto,' he answered with customary brevity.

'Pinto, this African business . . .'

'Yes, Minister?'

'Have you decided how we should play it yet?'

'I believe I have, Minister.'

'Good man, knew you'd come up with something. Shall we make it dinner tomorrow night?'

'I'd be delighted, Minister.'

'Splendid. My place, nine-thirty.'

It took Jack and Mercedes two and a half hours to drive to Salamanca. For once Mercedes did not seem hell-bent on breaking land-speed records. They felt relaxed, as though a burden had been lifted.

'Do you think Pinto will make good his threats?' she asked

'No. He'd be in the shit up to his neck if we spoke to the press.'

'Would we?'

'Probably not. But he couldn't risk it. He just needs us to be quiet until he's found his bloody gold and sorted out whatever he's plotting to do with it.'

'What do you suppose he's up to?'

'I don't know, Mercedes. Maybe it's better we don't know. There's something going on there that involves both Spain and Florin and I think we are best out of it.'

'What about Florin? How will you get the rest of the material? For the biography, I mean.'

Hadley had considered that at length.

'I reckon that by now Florin knows what happened in Saint Steven. Ivo would have told him. I'm sure he'll contact me again.'

They got to the flat and walked slowly up the stairs with their luggage. Mercedes inserted the front-door key in the lock but before she could turn it the door pushed open. Hadley dropped his bag and walked in past her. At first everything looked normal, then he noticed that the papers on his desk had been disturbed.

Hadley opened the top drawer as Mercedes came up behind him: it was empty. All his notes and documents relating to The Aztec had vanished.

'What now?' Mercedes asked.

'I've got duplicate sets of everything at the University. I'm going over to check they are still there.'

'I'm coming with you!'

'No need, but don't stay here either,' he insisted, 'Go to the café across the street. I won't be long. Meanwhile, you phone that Inspector Rueda.'

'Rueda? Are you sure?'

'I'm bloody sure. Our flat has been broken into. Let's do

what normal people do. Call the police, and wait in the café till they arrive.'

Hadley dashed down Cervantes Street, turned into Traviesa and ran to the History department. He climbed the stairs three steps at a time, watched by a bemused security guard. His room was unlocked and he went directly to the bottom left-hand drawer in his desk. The Florin files were there, complete and seemingly undisturbed.

He gave a sigh of relief, gathered his post and left the room, closing the door behind him. He wanted to hurry home and be there to meet Rueda. No friends in high places this time, he would tell the Inspector, just a bloody thief who broke into our flat. Find him!

He became aware of one bulky envelope with no sender details among his week's mail. He stopped halfway down the stairs and opened it. It contained a mobile phone. Hadley was puzzled and delved inside the padded envelope. He found a neatly folded note.

It is prepaid and pre-programmed with one number. Call me. Jesús.

Hadley was completely baffled. The phone implied urgency. Or secrecy: something you'd rather not put down on paper. He continued to speculate about the significance of Florin's request as he rushed back to the apartment before the police showed up.

Why did he want to talk on the phone? Had Florin somehow learned of Hadley's refusal to continue doing Pinto's dirty work?

He had just turned along San Pablo when he saw the

police car pull up outside his home and recognised the alighting figure as Inspector Rueda.

The policeman had the same resigned-to-his-fate appearance as the last time they had met in Salamanca's Police Headquarters but he brightened up unexpectedly as he saw Hadley approaching.

'Well, Professor Hadley, we meet again.' Rueda sounded quite genial.

When Mercedes joined them they walked up the stone steps together and pushed open the apartment's still-unlocked front door.

'I never thought you'd be calling *me*, I must say.' Rueda betrayed a little sarcasm as he shook hands with Mercedes.

'What seems to be the problem? Robbery, you said? Too menial for your influential friends in Madrid?' The Inspector pointedly surveyed his surroundings as if to say that the place did not look as if it had been burgled.

Hadley explained how they had just arrived home after a short visit abroad, only to find their door lock damaged and their home robbed.

'Have you established what's been taken?'

'Papers. So far as we can ascertain.' Hadley felt silly as he said it, which only increased his anger. 'Only papers.'

'*Valuable* papers?' Rueda was still playing the cynical cop.

'Yes, Inspector,' Hadley said defensively. 'Very valuable to me, *and* to my publisher. But valuable or not,' he continued, 'this is our home, it has been forcibly entered and, whatever was or wasn't taken, it's still intolerable.'

'Lots of things are intolerable, Professor, as we all know.' Rueda took in Mercedes too with that last comment. 'What do you suppose the thief or thieves would have been looking for?

'I don't know,' Hadley replied less than truthfully.

'Any jewellery? Valuables of any sort?'

Hadley shook his head. Rueda moved about the flat as they spoke, looking round as if for clues that only his trained eyes might spot but still wearing his overcoat and rainproof hat.

'Any . . . substances?'

'Inspector Rueda . . .' Hadley started to protest.

'Just asking,' replied Rueda without quite making an apology. 'Would your missing papers contain any sensational revelations?'

'Significant in a historical sense,' said Hadley, 'rather than sensational.'

'Not the sort of stuff the press would pay for?'

'No.'

'A competing author? Jealousy? It happens, you know.'

'No, I don't think so.'

'Well then, you tell me, Mr Hadley. Why would anyone want your papers?'

'As I said, Inspector, I don't know. But my home has been broken into. Are you proposing that we should do nothing?

'May I?' Rueda made towards the bedroom, then looked round the bathroom and the kitchen. He opened the bedroom window overlooking the churchyard and made a comment about the peace that could still be enjoyed in the centre of his city.

'No, I don't propose we do nothing, Professor,' he replied finally. 'There's a thing or two we can look at. How long were you away?' he asked.

'Four days,' replied Hadley.

'Both of you?'

They nodded.

'You might be in luck.' Rueda spoke condescendingly. 'There are two CCTV cameras on your street.' He tipped his head towards the front on the apartment building. 'One of them runs seventy-two-hour loops. Covers weekends, too.'

'Can we see the tapes?'

'You must,' Rueda said seriously. 'Let's see if together we can spot any strangers.'

'When?' Mercedes asked impatiently.

'You remember where my office is, I'm sure.' The Inspector smiled. 'Nine o'clock tomorrow sound all right?'

'Sure.'

'Good. Meanwhile I'll send one of my men,' he added, heading for the door. 'Have him go over the place, see if we can pick up some prints or anything useful.'

'And a locksmith?' Hadley asked.

'And a locksmith.' Rueda finally smiled. 'Who you'll pay for, naturally.'

When they were alone, Hadley showed Mercedes the phone and The Aztec's note.

'Are you going to call him?'

'Yes.'

'And then?'

'Then it will depend on what he wants, darling.' Jack pulled Mercedes close to him and gave her a long hug.

'I like Florin,' he explained, 'and I am sure there is a side to him that has not come through in anything he's given me to date.' He gently pushed her head away from his shoulder and looked into her eyes. 'I really want to get the measure of the true Aztec and in the process perhaps uncover bits of history that have never been addressed in the past.'

'Please be careful,' Mercedes pleaded.

Jack dialled the number and the call was taken on the first ring. Mercedes sat on their couch and listened quietly as Jack paced the room and asked monosyllabic questions — *Where? When? How?*

'But I've told him I'm done with him, Jesús!' Jack exclaimed, 'How can I go back?'

'Jack?' Mercedes could guess the Florin end of the conversation and she did not like the implications. Hadley brought a finger to his lips and pulled up a chair to their desk.

'Go ahead,' he said into the telephone.

'He wants me to see Pinto one more time,' Jack explained once he'd hung up, but Mercedes could see that his mind was already racing.

'Why? What can be gained?'

'He has sent me a package for Pinto,' Jack continued, 'setting out the full thing: recovery of the gold and what he wants in return.'

'And then? Once you've seen Captain Pinto?'

'Then, he said, I'm to go and meet him and he will give me all the missing portions that complete the Florin story, together with access to unique documents.'

'When would you go to Cuba?' Mercedes asked.

'As soon as I've seen Pinto. I'll be back within a week,' Jack assured her — without mentioning that it was not Cuba he'd be going to. 'Then we can resume our lives. I promise.' He sat next to her and hugged her once again.

'We'll have a peaceful summer by the sea; we'll have my children with us, like we said. And I'll get started writing The Aztec's biography.'

'I don't want to stay here while you are gone.' Mercedes left no room for arguments.

'You haven't finished your dissertation.' Jack seemed concerned. 'You've worked too hard to let it slip . . . Perhaps you could get a room at Fonseca?'

'I shan't. I won't stay in Salamanca till you are back.' She was not about to change her mind. 'I'll ask Ramiro,' she said, cheering up. 'I'll ask if I can stay in his house in Tordecillas.'

'It's fifty miles away,' observed Hadley.

'Perfect!' Her mind was clearly made up. 'One week, you said? I only have to be at the University for three days. Yes, I'll ask Ramiro. He'll let me.'

'What about Rueda?' asked Hadley, 'Tomorrow morning, he said.'

'I'll go. I'll point out anyone I see coming in or out who does not belong in this building. Then I'll leave him a set of keys for the fingerprints thing and go to Tordesillas from his office.'

20

Pinto and his team sat round the large table in his private conference room. Each place had a leather-framed blotter covered by individual copies of the briefing document.

There were two senior officers from Research: Diaz and Fuentes. Marcos Vega from the African desk and his Caribbean counterpart Javier Duarte sat next to each other. Hadley's debriefer, Minguez, completed the group.

Pinto invited Irma Diaz to summarise what they had so far. First she reviewed the items brought back by Hadley from Montenegro.

'The bag is genuine, Captain,' she said with conviction. 'Both the Bank and our laboratories confirm it. Approximately one hundred years old, the leather and the canvas are of the period and the bag itself matches archive photographs. There are also very faint traces of gold dust.'

The mention of gold got everyone's attention.

'And the other items photographed?' asked the Deputy Director.

'The crate remnants suggest that the original was identical to those sent to the Algameca in 1936. We have also spoken to one firm that packaged for the Government at the time. They assure me that those are pieces of their boxes. They say they are of the kind once used by the Colonial Service.'

'Do we all agree there's a strong possibility that, one,' Pinto counted on his fingers, 'the relevant time-frames make it perfectly feasible for the *Kursk* to have detoured to Budva and, two, that it is very possible that the missing gold was offloaded there and hidden in a cave under left-wing subversives' control?'

No one challenged their chief's conclusion.

'Then the next question,' continued Pinto, 'is when and how was it removed?'

'The broken crates and open bags' – Fuentes looked at the photographs in his folder – 'would suggest that the bags were unpacked.'

'But we still don't know by whom or when,' opined Duarte. 'Unless we take Florin's word that it was he who moved it in 1939,' he added, making reference to Florin's documents and photographs that had been given to Hadley.

'Can we believe that between 1936 and 1939 nobody touched this treasure?' asked Minguez.

'What are the alternatives?' Pinto wanted to know.

'Start with who might have taken it? Who had knowledge or access?' Again Minguez posed the questions.

'Florin was back in Spain, we know that,' Diaz read from her case file, 'and so was Mercer until the fall of Barcelona. That's January 1939,' she said looking up from her papers before continuing. 'The Yugoslav communists would have known, of course – they guarded the cave. And then there's

Orlov. He moved freely around Europe throughout the Civil War, though by 1938 he'd jumped ship and gone to America. Could he have dipped into the coffers?'

'This man . . .' Vega looked at his notes '. . . Klejevic, he says no. So does Florin.'

'And Mercer told me the same thing years ago,' Pinto confirmed.

'It really boils down to one thing, sir,' Marcos Vega summarised. 'Either we believe Florin or we don't. If we believe he's telling the truth, then the missing gold remained there until 1939 when he removed the lot.

'If we don't, we are back in the realm of myths and fantasy surrounding Moscow's Gold. We would have to ask ourselves, why is he so keen to convince us? What is all this *really* about?'

'And why was this substantial load of gold separated from the rest in the first place, since we only have Florin's explanation?' Minguez wondered why no one had asked that question.

'Again we must rely on Florin's version of events,' Pinto said. 'According to Klejevic the younger, it was a form of insurance, in case the Republic lost the war.

'Given that's how it turned out, we must assume that the gold was indeed retrieved, and again we have Florin's and Klejevic's confirmation. So where did it go after Montenegro?'

'Florin's version, since we are trusting him, says Mexico,' Minguez pointed out.

'No, it doesn't,' Vega corrected him. 'It says *he was told* to take it to Mexico.'

They all looked at their documents and leafed through the pages.

'What if he never made it? Because,' Vega added some logic of his own, 'if the gold had reached Mexico, the Republican Government in Exile – which was based *in* Mexico from 1939 to 1946 – would have taken control of it, converted it into cash and most probably spent it before any one of us in this room was born.'

'If that's the case we are wasting our time here. We are being set up. But set up for what?' Pinto could be blunt when necessary.

'So, if it didn't get to Mexico, where *did* it go?' asked Fuentes.

'Let's say we go along with Florin's story,' ventured Minguez. 'He removed the lot in 1939 to a place where it has remained, quite incredibly, ever since. And yet, we are told, a place where he needs our help' – he emphasised the last three words – 'in order to retrieve it. Where on earth is there a place that *we* can get to but Cuba can't?'

He let the question hang. Diaz and Vega instinctively glanced at the world map on the wall.

'Who says Cuba has anything to do with this?' It was Javier Duarte who first made the suggestion. The others looked at each other in wonderment. No one had considered the possibility: for almost half a century The Aztec had been synonymous with Cuba.

'Jesús Florin turning freelance?' Pinto almost laughed as he said it.

No one had ever suggested that The Aztec, a man who had shown nothing but disdain towards his own rightfully inherited wealth, might have the slightest interest in any missing treasure other than in the service of a cause.

'One has to admit it's odd,' Duarte persisted. 'For thirty

years we hear nothing from this guy and all of a sudden – one foot in the grave, so to speak – he wants us to help him retrieve his missing gold. Do we buy this?'

'We've always known that he's in intelligence, Javier,' Vega corrected his colleague. 'That's not the same as hearing nothing from him.'

'Sure, I don't dispute that, but we still have the unanswered question: why the hell does he want the gold now?'

'Maybe Castro has asked him. Like, Listen, Jesús, before we all croak, where did all that Spanish moolah go?'

Duarte made them laugh with his excellent imitation of a Cuban accent.

'In that case, why wait till now to ask?' Minguez did not readily agree with Duarte's theory.

'It might be easier to answer that if we knew where the gold ended up,' said Pinto. 'Imagine we are in 1939. The Civil War is over, the Second World War about to start,' he mused. 'We have a boat and we need to remove several tons of cargo from Yugoslavia. We set off for Mexico but something stops us from getting there.'

'Something like what?' asked Vega.

'Weather, engine trouble, mutiny, fuel . . . the list goes on. Take my word for it: anything can happen to a ship at sea.' Nobody was about to argue with the Captain in that area.

'Draw a line from the Adriatic to Mexico and then try to guess where you'd seek a safe haven if you needed it en route.' Pinto stood up this time and moved closer to the wall maps. The others followed him with their eyes.

'Back to Spain?' probed Vega. 'Surely there's enough coastline in Andalucia or the Basque country and sufficient Republican sympathisers left alive to unload a boat at night.'

'Too risky.' The military man in Pinto appeared to rule out that option, 'Same goes for North Africa.'

Spain still had its enclaves in North Africa, but in 1939, like the Canary Islands, they would have been firmly loyal to Franco.

'It's the Atlantic islands, then.' Minguez offered his own guess. 'The Azores, Madeira, Cape Verde . . .'

'Go on,' Pinto cajoled.

'Fernando Pó! West Africa!' It was Vega's turn. Now they were talking about his neck of the woods.

'Florin's diaries tell us that Mercer gave him a Republican Navy gunboat,' Pinto reminded them, 'and Klejevic confirmed it, verbally and with a photograph. I've looked into that.'

When the Civil War had broken out the Spanish Fleet had split according to location and each ship's officers' persuasion. Some never wavered, others eventually changed sides. But the Spanish Navy's archives documented the disposition of every single vessel in the Armada on 1 April 1939.

'Only two were unaccounted for,' Pinto explained, 'the torpedo boat *Mataró* and the minesweeper *El Saler*. I cannot tell the name of the gunboat in the photograph, but it is definitely a torpedo boat of the kind delivered to the Armada in 1931.'

There was silence around the table.

'We shall therefore continue with the assumption that Florin is, in this respect at least, telling the truth and move on to the next item on the agenda.' Pinto turned to Fuentes. 'What can you tell us about Jack Hadley that we don't already know?'

CNI had researched Jack Hadley from the moment when

Rosa's intelligence was delivered. Pinto had not revealed to anyone his last, discordant conversation with Hadley.

Objectivity was a quality the Captain believed in. In any conflict he endeavoured to understand his opponent's point of view.

He conceded unreservedly that it had been CNI who'd forced Hadley into this affair, albeit with good reason. Pinto had hoped at the time that the Professor's fortuitous securing of an interview could prove Rosa's intuition that The Aztec was ready to talk.

But beyond that, once the link had been established Pinto had expected to let a trained operative step into Hadley's place. So why on earth did Florin insist on Hadley running these 'errands'? Was there more to Hadley than met the eye?

Pinto had gone back to his staff and asked them to look at Hadley again, anything at all in the man's past, family, associates that could be useful to them. Anything that might suggest prior or even subsequent involvement with the Cubans, their aims or ideology.

'It's all in your briefing paper, sir,' Fuentes assured him. 'Born in Hereford, England. English father – a country solicitor – Irish mother. Two younger brothers and an older sister, all alive.'

'Irish?' Pinto opened his folder again; he hadn't picked up on that before. 'Has this been followed up?' Everyone knew there were connections between the Irish and the Basques.

'Family from Cork, sir – horse breeders, not a hint of anything untoward.'

'Student days? Activist?' Minguez asked the question.

'Not especially. Sheltered, Roman Catholic boarding

school in Somerset, followed by six years in the army including action in Kuwait and Iraq. St Catherine's, Oxford. Good history degree. Conservative type, I would say.

'Married one Jennifer Dalton, marriage broke up two years ago, just divorced. Two boys, eight and ten, who live with their mother. She's another academic: Renaissance Art.

'Both Hadley and his ex worked at University College, London. She still does. He, as we all know,' concluded Fuentes, 'is at Salamanca.'

'So,' Pinto asked the room for confirmation, 'nothing there to link him to Florin?'

They all shook their heads.

'What about the girlfriend?' Mingues's question once again.

'Ah, the girlfriend.' Irma Diaz smiled, pulling out two photographs of Mercedes from her folder. 'She's a bit more interesting.'

'You can say that again,' commented Vega, the *africanista* – then wished he'd kept his mouth shut when he caught the look on Pinto's face.

'Not so much her, as her family,' Diaz continued, ignoring the remark. 'She's pretty much what she seems: schooled by nuns in Xátiva, university in Valencia, five years with Santander including a stint in Geneva.'

'Any foreign influences while in Switzerland?' asked Pinto.

'None we can point at, other than the typical banker's international contacts.'

'Being a Spanish-speaking bank in Geneva,' Minguez suggested, 'they would have attracted clients from the Americas.'

'Yes,' agreed Diaz.

'Including, perhaps, Cubans?'

'Possibly.'

'Good point,' Pinto noted. 'We'll talk to Santander – off the record, of course, and without mentioning Miss Vilanova. See if their Geneva clients might include anything, shall we say . . . of interest to Spain?'

Notes were made and Pinto invited Diaz to continue with Mercedes's parents.

'A bit more interesting, as I said. The Argentine connection. Luis Vilanova, as we know, owns Vilanova Taronger in Valencia. We are talking millions here. But up until 1980 Luis Vilanova was a colonel in the Argentine Army.'

'So he would have served through the Dirty War,' Duarte observed. Argentina was not within the Caribbean Section's domain, but in South America during the 1970s Cuba and the mainland had been elaborately – often violently – intertwined.

'He did,' Diaz confirmed.

'Bloody hands?'

'More a case of sticky fingers, I suspect,' she replied, with a frown. When no one spoke she continued, 'The Vilanovas bought a lot of land in Xátiva in the late 1970s and throughout the 1980s. All with money from abroad. No laws broken in Spain that we know of but, well, we know historically that if the generals rule a country the generals get rich.'

'As do the colonels, it would seem.' Duarte tried to be a little humorous.

But if Vilanova came to Spain with a few million dollars under his belt, thought Pinto, *Judge Pinzón would surely be interested.*

Put another way, keeping the Judge out of the picture was worth some leverage.

'Could there have been any contact between Luis Vilanova and Jesús Florin?' asked Pinto.

'Not directly.' Duarte was sure. 'Florin was gone from Chile in 1973.'

'Yes,' Pinto agreed, 'but, as we know, he continued to run his networks in the continent from Cuba and to finance subversive movements – ERP, Tupamaros and the likes.'

'The very reason the military took over in Argentina,' Marcos Vega concurred.

'So, one would assume,' concluded Minguez, 'that any contact between Florin and Vilanova would have arisen from a mutual desire to slice each other's throats? Not a likely pair of co-conspirators.'

Pinto thanked the researchers for their input and it was agreed that they would delve a little deeper into Mercedes's time in Geneva and her father's army record.

Once Diaz and Fuentes had left the room, Pinto turned to Africa.

'I heard from Potro yesterday. He seems anxious to make his move. Do we trust him?'

The focus of CNI's attention was the tiny West African nation of Equatorial Guinea. Ruled by despots since independence and with its impoverished population terrorised by the police, it was nevertheless important to Spain, perhaps no longer for strategic reasons but for the more practical issue of its crude oil.

The former Spanish colony had it in abundance and Spain relied on imports for all its oil. History, tradition, connections and a common language put her in a unique position to secure regular supplies from Equatorial Guinea but the relationship had been put to the test more than once as democratic Spain and an outspoken press questioned the morality of paying out millions to murderers.

Spain's initial decision to give political asylum and a degree of quasi-official recognition to Celestino Potro had not endeared her to the Guinean ruling clan, either.

Potro, leader of the banned Guinean opposition, had effectively established a government-in-exile in Madrid and was reputed to have the necessary funding to launch a coup that would install him as his country's next president.

His backers would be rewarded with oil and mineral concessions and Spain, in turn, would be guaranteed a secure supply of vital energy fuel.

It should have been a simple power transfer that would give no one in the free world, let alone the Guinean people, cause to lament the Penang ruling family's demise.

But there was another complication: in its poorer days, Equatorial Guinea had flirted with Moscow and secured many favours. With the arrival of oil wealth, Penang saw a brighter future with America and was now courting Washington unashamedly. And the Bush administration relished the idea of a close friend in a traditionally hostile corner of Africa, at least enough to overlook the ruling clan's 'little peccadilloes'.

'We've looked after him for years, Captain.' Vega was personally involved in CNI's dealings with Potro. 'He's comfortable with us.'

Not quite, remembered Pinto. But he kept his counsel. A few years earlier the Conservative government, under pressure from Malabo, had withdrawn Potro's refugee status – a move that could have led to the aspiring president's deportation to his native Equatorial Guinea and almost certain execution. But the Spanish courts overruled the government and Potro was reprieved. He had since hedged his bets and moved to Switzerland but did he still bear a grudge?

'And we could make him quite *un*comfortable if he suddenly forgot who put him where he is,' concluded Vega.

That last remark did not need explaining. CNI had more than enough documents, tape recordings and bank records showing who'd paid what to whom and where Potro's assets were kept. *El Presidente*'s reign would be very short-lived if the oil did not flow directly north and unimpeded.

'Very well.' Pinto brought the meeting to an end. 'We shall meet again tomorrow. Meanwhile follow up on everything discussed today. Marcos,' he addressed the African desk chief, 'get me a full update on the entire region. I'm meeting the Minister tomorrow night and he expects my recommendation.'

Everyone gathered their papers and left the room. Pinto remained seated a while longer before walking back into his office where Rosa had been waiting for the last forty minutes.

The previous night Pinto had lain awake past midnight agonising about Rosa. If she was a double, the implications were not just dangerous but also personally hurtful.

She smiled as he walked into the office but straight away Pinto saw that she looked unwell. There was an unusual pallor to her face that the make-up could not mask and she seemed to have lost weight. Was she ill or simply worried about something? Pinto stared at her but Rosa betrayed nothing.

'Are you all right?' She asked the question, making Pinto realise that perhaps his own troubled expression gave away his concerns.

'Hadley's quit,' he said, perhaps a little too bluntly.

'What?' She looked at him in disbelief.

'You heard me. He won't work with us any more. Same goes for the girlfriend – they were both here yesterday.'

'What brought this about?'

'Their room got turned in Montenegro. Mercedes bumped into the intruder and the local boys shot him dead.'

'I can't believe this!' Pinto could see that her mind was racing; it always paid dividends, he noted, catching people by surprise. 'Are we talking about a thief or what?'

'No. We are talking about a Cuban trying to pass as a Mexican.'

'Oh my God.' Rosa looked genuinely disturbed and Pinto noted that she was definitely pale. 'May I have a glass of water?' she asked, reaching for her bag.

Pinto fetched the water from his sideboard in time to see her put three different coloured pills onto her palm. She pushed them into her mouth and drank the water.

'Thank you.'

'You are not well, are you?' he asked with some concern.

'No.' She didn't sound as if she wanted to discuss it.

'Any idea why the Cubans might be doing this?'

'None.' She really had no idea.

'Do you think we can persuade Hadley to stay on?'

'I don't know.'

'Will you give it a go?'

The colour seemed to be returning to her face.

'Me?' She seemed puzzled. 'What pretext could I possibly offer?'

'Look at it from his point of view: you work for the Government. You were just as involved as they were on the

night of February the thirteenth. We could be leaning on
you . . .' Rosa let the double entendre's implication pass.

'I'll think about it,' she said, but he took it as a yes.

'Good. And if he still won't play come back to me. We'll
up the ante a little.'

'If he won't play ball, Roberto, I suggest you give me
carte blanche.'

'Meaning?'

'Meaning I brought this one along in the first place. I'll
go back to my Cuban source and try approaching Florin
myself.'

Pinto stared at her silently for an instant. *We shall have
to see about that*, he thought.

Then he nodded and rose to his feet.

'You must go and get some rest now,' he said as Rosa
followed him to the door.

Perhaps Mercedes hadn't got it *quite* right when she'd
quoted Rosa. Pinto wanted to believe. But he would keep
an open mind.

21

Pinto's dinner with the Minister had gone well. For one thing, he was able to produce new and conclusive evidence that the already waning romance between Equatorial Guinea and Russia would soon be a thing of the past: the Americans were making their own overtures and a visit by Condoleezza Rice was being mooted.

While any sort of rapprochement was welcome by Western interests in general, if America took the lead American firms would reap the benefits. In Pinto's mind that meant not just oil but also lucrative infrastructure contracts that Spain felt, as the former colonial power and architect of the African nation's independence, should by rights come her way.

In the past, Spain's connection with Equatorial Guinea had become a source of embarrassment but now, given Spain's need for oil and trade, a less despicable regime in Malabo would be a welcome development.

So the Minister had given Pinto the proverbial nod and

wink and it was up to CNI to put the key players in place and apply its clandestine hand as the game unfolded.

In 1968 the colony of Spanish Guinea – which included the mainland settlement of Rio Muni and the island of Fernando Pó – became the Republic of Equatorial Guinea. The new independent nation – the only Spanish-speaking country in black Africa – was very prosperous at that juncture. It was a major exporter of cocoa and enjoyed one of the highest incomes per capita on the continent.

The Republic's new president, however, would soon put an end to that. Francisco Macías Nguema – he preferred to be addressed as 'The Only Miracle' – would spend the next ten years as its unchallenged ruler. In the process he would implement a reign of terror that even some of his more bloodthirsty neighbours would find hard to trump.

As literally half of Equatorial Guinea's population fled the country Macías wholeheartedly plundered its resources. Those who dared to raise their voices in protest were soon made to realise how ill-judged their outspokenness had been. Macías made his point visibly by staging a special Christmas show in the capital's football stadium, the centrepiece of which was the execution of one hundred and fifty of his adversaries while a military band played his favourite pop tunes.

But if the nation thought reprieve was at hand when 'The Only Miracle' was deposed in 1979, they were in for a major disappointment. The new President, Isidoro Penang, started as he intended to continue, taking Macías and his inner sanctum to Black Beach prison and having them shot within hours of their 'conviction'.

Thereafter Penang maintained and improved upon his predecessor's reign of terror.

In 1996 fate delivered an unforeseen bonanza into the despot's greedy hands: oil was found in Equatorial Guinea in sufficient quantities to give its population – by then down to half a million – as high a living standard as any country could hope for. Penang became wealthy beyond measure yet ordinary Guineans had to make do with incomes averaging one dollar a day.

Opposition to Penang's rule was dealt with ruthlessly and rumours circulated that he had sodomised a beaten opponent or had ordered a traitor's liver served up on his dinner table.

In Penang's Equatorial Guinea, torture, starvation and disease became the norm. His secret-police apparatus was among the most ruthless in the world, efficiently controlled by his most trusted lieutenant, Jorge Abad, the only man in the country whose own sadistic methods of repression might have been a match for his president's.

When Macías was deposed his top henchmen went to the firing squad with him. They included the top men in the state-security organisation.

Abad was then a rising star within the internal terror structure but, fortunately for him, had not yet risen high enough to warrant the same fate as his superiors. It did not take him long, however, to step into the vacuum and before the blood had dried on the walls of Black Beach prison's courtyard Abad was pulling further minor associates or unfortunate sympathisers of the late 'Miracle' into the terror-inspiring complex that the Western press referred to as 'Africa's Dachau'.

On a clammy Malabo afternoon Abad sat behind a functional metal desk and stared at the wretched man facing him from the other side. A guard stood silently inside the closed office door.

'Well, Mateo,' Abad asked, speaking slowly like a burdened man whose patience was reaching exhaustion, 'have you had time to reflect?'

'I've told you everything I know,' the man pleaded.

He was in a sorry state. The right side of his face was swollen, causing the bruised, blood-soaked right eye to be almost closed. His split, caked lower lip revealed several missing teeth. He sat opposite Abad, trying to stay upright to ease the pain caused by his arms being tied tightly behind his back.

Abad shook his head and shrugged. An occasional muffled scream from another room could be heard through the thick brick walls.

'Bring in Federico,' Abad ordered the guard, noticing the slight widening of the captive's good eye.

It was hard to know what to make of it, Abad considered as he waited. An informer had brought the Asuse brothers to Abad's attention. They were generally regarded as ordinary businessmen. They owned a large sanitary-ware business with showrooms in Malabo as well as Bata on the mainland. But they also visited Spain and other European countries regularly. Were these simply business trips?

Federico Asuse was hustled into the room and sat next to his brother. He was in slightly better shape than Mateo, but nevertheless he too bore the signs of torture.

'Federico,' Abad said, quite affably, 'Mateo and I have been making some progress.'

He saw the further look of alarm on Mateo's face but the wretched man did not dare speak. Abad seemed to be enjoying the game. You could achieve anything through terror, he knew. Some captives took longer than others to fathom, but eventually Abad would always find each individual's tolerance limit.

'But now I have stumbled upon a problem. You told me' – Abad made a display of looking at the notes on his desk – 'that you did not know Celestino Potro.'

'I . . .' Federico searched for words. 'I don't know him, Major – I mean, I've met him, but I don't know him. He doesn't know who I am.' He cast a fearful glance in his brother's direction. 'I'm telling the truth – I don't know him, I swear!'

'Then why,' Abad allowed his voice to rise slightly, 'am I told that you have knowledge of a Potro conspiracy against our country. Why?'

'I don't know.'

'Think! I've given you plenty of time to think. Why are people telling me "the Asuse brothers have spoken to Potro in Geneva", "the Asuse brothers know there's a coup in the making"? Why!' The last word was shrieked out.

'I don't know,' Federico repeated.

Abad gave him a look that suggested disbelief, pushed his own chair back and stood up.

'Follow me,' he ordered the brothers as he walked round his desk and towards the door. He gave little thought to the men being in leg irons and showed his contempt by leading the way without looking back.

Abad turned left outside the office and walked the length of the narrow corridor towards a sun-drenched doorway at its far end. Along the way they passed the open door to a torture room where an inert, well-beaten body hung upside down from a ceiling-mounted hook while a bare-chested soldier urinated against it as if to wash the blood away. Two of his confederates leaned against the far wall as they took a cigarette break.

The large internal yard's hard earth seemed dustier in the windless afternoon sun. The whitewashed walls, their monotony broken here and there by a steel-barred window or bullet pockmarks, did nothing to lift the Asuse brothers' spirits as they followed, their chains clanging, in Abad's steps.

The policeman walked to the centre of the yard before turning, arms akimbo, to watch his captives approach. When they came within a few feet from him, Abad took out his 9mm pistol from its holster and tapped its barrel on the palm of his open left hand.

'For the last time.' He gave a good imitation of a reasonable man who's tried everything but can no longer continue to offer his help. 'What can you tell me about Potro's intentions?'

The men looked down, avoiding Abad's stare.

'Federico.' Abad addressed the older brother, at the same time raising his pistol and, without looking directly at the target, placing it against Mateo Asuse's right temple. 'I know you boys met with Potro. What is he up to?'

'Federico . . .' Mateo started to speak but he was cut short by the blast of the handgun as Abad pressed the trigger. The bulk of Mateo's head jerked violently sideways as the rest of it spread out randomly in a mist of blood over two hundred square feet of dusty soil. His body left the ground briefly before hitting it with a gruesome thud.

'I wasn't talking to you,' Abad said, with a brief glance to his right before continuing. 'What did Potro say? *Tell me exactly.*'

'He didn't say what or when.' The man fell to his knees, crying. 'He didn't say. He just said there were mercenaries . . . white men . . .' He was sobbing uncontrollably. 'He said from South Africa . . .'

'What were these men plotting, Federico? You can tell me and we can end this misery.'

'I don't know, I swear.' The man looked up at Abad and saw that his questioner was smiling.

'I swear, Major Abad, I really swear, he was only boasting, we are not his friends, I don't know any more, I swear it.'

'I know, Federico,' Abad replied. 'I do believe you.'

He fired two rounds into Federico's head, turned on his heel and walked back, deep in thought, to his office.

There was definitely something afoot, Abad concluded. There were too many signs to just ignore them. Besides, that was not Abad's way. No organisation inside Equatorial Guinea had the resources to stage any sort of uprising. He had made sure of that by cutting down all potential opposition before it grew into a threat.

So, if Penang's time was drawing to a close, the action would come from outside. Mercenaries made sense. If they succeeded they would be paid and then the country would be handed over to the real instigators. If they failed they would be disowned.

But who was paying them? This was not the Russian way and Abad discounted them. Cuba? They had lost all influence in Malabo long ago. Could they be trying to regain it? Maybe – except that they would be unlikely to ally themselves with Potro, and vice versa.

Might this be a CIA operation then? It wouldn't be beyond them to court Penang and at the same time plan to replace him with a more palatable Potro. And then there was Spain.

They had never actively sought a change of Equatorial Guinea's government, and they would be less likely to do so with the Socialists back in power in Madrid. But if the Spanish empire builders had managed to obtain information about a *private* mercenary venture, they could certainly be wily enough to get chummy with the likely victor and regain some of their lost influence. And if Potro was involved, Spain was ideally placed to exercise some leverage.

All Abad could do now was to stay alert and wait. He would redouble his efforts with informers and step up his vigilance at Malabo docks and the airport. He would review CCTV cameras daily and post round-the-clock surveillance on key embassies. And for the moment he would not discuss this with Penang. Of late the President had taken to delegating matters to his wild nephew Dorito and Abad was certain that if he brought the hot-headed boy into his confidence he would screw everything up.

It was the sudden oil wealth that had provided the catalyst for change. With wealth had come the desire to enjoy it without having to escape the confines of an African man-made hellhole. So the Penangs started looking at ways to invest some of their fortune within their country, allowing some internal prosperity without relaxing their grip on total power.

Dorito, already with a string of homes in Spain and South America, super-cars, polo ponies and a lavish megayacht, was seduced by the idea of becoming a tycoon in his own country as well.

Start with the safe and obvious – hotels, utilities, transport – and move in on construction, leisure and that great dollar-earner, tourism. Western multinationals contemplating potential contracts might be persuaded to look the other way when Equatorial Guinea's human-rights record was discussed.

So the relationship with Moscow was allowed to cool while overtures were made towards America. If President Bush gave their regime even a hint of approval there was no reason not to start investing in their own country, and a good tourist infrastructure would present a better image of the country abroad. But, the way Abad saw it, the resulting influx of foreigners would inevitably undermine his own tight grip.

So Abad watched carefully as Penang's business advisers selected moneymaking projects. The latest and grandest was a massive development on the mainland portion of their nation, where the Muni River reached the ocean. It would include a yacht marina as well as luxury villas and apartments, all to be built on the strip of land bordered by the river on one side and the Atlantic Ocean on the other.

The location was only fifty kilometres north of the mainland capital, Bata, and on the same side as its airport. The Penangs were buying up all the land they did not already own, while the nation would build a road and improve the airport facilities. Marina del Muni would become a playground for the rich, a unique West African Riviera. Artists' impressions of the grand scheme had already been released to the world's press, a website had been set up and glossy brochures had been printed. Equatorial Guinea was about to join the twenty-first century.

And, Abad noted unhappily, the entire building contract would go to foreign companies whose own people would come into the country by the thousands. They would, undoubtedly, bring with them Western ideologies and the first curious members of their press in tow.

From then on Penang's days would be numbered. It had been tried before in other countries, this frivolous notion of despots seeking legitimacy. In the end there were too many scores to be settled. It simply would not work.

The Marina del Muni project could turn Abad's job into a nightmare.

22

Florin sat at his desk, savouring a late-night rum as he perused his charts. He had several maps of West Africa and naval charts of the Gulf of Guinea. He measured distances carefully with a scale and noted them on a pad.

Sergeant Truenos knocked gently on the study door and let himself in.

'General Ramos is here, sir.'

'Show him in,' Florin said enthusiastically, standing up to greet his friend.

'Jesús, you old fox.' Ramos opened his arms wide and they embraced. 'I came the minute I got your message.'

Though younger than Florin, Martin Ramos was still past retirement age. He had served for forty years in the Cuban Air Force but now he spent much of his time fishing off the Caribbean coast or partying with his cronies at his beach house in southern Camagüey.

'You are looking fit, Martin. Drink?'

'A beer,' he said to Truenos before looking at the charts on Florin's desk. 'What's this, planning a holiday?'

They laughed.

'Enjoying retirement, Martin?'

'Of course.' Ramos sounded genuinely happy. 'But there are times when I miss being in the thick of things.'

'Not a lot to miss any more,' Florin observed.

'Don't tell me you are still operational?' Ramos gestured towards the desk as he sat down.

'Not exactly.' Florin smiled but offered no further explanation. Ramos took the hint.

'You said you needed my advice, Jesús. How can I help?'

'It's to do with helicopters,' said The Aztec, pausing as Miriam came in with the drinks.

'Well, I don't have any to lend you,' Ramos joked. 'They took away my air force three years ago!'

'Don't worry,' Florin replied in the same vein, 'I can get one elsewhere; you are not the only friend I have with his own air force.' They laughed again; it felt comfortable being with friends.

'What I need,' Florin continued, 'are some facts and figures about these.'

He pushed a typed sheet across his desk and let Ramos read it. It listed half a dozen helicopter types, all Soviet-made. Ramos took just a few seconds to read it.

'I've flown the lot.'

'I thought you might have.'

'Some of these are very old,' Ramos said, looking at the list. 'We don't have them any more.'

'I wasn't thinking about us,' Florin acknowledged.

'Ah.' Ramos picked up his beer and swigged from

the bottle. Best to let Florin ask the questions, he thought.

'Range is my first question, Martin. How far can a helicopter go?'

'It varies from one aircraft to another. Is range an issue?'

'Yes.' Florin did not hesitate.

'This one has long legs,' Ramos pointed at the last entry on Florin's list, the Mil-17.

'How long?'

'Depends on weight, Jesús, but I'm sure you know that.'

Ramos picked up the list again. He'd been a helicopter pilot for three-quarters of his service time. Even after Fidel made him air force chief he still flew right-hand seat from time to time. Fifteen thousand hours, was it? He could rattle off the operating figures for any of those types.

'With full payload, no reserves,' he explained, 'the seventeen will do a thousand kilometres. How many on board?'

'Half a dozen, maybe eight.'

'This thing can carry twenty soldiers and their kit. Throw a dozen out and you can replace their weight with extra fuel – you'll get another five hundred kilometres.'

'How much weight can it lift?' asked Florin.

'Five tons, with four hours' fuel. Does it need to be armed? Rockets and the like?'

'No.'

'You can carry another ton if you remove the heavy weaponry.'

'Thank you, Martin.'

'Any time, my friend.'

'We must chat more often, you know, you and I?' Florin meant it.

'I don't come this way as much as I should. I must make a point of it,' Ramos promised.

'Camagüey treating you well?'

'I have everything I need, and plenty of visitors. Perhaps you'll honour me one day?'

'I don't get about much these days,' Florin lamented. 'But yes, I must.'

'We'll fish and cook on the beach. Nice women, too.' They laughed.

'Do you still have your boat?' asked Florin.

'You bet! Come and visit – we'll fill the boat with rum and women, go deep-sea fishing and party.'

'I just might do that,' Florin promised.

'Do you see much of Fidel and Raul?' Ramos asked.

'Raul stops by regularly. Not Fidel. Haven't seen him for a while.'

'Some say he's not well,' Ramos ventured.

'We are all past our prime, Martin.' The Florin laugh filled the room, 'Fidel no exception. But there are a few years yet in the *Comandante en Jefe*. Are you going back to the coast tonight?'

'No,' replied Ramos, 'I'll be staying in the Club. I'll spend tomorrow with my daughter and grandchildren.'

'Then dine with me before you go,' Florin demanded.

They spent a couple of convivial hours together. They remembered both the good and bad times and in between Florin asked more questions about the Mil-17.

At around ten Florin walked Ramos to his car and watched him drive off towards Havana. Then he went back to his desk and charts. He assumed that Miriam had gone to bed so he asked Truenos to fetch him a surreptitious nightcap.

Armed with the knowledge imparted by his air-force friend, Florin returned to taking measurements and making notes. It was close to midnight when he took out his address book from the safe and dialled a number in Kinshasa.

'Massama.' The phone was picked up on the second ring.

'How nice to hear your voice, *mon général*.' Jesús spoke in French.

'Jesús?' he could not hide his surprise.

'And how are you, *polisson*?'

'Jesús! I can't believe my ears! Where are you?'

'At home, in Cuba.'

'*Mérde!* How long has it been? Ten years? *Putain!* I keep asking people if you are dead!'

'What do they answer?' Florin wanted to know.

'That you are plotting revolutions in hell!' Massama's voice cracked with laughter.

'I'm alive and well, my friend. Older, a bit tired, but alive and well. And you? Prosperous, I'm told by *my* inform-ants who are, *obviously*, better informed than yours.'

Massama chuckled.

'So what is this? Are you calling to wish me a happy birthday?'

'Not exactly, but Happy Birthday anyway. How old is that?'

'Fifty-eight.'

'Still a child, then,' Florin joked.

Massama was a survivor. From boy soldier with one faction to army general with another, he had fought his way through the massacres of the Belgian Congo's transition from down-trodden colony to corrupt Zaire. In Mobutu's time he had benefited from being close to the seat of power and had somehow distanced himself from his past to become a wealthy man. After Sese Seko's fall, Massama reclaimed his freedom-fighter credentials, fought with the victors in the bloody Second

Congo War and continued to prosper in the new Democratic Republic while remaining active in the army – which he'd discovered was the best form of life insurance in troubled Africa.

'Jesús, really, you need something? Anything I can do? Like you say, I am a man of great means.' He chuckled again. 'And in these parts even a little power.'

'As a matter of fact, I do, my friend. I need a helicopter.'

Massama guffawed. 'Can't get any from Mother Russia any more?'

'I need one in Africa.' Florin stopped joking.

'Africa is a big place, Jesús.' Massama, was equally serious now. 'Tell me more.'

'I need to borrow a Mil-17 for a day or two.'

'We have some,' the Congolese confirmed. 'They are huge bastards,' he added more jovially. 'What do you need to carry? Gold bullion?' Massama laughed.

'Not quite.' Florin smiled at the irony, 'It's more a question of range.'

'So where do you need to go?'

'To Bata. On the Guinean coast. I need a helicopter, a crew and enough fuel to fly from Boma to Bata and back. That's one thousand kilometres.'

'When?'

'Soon. I will let you know,' Florin said, knowing Massama would deliver. 'And I can't pay you, by the way.'

This time Massama did not laugh.

'You've paid enough already, my friend. This will be my pleasure.'

'Thank you, Bienheuré.'

'Will you tell me what it is about?'

'Of course. When I see you in Kinshasa.'

* * *

Florin turned his attention to the papers on his desk. The original tip-off, from South Africa, had made the rest of the plan possible.

Were it not for how much was at stake for Florin personally, he might have allowed himself the luxury of a smile. They were amateurs. Tough, maybe, even experienced at soldiering. But African coups are best left to Africans, with outsiders sticking to investments and rewards. Cuba had learned that lesson the hard way.

Thabo Mbeki would never countenance such an operation being launched from South Africa so they'd have to go from somewhere else. Florin put the questions out, not officially, not through Sierra's office, but through his own private network from the old days, which he could still call upon when needed even if he seldom had reason to.

They'd launch from Zambia, Florin's jungle drums told him, in a beat-up 1960s-vintage Boeing 727. They would make a stop in Harare – where bonded freight awaited them and officials had been suitably bribed – to load the boxes full of equipment and weapons flown in from Oostende.

Florin would not approach Mugabe directly. Mugabe could construe this as a Cuban operation and would expect something in return. Florin needed a credible intermediary and he knew just the man.

'Leonid Florin's blood is part of this nation,' he'd once said, 'and Leonid's father will for ever be one of us.' Angola had good relations with Zimbabwe and Florin's contact was its President. Florin would ask him to make the call to tell Mugabe about the weapon-carrying, white-mercenary aircraft, to hint at the likelihood of a pile of cash on board, and to suggest the opportunities that could arise from currying favour with the wealthy ruler of an oil-rich African country.

Once again Florin returned to the charts. Happy that the facts were clear in his mind he could now plan the operation. First a location that was both tactically suitable for his purpose and credible in more sense than one. A cutting from *El País* had given him the idea.

He called up the Earth Viewer and started an aerial reconnaissance of the mainland sector: Rio Muni. The city of Bata would be the focus of the operation. Its airport lay just to the north and Florin followed the coast past it until he came to the river mouth.

He compared his computer readings with his naval charts and carefully noted the location at Utonde. 1° 56' 13" North by 9° 48' 49" East. He marked the spot with a cross. It would do.

Florin switched off his desk lamp and stood up. He picked up his drink and walked out onto the back veranda. It was a cool starry night. For the millionth time the awesome magnitude of the galaxies in a clear moonless sky spurred memories to the surface, thoughts that he had spent thirty years trying to suppress if only to retain a modicum of sanity.

How many nights in how many places had he shared those skies?

With Natalia, Yuri and Leonid.

With Lucía.

With María Luz who had been taken from him before he'd had a chance to teach her the names of the stars.

And with a thousand others whose death-mask faces were slowly fading into the mists of time.

Not long now, Florin told them silently. *I'm almost done.*

23

Pinto looked at Hadley as if gauging the man. He leaned back on his chair and studied the neatly typed sheets of paper that the Englishman had brought along. Nothing to tie them to anyone. Plain paper, no signatures, no attributions. They could have come from anywhere.

'These just arrived by courier?' asked Pinto.

Hadley nodded.

'No sender details? No courier receipt?'

'No.'

'And you did not see the delivery man?'

'I was not at the University when the package arrived.'

'But Florin had told you over the phone that you should expect it, you said?'

'Yes.'

'And bring them to me?'

'Correct.'

'What made you change your mind?' Pinto changed tack.

'Florin. He said the entire operation so far would have been pointless if we did not take it to its logical conclusion.'

'Mrs Uribe did not persuade you to come back?' Pinto probed.

'I haven't seen or heard from Mrs Uribe since we parted company in this building back in February.'

'Any other reason?' Pinto ignored the remark.

'Yes. The biography.' Hadley saw no point in lying. 'I need the rest of Florin's manuscript.'

'Ah, poor Professor Hadley,' Pinto quipped in mock sympathy. 'Do you feel blackmailed yet again?'

'Far from it.' Hadley was finding Pinto particularly irritating this morning. 'But there are many aspects of Florin's life that I believe must be told, including recent events,' he said, hoping that the last remark would annoy the Captain, 'and I intend to do just that.'

'Let's go over this once more' – Pinto disregarded the insinuation – 'starting with the gold.'

Almost exactly as Pinto himself had predicted, Florin revealed that the Spanish torpedo boat had never completed her voyage between Budva and Veracruz. Beset with engine problems she had barely made it through the Strait of Gibraltar before she'd had to contend with increasingly rough seas.

The weather to the north was menacingly uninviting, with developing thunderstorms and gale-force winds effectively ruling out Florin's preferred alternative round the Bay of Biscay and on to England.

Any attempt to reach Mexico was doomed to fail: should the engine fail completely they would at best be condemned to drift in the growing swell until the food and water ran out or, more likely, to perish as the powerless vessel eventually capsized.

That made a southerly course the only alternative, following the coast of Africa.

'Not a bad choice,' Pinto commented, 'considering how little Florin would have known about sailing. I wonder who commanded the *Mataró*?'

'No names are mentioned anywhere,' Hadley replied, 'but that's the sort of gap I'll want to fill.'

Morocco would have been a Franco stronghold and thus out of the question. Nor had Florin gone for the Atlantic Islands as Minguez had speculated. It was Marcos Vega the *africanista* who had come closest when he said Fernando Pó.

The island colony, twenty-five miles off the coast of Cameroon, could have provided safe harbour at Santa Isabel. It was lightly garrisoned, the inhabitants spoke Spanish and there would have been plenty of sheltered coves in which to make repairs and wait for better weather. They could easily have taken the gold ashore and hidden it. But there would have been a real risk of coming up against a Nationalist Navy vessel and being forced to fight it out or surrender – either way jeopardising Florin's ultimate mission of delivering the gold to the Republican government-in-exile.

So Florin had opted for giving Fernando Pó a miss and continuing a further 370 miles to the next Spanish enclave, Rio Muni, on the African mainland.

As Florin's ailing gunboat arrived in the Muni River estuary in 1939 the colony was a quiet backwater and the perfect hiding place for his valuable cargo.

Pinto looked at a photocopied section of a naval chart

that Florin had appended. It looked like a 1:20,000 British Admiralty chart covering the Gulf of Guinea.

'What he seems to be saying,' Pinto said, 'is that what remains of the gold is buried here.'

He turned the chart around and invited Hadley to inspect it. Florin had put a cross next to Utonde, a small settlement on the river's left bank close to where the river discharged onto the Atlantic Ocean. A pair of coordinates had been written on the chart in red ink.

'That's what he says,' observed Hadley.

'All of it, do you think?'

'He said he kept some' – Hadley pointed at the typed sheets – 'to get his crew away.'

'Quite.' Pinto sounded non-committal.

'If it's not true, why bother?' Hadley asked him. 'Why go through all this chicanery?'

'You tell me.' Pinto still spoke as if he did not believe a word on the typed sheets that Hadley had delivered.

'And after hiding the treasure in Rio Muni,' Pinto continued, glancing briefly at the notes, 'he sails this ailing vessel another hundred miles to French territory in the Gabon and dumps the gunboat close to Libreville from where he and his crew make their way home, happily flogging sovereigns along the way.'

'I've no reason to doubt him.' In fact, Hadley did have some doubts but he was not prepared to agree with Pinto about anything.

'Let's turn to Florin's proposal.' Pinto shuffled the papers and selected one sheet, which he moved to the top.

The deal, of course, was quite attractive: Florin had somehow learned all about the coup attempt being hatched in South Africa.

'How do you suppose Florin got this information?'

'I'm told he has eyes and ears all over Africa.'

'By whom?'

'Florin himself,' Hadley had to admit. 'And given that his information seems to be true,' he added in response to Pinto's cynical smirk, 'perhaps he is as well informed as you are.'

'And he demands that we recruit this man.' Pinto placed a further sheet from Florin's wad on his desk and looked at it studiously. 'What do you think, Hadley?'

'Look, I've no desire to be here in the first place, let alone to get involved in your murky business—'

'Yes, so you said,' Pinto interrupted sharply. 'But like it or not, Jack Hadley, you *are* involved. You have read all this,' he waved his right hand at the papers on his desk, 'and are therefore privy to state secrets. Now, *I'm* not happy about *that* but I'm stuck with you. So let's try to find a way to live with these facts or I shall be forced to detain you in isolation until this business is over!'

'So what the hell do you want me to do, Pinto?' Hadley raised his voice.

'First,' Pinto spoke slowly, supported by his habitual finger-counting, 'you give me your word, as an officer and a gentleman, that what you have learned about Equatorial Guinea will not be discussed with anyone – and that includes Miss Vilanova, by the way. Has she seen this?' Again he pointed at his desk.

'No.'

'Good, let's keep it that way. Secondly,' continued Pinto, 'you start showing some sort of respect, if not loyalty, towards your adoptive country and try to think beyond the bare facts. I want to know what you think of The Aztec, whether or not you believe he can he be trusted, and why.

'You have, after all – and in no small measure thanks to us – the unique privilege of having recently spent several hours in conversation with him. So, do we have an agreement?'

'OK. Until this African business is over.'

'I have your word?'

'You do.'

'Sign this, anyway.' Pinto took an official-looking document from a drawer in his desk and pushed it across to Hadley, together with a pen.

'So much for the gentlemanly bit,' Hadley muttered as he signed his name. Pinto took the pen and paper back and ignored the gratuitous comment. 'Can I ask you a question, if we are going to be candid?'

'Go ahead.'

'Does Rosa Uribe work for you?'

'She works for ICEX,' Pinto replied, 'but she's . . . known to us. That's all I'm going to say. Now, let's get back to this man in Malabo . . .' he looked at the photograph '. . . Major Abad.'

Florin had been explicit in his appraisal of the situation: the military coup would probably succeed, but not for long. The people of Equatorial Guinea had been used to untold repression ever since they'd gained independence from Spain. A group of foreign mercenaries would not be able to replace that brutal set-up.

If Penang was deposed, his successor Potro would be viewed as Spain's choice. But if the collapse of Penang's terror apparatus meant wild rioting and civil disorder, then undoubtedly Cameroon or Congo would invade – to preserve lives, naturally – and become de facto custodians of the nation's oil wealth while inviting an *African* debate on Equatorial Guinea's future and throwing all non-Africans, Spain included, out of the country.

Florin's plan called for removing the Penang clan but keeping Abad to secure a smooth transition. Abad could be bought, and Spain was ideally placed to buy him. Let CNI's Malabo office make the overture and Abad would be sure to side with the winner.

Though CNI did not have a lot on Jorge Abad, Pinto felt they had enough to make the necessary approach. Years ago, when the previous president had been deposed, Abad had cleverly changed loyalties – and then secured the top job.

Pinto looked at the photographs in Abad's file. They'd been taken with a telephoto lens but they were clear enough. He was a slim man in a plain beige uniform. His skin was brown rather than black, suggesting mixed blood not uncommon in Equatorial Guinea, but his slicked-back jet-black hair and distinctive facial features pointed towards a Polynesian rather than ethnic African origin.

And, more importantly, Marcos Vega's annotations concluded that the man would sell his own grandmother if that was what it took to hang on to power. They also provided incontrovertible evidence that he was not beyond accepting cash inducements to protect selected parties whose interests did not directly clash with his own.

'What do you think, Mr Hadley?'

'I'm no expert on Africa.'

'Think of Iraq, then.'

'You need locals to kick the locals. They know how to.'

'Florin's right, then?'

'I guess.'

'And then,' Pinto rifled through the papers till he found the right one, 'we are to make a deal with Potro now, before he becomes *el Presidente*. Spain gets contracts for the oil and a large piece of the growing infrastructure. Specifically, we sign a memorandum of understanding before he leaves Switzerland for Malabo that gives our construction boys the entire Marina del Muni development.' Pinto looked up at Hadley and smiled.

'Meaning what?' Hadley demanded.

'Do you know where Marina del Muni is?'

'No.'

'Right here.' Pinto put his finger on Florin's little *X* on the Admiralty chart. 'A hundred villas, twice that number of flats, shopping mall, country club, five hundred yacht berths.'

'I see . . .'

'Tons and tons of earth to be excavated. Including the very spot where our Aztec friend says he once buried two hundred million dollars in gold coins!'

'Christ!' Hadley was incredulous.

'Still, seems cheap to me . . .' mused Pinto.

'Two hundred million dollars? Cheap?'

'Half! Remember what you said after your Cuban visit? Spain only gets half! But it's not what we get that troubles me.'

'What, then?'

'We get half a billion euros' worth of public works, a long-term crude oil contract, a conveniently friendly despot in charge of a former colony of potential interest to Spaniards and a little kudos with both the UN and OAS. All that in addition to the gold!'

'What the hell does Florin get? Or Cuba? Or anyone else, for that matter?' Pinto made Florin's offer sound implausible.

'A shitload of gold sovereigns?' ventured Hadley.

'What for? What does an octogenarian freedom fighter want to do with a hundred million bucks?'

'I've no idea.'

'Well, think. Because unless we can understand why the hell this windfall is being pushed our way the natural cynicism that comes with years on this job, Mr Hadley, sets alarm bells ringing!'

'So do you think you can do what he suggests?' asked Hadley.

'Does he want a response?'

'Yes. I'm to deliver it in person if I'm to get the rest of his material.'

'We are not paying for another trip to Cuba, Mr Hadley.'

'I'm not asking you to pay.'

'Are you taking your girlfriend?'

'No.'

'Well, you can tell him we'll play. I'll send the Head of my Africa Section to Malabo to seduce the Major. Our mutual friend at ICEX will know exactly how to draft the Marina del Muni memorandum. I'll make sure *el presidente* sees her and signs it. You may tell The Aztec that.'

I'll also make sure el presidente *does not get a copy of what we signed until after he's succeeded*, Pinto told himself. *If the coup fails I'll shred the lot.*

'And you and I? Where do we stand?'

'The slate's wiped clean, Professor.' Pinto stood up and pressed the button. 'Good luck with the biography. I shall look out for it.'

But without quite knowing why, Pinto was right to question this particular gift horse. Florin's real intentions were not exactly as set out in the couriered package.

He *did* intend to share the remaining gold with Pinto and Spain would *definitely* come out of this smelling sweet, as he had promised Rosa.

But the *coup d'état* would not succeed and Celestino Potro would never set foot in Equatorial Guinea. Florin and his friends would make sure of that.

24

'Miriam, I need to pack,' Florin announced halfway through his lunch. He was picking at a chicken salad while reading the latest issue of *Granma*.

'Pack?' She looked at him, wide-eyed. 'And where might we be going?'

'Fishing,' he replied without lifting his gaze from the paper. 'I'm going fishing with General Ramos in Camagüey.'

'Why wasn't I warned?' Miriam chided.

'Because I've only just decided, that's why.'

'General Ramos has no wife,' she persevered. 'Who's going to look after you while you are there?'

'We are taking a load of women on the boat,' he told her, looking up with a defiant smile. 'They'll know how to look after me and the General.'

Nurse Miriam made a despairing gesture and turned away, muttering something about the clothes he'd need to take.

'I'll need two sets of fatigues, blue and khaki,' he called after her.

'I thought you said *you* needed to pack,' she pointed out as she left the dining room.

'It was a figure of speech,' he retorted, loud enough for her to hear, 'like you asking where *we* are going.'

Florin's elaborate plan had been made easier by a stroke of luck. The previous week, Nurse Miriam and Sergeant Truenos had come into Florin's study together. They'd stood nervously, side by side, as they'd informed their employer of their intention to get married.

'About time too,' Florin replied, making Truenos grin sheepishly and Miriam blush.

Florin then telephoned the Deputy Commander's Office, broke the good news to his nurse's distant uncle and invited him round to toast the couple. Raul agreed to come over – on the day before Jesús planned to leave for the south coast.

Truenos stood in his best uniform as the two-vehicle convoy pulled up outside The Aztec's bungalow. He saluted and Raul Castro returned the formality before following it with a congratulatory embrace.

Indoors, cool drinks and an array of cakes and sandwiches that Nurse Miriam had prepared were neatly laid out on the dining-room table. After the usual niceties, while the visiting retinue enjoyed the offerings and made polite conversation with the happy couple, Florin and Castro walked out to the back garden.

'Are you keeping well?' Castro asked, casting an approving look at Florin.

'Very. I'm about to take a break, as it happens.'

'Oh?' Castro appeared pleased.

'I'm off tomorrow, on Martin Ramos's boat.'

Castro laughed, taken completely by surprise.

'It's a floating bordello, from what I hear. You'll need to take along the magic pills!'

'We are going fishing,' Florin explained in the same vein.

That made Castro howl. 'Well, you be sure *not* to catch anything,' he warned Florin merrily. 'Say hello for me.'

They continued jesting for a while as they took a gentle stroll towards the beach. A bodyguard followed at an unobtrusive distance. They talked about Ramos and reminisced about the old days.

'I heard from an old contact in Yugoslavia the other day.' Florin let the subject drift in casually. Castro looked at him but remained silent.

'Ivo Klejevic,' Florin explained. 'No one you'd know. His late father, Stefan, was a good friend of mine. Fought at Leningrad.'

'I see.'

'Ivo is an important man now, with state security in Montenegro. I expect he'll run the service once his country separates from Serbia.'

Florin recognised the change in Castro's facial expression. He was suddenly interested.

'He told me something I can't quite make out. I was going to pass it on to Aquiles Sierra, but since you are here . . .'

Castro smiled.

'You still don't like Sierra. Do you?'

'No,' admitted Florin.

'He does a job, and does it well. They think differently from us, the new generation. But remember that the Cuba they will have to live in will be different from ours.'

'Sure. I don't interfere, Raul. I simply don't like him.'

'That's fine, too. So what did Klejevic have to say?'

'A man was shot dead by Ivo's men last week,' Florin explained. 'Carried a Mexican passport in the name of Pascual Lagos.'

'Why was he shot?'

'He was caught in the middle of a burglary. Tried to run; fired a shot at the police and they shot back.'

'I see. Did your friend say why this should interest you – or interest any of us, for that matter?'

'Yes, on both counts.'

Castro stopped walking and took a deep breath, stretching his arms.

'I love the fresh air here,' he said. 'I spend too much time indoors. Maybe I should do like you and go fishing.' They turned back towards the house.

'The man he was trying to rob was an Englishman called Hadley. He's a professor teaching at Salamanca University. He's also writing my memoirs.'

'Is he now?' Castro feigned mild surprise, but he had been told about Hadley and made no further comment.

'He was in Montenegro researching my time there,' Florin continued, speaking calmly. 'He was in Budva, where I visited in the 1930s. He had been asking questions about the old Republican gold.'

'That was sixty years ago!' Castro looked puzzled. 'What the hell can the Mexicans want with that? It was all removed to their country anyway, wasn't it?'

'Yes,' Florin agreed.

'Well then?'

'It's just that Ivo's department had a file on Lagos. They are sure the name is phoney. They are not even convinced he was Mexican.'

Castro gave Florin a concerned look.

'Quite.' Florin read his mind, 'They have him down as one of ours.'

'No one's said anything to me.' Castro sounded unhappy and Florin knew that by *no one* he meant Sierra.

'There's more . . .' Florin could see that his old friend did not like where this might lead, 'Hadley called me two days later. When he got back to Spain, he found that his apartment in Salamanca had been burgled.'

Castro looked at Florin inquisitively.

'There was only one thing stolen: the manuscripts I'd given him to help with the biography.'

'Do you have any ideas?' Castro looked puzzled.

'No. My guess would have been the Spaniards poking their noses in. There are one or two in Madrid who still have a bee in their bonnet over the gold. And over me,' Florin added, making light of it. 'But Ivo is a chip off the old block and he didn't get where he is by talking nonsense. And he reckons the phoney Mexican is Cuban.'

'Was there anything in your notes or about . . . what's his name? Hadley? Anything that might be damaging to Cuba?'

'Nothing that I can think of. I believe Hadley to be genuine.'

'Good.' Castro appeared unruffled but Jesús knew him well: he was very displeased with what he had heard.

'I'll see what I can find out, Jesús.' Castro smiled, as if concluding the matter. 'Leave it with me.'

'Thanks, old friend. Maybe Ivo's got it wrong. Maybe it's the Spaniards after all.'

'And, Jesús . . .' Castro looked probingly into Florin's face.

'Yes?'

'You are not about to go poking *your* nose into Yugoslavia, or even into Spain for that matter, are you?'

'No way!' exclaimed Florin, visibly shocked by the suggestion.

'Good.' Castro nodded his approval and gestured at Florin to lead the way back into the house.

Next, Florin hoped, Castro would assume that Sierra was running a private operation and would give the bastard a very hard time. Sierra would be forced to think twice before meddling with Florin's affairs – at least in the short term, until the dust settled, which was all that Florin needed in order to get away without having to watch his back.

On Saturday morning Truenos requisitioned a car to drive Jesús Florin halfway across Cuba to Santa Cruz del Sur.

The previous night Florin had opened his safe and transferred three passports, several maps, overseas contact details and two envelopes stuffed with hundred-dollar bills into a rucksack.

In an apparently spontaneous last-minute gesture, Florin asked Miriam if she too would like to come along for the ride. Their destination, in the south-western province of Camagüey, was two-thirds of the way to Miriam's own native Guantánamo region so he suggested that Miriam should take her fiancé there for a few days and show him off to the extended family.

In fact, Florin wanted no one in his home who might have to answer questions should Sierra still have the gall to come snooping after Castro quizzed him on his – deniable or not – dead agent.

They set off early in order to cover the five hundred and fifty kilometres in one day, stopping for lunch at a simple *mesón* in Ciego de Avila where staff and local patrons made a point of shaking hands with Florin and where, inevitably, they refused to let him pay.

They reached General Ramos's seaside home in the early evening and, after taking some refreshments in his kitchen, Truenos and Miriam wished the old soldiers happy fishing and set off on their own journey.

'About a week, depending on how we get on,' Florin told them as they prepared to leave. 'I'll call when I'm ready to go home.'

Ramos lit the barbecue, then pulled up a garden chair next to Florin's and passed him an open bottle of Cristal.

'It's so good to see you here, Jesús,' Ramos said. 'We are going to relax and have fun.'

'Raul sends his regards,' Jesús said, smiling appreciatively. 'Says he might go fishing himself one of these days.'

'He knows he's always welcome here.'

Ramos's house was on a hillock, close to the shoreline and sufficiently high up to enjoy an unimpeded view of the Caribbean. As dusk set in they could see the sporadic flashes of a distant thunderstorm.

'How far away are those?' Florin asked.

'Over a hundred miles, I'd say,' ventured Ramos. 'Around the Caymans.'

'Ever been there?'

'Sure.'

'In your boat?'

'No,' Ramos laughed, 'on Cubana. But I could go with the boat if I wanted to.'

'How long would it take?'

Ramos looked at him apprehensively.

'You are not suggesting that I take up smuggling, are you?'

'Hardly.' Florin smiled knowingly. 'But, seriously, how long?'

'Six, seven hours.'

They heard the sound of tyres on gravel, followed by excited female voices. Jesús looked up at his friend in mock amazement as the doorbell rang.

'Do you still have a bad back?' Ramos grinned as he went to the front door.

They were just what Florin expected: young, in tight-fitting jeans and T-shirts, clearly fond of the General's generosity. Florin decided to play along for the moment and leave the true purpose of his visit until morning.

'Yes,' he said, grimacing and feigning discomfort, 'I have a very painful back. You are not about to tell me that one of these lovely ladies is a physiotherapist, are you?'

In the morning Ramos made a fuss over cooking a traditional Cuban breakfast. He laboured over fried eggs, fish croquettes and black beans as one of the girls cut up fruit and another laid the table. The third girl had been sent into the village to buy bread and pineapple pastries.

Florin came into the kitchen wearing army shorts and a khaki vest, drying his hair with a red towel.

'Is the idea that we throw up all over your boat?' he joked looking at the smoking stove.

'Puke at your peril,' threatened Ramos. 'That goes especially for you lot,' he said to the girls.

'Where are we going?' the plumper one, Teresa, asked as she tucked into the *pastelitos*.

'Wherever there's fish.' Ramos dismissed her.

'I have some ideas which way we could go,' offered Florin and Ramos gave him a worried look, 'but we'll talk about that later.'

The girls were ordered to wash up and tidy the house while Ramos and Florin went outside for a smoke.

'You are not here for the fish, are you?' Ramos asked when the two men were alone.

'You know me well, old friend. Sorry.'

'Tell me, then.'

'I need you to drop me off.'

'Not the goddamn Caymans! Is that why you were asking last night . . .'

'No. Not the Caymans. Bit nearer,' Florin laughed.

'*Donde mierda?* Where the hell?'

'Montego Bay.'

'What for?'

'I have to do something, Martin,' Florin explained. 'It has to be covert and it's all in place once I reach Jamaica.'

'How long do I have to wait?'

'You don't. I'll fly back openly into José Martí. There'll be no more need for secrecy by then.'

'So you want me to drop you and come back? Is that it?'

'No. You drop me and then you take the boat and the girls and float around the Cuban coast for five days. In sight of land, but you don't dock.'

'*La gran puta*, Jesús, we are good friends – but five days? What the hell am I supposed to do for five days on a bloody boat?'

'What you've always done, Martin: fish, drink and fuck!'

They sailed in the early afternoon. The harbour master at Santa Cruz paid little attention. He was used to seeing Ramos and his women on the boat, though he did note Florin's presence and his respect for General Ramos was accordingly enhanced.

While the girls transferred provisions into the *Tiburón*, Ramos let it drop into the conversation that they would be heading east along the south coast, past Santiago de Cuba and eventually turning north to Baracoa.

'I hope you've brought along plenty of hard currency,' Ramos said as they set a south-westerly course. 'We'll need to buy fuel for the return journey.'

Jesús nodded and sent Lucrecia below to fetch two beers.

'You needn't worry, Martin, everything's been thought out. There will be no problems.'

They cut across the Gulf of Guacanayabo and an hour and a half later reached Cape Cruz. Along the way and for the benefit of any nosy onlookers, Ramos fitted four fishing rods into their holders, lines trawling behind the moving boat. He steered the *Tiburón* two miles or so past the point, as if to turn east at a prudent offshore distance. He scanned the coastline with binoculars, then locked the autopilot on a southerly heading and opened up the throttles for the eighty-mile run to Jamaica.

Powering its way through a dead-calm Caribbean and with hardly any wind, the cabin cruiser made its destination in well under three hours. Only Teresa had thrown up and even then she managed to do so over the side.

A mile from the shore Ramos identified the jutting Sunset Beach peninsula. He knew they would find the Yacht Club on its southern side.

He rounded the north-western corner and soon enough the club's jetty came into view. There were about thirty boats moored along its sides with a further twenty tied to submerged moorings or lying at anchor nearby.

Jesús borrowed the binoculars and inspected the pier.

A lone figure dressed in denim chinos and a white shirt and with a navy sweater tied around his neck stood at the jetty's tip.

Florin nodded approvingly as he recognised Jack Hadley, who was shielding his eyes against the sun with a hand across his forehead as he gazed in the direction of the approaching *Tiburón*.

25

Aquiles Sierra could barely contain his anger as he returned to his office in Havana. Raul Castro had not minced his words. The security chief had been summoned by the Deputy Commander and made to feel most uncomfortable by Castro's unexpected line of questioning. He was left with little option but to make a tactical retreat.

'It's not my operation, sir.' Sierra was emphatic. 'Although we have used someone by that name before, I do recall,' he added just in case.

'So what the hell is going on there?'

'I don't know, sir. If there is a suspicion of Cuban involvement I am surprised that I haven't heard.'

'Do you know this man Hadley?' Castro was not about to beat around the bush and Sierra could sense it.

'Yes, sir. Jack Hadley. An Englishman. He was in Cuba recently as a guest of Havana University, sponsored by Dr Hugo Asencio of the History Faculty. I met him there. Also, I believe, he had meetings with Jesús Florin.'

'In that case it would be too much of a damn coincidence, wouldn't you say?'

'Is there a problem associated with Mr Hadley's visit, sir?'

'I don't know. There have been two attempts to rob him – one in Montenegro and the other in Spain, both of them since he visited Cuba.'

'Rob him of what?' Sierra thought he should ask the question.

'Papers,' replied Castro. The look on his face conveyed a degree of bafflement but he was still not dropping the interrogator role.

'May I . . .' Sierra hesitated. 'May I ask the source of this information?'

'No,' the Deputy Commander replied immediately. 'But I want to know if these two incidents are in any way linked with Cuba.'

'Yes, sir.' It had to have come from Florin, Sierra was certain.

'Any names you can think of?'

'Perhaps CNI?' ventured Sierra. 'Could they be interested in Hadley and his visit here?'

'And Montenegro? Where's the Spanish connection there?'

'I don't know. Other than Hadley. There is, of course, a rumour . . . but it would be so far-fetched . . .'

'Well?' Castro was not in the mood for guessing games.

'There were always these whisperings about Jesús Florin, Montenegro and missing Spanish gold . . .'

Castro nodded, with a barely audible grunt. This was the second time this week that the gold business had been mentioned.

'So? What's this to do with a dead Mexican?'

For once Sierra seemed to have no answer but Castro knew better than that.

'You find out about the Mexican, Cuban, or whatever he is,' he ordered. 'Also see if you can get anything on the theft in Madrid.'

'Yes, sir.'

'And stay clear of Jesús Florin, understand?' Castro's voice became harsh as he stood up without waiting for Sierra's reply. He was clearly far from satisfied.

'I believe I have said this before,' he ended firmly and unequivocally, waving an index finger as if recalling the precise circumstances. 'But I shall say it once again: General Florin is outside your remit.'

Ever since Rosa Uribe's visit last December, Sierra had kept Florin under discreet surveillance. He was not about to risk repeating the bugging fiasco of a decade earlier but neither was he willing to look the other way when he knew full well that Florin was up to something.

Whatever views the Castros might hold about The Aztec, they would have to bow to Sierra's evidence – and be thankful for it – the minute it was put in front of them.

But it was still a case of the chicken-and-egg conundrum. To gather the evidence, Sierra needed to keep tabs on Florin, yet if he were found out his actions could spell the end of his career. Sierra would not take that chance, certainly not after the explicit warning he'd been given by the Deputy Commander himself.

Still, it was very reluctantly that the security chief picked up the phone and pulled the twenty-four-hour rotations that kept watch on Florin's house.

What angered him most was the obvious nature of Florin's deception – obvious to anyone with a bare modicum of intelligence but perhaps not to the bunch of ageing caudillos who refused to stop living in the past.

The Hadley man with his amateur minders in tow was no coincidence, Sierra was certain, and you would have to be naive beyond measure to think the ancient half-escudo coin was anything other than a covert message to the CNI.

If Florin left the country Sierra would have no problem tailing him. Cuban ports and airports were so tightly controlled that no one – especially a high-profile figure like The Aztec – could slip through.

The Yugoslav business, however, was another matter. The trip to Montenegro had come as a surprise and Sierra had been forced to use a second-rate freelancer who had only managed to exacerbate the problem.

A Cuban-born ex-policeman of Macedonian extraction, Sierra's spy had returned to the land of his ancestors when Yugoslavia broke up. He had set himself up as a private investigator in Skopje and offered his services to anyone who could afford his fee. At least he had heeded Sierra's advice to carry false identification and, luckily for Sierra, when he'd botched the job he had managed to get himself killed.

What his death had achieved, however, was to confirm to Sierra that he had definitely been on the right track: Hadley would not have had that sort of armed protection unless he was in Montenegro with official sanction. He had to be in cahoots with Florin.

Add the Spanish woman to the equation – and Sierra

knew that she worked for her government – and there could only be one logical conclusion: The Aztec and the CNI were running a joint operation and the famous missing gold had to be at the heart of it.

Sierra's second operative, the one in Salamanca, had been more successful and had managed to retrieve a full set of Florin's documents. Sierra was going through them when his phone rang.

The caller was one of his informers within the State motor pool: a Niva Roadster, the Russian built four-wheel drive so favoured by government apparatchiks, had been requisitioned by Sergeant Wilson Truenos. The chit requesting two weeks' use of the vehicle stated the purpose as 'personal' and had been authorised by General Florin.

Sierra countermanded his original order. He asked three different vehicles, at one-hour intervals, to pass by Florin's house and a similar number of foot operatives to take a walk along the beach and look for signs of life. By late afternoon all had reported the same findings: the Florin bungalow was deserted.

The Aztec was on the move. Sierra had to find the car. He telephoned his man at the car pool and gave him further instructions: move Florin's requisition chit to a different car, one of the same make and with a similar registration. Then remove the card for Truenos's vehicle and report the car as 'missing'. A simple case of a stolen vehicle. Pass the information to the police, nationwide: do not approach or intervene, simply locate and contact State Security, immediately, day or night.

They would start by checking every airfield and harbour on the island, but it was not until the following morning that they found what Sierra wanted: the dark green Niva was parked close to a remote beach at Barlovento Point, east of the American military enclave at Guantánamo Bay.

The policeman who spotted it behaved as instructed and took no action other than reporting his find to his own chief. He did, however, add his own observation that the car might belong to what looked like a family group picnicking on the beach as there was no one else in sight.

This information reached Sierra within thirty minutes of the policeman's discovery. It was a long way to Guantánamo but he was going to handle this in person. He ordered the local police to keep a watch on the car and report with a description of the people on the beach and, above all, not to lose them.

The city of Guantánamo was five hundred miles from Havana. Sierra had himself driven to Baracoa Beach Air Base where he'd asked for a small aircraft to be made ready. There was an airstrip at Los Caños, north of Barlovento Point, and he could be there within a couple of hours.

As he was about to board his plane further information arrived. The group was made up of six people, two of whom matched Miriam Mercado's and Wilson Truenos's descriptions. But no mention of Florin. For one ghastly instant Sierra considered that this could be a decoy planted by Florin, meant to lead Sierra's forces on a time-consuming wild-goose chase while the wily Aztec slipped away in a different direction. But once again Sierra reminded himself that all ports and airports were covered, that getting out of Cuba was not that simple, that the days of the boat people were over.

During his flight Sierra decided that he would only show his hand if he could establish what Florin was up to. He'd be close by, but he would have to make the approaches seem casual. Anything out of the ordinary would be undoubtedly reported to Florin by his loyal Sergeant Truenos.

The two policemen ambled down to the beach. Three men and three women, they noted, not dangerous they had been told.

Warm greetings were exchanged.

'Is that your car up on the road?' one officer asked, waving his hand back over his shoulder.

'It is,' replied Truenos. 'Any problem?'

'No, none at all.' The policeman was friendly. 'Just a routine check, you know?'

'Sure thing.'

'Would you like some refreshments?' Miriam invited them.

'Thank you.'

Both policemen sat cross-legged and gratefully accepted the beers from Nurse Miriam's cold box. They too were *guantanameros*, like Miriam, and it soon transpired that they knew each others' families.

'Were you not working in Havana?' a policeman asked her.

'I still am,' she replied.

'I heard you worked for Don Raul Castro – is that true?' asked the second officer.

'No.' She smiled, then added proudly, 'My fiancé and I both work for General Florin.'

The policemen were impressed. Whoever at headquarters had suggested that these people might have anything to do with a missing car had obviously got the wrong end of the stick, a view that was only reinforced on learning that Truenos was a serving Sergeant, First Class, in the nation's Revolutionary Army *and* that he and Miriam were Florin's *personal* staff and lived with him near Havana.

'What's he like, The Aztec?'

'Demanding but fair.' Truenos passed judgement.

'Nice of him to let you both go on holiday.'

'He's on holiday too,' Miriam explained. 'That's how we got the car. We had to drop him off in Santa Cruz del Sur along the way.'

'Never been to Santa Cruz,' one of the policemen commented. 'Is it nice?'

'We didn't stop long. General Florin was going fishing with his friend General Ramos. Maybe we'll see a bit more when we return to pick him up.'

They quickly ate some of Miriam's sister's cake and got back on their feet for a round of handshakes before heading back towards the road. The beach was nice but with only a light breeze and not a cloud in sight a bit uncomfortable even for local men when they were in full uniform.

They got back into their vehicle and a kilometre up the road pulled up next to Colonel Sierra's car. He listened to them attentively without betraying any emotion as the two policemen competed to deliver the good news.

He bid them goodbye with a brief thank-you and ordered the driver to take him back to Los Caños.

Martin Ramos. *Another General, yet another Castro crony*, reflected Sierra, *another one of the bloody untouchables.* But Sierra had a file on Ramos too. He might not be approachable, but Ramos had a weak spot: women. They would talk.

Fishing. Ramos had a boat. Sierra was furious. Boat

people. As soon as he reached the airfield he clambered onto the plane.

'Back to Havana, sir?' asked the pilot.

'No. We shall stop first at Santa Cruz.'

26

For the second time Hadley found himself driving The Aztec along unfamiliar roads on a Caribbean island, only this time the island was not Cuba but Jamaica.

The *Tiburón* had arrived just as Florin had said it would. Hadley had recognised The Aztec's upright figure from afar, long before the cabin cruiser pulled up alongside the floating jetty at Sunset Beach.

Florin smiled down at his co-conspirator while General Ramos squeezed the bow thrusters and issued a barrage of orders to three bewildered young women who did their best to drop fenders over the side.

'Hadley.' Florin greeted him effusively as the engines shut down. 'I'd invite you on board for a cold Cristal but I'm afraid we have no time.'

Florin wore jeans and a dark red denim shirt and had slung a small canvas rucksack over his shoulder. His scalp had been protected by a peaked white cap during the sea crossing but Hadley could see the ever-present black beret that would soon replace it tucked into his webbing belt. He looked as if he was ready to jump ashore before the passerelle was lowered. Hadley shook his head in disbelief. Did this man ever tire?

'This is my English friend Hadley,' Florin told his fellow sailors. 'He speaks Spanish – you can say hello!'

Ramos shook hands with Hadley and passed him Florin's only piece of luggage, a soft-sided olive-coloured army kitbag. The girls looked at the dark-haired green-eyed stranger and beamed interested smiles.

'Well, I'm here as you asked, Jesús. What next?'

Hadley had speculated endlessly since The Aztec had summoned him. What was in Jamaica? There were no direct flights between Spain and Jamaica. He had been forced to fly from Madrid to London and catch a Virgin flight to Montego Bay. 'Don't hire a car, Hadley,' Florin had said over the phone. 'We shan't be needing it.'

A Yacht Club employee and a Jamaican official strode up to inspect the vessel's papers and collect a mooring fee. Ramos explained that they would not be staying long and ordered fuel. He conspicuously took from his pocket a large bundle of US dollars – given to him earlier by Florin – suggesting perhaps that the absence of bureaucratic nonsense would be generously recompensed.

Jesús produced his passport – Mexican – and the official gave the photograph a brief glance before returning it with an obsequious 'Thank you, Señor Fernández' that produced a fleeting exchange of amused looks between Ramos and Hadley.

The men shook hands and Florin pecked each girl's cheek

in turn while the club's steward was sent off to order a taxi. A few minutes later Hadley and Florin were on their way to Sangster Airport.

'Do I get to know where we are going?' Hadley enquired lightly.

'Of course, Hadley,' Florin replied jovially, with a cautioning nod towards the driver. 'All in good time. But, as you must realise, a man my age needs to be chaperoned.'

'You should have asked Nurse Miriam to come with you,' Hadley joked.

'Miriam is getting married – did I not tell you?'

'No.'

'She is. To my man Truenos. Good idea. I approve.'

Hadley paid the taxi driver and they entered the busy airport concourse.

'There's a flight to Brussels at nine-thirty,' Florin said casually. 'Buy two Business Class tickets for us.'

'What? I've just come from Europe!'

'I can't travel on my own, Hadley. An old man flying on his own draws attention. They start asking for medical certificates and the like.'

'So who am I travelling with? Señor Fernández?'

'Emiliano Fernández Bueno, *para servirle*.' Florin smiled and handed him the passport. 'Now leave me somewhere where I can get a beer and you go buy the tickets.'

Hadley was gone half an hour. When he returned Florin was on his second Red Stripe.

'They don't sell Cristal here,' he grumbled.

'So why do we need to go to Brussels, Jesús?' Hadley asked, putting up two fingers of one hand and pointing at Florin's empty bottle with the other in a silent message to a laid-back nearby waiter.

'I'll explain once we are airborne. It's a long flight. Now, you tell me about Pinto. I know he has accepted my proposals, but do you believe I can trust him?'

'Trust is a big word, Jesús,' Hadley commented after a moment's reflection. 'But, much as I resent the way that Pinto's sucked me into his games, I think he's straight.'

Florin nodded pensively.

'Provided you are,' added Hadley. 'Are you genuine, Jesús?'

'I haven't lied to you,' replied Jesús, with a smirk. 'I have not necessarily told you everything, but I haven't lied to you yet!'

The charter plane was an old DC10 but the Business Class seats were large and reclined almost horizontally. Florin and Hadley ate lightly and prepared for a night's sleep.

'You were going to tell me why we are going to Brussels,' Hadley reminded The Aztec as Florin asked him to turn off the overhead light.

'Because it is the quickest way from Montego Bay to Kinshasa.'

'Kinshasa? What Kinshasa? In Africa?'

'The easiest way would be on Cubana, of course,' Florin continued, 'from Havana to Kinshasa direct. But then I'd have to show my hand. Can't risk it.'

'Where the hell *is* Kinshasa, anyway?'

'Congo, Hadley. Democratic Republic of the Congo.' He looked at the Englishman who was trying to recall what he knew about the DRC. 'Used to be called Zaire. Belgian Congo in my day.'

'So why are we going there?'

'Because I have friends in Kinshasa who will help me with my mission.'

'How far is Congo from Equatorial Guinea?' Suddenly Hadley had an inkling. 'Surely you are not going to dig up this gold personally? Are you crazy?'

'No, Hadley, I'm going to go there in a borrowed helicopter, collect a passenger and go home.'

'Where do I come into this?'

'I told you, Hadley, I can't travel on my own.'

Nearly twenty years had passed since Florin had last set foot in Africa. As the aircraft door slid open the steamy evening air brought in scents of the jungle, smells and tastes that conjured up turbulent images of bygone times.

A smartly uniformed army captain entered the cabin before anyone was allowed to deplane. He was leading a middle aged African man in a smart silk-woven suit whom he addressed as 'mon général' and, judging by the deference the man was accorded, he was no ordinary Congolese.

Jesús was already on his feet when their gazes met. The African walked directly over to him and locked him in a warm embrace.

'Welcome home,' he whispered into The Aztec's ear. Then he and the captain shook hands with Hadley before all four walked down the steps. A large Mercedes saloon was parked next to the plane. Hadley identified his and Florin's luggage and it was moved directly from the hold into General Massama's car. The captain took the driver's seat and eased the car towards the exit.

There were no formalities, no Customs or Immigration. Men simply saluted as they went through. Thirty minutes later they reached Massama's home in Kinshasa. There had been no debate about where the two visitors would be staying.

It was a large house in the elegant Gombe district, surrounded by extensive gardens and completely enclosed by high walls. The captain excused himself and disappeared from view. Servants in white cotton jackets moved around unobtrusively.

'Is your family well, Bienheuré?' Florin asked as they sat outdoors and took refreshments. The private compound belied the fact that it was within the confines of Africa's second-largest city. The vast Congo River flowed mightily nearby and from its banks you could see the lights of Brazzaville gleaming across the border.

'They are. Three boys and two girls now,' he replied proudly. 'They're with their mother, visiting their grandparents in Kananga. We have the house to ourselves.'

Hadley wondered whether the family had been intentionally removed lest they reminded Jesús of his own.

They spoke briefly of their bush days, mainly for Hadley's benefit, and Massama told war stories as old soldiers do.

'He was a crazy bastard,' he recounted between fits of laughter, 'always trying to get us killed. But he failed, as you can see!'

'I'm not done fighting yet,' said Florin and his famous laugh filled the night.

'I'd be worried now,' Massama too joined in the laughter, 'if I didn't know you were joking.'

'I'm tired.' Jesús stood up. 'Can we talk in the morning, Bienheuré?'

Hadley and Massama remained outside a little longer.

'Do you know what all this is about, Jack?' asked the General.

'Not entirely. I presume you know about the helicopter?'

'I'm providing it.' Massama smiled.

'Then you know more than I do. All Jesús said to me is that we are to fly into Equatorial Guinea, collect a passenger and come back.'

'What's your role, if I may ask?'

'As far as I know' – Hadley shrugged incredulously – 'I'm to keep him company. He says he's too old to travel on his own.'

That made them both laugh.

'Did he say who this passenger might be?'

'No.'

'A *willing* passenger?'

'Oh, hell.' Hadley sat up. 'I had assumed that!'

'He never mentioned anything about cargo, did he?'

'Not to me – why?' Hadley was puzzled by the question.

'May be nothing. But when we spoke he wanted a particular type. It's a big weight lifter.'

'Is that its main attribute?'

'Yes – though range and speed are also pluses.'

Hadley wondered whether The Aztec had it in his mind to recover his gold. '*A long time ago, Hadley, I lost something of great value.*' Had those been Florin's words that day on the beach?

'I don't know. I really don't know,' he said sincerely. 'Perhaps he will let us into his confidence in the morning.'

'Whatever it is,' Massama said as he stood up, 'whatever he wants, he knows – and you should know – you can count on me. Jesús Florin is like my father. He gave me life. *A* life, in any event. So,' Massama smiled, 'it will be my pleasure to help him get whatever it is he's after.'

Over breakfast the next day, Florin laid out his plan. They would launch from Boma, on the narrow strip of land between the former French Congo and Angola, where the Democratic Republic's only shoreline touched the Atlantic coast.

'That's all arranged,' Massama assured him. 'Your helicopter is at Ndolo aerodrome, right here in the city.'

'It needs to be painted like this.' Florin produced a pair of colour photographs from deep inside his rucksack and passed them to his friend.

'We can do that,' Massama said. 'But do you intend to fly into Equatorial Guinea with those markings?'

Jesús nodded. Massama passed the photographs to Hadley who raised his own eyebrows in turn.

'Along the coast or through Gabonese airspace?'

Florin shrugged.

'Better not crash my aircraft outside DRC territory,' Massama warned, 'or they will be an awful lot to explain.'

'If we crash, Bienheuré,' Florin retorted, 'I promise to burn to a cinder or drop deep into the ocean.'

'How reassuring,' was all Hadley could think of saying.

At that moment a telephone rang inside Florin's rucksack. He pulled out an Iridium 9505 Satellite Phone and took the call.

'Jesús?'

'*Malinche?*'

Florin listened silently for a while but he rapidly turned visibly pale. He stood up and walked away from his two friends, speaking in a low voice.

When the conversation ended he continued pacing on Massama's terrace for another ten minutes. He dialled a number and talked on the phone again before finally rejoining his friends who had remained at the breakfast table.

'Is everything all right?' Hadley asked.

'There's been a change of plan.'

'You still need the helicopter?' asked Massama.

'Oh yes, the flight goes ahead as planned. But you, Hadley,' he turned to face the young Englishman squarely, 'you won't be on it.'

'I can't say I'm bitterly disappointed.' Hadley decided to make light of it.

'No, I'm going to need you at the other end. I'll give you one of these,' Florin pointed at the Iridium, 'and send you ahead to Malabo.'

'Malabo?' asked Massama, 'You did say the helicopter would go to Bata?'

'Correct.' Florin was clearly in control

'So what am I doing in Malabo?'

'The crew.' Florin disregarded Hadley's question. 'All black?'

'Yes.'

'I need at least one more white man. You have no white pilots?'

'No.'

'Arabs? Any non-Africans?'

'Not pilots. Why?'

'I need some white faces in that plane. Now that Jack won't be on it.'

'I can give you two Algerians. From an airborne unit, but they can wear flying suits. OK?'

'Thank you.'

'Good. Let's go over the details.'

27

Jorge Abad returned to his office in downtown Malabo, closed his door and asked not to be disturbed. He had just spent an hour in the Spanish embassy attending a pre-arranged meeting with a 'visiting security expert' from Madrid before joining him for lunch.

Since Al Qaeda's attack on the Americans three years earlier, 'national security' and 'anti-terrorist measures' had become bywords with governments worldwide. Officials tasked with security, even those from pariah states like Equatorial Guinea, were suddenly exchanging hitherto well-guarded information and were being invited to participate in all manner of international cooperation schemes.

Following the Atocha Station bombings in March, Madrid had additionally launched a separate initiative within the Spanish-speaking world. It was therefore not surprising that an expert from Madrid should come to Malabo for discussions on the subject, nor that he should ask for a private meeting with Abad himself.

But Abad also knew this was not going to be an ordinary meeting: his daily review of the video cameras at Santa Isabel airport told him that the face that went with the name Arturo Blanes – the so-called expert – belonged to Marcos Vega whose true position was Head of the Africa Section in Spain's CNI.

Blanes's diplomatic passport, of which Abad now had a scanned copy on his desk, was as fresh as it was phoney and if his visit needed to be shrouded in at least a modicum of deception, Abad suspected that the problem of Al Qaeda might be just a cover for a different sort of business to be discussed.

They are coming to me, Abad reasoned. *I wonder what they have in mind?* Had he known from the outset that Vega was coming Abad might have insisted on meeting him at Police HQ where he could have recorded the conversation and had him X-rayed as he entered the building.

With an embassy meeting the tables were turned. Abad would need to be cautious but undoubtedly Vega would expect that. The Guinean was therefore taken by surprise when, after exchanging a few pleasantries and sitting down with his host in a first-floor office, Vega pushed a sheet of paper across his desk and turned it round for him to read.

This room is bugged, the Spaniard had handwritten on it. *Let's chat here for a while and then you can invite me to lunch. We'll talk outside. OK?*

So for the best part of an hour they discussed the independent cells of Al Qaeda sympathisers that had caused mayhem in Madrid and their subsequent death by suicide, as well as intelligence reports suggesting the presence of training camps in Africa and matters concerning the funding of terrorist activities.

When Abad brought up the question of lunch Vega quickly suggested a restaurant close by, one they could walk to despite the equatorial heat. He complained that he spent his life either trapped behind a desk or cooped up in an aeroplane and therefore any opportunity to stretch his legs was very welcome, heat or no heat.

They walked slowly and they talked, Abad in his characteristic lightweight uniform with no embellishments of rank, Vega in a rumpled linen suit and Panama hat.

'There are rumours of an externally driven coup.' Vega was certain that Abad too had heard them. It was safe to bring up the subject.

'There are always rumours.' Abad was dismissive.

'You've heard, then?'

'What I've heard,' Abad dispensed with niceties, 'is that your friend Potro is plotting against my government with your government's agreement.'

'Potro is not our friend, Major. He's anybody's friend. He's for sale. And Madrid's is not the fattest chequebook.'

'Then who?'

'We are concerned that the Americans might be up to their usual shenanigans. Not what Spain would wish.'

'The Americans are well disposed towards our government.'

'The Americans want Equatorial Guinea in their camp. They don't give a damn *who* runs it.'

'Why are you talking to me?' Abad turned to face the Spaniard, 'You should be talking to the Foreign Minister or President Penang.'

'Major Abad, you of all people must understand that President Penang's days are numbered. Please let me finish,' he asked when he saw that Abad was about to interrupt.

'You can only withstand, indeed suppress, *internal* threats. What I'm talking about here is much bigger.'

'Our neighbours would not tolerate an invasion,' Abad argued with some logic. 'They would come to our aid.'

'Of course.' Vega nodded and smiled knowingly. 'They will come in to help you and then take their time leaving. No one walks away on half a million barrels a day.'

'Very well.' Abad thought that the conversation should end. 'I shall report your warning to my Minister and let you know what he says. I shall tell him that Spain came to us in friendship.'

'Thank you for that. You may speak to the Minister if you wish, Major Abad, but you might want to consider another option.'

'Such as?'

'*If* the President was overthrown this country would sink into chaos. That wouldn't suit Spain at all. I imagine it wouldn't suit you either.'

'Go on.'

'Spain's concern is that Equatorial Guinea should not descend into chaos. Consider this, Major Abad: a highly mobile, well-equipped and capable mercenary army carries out a commando raid into Malabo. They kill the President, the Cabinet, a few key people.' He paused before the last phrase and stared into Abad's eyes. He detected no fear, but enough anger to confirm that his target understood the implication.

'Not a tear would be shed, Major, and the world would applaud the passing. But before a new president could be installed – call him Potro, if you wish – the populace goes on the rampage.'

Vega accepted a cigarette from the Guinean who put

one between his own lips before lighting the Spaniard's. *Mercenaries*, Abad was thinking, *just like Francisco Asuse had confessed.*

'Usual round of statue-toppling and shoplifting follows,' Vega continued. 'No big deal so far, just what you'd expect, dancing in the streets and all that. Except for one small detail.' Vega paused. 'With me so far?'

'Please continue.'

'Oil, Major. Twenty-five million dollars a day gushing out of the Zafiro, Ceiba and Alba fields, their previous owner dead and the new landlord not yet in situ.

'Hell, Major,' Vega laughed, 'Exxon and Mobil wouldn't even know who they should be taking care of!'

'Are you saying to me that Spain supports a change?'

'I'm saying that a European-led future would be more beneficial to Equatorial Guinea than any American initiative that – like everything else they do in Africa – is certain to end in tears.'

Not just in Africa, thought Abad. Years ago he had placed his trust in the CIA and carried out their dirty work as asked but when the time came to accept responsibilities they had disowned him.

Abad had for some time been concerned about the Americanisation of Equatorial Guinea, though he did not tell Vega. He had already made up his mind that if the country opened up the way Penang and Bush were suggesting it should, he might as well look for a life elsewhere.

'So what do you want, Vega?' he asked bluntly.

'Stay in place. Work with the new president. Keep your security apparatus intact and therefore the peace in Equatorial Guinea. A smooth transition of power with just the Penang clan taken out. Like you did with "The Only Miracle".

The oil will flow unimpeded and the building contracts will be undertaken by Spaniards and Guineans, not Yanks.'

'I'd want guarantees,' Abad demanded. 'In writing. Top-level. If anything goes wrong the world press gets to see your attempt to interfere in our affairs.'

'You'll have them.'

'And payment. In advance.'

'We'll put a hundred thousand euros into any bank account you wish. Today.'

'A million.' They had reached the restaurant. Abad stopped by the entrance and waited for an answer.

'I would need to refer that.' Vega had expected the bastard to get greedy.

'A million or no deal.' Abad appeared inflexible.

'OK, a million it is. Half today, half when the new president is sworn in. You can have it in writing. After lunch.'

They shook hands and entered the restaurant. Vega went to the lavatory and switched off his tape recorder. It was the very latest technology. Miniature stuff.

Ever since his discovery in Guantánamo, Aquiles Sierra had been trying to establish where the *Tiburón* had been. She had sailed from Santa Cruz and turned east, following the coast. Beyond that nobody could say. Sierra had checked the obvious ports in south and eastern Cuba but there was no record of her so he had posted a team in Santa Cruz and was left with no option but to wait.

Martin Ramos intended to do as Jesús had asked of him, sailing east to round the tip of Cuba before retracing his route back towards Santa Cruz. But on the trip back from Jamaica, Teresa became ill. Initially the General put it down to overindulgence with food and drink but after two days it became clear that the girl was seriously seasick. Even slowing down or allowing the boat to drift gently with its engines idling did little to improve her condition.

So Ramos elected to cut the voyage short. He was conscious of Florin's request that he should stay away for five days, but three and a half would have to do. He would lie low for the next forty-eight hours just in case and if anyone came round to the house asking questions Ramos would tell them where to go. Not many people in Cuba would wish to take on General Ramos.

But the girls were a different matter altogether. Sierra chose which one to target. His assigned interrogator met her on her way to market, ordered her into a patrol car and drove her in terrifying silence to a remote police station.

'Do you know it is a crime to leave the country without permission?' the interrogator asked bluntly in a manner that suggested the dire consequences of such an action.

'I didn't know,' she blurted out, on the verge of tears. 'I didn't know where we were going. It was fishing, that's what the others said. It was Lucrecia who told me, I swear.'

'You wouldn't lie to me, would you, Teresa?'

'No, sir, I swear.'

'Did you go ashore?' he asked without looking at her, making notes as he spoke.

'No sir, I stayed on the boat, the others can tell you. It's the truth.'

'Who were the others, Teresa?'

The interrogator sensed her hesitation and looked up from his writing, delivering a blazing stare that evaporated all resistance.

'It was me and Lucrecia and Magdalena, sir. Nobody else.'

'Just you three and the generals? Is that right?' He looked at her questioningly, yet implying that he already knew the answer.

'Yes, sir, General Ramos and General Florin.'

'Well, as you know, Generals Ramos and Florin are two of our most illustrious heroes. We certainly do not wish to upset them.'

'No, sir.' Teresa seemed relieved.

'Or to annoy them with tales of young ladies on their boat who go abroad without the right papers and visas, right?'

'No, sir. No.'

'Good.' The interrogator stood up. 'We shall take this matter no further.' He watched her smile. 'And we shall keep this conversation between you and me. Agreed?'

'Yes, sir.' Teresa did not need much persuading.

'Let me walk you to the car.' He talked to her as a friendly uncle might. 'My driver will drop you close to home.'

'Thank you, sir.'

'Do you remember the name of the place where you left General Florin?'

'It was Jamaica, sir – they spoke English there.'

'I know it was Jamaica,' he lied. 'I meant the name of the port?'

'I think they called it Montego.'

'And who came to meet the General?'

'I don't remember his name, sir. He was English, they said, but he spoke in Spanish. And he was very good-looking and knew General Florin, I think.'

'Good girl.' The interrogator held the car door open for her. 'Perhaps you should decline the next invitation to visit

General Ramos.' He looked menacingly into her eyes. 'Yes, I think that would be a good idea. Let another girl go instead.'

He closed the passenger door firmly and turned sharply on his heel. Colonel Sierra would be pleased.

Hadley did not know what to expect in Malabo. He had never given Equatorial Guinea much thought. Florin's words about his mission did not do much to assuage any fears he might have had.

The country was made up of two main parts: the island of Bioko which contained the capital, Malabo, twenty miles off the Cameroon coast, and a mainland region three hundred and fifty miles further south along the coast.

Hadley had only just become aware of the country's oil wealth and as they approached Santa Isabel airport he peered through the aircraft window, trying to study the lay of the land.

There seemed to be a mix of the old and the new – the old being neither historical nor traditional but just that: old, plain buildings erected during the pre-independence 1950s that had been followed by years of abandonment until the oil arrived. 'New' meant showcase projects: the ministries and palaces and the grand houses of the very rich.

It had taken Hadley all day to get there from Kinshasa. First he'd had to go by road and ferry to Brazzaville, then fly to Libreville in Gabon where he could finally get a plane to Malabo. Both his flights had been delayed and all three airports were chaotic so he was pleasantly surprised to discover that the planes at least were modern and of Western manufacture.

But the convoluted journey had given him time to

reappraise the task ahead and to question the wisdom of accepting it. After the disturbing phone call from *Malinche* – Florin had refused to tell him or Massama who *Malinche* was – Florin had been forced to, as he put it, reassign the deployment of his assets.

'I'm one lieutenant down in Malabo, Hadley,' he announced. Then he added unflatteringly, 'You are all I have to fill the slot.'

Florin went over what was about to unfold, much of which Hadley already knew. Massama, who had never demanded explanations from his friend, listened in attentive fascination. It had been a long time since white soldiers of fortune had played any sort of part in the fragile world of black African politics. Hired armies were now made up of local boys – cheaper, tougher, hungrier and ten times more determined.

'The harsh reality,' Florin assured them, 'is that this idiotic amateur intervention is going to fail. The greedy fools who backed it will lose every penny they've put up or borrowed and the actual perpetrators will either die on the spot or spend the rest of their days festering in the world's filthiest jails.'

'So,' Hadley thought of his last visit to CNI headquarters, 'poor old Captain Pinto's not going to get his gold!'

'Gold?' Massama latched onto the hypnotic word immediately and even Florin laughed. 'You never told me there was gold in this!'

'Gold has nothing to do with you, *polisson*.' He addressed Massama first, then turned to Hadley. 'And Pinto will get his share no matter what happens – I gave my word.'

'And Spain? Pinto is backing Potro at your behest . . . Shit, Jesús, you got me to go back to Pinto . . .'

'Spain too will come out of this on the winning side,' Florin cut in. He was no longer joking as he spoke now. 'I gave my word too in that respect, to someone far more worthy than Captain Pinto.'

'Who would that be?' Hadley wanted to know. 'I'm supposed to be writing your biography, remember?'

'Which reminds me.' Florin delved yet again into his rucksack. 'Here's all you'll need.'

He handed Hadley a wad of US dollars – 'Expensive place, Malabo,' he said – and a plain white envelope. A name and address in Luxembourg were written on the outside. Hadley felt the envelope: it contained something hard.

'There's a key and a code. I should keep the two apart until you are ready to use them. Together they open a safe deposit box. Everything you need to know to complete my memoirs is inside it. There's only one chapter missing. You'll have to work it out for yourself. It starts on the day you first came to me in Cuba.'

'And when does it end?'

'In a couple of days.'

Hadley took an overpriced taxi from Santa Isabel for the ten-minute drive to the only passable hotel in Malabo. It had once been an eighteenth-century cloister of traditional colonial architecture, now sympathetically converted into a semi-luxury hotel by a French chain.

Tourism, concluded Hadley as he registered for his € 500-a-night stay, was evidently not encouraged in Malabo. He went to his room and phoned Mercedes to tell her his whereabouts and reassure her that the plan was still to be home within the week.

'Ramiro is being a magnificent host,' she said. 'He's even taken time off work to keep me company.'

'Send him my best wishes – and say thank you for me, too.'

'Will do. Hurry home.'

'Did you get anywhere with Inspector Rueda?'

'Yes, I forgot to tell you. I pointed out three people I'd never seen before. They may be quite innocent, he said, but he'll check them out.'

'OK. I'll call you again tomorrow.'

'Where are you staying?'

'Sofitel Malabo.' He gave her the telephone number.

Hadley turned on the shower and undressed. He saw his tired face in the mirror and wondered in amazement how Florin could keep up. He also noticed the brass key, its stem hanging next to the golden St Christopher medallion round his neck. He had e-mailed the Luxembourg address and code number to himself from Massama's home.

Next he needed to make contact with Jorge Abad. He hoped that Florin's assessment was right.

Abad, however, was already looking into Hadley. The passport scan had come in from the airport. An unknown Briton, claiming to be on holiday, staying three days. In from Kinshasa via Gabon. A mercenary scout? A spy, perhaps? Enough unanswered questions to warrant a closer look.

The Aztec's day of reckoning started shortly before sunset when the well-worn Boeing 727 of early 1970s vintage with a freelance Egyptian three-man crew took off from a remote airfield in southern Africa, bound for Lusaka International Airport in the Zambia.

The aircraft, sporting service records dubious enough

to deny it entry into most of the world's airways, was registered in Cameroon, the flag of convenience for planes too tired to meet international standards.

This particular plane, however, was not going to stray outside sub-Saharan Africa and its passengers were not too concerned with safety standards.

All one hundred of them, in civilian clothes and carrying hand baggage, would await the aircraft's arrival in Lusaka where they would clamber aboard for a thirty-minute hop to neighbouring Zimbabwe.

In that country's capital, Harare, they would load onto the 727 a cargo of weapons and ammunition that was awaiting their inspection and acceptance, a consignment safely packed and tucked away behind a wall of greenback bribery.

At one-thirty the following morning the 727 would set off on the final leg of its outbound journey, a two-thousand-mile flight to Malabo, where the mercenary army intended to take over Equatorial Guinea.

The men, mostly white, were a mixture of Europeans and South Africans, all with solid and wide-ranging military experience and equally well versed in the intricacies of African warfare. Their cocksure attitude towards their mission, on the other hand, might have suggested they were less well informed about the realities of African politics.

As the Boeing lifted off the runway in Lusaka, its ancient non-bypass turbines thundered unconcernedly through the ominous calm of the African night. The plane's occupants cheered and uttered battle cries as the wheels left the tarmac, ritually boosting their spirits, their bullishness encouraged by their commanders' understanding smiles.

The waiting was over: the time had come to collect their

tools of trade, get down to business, savour the intoxicating taste of victory and go home with a generous, well-earned reward.

At a dirt strip near Yaoundé in the Republic of Cameroon, a second aircraft – a smaller Soviet-built Antonov 24 that had served with the Angolan air force in the late 1960s – was being prepared.

It would carry an advance party of twenty-five mercenaries tasked with securing Santa Isabel airport in Malabo and holding it for a couple of hours until their comrades in the Boeing arrived. The Antonov would need to set off at three in the morning in order to reach Equatorial Guinea's capital by four.

There was a third plane involved, a modern and luxurious private jet loaned by an enterprising Spanish businessman to Equatorial Guinea's next president.

Celestino Potro and three of his Cabinet Ministers designate – Defence, Finance and Mineral Resources – together with the jet owner's watchful agent, were scheduled to depart Geneva airport at six-thirty in the morning, receive radio confirmation by nine that the *coup d'état* had been successful and land in Malabo at noon when President Potro would deplane wearing the mantle of the nation's saviour and deliver an elevating speech replete with promises before stepping into Penang's – hopefully by then the *late* Penang's – vacant shoes.

Florin's own journey would begin from another airfield, this time one in the northern outskirts of Boma, the riverside former capital of the Belgian Congo. Boma was now a city of half a million people, twenty miles east of where the mighty river that once separated the French from the Belgians poured itself into the Atlantic Ocean.

The Mil-17 had been painted to Florin's requirements and positioned to Boma the day before. Though the helicopter might not have passed muster at an Armada inspection, the blue fuselage with its white lettering and gold insignia was unquestionably up to the job.

Florin too had travelled to Boma the previous day. With his friend Bienheuré Massama and accompanied by two Algerian paratroopers serving in the Congolese army who had been ordered to guard Florin with their lives, he had been driven 180 miles in the big Mercedes. With a heavy heart, Florin watched the scars left along the country's main highway by the Second Congo War.

'Are you sure you don't want me to ride with you, Jesús?' Massama offered yet again.

'You can't, Bienheuré.' Florin shook his head. 'If you were caught or killed in Guinea it would create an explosive international situation. I wouldn't dare go home!'

'We've created plenty of those before,' Massama laughed. 'Why worry now!'

'Still a wild child,' Florin teased him. 'But in this instance I must say no. Thank you all the same. I'm sure your troopers here will take good care of me.'

'They will, Jesús. I assure you that they will.'

28

Mercedes sat on the terrace soaking up the remains of the day's sun as Ramiro busied himself in the kitchen. From her vantage point she could look over Treaty House's tiled roof and admire the pale brick buildings of Tordesillas.

'Heard anything from Rosa lately?' she asked casually, raising her voice sufficiently for Ramiro to hear her through the open sliding doors.

'Not a word,' he replied, not quite managing to conceal a measure of displeasure. 'Let's give her a ring.'

'You phone her,' suggested Mercedes. 'At least she might take *your* call.'

'What nonsense,' protested Ramiro.

He came onto the terrace carrying a chilled bottle of Finca Dofí and a plate of his finest olives. He topped up their glasses and sat down beside Mercedes on the brightly cushioned cane sofa.

'She has successfully avoided me since February, Ramiro.'

The Aztec

Mercedes was quite categorical. 'I see no reason why she might alter her behaviour now.'

'Did something that I should know about transpire between you two?' Ramiro sounded genuinely alarmed.

Mercedes pondered the question that conjured up all manner of mixed feelings – from the genuine instant rapport she had shared with Rosa on Friday the thirteenth to her misgivings about Pinto's murky world.

'I don't know,' she answered sincerely. 'I don't think I've quite fathomed your dear cousin.'

'She's really one of the nicest people on earth,' said Ramiro as if he was speaking to himself.

Mercedes was surprised by the transparency of his statement. She had always perceived Ramiro as a somewhat shallow man. Great fun, for sure, and an unquestionably generous and loyal friend too, but perhaps a little frivolous – comic, even – a product of his class, a throwback to a bygone era.

She and Jack had at times wondered whether Ramiro was gay and the short-lived occasional relationships with girlfriends a contrived decoy, but then there were no male friends to be singled out either. Perhaps, they'd concluded, he was more asexual than anything else: a content and self-sufficient man.

Ramiro extracted a cellphone from his shirt pocket and pressed two keys.

'It's ringing for you,' he said, smiling as he passed Mercedes the phone.

'*Dígame.*' The voice that answered was not Rosa's. A housemaid, perhaps, guessed Mercedes.

'Mrs Uribe, please.'

'Mrs Uribe is not here.' Mercedes perceived an unexpected tension in the voice. 'Who is calling, please?'

'Mercedes Vilanova. Do you know when she might be back?' Again the pregnant silence.

'One moment, please,' Mercedes demanded, then quickly passed the phone back to Ramiro. 'She's not there,' she said, 'or else she's still avoiding me.'

'Ramiro de la Serna. Who am I speaking to?'

'Ah! Don Ramiro.' The woman seemed relieved by the sound of a familiar voice.

'Oh, Don Ramiro.' Her tone of voice changed. '*La señora* is not well, Don Ramiro – they've taken her to hospital.'

'Isabel?' He recognised the maid's voice. 'Is Dr Max there?'

'He's with *la señora*, Don Ramiro.' The poor woman seemed on the verge of tears. 'Oh, she is not at all well, Don Ramiro.'

'Where have they taken her?' Ramiro asked as Mercedes looked on in puzzlement.

'What's happening?' Mercedes became concerned as she saw the expression on Ramiro's face.

'It's Rosa,' he exclaimed. 'She's ill again – they've taken her to hospital.' Then he jumped to his feet. 'I must go to her, right now!'

'I'll take you . . .'

'No, no, I must go straight away! I'll take the train.'

'I'll drive you, Ramiro.' Mercedes stood up and took his arm. 'I want to see her too.'

Mercedes managed to reach Madrid before dark, pushing the Porsche hard, well above permitted speed limits. Ramiro, who ordinarily might have protested, was submerged in thought and took no notice.

They parked next to the modern building that housed

the Anderson Complex and walked into the hospital's serene reception area.

'Mrs Uribe cannot have visitors at this time,' a polite but firm nurse explained. 'Perhaps if you could take a seat while I make enquiries. Are you family?'

'I am. Ramiro de la Serna. This is Miss Vilanova, a very close friend.'

The nurse walked away purposefully down a long corridor before turning left and disappearing from view.

'This is a cancer centre, isn't it?' Mercedes asked.

'I think so,' replied Ramiro, looking around the hall. No matter how welcoming or luxurious these places were made to look they still failed to conceal an undercurrent of pain.

'Was that why she had the hysterectomy? You told us about it, remember?'

Before Ramiro could answer Máximo Uribe approached them from the direction in which the nurse had gone. He looked exhausted and his bloodshot eyes evinced he had been crying.

'Ramiro,' he said, as his wife's cousin stood up and hugged him.

'Do you know Mercedes?' Ramiro made the introduction and their gazes met. Mercedes sensed that Rosa's husband knew something about her.

'She's not well,' Max lamented, 'really not well. But she wants to see you.' Max looked briefly at Mercedes as he spoke but quickly corrected his faux pas by smiling at Ramiro and gesturing for him to lead the way.

Rosa lay supine on a narrow surgical bed. Her face was shockingly pale but the pallor could not quite manage to suppress the striking features of the beautiful woman that she was. She breathed slowly with her eyes closed. A tube delivered oxygen to her nostrils from a pair of bedside tanks. Two long cannulas ending in needles descended from clear plastic bags hung on hooks next to her bed and disappeared under taped gauze on the back of her left hand while space-age devices bleeped and painted sinusoidal patterns on a cathode tube.

Max pulled up a chair close to Rosa's bed and invited Mercedes to sit down. Ramiro stared silently at his cousin as a tear rolled down his cheek.

Max whispered something into Rosa's ear and she opened her eyes slowly. She gave her husband a faint smile and turned to Mercedes.

'Are you all right?' She barely managed the words, still weary from the effects of anaesthesia.

'Of course I am.' Mercedes touched Rosa's arm gently. 'It's you that needs to get better.'

Rosa smiled and closed her eyes again.

'There's so much I need to tell you,' she whispered.

'Not now, darling. Just rest.'

'Where's Jack?' she asked, eyes still closed.

'With Florin again,' Mercedes replied casually. 'He's obsessed with his research for The Aztec's memoirs. He called last night.'

Rosa opened her eyes wide.

'Where? Where did he go?' Her voice came out hoarsely and she looked pleadingly at Mercedes.

Fear had suddenly appeared in Rosa's eyes and it was not on account of her illness.

'He's in Africa now, a place called Malabo. He said it's a dump!' Mercedes tried to make light of it.

'Tell him to come back,' Rosa said with dread in her voice. 'Tell him to come home now. Please, Mercedes.'

'Is he in danger?' Mercedes looked at Max and Ramiro for reassurance.

'I don't know. Just don't let him stay there.'

The monitoring machine's graphics changed shape as Rosa's pulse picked up. The bleep turned into an alarm and a nurse rushed into the room, followed closely by a duty doctor.

'Everyone outside, please.' The doctor was firm, adjusting a surgical mask over her face.

'Max!' Rosa called out.

'You must leave now.' The nurse repeated the doctor's order. 'I'll let you know the moment the doctor has finished, Mr Uribe,' she added.

'Tell me, darling, anything you want.' Máximo Uribe ignored the others and took Rosa's hand.

'Get Captain Pinto. I must speak to Pinto. Please!' Rosa implored.

'Pinto?' Max was surprised.

'Yes, get him now.'

'Please, you must wait outside. I need to examine Mrs Uribe,' the doctor said as she prepared additional sedation. The nurse ushered the visitors towards the door.

They stood in stunned silence in the corridor.

'What is going on here?' Only deeply rooted good manners prevented Max from venting his anger. 'What's between this Jack of yours and Roberto Pinto?'

'I'm not sure.' Mercedes met his stare. 'All I know is that Pinto has been forcing Jack to spy on Jesús Florin. Jack only wanted to interview him for a book.'

'So why should my wife want to see that ghastly man as she hovers between life and death?' he exclaimed.

'I'm sorry, Max.' Mercedes spoke softly. 'We don't even

know what's wrong with Rosa . . . we only just heard she was here . . .' She broke off, evidently distraught.

'She had exploratory surgery this morning,' Max explained. 'They closed her up. It's not good. Metastases . . . it's every-where.'

Max was also finding this too emotional; Ramiro took an involuntary deep breath.

'I'm so sorry, Max,' Mercedes said.

'Why does she want Pinto? Do you know?' Max insisted.

'Does . . .' Mercedes chose her words carefully. 'Does Rosa work for Pinto, Max?'

He thought about it for an instant, then nodded.

'You'd better do as she asks, Max, please. I don't know any more than you do. But we all trust Rosa. She must have a reason and I think Jack might be in danger. Excuse me now.'

With that Mercedes walked rapidly towards the exit. Once outside she switched her phone back on and dialled her father's number.

'Dad? I need your help,' she said, trying to sound calm. 'I think Jack is in trouble. I must go to him. Please help me.'

'Where's Jack?'

'In Africa. Equatorial Guinea, I think,' she added, suddenly remembering where Malabo was.

'And where are you?'

'In Madrid.'

Luis Vilanova fell silent for an instant.

'Go to Cuatro Vientos,' he told her. 'I'll be there in two hours. I'll call you from the plane.'

Shortly before four a.m. the chartered Boeing's captain radioed Harare Tower and requested engine start-up. It was uncomfortably hot and muggy inside the aircraft even at this hour of night. Ten minutes later he called for taxi clearance but was told to stand by.

It was already after two in the morning in Malabo. The mercenaries were running half an hour behind schedule and they still had a four-and-a-half-hour flight ahead. The hundred men – ninety-nine, in fact, as one had been carted off to hospital in Lusaka with suspected appendicitis – had finished loading their cargo. Most of the weapons and ammunition were of necessity in the aircraft's hold, but they had managed to secrete several pistols and hand grenades in the cabin inside two catering trolleys. Once in the air they would shed their civilian clothes and dress like soldiers.

After five minutes waiting and burning fuel, an impatient captain enquired about the reason for the delay but once again he was ordered to stand by. There were no other aircraft in radio contact or manoeuvring on the ground. Captain Al Swami was about to demand an explanation for the hold-up when the ramp lighting was suddenly turned on full and a convoy of military vehicles entered the apron and encircled his plane.

An hour earlier, President Mugabe had been woken up by a call made to his private line by his counterpart in Luanda.

The Angolan president apologised for disturbing his 'dear friend Robert' in the middle of the night but, he explained, a grave matter which needed urgent and decisive intervention had just been brought to his attention.

Thanks to intelligence supplied by the Spanish Government who had in turn asked him to alert his good friend immediately, he had learned that an aircraft full of mercenaries, weapons and a fair amount of cash was at that very moment preparing to leave Harare to spearhead a *coup d'état* in Equatorial Guinea.

The mercenaries were white men, mostly Britons and South Africans, working for multinational paymasters. The Angolan president was certain that the African people could count on the great Zimbabwean leader to stamp out this intolerable and arrogant effrontery which was nothing short of a cynical attempt to return to colonialism.

Mugabe listened patiently and got out of bed, suddenly fully awake, as the significance of the information he'd been given sank in. He assured the Angolan president that Zimbabwe could not and would not tolerate this violation of her sovereignty and then he excused himself as he would need to act immediately.

He put on a dressing gown and ran out of his bedroom, barking orders and ignoring his wife's questions. This was a godsend. Not only would he have a chance to strike back at the British by parading their mercenaries in chains through Harare's streets but in the morning he would be able to telephone one of the wealthiest men in Africa and inform him that he, Robert Mugabe, had just stamped out a plot by powerful foreign factions to invade Equatorial Guinea, murder him and his family and seize his country's oil wealth.

He would promise to obtain more information once the captives had been questioned. He wasn't sure what Spain expected to get out of this but that was not the issue: Mugabe could still announce that he was acting against British imperialism in response to Spain's and Angola's pleas – living proof that Zimbabwe was still very much a respected player in the international political arena.

The Angolan president hung up the phone with satisfaction. He knew that Mugabe would do what was expected of him admirably. For forty years, the president recalled, Jesús Florin had been a good friend. They'd fought side by side in the years of the Movement and he'd enjoyed Jesús's support – even after he had left Africa – all the way to Independence. Until now, The Aztec had never asked for anything in return.

When he'd phoned so unexpectedly – from Bienheuré Massama's house in Kinshasa of all places – the President was as delighted as he was surprised. Of course he would do as asked! And do it personally! Twenty-five years as President might have hardened him and taught him to play politics. But not when it came to Florin's friendship.

Earlier that night Pinto had arrived at the Anderson Clinic in a flustered state. He had received the message to go there immediately. He did not know the nature of Rosa's illness. It was Victoria who had told him that Max's wife had been taken into hospital for some sort of cancer tests.

The last time Pinto had seen Rosa she had admitted to being unwell but he had put it down to exhaustion or some minor ailment.

The Pintos and the Uribes were acquainted, but were not friends. On learning of Rosa's hospitalisation he had sent flowers and get-well wishes, but had signed the card 'Roberto and Victoria'. The Deputy Head of CNI did not make a habit of appearing in public with his clandestine operatives.

So when Rosa's husband phoned to say that despite her serious condition she needed to see him urgently, Pinto knew it would be something serious. He had been in Bilbao at the time and did not get back to Madrid till late that night.

An eerie calm reigned in the clinic as he entered it but as soon as he gave his name to the somnolent receptionist she jumped to her feet and acknowledged that the Captain was expected.

Rosa was asleep in her darkened room. Her husband sat by her bed, holding her right hand as a nurse read the monitoring devices and copied figures onto Rosa's chart. Max looked at Pinto with unconcealed distaste as he was ushered in.

'You can't wake her now.' The nurse was unyielding.

'I can wait,' Pinto replied promptly while Max hesitated.

'She said she had to speak to you,' Max whispered. 'Very urgently. I don't know why.'

'Max.' Pinto measured his words. 'I don't expect you to trust me or even accept that I've always had the highest possible esteem and respect for your wife. I apologise for intruding upon your privacy. The only thing I can say, *must* say, is that if Rosa has sent for me in these circumstances she must believe there's something urgent that I have to know. So, with your permission, I'll stay here until I can talk to her.'

Max looked at the nurse who shook her head.

'As I said,' Pinto repeated, 'I'll wait. As long as it takes.'

They pulled up another chair for Pinto and both men sat down.

'What . . .' Pinto ventured. 'Did anything happen yesterday that made Rosa send for me?'

'I'm not sure. Rosa's cousin Ramiro and Mercedes Vilanova were here at the time. Do you know them?'

'I know Mercedes.'

'They were talking about her boyfriend Jack.'

'What about him?' Pinto tried not to sound alarmed.

'Something about him being in Africa. Malabo, I believe they said.'

Pinto looked instinctively at his watch. Ten to one. There was time. If she was still asleep by two-thirty he would need to have her woken up, but there was no need to announce that yet.

'Let's wait,' said Pinto, settling back into his chair and folding his arms.

The Vilanova Taronger Citation jet put down gently at Tenerife's Reina Sofía airport and requested food, water and full tanks.

Three hours earlier Mercedes had sat eating a sandwich in Cuatro Vientos airfield's cafeteria. Downtown Madrid, five miles away, glowed brightly to the east. She wondered how her father would react. Luis Vilanova had warned them more than once not to get involved with Florin and now she would have to ask his help to extract Jack from some awful situation.

But Rosa's words had terrified her and her father was the only person she could turn to for advice. '*Tell him to come home right now*,' was what she'd said, but the frightened look in her eyes had been more eloquent.

Mercedes's spirits brightened when she spotted the distinctive orange markings on her father's plane as it entered the parking area. The engines had not quite stopped when the front door opened and Vilanova stepped out. He saw her on the terrace and waved, then spoke to his captain through the jet's open door before entering the terminal.

'Tell me again, from the beginning,' he told his daughter after she finished relating the day's events. Mercedes told him about Hadley's trip – supposedly to Cuba – his call from Africa announcing the change of plans, and Rosa's warning.

315

'Have you tried calling Jack tonight?'

'I have. His cellular phone has no signal. And the hotel says he's out.'

'When did you last call?'

'An hour ago – I left a message.'

'Give me the number.'

Vilanova called the Sofitel and spoke to the receptionist. From him he learned that Hadley had been in the hotel most of the day – the receptionist had seen him by the pool in the early evening and leaving the restaurant at ten. But he insisted that Mr Hadley had gone out after dinner and had not yet returned. That was what he'd been told to say.

'You are worried, right?' he asked Mercedes after hanging up. In another place, Vilanova reasoned, Jack Hadley might have gone out for a drink, a show, a night-club, whatever a bored man did when travelling on his own. But in Malabo? The only place – as well as the safest – to be in Malabo at night was his hotel. What was Jack up to?

'I'm very scared, Dad. It was the way Rosa said it.'

'OK.' Vilanova smiled at his daughter. 'Let's go fetch him.'

'Now?' Mercedes had been unprepared for that.

'It's past midnight. No point phoning consulates and the like at this time. I've nothing pressing tomorrow – let's go to Equatorial Guinea.'

Vilanova summoned his captain and told him his intentions. They would have to refuel along the way, so they opted for Tenerife as the simplest option. Just a flight plan to be filed, no Customs or formalities for a domestic flight – the Canaries were in Spain.

It was three in the morning and they called Hadley's hotel again with the same result as earlier. Now Vilanova himself was growing concerned.

They waited until the Citation was ready and boarded again. They should reach Malabo by seven a.m.

29

Close to three in the morning Pinto decided that he could wait no longer. The nurse protested but Max remembered his wife's pleading look and backed Pinto's request.

Rosa managed a pained smile and asked for a drink. The men looked on quietly as she sipped slowly through a straw. She asked to be propped up slightly and grimaced as the nurse used the control. She closed her eyes for a moment before speaking.

'Roberto,' she addressed Pinto. 'The Malabo coup will fail.'

Pinto looked on impassively.

'Please, don't let Jack Hadley be killed for no reason.'

'What's Hadley got to do with this, Rosa?'

'Florin sent him in my place. *I* was supposed to be in Malabo.'

Pinto's face betrayed no emotions even though Rosa was effectively telling him that she had a master other than him.

'Do you work for the Cubans?'

'No.' She shook her head almost imperceptibly and smiled.

'So what would you be doing in Malabo?'

'Telling Abad that the game was up and that Spain would spirit him to safety.'

'On whose authority?' Pinto almost raised his voice.

'Are you sure you want to continue?' A concerned Max took his wife's hand and looked fiercely at Pinto.

'Yes, my love, I must.' She squeezed his hand with what little strength she had left.

'Nobody's authority. It's a personal issue. Florin wants Abad. He'll get him out of the country.'

'And you betrayed your country for Florin?'

'On the contrary.' Rosa spoke slowly but with remarkable clarity despite the morphine, 'The plot was doomed to fail from the outset. The mercenaries will never get past Zimbabwe. Florin is about to save the day for you. He only wants Abad. Spain will take the credit for the coup's failure.'

'How?'

'Three presidents will tell Penang tomorrow.'

'And Hadley?'

'He's trying to do my job. Get Abad away. I fear Abad will see through him and kill him.'

'And you think *you* could have done it?'

'I'm a diplomat, Roberto. I work from the Embassy. If I told Abad that a Navy helicopter would pick him up he'd believe me. He'd have no choice once the coup went down.'

Pinto didn't ask where the Navy helicopter would come from.

'What do you expect from me?' Pinto did not mean to sound blunt but time was running out. If indeed the plane was to be detained in Harare, he would find out any minute now.

'Get Marcos Vega to do it. Hide Hadley in the Embassy and get Vega to send Abad to his pickup in Bata.'

Rosa closed her eyes for a moment, took a few short breaths and sipped some more water.

'I'm dying, Roberto. You have to believe what I say.'

'Don't talk like that, darling.' Max's voice was breaking. He turned to Pinto, 'I think that's enough.'

'I'll try,' Pinto told her and promptly left the room.

After dinner Hadley had gone to his room, lain down on the bed and switched on the television. He placed his phone next to him and thought about the task ahead.

He had a photo, two addresses and three phone numbers for Jorge Abad. He would try to contact him around midnight. Hadley admitted he was nervous. In the short time he had been in Malabo the place had given him the creeps. Even the contorted branches of the silk-cotton trees looked menacing.

Flags, anthems, slogans, pictures of the great man himself were everywhere. It seemed as if all tyrants adhered to an international code. It didn't matter where you looked: Baghdad, Pyongyang, Rangoon, the faces and languages were different, but the messages were always the same.

'Don't fret,' Florin had said in Kinshasa. 'He'll be jittery as hell. Any message from a foreigner on the night will get his immediate attention. Just be sure you are with him when the news comes from Harare.'

Hadley had been told not to approach the man too early: the longer Abad was able to ask questions the greater the risk of a slip-up.

'We've already made him rich with Pinto's money, Hadley, and rich people like to live. You'll simply need to convince him that if he wants to enjoy his money he'll need to run.'

Florin made it sound simple enough. '*If the coup fails, the conspirators will talk. They have Abad's name as their contact in Malabo, the man who'll keep the locals in line. If Abad stays put, his liver could be destined for Penang's dinner table.*'

'Tell him that Spain looks after her own – but she can't waltz into Malabo in the middle of the turmoil.

'If Abad can get to Bata – and that should not prove too difficult for the country's top policeman – the Spanish Navy will pull him out.'

A propaganda feature extolling Dorito Penang's many virtues caught Hadley's eye and he watched with mild amusement. The thirty-three-year-old heir apparent was known around the world for his excesses, and at home for his murderous disposition. The programme makers extolled his many virtues, which was not surprising as Dorito was Director General of state television.

There was a knock on Hadley's door. He ambled towards it absentmindedly, keeping one eye still on the TV. Two uniformed policemen stood outside and they looked like they meant business.

'You come with us,' the taller one said, clearly unaccustomed to giving explanations. Hadley gathered up his wallet, passport and cellphone under their watchful gaze and followed the officers down the stairs. A third policeman was talking to the receptionist.

They did not go to police headquarters in the city as Hadley had anticipated. They drove instead to a northerly suburb and into the single-storeyed complex of buildings known as Black Beach.

*   *   *

Colonel Sierra realised he might not have a lot of time but he was giving it his best shot. The reward could be magnificent. Expose Florin and he'd become untouchable himself. Locating the gold would be a bonus.

Jamaica had been simple. Sierra had good contacts there. Most flights from Montego Bay went to the United States so he ignored them. That left only a handful to be looked at for the day in question: flights to Canada, England, Germany and Belgium. One to Havana he would skip as well. An hour later he had his lead.

'There was a Jack Hadley on the flight, Aquiles,' his informer reported. 'No Florin, of course' – they had not expected The Aztec to use his real name – 'but the English guy travelled with a Mexican: Emilano Fernández Bueno.'

'Where to?'

'Brussels.'

'No connection?'

'None shown.'

'Thank you. I'm in your debt.'

'Any time.'

Brussels proved more difficult. A British passport would barely be looked at and an elderly Mexican would hardly draw attention. It just depended on where they went from there. If they'd left by road the trail would end.

Sierra used a private detective agency in Brussels that did regular work for his government. He would have to be careful with his brief. No mention of Florin. But Jack Hadley and Emilano Fernández Bueno should be safe enough.

He rang the agency up and gave them twenty-four hours.

* * *

Hadley was taken directly into Abad's office. Few lights were on within the prison compound and an eerie silence reigned briefly over the house of screams.

The Guinean wore his customary plain uniform and sat at his austere desk. He did not stand up for Hadley nor did he offer to shake hands. The guard remained inside the office and closed the door. Hadley sat down on the chair recently occupied by one of the late Asuse brothers.

'Passport?' Abad put out his hand and Hadley handed him the document.

'Why am I here?' he asked, trying to sound annoyed.

'You tell me. Why *are* you here, Señor Hadley?'

'Because your thugs brought me here,' he replied before he could think of being more judicious.

Abad stood up and in one smooth rapid movement swung a four-foot cane that he had concealed behind the desk, striking Hadley on his left cheek.

The Englishman had been so surprised that he had barely tried to move out of harm's way. The shock temporarily obliterated the pain but the room went dark and the next thing Hadley new he was being pulled back on the chair by the guard.

'I ask you again.' Abad seemed totally unruffled. 'Why are you here?'

'To protect you, *cojones*!' retorted Hadley. He would have preferred to say it without the guard there, but it was out now.

Abad frowned, but his right hand was out of view and he could strike again.

'Should things go wrong tonight,' Hadley added quickly in a lower voice, hoping it would stop the cane from being wielded again.

Abad looked past Hadley and made a small movement of his head. Hadley heard the door open and close again as the guard repositioned himself outside.

'You'd better make some sense.' Abad opened a drawer and put his Beretta pistol on the desk.

'I've come from Spain, Major Abad.'

'You've come from Kinshasa,' Abad corrected him and moved his right hand closer to the pistol.

'Equatorial Guinea is not my only business,' Hadley said, improvising. 'If things go well I'll be back in Madrid tomorrow and we can forget *this*.' He pointed at the cut on his cheek.

'What things, specifically?'

'By this time tomorrow this country should have a new government. If that's the case, you and I are done.'

'But?'

'But if something should go wrong and you needed to get out, I'm here to arrange that.'

'You? Arranging things for me in my own country?' The words hissed through Abad's lips.

'It will cease to be your country if things go wrong.' *And how I'd like to put my fist through your stupid face*, Hadley thought as his cheek started to throb.

'I have orders. We are worried about this operation's security. If it's compromised we'll pull you out. Others wouldn't.'

No, thought Abad, *they wouldn't and they didn't*. His hatred of the CIA surfaced again.

'So what were you planning to do had I not brought you here?'

Hadley opened his wallet and passed Abad a piece of paper.

'Your phone numbers. I was about to call you.'

Abad checked the numbers and nodded. 'And then?'

'Then we wait.' Hadley put the yellow phone on the table. 'Until this rings. You'll know then that I'm telling you the truth.'

Jesús Florin went to bed at midnight. Massama insisted that he would call him in the morning and take him to the helicopter. Timing was crucial: by the time the Mil-17 reached Bata, everyone else involved in the operation should have done their bit.

While Florin slept, Massama sipped a whisky and kept the satellite phone by his side.

At two in the morning it rang for the first time. His old friend José Eduardo was calling from Luanda to confirm that he had spoken to 'Roberto' and the dice were rolling.

Forty minutes later the military attaché at the DRC Embassy in Harare advised him that there was indeed a commotion taking place at the International Airport. Apparently a jet airliner had been seized by the authorities and all its occupants, over one hundred it was rumoured, were being bundled off to Chikurubi Prison under heavy army escort.

Then Massama dialled Hadley's number and confirmed that Harare was down.

Sierra's detectives put three men on the job and came up with a positive result eight hours later. They had spent their entire time at Brussels Airport checking airline lists, immigration records and ticket sales – not forgetting waiters, porters, anyone who might remember a fit Englishman and an old Mexican travelling together. Sierra had e-mailed photographs of them both.

Being ex-policemen with vast airport experience they knew exactly where to look, especially when it came to bypassing official channels to obtain confidential information.

Since the arrival of the suicide bomber, airline employees were trained to reveal nothing and suspect everyone, but conversely they had also learned to be more communicative with security agencies. Private eyes hardly warranted that classification but with former coppers the line was blurred.

The agency called Sierra the following morning, told him they had been forced to put eight people on the case but, with positive results in one-third of the time allowed, it equated to money saved.

Mr Jack Hadley and Señor Fernández Bueno had travelled on Air Brussels to Kinshasa.

It was also noted that neither Señor Bueno nor Mr Hadley had DRC visas which was why the ticket office remembered them so well. It seemed that Señor Bueno, who carried a bright yellow phone with him, had made a call to some big wheel, because forty minutes later in had rolled this vice-consul from the Democratic Republic of the Congo's Brussels representation and stamped both men's passports with the necessary visas there and then.

Sierra was clearly pleased with the findings and he said so. The chief gumshoe in Brussels was equally happy with the large suitably-padded bill he would submit to the Cuban Government.

Cuba, unfortunately for Sierra, had no influence or even a legation in Kinshasa. But they did have a full embassy across the river in Brazzaville. To send French Congolese to do your dirty work in the Belgian Congo was never a good idea, but Sierra had no choice and time was running out.

What the hell were Florin and Hadley doing in the Congo? If the pot of gold had been hidden there it would be long gone, concluded Sierra. He remembered reading how people got chopped up in Sierra Leone – or where was it? – for a few ounces at a time. And that was just the kids.

That afternoon a hastily briefed Congolese operative took the ferry from Brazzaville to Kinshasa and on entering the DRC went directly to N'djili Airport.

Like his counterparts in Brussels, he too did the rounds of the airlines, ticket offices, Customs and Immigration. He carried a fistful of folded banknotes in his hand and peeled off one or two at a time whenever a satisfactory answer was given, or even a suggestion of who to ask was made.

Eventually the operative got to the man who knew all the answers. He was well aware that Jack Hadley and Jesús Florin had arrived on Air Brussels, that Mr Bueno was a false name, that they had been met by General Massama and that they were staying in the General's home in Kinshasa.

He knew all this because General Massama had personally tasked him with making the necessary arrangements to ensure a smooth passage through N'djili for his VIP guests. So when the visitor from Brazzaville – he gave his name as Gaston – put his questions to him the man smiled, invited him into his office, then locked the door and called the Military Police.

Gaston was taken to an army camp close to the airport, softened up in accordance with the General's instructions and thrown into a cell. When Massama eventually arrived, his subordinates had already been able to establish that Gaston came from the Republic of Congo, that he was working for the Cuban Embassy there and that he was trying to establish Florin's and Hadley's whereabouts.

Gaston was lying on the concrete floor when Massama entered his cell. His face and body were bruised and bloody but he was not seriously hurt. Massama crouched sufficiently to look the man in the eye and pushed the barrel of his pistol into the captive's mouth.

'Can you read and write?' he asked. Gaston nodded, his bulging eyes trying to focus on the gun.

'Good. What I want you to do is write a confession. Everything you know, everything you can think of that might interest me. People at the Cuban Embassy: names, contact methods, other jobs you've done, jobs others have done. Are you with me?'

Gaston nodded again.

'With special attention to anything concerning General Florin. If you want to stay alive, keep writing.'

Gaston made an undecipherable sound. Massama pulled his gun out of the man's mouth and stood up.

'When he stops writing,' Massama told his men out loud, 'shoot him.'

Once outside the cell he countermanded his last order.

'We'll decide what to do with him later. General Florin may wish to speak to this man when he returns.'

But Gaston's confession would make a nice little dossier for Jesús to take back to Cuba. It might help him to sort out whoever was gunning for him back home.

The yellow phone rang first. Hadley listened to Massama's brief message, keeping the phone turned slightly towards Abad to show that he was hiding nothing.

'That's it,' he told Abad once he rang off. 'They've been

arrested in Harare. The plane with the mercenaries will not be coming.'

'Am I to take that on your say-so?'

'It'll be in the news. It's a big story,' replied Hadley, forgetting briefly where he was. The only radio station in Malabo was owned by Dorito. State TV was not much better and was not on air during the night. And there were no internet connections at Black Beach.

'There must be some way to communicate with the outside world,' Hadley demanded.

Abad thought for a moment. He lifted his own telephone's receiver and dialled Santa Isabel airport. It answered after several rings.

'Tower.'

'Major Abad here, who's on duty?'

'Murta, sir. Good evening, Major.'

'Everything quiet there?'

'Yes, sir.'

'Expecting anything?'

'A charter from Harare due in at six, sir, and then the schedule from Lagos at six-thirty.'

'Do something for me.' Abad made it sound more like an order than a request. 'Contact Harare. Ask about the charter.'

'Sir.'

'What sort of plane is it?'

'727, sir.'

'Passengers?'

'Says 103 on the flight plan.'

'Call me back at the Beach.' Abad hung up.

Two hundred miles away in Cameroon, news of the arrest of the main forces in Harare had not reached the advance group. At three a.m., exactly as planned, they took off from their dusty jungle airstrip, armed to the teeth and with their faces suitably blackened, determined to capture Santa Isabel airport and hold on to it until their colleagues arrived.

They landed at 03:47 and taxied directly to the base of the control tower. The duty controller, Murta, already angry and threatening all manner of sanctions because he had not received any advance warning of the movement and could find no trace of a flight plan, was now hurling abuse at the Cameroonian crew who spoke no Spanish and had difficulty communicating in English – the official language of air traffic control worldwide.

Murta watched in dismay as the crew misunderstood or ignored his instructions to park opposite the terminal building. He came out on the tower's balcony with a megaphone, calling them *huevones* and similarly unpalatable names imported from the Peninsula centuries before.

A twenty-year-old Swazi with blue eyes and curly blond hair who could drop an aardvark at a thousand metres with an ordinary hunting rifle was the first to exit the Antonov. He put the cross-hairs of his telescopic sight on Murta's head and shot a 9mm brass-encased high-velocity bullet cleanly though the man's brain without even scratching the megaphone.

The rest of the advance party disembarked quickly and set about securing their objectives within the almost deserted airport that, thanks to the internet, had about as many surprises for them as their own backyards.

By 04:30 the airfield was in their hands. A South African who had once worked in Durban Airport's tower took the dead controller's place and tried to raise the inbound Boeing 727 on a prearranged frequency but got no reply, leading him to conclude that it was still out of range.

A group of mercenaries set up a heavy-firepower base on the airport's approach road, including a shoulder-launched anti-tank weapon that would give the first defenders to react some food for thought.

For the rest of them there was not much to do but wait in their assigned positions and perhaps rifle through the unattended duty-free shops for a nice pair of Ray-Bans or an iPod.

Minutes later a policeman cycled up to the front of the terminal building. The approach-road unit let him pass. An old lady had reported hearing a gunshot from the direction of the airport. The policeman tried to enter the terminal but the doors were still locked. There should have been cleaners at work, lights in the control tower and a van on runway inspection in preparation for early arrivals. That wasn't how it looked to him but if indeed there had been shots fired he was not about to get shot himself gratuitously. He whistled a tune to appear nonchalant, got back on his bicycle and hoped that he could get back to the station unimpeded. Best to let the army check things out.

'*Anything, anything at all unusual in or around the airport gets reported back to me immediately*', Abad had ordered, '*or the person responsible will be my guest at Black Beach.*'

Soon after the policeman had pedalled away down the lane, an inbound flight from Lagos called Malabo Tower to request the latest weather. The South African informed them that the airport was closed and suggested a diversion to Port Harcourt. He then changed frequency and tried unsuccessfully to raise his own plane again. He was starting to worry. The Boeing was supposed to land within the hour.

30

At six o'clock Florin awoke to find that the Algerians were already up and finishing their prayers. With Massama at the wheel they drove silently to the airfield where the pilots had the Mil-17 ready to go.

'Don't you dare die on my watch, Jesús,' Massama whispered in his friend's ear as they parted.

'No chance, *polisson*,' he replied jovially. Never before, in decades of bloody fighting, had Florin been so certain that he would survive.

The Algerians helped him board the aircraft – the step up to the door was high and for an instant Florin looked his age. Once aboard he tidied his denim blue Navy tunic and, flanked by his seconded bodyguards, waved at Massama as the large rotor raised a whirl of dust and the shuddering monster staggered into the air.

Though stripped of weaponry and carrying only five people, the Mil-17 still used six hundred kilogrammes of fuel an hour. The trip to Bata was estimated at three and a half hours each way and there would be no chance to refuel there.

The aircraft had to carry almost five tons of fuel and had been hastily fitted with additional tanks made up of a dozen barrels strapped together in the cabin after most of the seats had been removed. It would become lighter as the fuel was burned but on departing Boma the helicopter weighed more than its maximum certified thirteen tons.

The stench of kerosene abated as the aircraft picked up speed and air passed through the cabin. They flew a north-westerly course over the awakening Congolese rainforest, the low sun of dawn projecting long dark shadows towards the coast. Thirty minutes after lift-off they crossed the Angolan enclave of Cabinda and continued to Pointe Noire where they would coast out and fly parallel to the shore-line until they reached their destination.

Florin tried not to think about Lucía and María Luz but it was proving impossible. He could hear his wife's pleading voice begging him to turn round and go home but he felt irreversibly committed.

To pass the time he decided that he would teach the Algerians a few useful Spanish phrases like 'over here', 'run', 'stay still' and 'shut up or I'll blow your head off'.

'What are your first names,' Florin asked them. They both had Muslim names.

'You'll need Spanish names for this mission. You shall be Pepe and you Paco.'

The phone rang again but it wasn't Hadley's satellite set this time. Abad picked up his landline and grunted. After listening for an instant he straightened up and looked at Hadley through furious eyes.

He slammed down the phone, raised the cane and hit out again, only this time Hadley saw it coming and deflected much of the impact with his forearm.

'Who the fuck is playing games with me? You hear?'

The guard outside opened the door when he heard Abad shouting but was rewarded with a vitriolic order to get out and stay out.

'Cut the crap, Abad,' Hadley shouted back, 'Tell me what's going on or I guarantee you'll end up dead today and it won't be me who kills you.'

Abad had become a man incapable of reasoning until he had vented his anger. But he was also a man accustomed to beating up defenceless, terrified civilians – he wasn't a trained soldier. Hadley took the blow as the cane came down a third time, dived across the desk at Abad and picked up the Guinean's pistol on the way.

Abad shouted once but this time the guard did not dare come in. Hadley lay on the floor on top of the police chief and pressed the Beretta's muzzle against Abad's temple.

'Talk to me! Who called?'

'I'll fucking kill you!'

'Who called?'

'The coup has succeeded,' hissed Abad. 'That was one of my men. The rebels have taken the airport. You are dead.'

Hadley thought quickly. It was impossible. Massama had been clear. It had to be the Cameroon detachment. The fools had gone ahead alone!

'That's not the main force,' he said harshly. 'They've been busted in Harare! That's only the airport platoon. Twenty-five guys. We must go to the airport! Until the Zimbabwe lot betray you, you are still in charge.'

'No!'

'Abad, you have to take back the airport,' Hadley persisted. 'They'll surrender when they know their colleagues' fate. I guarantee it. You'll win both ways: either as the hero who took back Santa Isabel from the rebels, or the one to open up our escape route to Bata if necessary. We must get there by mid-morning for the evac chopper.'

Despite his fury, Abad considered his options. Then his phone rang.

'Take it,' ordered Hadley, pressing the gun harder against Abad's head.

'Major Abad? Arturo Blanes. Is this line secure?'

It took Abad an instant to remember Marcos Vega's alias.

'Tell me what's going on.'

'Complete fiasco, I'm afraid. Not our end – South African cock-up, we believe.'

'So?'

'The inbound group has been seized by Mugabe. It's all off.'

'Where does that leave me?' Abad could barely control his anger.

'We are keeping quiet. You have your pay. We are sending a man to fetch you. Jack Hadley. We need to get you to Bata; our Navy will pick you up. Can we meet at Santa Isabel right now?'

'Santa Isabel is in rebel hands,' Abad replied, looking at Hadley. 'But not for long. Yes' – he made up his mind – 'I'll meet you there. I'm going to take back the airport.'

The Mil-17 passed Banio Lagoon at Mayumba in Gabon and reached the halfway point of the outward journey. After an hour of Spanish lessons – with some amusing results – Florin had settled on a rear seat and taken a nap.

He woke up to see the Algerians rolling out the empty fuel drums and throwing them into the sea below.

'Pilot asked if you could go up to the cockpit, sir,' Pepe told Florin.

'What's the problem?' Florin asked, leaning into the flight deck. The day was getting warmer; to the right Florin could see the interminable Gabon coastline with occasional settlements or fishing villages tucked in along the way. Ahead and to the left just the vastness of the ocean. The helicopter flew low, keeping a mile or two offshore, undetected.

'We are burning more fuel that we thought, sir,' the second pilot explained.

'Can we still get there and back?' Florin asked, but his mind was unflinchingly made up: they would go to Bata, conduct their business and worry later about getting back.

'It could be close, sir,' the pilot replied. 'Depends on what winds we encounter.'

'Anything we can do to save fuel?'

'We could go direct to Bata from here. It would save eighty miles.'

'Over Gabon?'

'Yes, sir. We fly fast and low, avoiding towns. By the time anyone hears us we'll be gone.'

'Go ahead.'

Florin returned to his seat as the aircraft banked right and set a new course. They were over the jungle in five minutes. The ride got bumpier and the scenery changed from majestic to awesome.

Florin called the Algerians over and suggested a game of cards.

*   *   *

The airport was taken very quickly. Abad rounded up an infantry regiment from Black Beach barracks and barked orders at their colonel – who might have outranked Abad but knew better than to argue with the President's chief executioner. Twenty minutes later the convoy set off for Santa Isabel.

Abad had a truce of sorts with Hadley; he would decide what to do with him later. For the moment the Englishman seemed to be telling the truth and Abad might need him to make good their escape.

'You have no more than a couple of hours,' Hadley had told him. 'If Mugabe has the leaders it won't be long before they talk.'

'Who knows about me?'

'Just the officers. They were to rely on you once the shooting stopped. I expect they'll be tortured first.'

Hadley had refused to return Abad's Beretta. Before agreeing to leave the policeman's office he had loaded a round into the chamber, put the safety on and slipped the pistol into his trouser pocket. *If this viper strikes again*, Hadley decided, *I'll take him with me*.

'Don't try anything, Abad,' he warned him for good measure. 'Without me you are fucked!'

Approaching the airport the army colonel and three of his NCOs were pulverised by an anti-tank missile fired from some bushes to the left of the road.

A livid Abad shouted at the soldiers to take cover. Hadley urged them to leave the road and cut their way in through the perimeter fence. There were only two dozen defenders, he assured them. When they saw the numbers they were up against they'd surrender or run.

* * *

At that moment the fax machine in the control tower started printing a message. It was Harare Tower responding to an earlier request by Murta.

Harare Airport is closed. The Boeing 727 charter plane scheduled to depart for Malabo at 01:30 UTC has been detained by the authorities and should not be expected. Flight plan cancelled.

The South African in the tower ran down three steps at a time to alert his commanding officer and the order was given to abort.

'Everyone pull back to the Antonov. Let's get out of here!'

As the mercenaries closed in on their plane it was hit by a barrage of Guinean machine-gun fire. Glass and bits of aluminium flew in all directions as the bullets struck. The left undercarriage collapsed and the plane crashed onto its port wing.

The mercenaries knew they were beaten. They stood defenceless on the apron, dropped their weapons and raised their arms.

A hundred and fifty miles south of Bata, the Mil-17 changed course again. It was approaching Libreville and the captain decided not to overfly it in case the Gabonese scrambled an interceptor. The safest route was out to sea. They turned west over Wonga-Wongue National Park and coasted out south of Pointe Pongara.

Florin picked up his gun holster and belted it round his waist. He pulled out a Russian GSH-18 pistol loaded with eighteen rounds of armour-piercing Parabellum ammunition. The Algerians looked at it admiringly.

'A gift from *le Général*,' he told them. 'Ready?'

They knew the routine. Florin stood by the open door and fired a couple of shots, then flicked on the safety catch and put the weapon back in its holster.

Pepe and Paco followed suit and squeezed off a few rounds from their AK-47s.

When the fighting stopped at Santa Isabel, the Vilanova Taronger Citation was twenty-five miles out – just minutes away from landing.

The captain was concerned that he had not been able to raise the Santa Isabel tower. There were no NOTAMS – notices to airmen – posted to suggest the field was closed.

He called them again and got nothing. He pressed the intercom button and spoke to Vilanova.

'Make a low pass and take a look,' his boss suggested. 'If it looks safe we land.'

'Right, sir.'

'What's happening?' Mercedes asked her father.

'We are not sure. There's no response from Malabo Airport. We are going to take a look, make sure the runway's not blocked.

'Don't worry, we'll be careful.' He took her hand again. 'If Jack's here we'll find him and take him home.'

Earlier, Vilanova had gone into the small toilet compartment in the back and unscrewed a plastic covering. Behind it, held in place by masking tape, Vilanova kept a snub-nosed revolver. It fired low-velocity close-quarter shells of the type issued to air marshals. He had decided after 9/11 that if any terrorist tried to take over his plane he would not go out like a lemming.

He took the gun out and replaced the cover, then

wrapped the weapon in a linen towel and carried it back to his seat. He lifted the narrow storage bin under the right armrest and dropped the gun into it.

Hadley and Abad looked up as they heard engine sounds. A small white jet was approaching but looked a bit high to land.

The mercenaries had been rounded up and shoved violently into army trucks. As the sound of the jet increased everyone looked up. It overflew the runway at about three hundred feet and Hadley was rendered speechless. Its tail was painted in the distinctive colours and markings that he had seen in the Xátiva lorry park: Vilanova Taronger. It couldn't be a coincidence. He had to act quickly – there was no telling what Abad's trigger-happy troops, already excited by their 'victory', might do next.

'A Spanish plane, Major,' he said. 'I don't know what it's doing here, but that's our ticket to Bata.'

Abad did not argue. The plane climbed away and started a gentle circuit over the sea to reposition itself for landing.

'Get a man in the tower. Flash the green lantern at the plane. It will land. And make them hold their fire. We'll be out of here in minutes.'

They were interrupted by Marcos Vega's arrival. He was escorted to where Abad and Hadley stood.

'Madrid's been on the phone,' he started to explain as he got closer. Then he saw the cuts and bruises on Hadley's face. 'Christ! Are you OK?' he asked.

'I'm fine. Please carry on'

'Captain Pinto himself,' Vega added.

'What the fuck went wrong?' Abad demanded to know.

341

'They don't know yet. Someone leaked the operation to Zimbabwe. We don't know who or why. Now, we need to get you to Bata straight away.'

Vega stopped talking as he saw all eyes looking north. The white and orange jet was on final approach, gear down, lights on.

'Who's that?' he asked

'Spanish plane. Civilian,' replied Hadley.

'As I was saying,' Vega continued, glancing occasionally at the landing jet, 'we need to get Major Abad to Bata and you, Mr Hadley, are to go to the Embassy in Malabo.'

'He comes with me!' Abad overruled him.

He waved his newly acquired gun about as he spoke. Hadley still had the Beretta in his pocket. *You'll have to shoot me in the back if you want to take it*, Hadley had implied.

'Major Abad, I have my own orders!' protested Vega.

'It's OK,' Hadley said, intervening. 'I was given the job of escorting the Major. I intend to do so.'

As the little jet taxied in Hadley thought he saw Mercedes's face through a window. What the hell *was* going on? Abad started walking towards the plane. Hadley pulled out the Beretta.

'I'll commandeer the plane,' he told Abad, then started moving towards the aircraft, leaving no room for argument. 'You make sure your troops don't shoot and that they understand clearly that we are leaving right now. Don't keep me waiting.'

Abad turned to Vega. 'You haven't heard the end of this,' he threatened, still waving his gun around. 'I still want the rest of my money and compensation for your fuck-up. I shall see you in Madrid.'

*   *   *

'Two minutes to Equatorial Guinea, General,' the Mil-17 captain called.

'Thank you. And please drop the "general" when the passenger gets here,' said Florin, pointing at his Chief Petty Officer epaulettes. 'How far is Bata?'

'Eighty miles. We'll put down in thirty minutes. I shall need to call them, sir – I need your Spanish voice.'

Florin moved over to the jump seat behind the pilots and put on a headset. They had written it all down for him.

He had travelled a long road. He had called upon his friends of old to make it possible and they had stood by him. He had also encountered pure goodness where he'd least expected it. He thought of Rosa Uribe and smiled.

Today would be a special day. A deserved execution and a belated rebirth. On cue he pressed the transmit button and made his call.

'Bata Approach, Helicóptero Armada 35, buenos días.'

'Bata Approach, Echo Victor Tango, buenos días.'

The Vilanova Taronger Citation requested landing clearance. If he encountered the slightest reluctance to let them land the Captain would declare a fuel emergency which under international law would require an immediate clearance.

It had all happened so quickly that they were still in a state of shock and confusion. First Jack Hadley had appeared out of nowhere, yanked open the Citation's door and stormed into the cabin brandishing a gun.

'Jack!' Mercedes had jumped out of her seat and made towards him but he pointed his gun at her as her father stared in utter disbelief.

'Sit down! Listen to me!' Hadley shouted, holding up

the gun so that Abad could see him through the open door. The police chief was still remonstrating with Vega and an army officer who had joined them but his body language said he wouldn't be long.

'You don't know me, OK?' he pleaded, 'There's a nasty guy boarding in a second — you have to trust me. You've never seen me before in your lives. We are commandeering your plane. I'll try to get you off it, but if I can't we are only going to Bata on the mainland. Then I'll tell you everything.'

'Jack—' Mercedes started to say.

'You don't know my name!' Hadley stared at Mercedes. 'Trust me. He's coming now. He's armed.'

As Abad got to the jet, Hadley had turned his gun on the crew. 'We are going to Bata,' he shouted. 'Start the engines now!'

Abad came on board and shut the door behind him. Vilanova glanced at his armrest bin.

'Let's get rid of these people, Major,' said Hadley.

Abad studied Vilanova and Mercedes.

'They look important,' he said, with a smirk. 'They stay as extra insurance.' Then he turned to the pilot. 'Didn't you hear? Start your engines.'

'We are short of fuel, sir,' the captain said. 'I'm down to reserves.'

'I say go!' ordered Abad.

'Do as he says, Sabastián,' Vilanova intervened, 'How much fuel have we got?'

'Forty-five minutes' worth, Mr Vilanova.'

'How long to Bata?'

The captain looked at his co-pilot who had been entering data in the flight-management system.

'Thirty-four minutes,' the younger man said.

Vilanova nodded.

'Vilanova?' asked Abad. 'Of course, the plane is the same colour as the cartons in my fridge!' He looked around the cabin. 'You must be very rich.'

'I am,' Vilanova held his stare.

'Why are you in Malabo?'

'Business,' he replied and Abad eventually looked away. Hurting an influential Spaniard would not be advisable if he planned to seek asylum in Madrid.

The captain said they would taxi on one engine and light the other just before take-off. Hadley took the opportunity to preempt any deadly mistakes.

'My name is Jack Hadley,' he told the Vilanovas. 'I work for the Spanish government and so does Major Abad here. This is a national emergency. You will not be harmed. We will go to Bata where you can refuel and go home. We'll be done there. Thanks for your cooperation. Please do not leave your seats – it is a short flight.'

Abad holstered his gun and sat on the front seat by the door. Vilanova thought he could easily retrieve his pistol and put a bullet in the back of the man's skull.

What kind of soldier sits with his back to the people he'd just taken hostage? Vilanova asked himself. He knew the answer, of course, he'd encountered that sort before: the kind of soldier that only fights unarmed civilians. They exuded the same disgusting arrogance wherever you found them on the globe.

Vilanova and Mercedes sat in the second row, one each side of the aisle. Jack took a seat behind his girlfriend. He did not want to look at her, lest either of them betrayed their feelings.

345

Twenty minutes after take-off an alarm went off in the cockpit. A fuel-warning annunciator flashed its red light. The crew reset it and made their call to Bata.

'*Echo Victor Tango, Bata,*' came the immediate reply. '*We have no flight plan for you, sir. Where have you come from?*'

Vilanova's captain declared a fuel emergency and asked for a straight-in approach. He ignored further requests for his flight details.

Ten minutes later the red lights came on again, both sides this time, flashing ominously. The crew extinguished them again and lowered the undercarriage. The passengers leaned towards the aisle and were relieved to see Bata's runway straight ahead.

31

Just as the Vilanova Citation made its final approach into Bata, would-be President Potro was sitting in the lap of luxury, sipping sherry from a crystal *copita* at Flight Level 410, halfway between Geneva and Malabo.

The crew received the expected radio call and wrote the communication down verbatim for the stewardess to take to Potro. Far from confirming the success of the military operation in Malabo, the message suggested that young Dorito and a specially convened firing squad were on their way to Santa Isabel airport to await Potro's arrival.

The aircraft owner's agent excused himself from his guests and moved to the Gulfstream's private cabin in the rear. He picked up the wall-mounted handset and spoke to the cockpit first. As he was dialling his second call, to his boss in Madrid this time, the plane turned around 180 degrees, descended 1,000 feet and headed for home.

*   *   *

The Citation touched down in Bata and taxied to the terminal building. The computers estimated six minutes' worth of fuel left. A hundred metres away, on a corner of the apron, a Spanish Navy helicopter was standing by.

A captain and a corporal with automatic rifles approached the plane and shouted at the occupants to disembark. They made no effort to hide their surprise when the first person to emerge from the jet was Abad.

'Major Abad, sir!' They both lowered their guns and saluted. 'What a relief!' the captain said. 'We don't know what's going on, sir.'

They had heard there was trouble at Malabo airport and that a state of emergency had been declared on Bioko Island.

'It's all sorted now,' Abad boasted, 'The terrorists have been caught.'

The problem with dictatorships, thought Hadley as he stood at the jet's door, was that they suppressed information to the point where their own people had no mechanism for verifying the truth. This was the second instance in a few hours. But this time it would work to Hadley's advantage.

'And there's this Spanish helicopter,' explained the captain, pointing up the ramp. 'They say they are here on orders from the presidency. We can't confirm that. What do you want us to do, sir?'

'You are doing fine. Here's what you'll do next.'

Abad had his gun in his hand again as he put his arm over the captain's shoulders.

'You will seal this airport completely. Nobody comes in or out, nobody lands. Block the runway with a truck.'

'Yes, sir.'

'Mr Hadley and I,' he indicated the tall man behind him,

'are going in that helicopter. Wait for further orders. Understood?'

'Yes, sir!'

Abad walked back to the plane and leaned into the cabin.

'You all go and sit in the terminal. You'll be there some time. If you cause trouble you'll be arrested,' he said. Then he took Hadley's arm, put his gun against his ribcage and pulled him along. 'You are coming with me.'

The Mil-17's rotor blades started turning, the whine of the the gas turbines gradually growing louder as Abad and Hadley approached. Florin stood by the door with a flying helmet on. The two Algerians in their naval uniforms tensed up, ready for action.

'One man are my orders,' Florin shouted above the din. 'Which one of you is Major Abad?'

'I'm changing those orders, Petty Officer,' Abad insisted, waving his gun around. 'This man comes with us.'

Hadley winked at Florin as he clambered aboard first, followed by Abad.

'Let's go,' Abad shouted at the pilots.

Florin nodded at Hadley and indicated the open door. As the aircraft's wheels eased off the ground, Florin passed between Abad and Hadley.

'Now,' he shouted.

Hadley threw himself out of the door and tried to roll back under the helicopter. Abad sprang to his feet and ran to the open door. Holding on to the overhead rail he fired his gun at Hadley but the helicopter rotated clockwise and banked to the right, hiding the Englishman from view. Pepe leaped forward, hit Abad on the head with the butt of his AK-47 and grabbed him as he went down.

Florin kicked Abad's pistol out of the helicopter and just caught sight of the girl running across the tarmac towards Hadley, with a soldier in pursuit. The two Algerians dragged Abad to a seat and forced him down.

'Five miles out, one thousand feet,' Florin told the pilots.

Abad came round quickly. The aggressive look was still there but there was an element of fear in his eyes.

'What the hell is going on?' he demanded.

There were six seats at the rear of the cabin, arranged in two rows facing each other. Florin sat opposite Abad, Paco stood guard behind the Guinean and Pepe stood at the front by the cockpit.

'Where exactly are we going?' Abad could see the shoreline to the east. They were flying south. 'Where's your ship?'

'We are going to Kinshasa, Major Abad,' Florin replied. 'Well, at least my comrades and I are going to Kinshasa,' he said and let out a Florin laugh. The Algerians had not quite understood what Florin had said, but they smiled anyway.

'I could, of course, say "What makes you think we are going anywhere?"' Florin stared at Abad.

'Who the fuck are you?' Abad suddenly got aggressive again. 'Where's your officer?'

'My name is Florin, Major.' Florin removed his helmet, then ran an index finger over the faded stencilled name above his shirt's left pocket. 'There are two officers in the cockpit, but frankly I don't think they'd be interested in what you have to say.'

'Florin?' Abad's brown skin turned pale. 'What Florin?' Now he was mumbling.

'How many Florins do you know, Major Abad?'

Abad remained silent. His stare darted all over the cabin,

like that of a trapped fox that had always managed to find an escape route in the past.

'Or should I say Major Ortiz?' Florin's voice would have sliced through steel as the name came out.

'That was a long time ago, Florin. There was a war!'

Florin remained silent for a moment. The helicopter continued on its course. There were no voices now. It was him, Jesús Florin, alone with his conscience and his ghosts. The sounds of real life receded. There was only the monster sitting there five feet away.

'Was my wife a combatant, Ortiz?'

'It was an accident. There were witnesses!'

'Was my daughter a combatant in that fucking war of yours, you scumbag?'

'I saved her life!' Abad shouted the claim, like a wronged man facing a callous judge.

'I know exactly what happened, Ortiz.' Florin's tone changed from hatred to contempt. 'There was a young conscript with you. A good boy trapped by circumstances. He wrote it all down, Ortiz. Then he took his own life. But what he wrote lives on. And I have read it.'

The helicopter hit a patch of turbulence and Paco tumbled forward. As he steadied himself on the back of Abad's chair, the Guinean grabbed the muzzle of the Algerian's AK-47 and yanked it away from him.

Florin went for his pistol but Pepe was ahead of him and raised his gun. Abad saw the danger coming and reacted first. He squeezed the AK-47's trigger and thirty rounds of 7.62mm bullets sliced diagonally across the cabin.

Pepe took the brunt of the barrage as his chest exploded in a bloodbath. The co-pilot, sitting on the left-hand seat, took eleven rounds in his back and skull. Most of the bullets, having passed through one or another body, struck the cockpit, shattering the windscreen, the left-hand-side flight instruments, the entire communications panel and half the navigation equipment.

Paco, beside himself with grief, put his entire body weight behind his right elbow and delivered a mighty blow to Abad's temple, retrieving his rifle as the Guinean passed out.

'Guard him,' Florin ordered, trying to restore Paco's pride. He made his way to the front.

'Are we going down?' he asked the surviving pilot.

'Not at the moment, but forget Kinshasa, sir. We need to land.'

'Can you get back to Bata?'

'I think so, General.'

'Go for it,' Florin ordered and returned to the rear.

When Abad came round, Florin spoke softly. This time Paco leaned against the cabin wall with his shouldered weapon aimed at Abad's chest.

'We are going back to Bata,' he said, 'thanks to you. Dorito will be pleased. He wants to see you. Thinks he could enjoy you for weeks at Black Beach.'

'I'll give you a million euros. I have it in the bank.' It was Abad's last plea.

Florin laughed. He leaned closer to Abad, this time with his pistol pressed against the man's groin. 'I'm fucking rich, Ortiz. I piss on a mere million.'

Florin stood up.

'Bring him forward, Paco.'

'What are you going to do? Throw me out?' Abad was panicking.

'We can do better than that,' replied Florin. He held

his pistol with both hands and fired a high-velocity round. The sleek bullet went straight through Abad's boot, his foot and the helicopter's floor, before vanishing towards the ocean. Abad screamed and fell to the cold metal floor, his eyes wide open in pain and terror.

'Put a light tourniquet on that leg, Paco,' Florin ordered the Algerian. 'We don't want him to *bleed* to death.' He turned to the pilot, 'Ten feet and hover, captain, please.'

'The right foot is to help you swim, Ortiz,' Florin explained without a trace of emotion in his voice as the sea spray stirred by the rotor drifted into the cabin. 'The bleeding left foot is to make sure the sharks don't miss you.'

He turned to the Algerian, 'Will you do the honours, Paco?'

'My pleasure, sir!'

Paco handed Florin his AK-47, gripped the overhead rail with both hands and, placing his feet on Abad's hip and ribcage, shoved him out through the aircraft's door.

Florin nodded at the captain, waved a hand in Bata's direction and walked back to his seat.

In Madrid, Captain Pinto took a call from Marcos Vega who was able to confirm that everything was unfolding as Rosa had predicted.

President Penang, having already been telephoned by the presidents of Zimbabwe, Angola and the DRC, had invited the Spanish Ambassador to lunch to express his gratitude and discuss further cooperation between their two nations.

Pinto then phoned his own Minister, apologised for not having kept him in the picture blow by blow, explained that CNI alertness had unearthed Potro's double-dealing and that therefore he had decided to adopt their carefully laid out fallback position to run with Penang.

If proof was needed of the CNI initiative's success, Pinto explained, the Foreign Minister would be able to confirm that on this very day his Ambassador would be feasted as the President's very special guest.

With the politics disposed of, Pinto left his office and took a taxi to the Anderson Clinic. Unfortunately he wasn't able to give Rosa the good news. She was already unconscious when he arrived and her husband had no more time for him. Ramiro sat on a chair outside her room, looking forlorn.

Pinto left the clinic troubled and downcast on a day when he should have been toasting his organisation's success. The following morning, with Max and Ramiro by her side, Rosa Uribe passed away.

After the helicopter had left Bata, Vilanova's pilots tried in vain to obtain fuel for their plane. Hadley still had his yellow phone so he called Vega in Malabo and enlisted his help.

The order had just come in from the Armed Forces commander to let the Citation have whatever it required when the damaged helicopter staggered in. It landed where it had been parked before but only three people climbed out.

'Get the bodies out,' Florin ordered. 'Then topple one of those fuel drums and set this thing on fire.'

He didn't want photographs of Massama's artwork appearing in the world's press. The two dead comrades would have to be left behind. The army captain promised Florin that they would have soldiers' burials.

He did not ask about Major Abad. The army chief had

told the captain that if Abad showed up he should be shot on sight.

With six passengers and two crew, the Citation could not carry full tanks of fuel, Vilanova's pilot explained.

'We can't make it to Tenerife.'

'Let's go to Kinshasa – it's less than half the distance at a guess,' suggested Florin.

'Hmm.' The captain wasn't sure. 'The DRC is difficult. We need visas, pre-approvals, far more documents than we've got.'

'Captain,' Florin promised, 'you take us to Kinshasa and I'll have the runway there sprinkled with rose petals in your honour.'

Then he grabbed his own yellow phone and spoke to his good friend Bienheuré.

They all piled into the Citation. The centre seats were arranged Club style with little pull-out tables in the middle. Vilanova sat next to Mercedes, facing forward, and Florin sat across from her. Hadley had the fourth chair. Paco and the helicopter pilot sat together in the back row.

They sat silently at first and did not hide their relief as the plane finally lifted from the runway. When the seat-belt signs disappeared Mercedes spoke first.

'Would anyone like a drink?' she asked, stepping down into the aisle.

'Do they serve beer in private jets?' Florin asked.

'They do, Mr Florin,' she laughed. 'We have Sol – it's Mexican.'

'No Cristal?' joked Hadley.

She brought beers for Hadley and Florin, a whisky on

ice for her father and a glass of VT orange for the pilots, the military men and herself.

'You are not at all what I expected,' Vilanova said.

'Oh?' Florin was surprised. The others held their breath. Mercedes knew her father's views on terrorists.

'Your fame precedes you, Mr Florin . . .'

'Jesús, please.'

'Thank you, Jesús. I guess you and I have spent our lives on opposite sides of the fence. I never envisaged sipping drinks with you in my plane.'

'If it's any consolation,' Jesús smiled at Mercedes before continuing, 'this is my first time in a capitalist's private jet.'

'Was it worth it, Jesús? All the fighting?'

'Someone always has to fight. Were you ever in uniform, Luis? May I call you Luis?'

Vilanova nodded.

'I was, in Argentina. But I never had to fight.'

'Then you were lucky. We fight because we have to. Doesn't mean we like it, does it, Hadley?'

'Not necessarily,' Hadley replied, looking at Mercedes.

'When did you live in Argentina, Luis?'

'From birth until 1980.'

'Then you would have been there when I was in Chile.'

'When was that?' Mercedes asked.

'1971, 1972 . . .' Florin said, remembering. Happiest years of my life.'

'Not mine,' Vilanova admitted. 'It was the beginning of my disillusionment, but it took me another nine years to get out.'

'Let's talk about cheerful things, please,' Mercedes interjected. 'We've been through hell today and we are all alive.'

The minute she said it she blushed. She remembered the two men behind her who'd lost their colleagues.

Florin noticed. He took her hand and held it tight. 'It's all right,' he said. 'They don't speak Spanish.'

'You must come to see us in Spain,' she said. 'Next year, for the book launch. Your biography!'

'Hadley has to write it first.' Florin gave a nervous laugh and let go of her hand.

Vilanova noticed and looked at him silently.

'You could come with us now,' Hadley suggested, 'and help me write it.'

'No chance at all of that.' Florin's infectious laughter lifted everyone's spirits. 'I have unfinished business in Cuba. Next year,' he said, still looking at Mercedes. 'Next year, perhaps.'

They landed in Kinshasa and were greeted by General Massama. He hugged Florin and refused to let him go.

'Finest man on earth,' Massama told the others, looking over Florin's shoulder. 'We are lucky to even know him. What do you all want to do?' he asked.

'Let my poor pilots get some rest and make arrangements to go home tomorrow,' said Vilanova.

'You can all stay in my house,' proclaimed Massama, and then barked a few orders. While they waited for extra cars to arrive, Massama took his two survivors aside, spoke to them in private and placed them in the care of his aide-de-camp.

The rest of them drove directly to the Massama compound in Kinshasa. Florin, Vilanova and the pilots rested in the afternoon while Jack and Mercedes spent their time in and out of the swimming pool. Later, Vilanova and Florin were seen walking slowly through the garden, deep in conversation, keeping to the shade.

'Mum will never believe it.' Mercedes smiled from her sunlounger, propping herself up with one arm. 'Dad and the terrorist!'

'Guerrilla, I think she called him,' jested Hadley without opening his eyes, '*Guerrillero*.'

They dined together under a garden pergola. Massama went to bed at eleven and Vilanova took himself upstairs at midnight. Hadley and Mercedes stayed up, talking to Florin. At two in the morning she kissed The Aztec on both cheeks and went to bed herself.

Hadley called it a day thirty minutes later.

'You haven't lost the Luxembourg key, have you?' asked Florin as Hadley stood up.

'No chance,' said Hadley, smiling as he pulled the chain from under his shirt.

'When you go there to collect your box of papers . . .' Florin continued.

'Yes?'

'You must promise me something.'

'Of course. What would you like, Jesús?'

'There's a brown quarto envelope in amongst my papers.' He described the shape and size with his hands. 'Quite thin. Just the one.'

Jesús was silent for a moment and Hadley did not interrupt.

'I want you to separate that envelope from the rest of the papers and destroy it.'

'Destroy it?' Hadley was shocked by the request.

'That's right. I'll have to trust you, Hadley: don't open it.

Shred it, burn it, it's for the best. I've thought about it carefully. Please promise me that you'll do as I ask.'

'As you wish, Jesús.'

'It's more than a wish, Hadley. I want your word. Swear it.'

'I swear, Jesús: you have my word.'

'That's good. That's very good. It's been a good day, Hadley.'

The Aztec looked up to the stars and searched for Lucía but he could not find her. Maybe she was resting at long last.

'Goodnight, Hadley,' he said, with a melancholy smile. 'You and that girl take care, now.'

In the morning they were driven to N'djili airport. Jesús did not join them. He sent a message saying that he was suffering from a bad hangover and would remain in bed till lunch.

Massama explained that The Aztec had decided to stay in Kinshasa an extra night. He wanted to get drunk one more time with the last of his old friends before he returned to Havana.

1973

32

Chile's own version of a tragic 9/11 took place in 1973. In the early hours of the eleventh of September, the Chilean fleet – supposedly out on manoeuvres with those of neighbouring countries – appeared unexpectedly off Valparaíso.

Shortly after, several detachments of marines deployed throughout the city, occupying key positions and taking control of its transport, communication and broadcasting infrastructure.

As this was taking place, at around seven-thirty in the morning, Lucía Florin was driving along the coastal road towards Valparaíso for an early meeting with union leaders in the city's Portales district.

Once across Casino Bridge she saw a group of marines placing metal barricades across Avenida España ahead. She immediately switched on her car radio – combat uniforms in the city's streets could have only one implication – and Lucía's fears were instantly confirmed when, instead of the usual repartee of early-morning news and chatter, the sound of strident martial music filled the car.

'*Should it ever happen while you are in Viña,*' Florin had said, '*go home, close the door and stay there. If you are in Santiago, take María Luz and go to any friendly embassy. You are not just another Chilean. You are my wife. You are entitled to Mexican, Cuban or Soviet citizenship any time you want.*'

They had been speaking hypothetically. Lucía might have shrugged off the suggestion. *This is Chile*, she thought at the time, *we don't have revolutions*. But she was conscious of how much her husband had been through and she did not wish to invite controversy on that subject.

'I'll be fine,' she'd said, smiling. 'I'll look after us if you are not here.'

She brought her car to a halt fifty metres short of the barriers, turned round before any of the marines had time to react and headed back north towards Viña.

She only just made it. Five minutes after she entered the resort, barriers identical to those erected in Valparaíso sealed off Viña de Mar.

Lucía's mind raced as she turned along her clifftop bungalow's short driveway. Was this local or was it happening everywhere?

Eva Bamberg came round the house along the garden footpath, smiling inquisitively.

'What have you forgotten today?' she teased her daughter.

'Have you heard any news?'

'What news?' Eva saw Lucía's alarmed look and became concerned in turn. 'What's happening?'

'I don't know yet, Mum.' Lucía led the way towards the sea-facing porch. 'I think there might be some sort of military uprising.'

They stood in the living room, feeling the ocean breeze blowing gently through the open French windows, and searched the TV channels in vain for any sort of information. Nothing. Just the rousing sounds of a military band and the red, white and blue of a Chilean flag with its single white star, flying imperviously against a clear blue sky.

In her room next door, perhaps woken by the sound of drums and bugles, María Luz cried.

Lucía tried the telephone but the line was dead. Eva went into the child's bedroom and came out with her granddaughter in her arms.

'What do you think is happening?' Eva asked, gently rocking the child at the same time.

They did not have to wait long for an answer. At 07:30, as Lucía was setting off for Valparaíso, the army Commander-in-Chief had taken over the Peñaloén Communications Centre near Santiago and effectively had seized control of all broadcasting in Chile. At the same time, President Allende and most of his Cabinet, made aware of what was taking place in Valparaíso, arrived in ones and twos at the Moneda presidential palace.

At 08:45 General Pinochet informed the nation that the Allende regime had been given an ultimatum and that the armed forces were in control.

'We'll have to sit it out, mother.' Lucía took charge. She had a satellite phone in her cupboard. If necessary she would use it to call Jesús, but not yet. The news would be reaching Cuba too and events in Chile would be closely monitored.

Lucía felt heartbroken. She wanted to cry out for Chile, she wanted to shout that a dark CIA-sponsored future was not what Chile deserved. But at no time did she even remotely imagine that either she or any member of her family might be in danger. Had she considered that option she might have run, hidden, taken whatever measures she could to protect her daughter's life. But at that time, in the peaceful reassurance of a costal resort's spring, with the smell of fresh flowers mingling with sea salt in the breeze, Lucía Florin could not imagine that the very incarnation of unspeakable terror was about to descend upon her home.

In Santiago events were following a resolute course. At 09:55 tanks surrounded the Moneda Palace and opened fire.

At 10:15 Allende managed a broadcast through the only radio station still on air and out of rebel hands. He confirmed that an attempted *coup d'état* was afoot and vowed never to surrender the mandate given to him by the Chilean people. It was, as it turned out, a farewell address.

At 11:52 Air Force jets launched a rocket attack, setting the Moneda Palace on fire, shattering any doubts that the military meant business and that they were prepared to use their weaponry to whatever degree they deemed necessary to achieve their aim.

Across the square from the burning palace, tourists, visitors and journalists watched the surreal *mise en scène* from the windows and balconies of the luxurious Hotel Carrera.

At 14:38 the Moneda Palace was taken. Allende's body was found in his office, the top of his skull missing because in a last act of defiance he had fired his own AK-47 – the very same gun presented to him by Jesús Florin two years earlier – upwards through his chin.

At 15:00 a curfew was put in place throughout the nation and broadcasts by the new regime began.

'All traitors to the Motherland are to be denounced immediately . . . All office holders must report to the nearest police station as soon as the curfew is lifted in the morning . . .'

It had been planned for some time. The arrests began immediately. Over the next few days anyone associated with the Allende regime was rounded up and taken to Santiago football stadium before being transported to a place of interrogation, torture or execution.

For some – outspoken influential communists who actually had little useful inside knowledge – the bullet would be swift.

For those actively involved in the establishment of a socialist-communist society in Chile, death would be delayed until the torturers had managed to extract every piece of information that might lead to further arrests and a repetition of a cycle that would only end when no vestige of the Allende era remained. In those first few days over two thousand civilians died.

In Santiago, an Intelligence Service colonel had gone through some of the names on the 'most wanted' list. Special units would be out with orders to arrest them at any cost and prevent them from going into hiding.

'This one,' he explained to the eager young officer handing him a dossier, 'given time, could lead us to the entire Cuban network.'

'I can take her to Villa Grimaldi, sir . . .' the Captain volunteered.

'No, Ortiz. Unfortunately we don't have time. We can't hold this bitch. Someone would eventually find out and we could have a major problem on our hands. That's from the very top.'

'What are my orders, Colonel?'

'You have today: that's it. Do your best.' He said it in a way that left little doubt: results expected.

'Sir!'

'No witnesses and no trail, Ortiz. She's just another Chilean – and a filthy traitor at that – whatever the bastard she cohabits with might think.'

Lucía sat on her sofa and buried her face in her hands while her worried mother looked on.

'Do you think you'll have the leave the country?' Eva asked her daughter.

'Probably,' she replied sadly. 'I don't think Jesús will be allowed back in.'

'He is a diplomat . . .' Eva started to say.

'They won't let him in, mother.' Lucía was certain. 'I doubt Castro will allow him to leave Cuba in the first place. The embassy will be thinned down for sure, even closed.'

'Poor Allende,' said Eva. 'He only appointed Pinochet last month!'

'I know,' Lucía said but her mind was moving on. 'Office holders' must report . . .' She knew what that meant. All Allende's cadres: the organisers, the union people, the social reformers, the entire apparatus of socialist Chile were to deliver themselves to their new masters for immediate detention and goodness knew what else.

She thought of her office colleagues and started to reach for the telephone before stopping in her tracks as she remembered that the lines were cut.

There was a loud knock on the door that made both women jump. Lucía asked her mother to stay with the baby and went to open the front door.

'Mrs Florin?'

The man standing in front of her had the name Ortiz stencilled on his combat tunic and sported a Captain's pips on his epaulettes. Three helmeted young men, a corporal and two conscripts, stood haughtily behind him. They all carried side arms but no rifles. Army, she noted, not marines.

'Follow me,' the officer said, pushing past her. The three soldiers entered the house behind their young leader, almost driving Lucía along.

'What do you think you are doing?' she protested.

'Dealing with traitors and scum.' He turned and faced her, an embittered look on his face. 'Are you a traitor, Mrs Florin?'

'Certainly not!'

'What is happening, dear?' Eva came into the hallway, still holding little María Luz in her arms, and recoiled in shock when she saw the troops entering her daughter's house.

'Then you've nothing to worry about, have you, Mrs Florin?' The officer said it with an evil smirk.

'What do you want?' Lucía spoke firmly. As a lawyer she was used to dealing with uniformed officials impressed by their own authority.

'Where's your husband?' he demanded.

'None of your business,' she replied.

Ortiz slapped Lucía hard across the face and her mother let out a horrified scream. María Luz started to cry.

'Respect,' Ortiz explained viciously through clenched teeth, 'is what your kind is going to show in future. And the future,' he raised his voice, 'starts now!'

'My husband, Captain . . . Ortiz,' Lucía spoke slowly

but firmly as the left side of her face turned red, 'is a foreign diplomat. And even your superiors, whoever they might be, will appreciate the implications of your actions.'

'Your husband,' Ortiz said, 'is a foreign agitator given to acts of terrorism. He has long lost the rights and privileges accorded to real diplomats.'

He ordered both women to sit on the sofa and turned to his men.

'Search this house,' he commanded.

Lucía's head was throbbing from the slap. *María Luz! Dear Lord, how to get María Luz out of harm's way?*

'*It's best that you know nothing,*' Jesús had counselled his wife in the peace of their darkened bedroom on a cool Pacific night. *Then you'll have nothing to tell if you are asked.*'

Lucía knew that her husband was no ordinary diplomat. He worked in the Cuban Embassy's political section and ran a network of agents that covered the length of Chile from the Atacama Desert to Cape Horn.

'*You don't fight the CIA with niceties,*' he had replied when she'd pooh-poohed what she called his penchant for the political underworld.

'I want to speak to your commanding officer,' Lucía demanded. 'Take me to him now.'

'I will tear this house apart if necessary.' Ortiz ignored her request. 'I'll rip off partitions and pull up the floorboards.'

'There's nothing here,' Eva volunteered. She was on the verge of tears.

The men went about the house opening cupboards and drawers, emptying contents on the floor with little care or regard.

'Is your name Lucía Irene Bamberg de Florin del Valle?'

Ortiz started his aggressive questioning. He knew they always broke in the end.

'I prefer Lucía Florin.'

'I'm not interested in your preferences. Are you a member of the Communist Party of Chile?'

'I am.'

'Are you a member of Comintern?'

'I am, and well you know it!'

'Do you associate with the subversives Gladys Marin, Pablo Neruda and Victor Jara?'

'Ha!' Lucía let out a cry that was half despair and half laughter. 'I'm proud to know Congresswoman Marin, Ambassador Neruda and Maestro Jara.'

Lucía could hear the obscene sounds as the house got ripped apart. Wooden panels were taken down and floorboards lifted just as Ortiz had threatened. All papers found were brought into the living room and placed on the central coffee table: legal files, passports, deeds, domestic bills, but nothing of immediate interest to Ortiz.

He spent a few minutes reading the entries in an address book but promptly threw it onto the pile.

One of the soldiers came into the living room. He carried Florin's satellite telephone in his hands.

'What is this?' asked Ortiz

'A telephone! What else?'

Ortiz studied the unusual contraption. A handset sat on a large battery pack. A directional antenna could be extended and aimed at the skies. He drew out the aerial and turned the power on. They were all taken by surprise as the phone rang. Ortiz lifted the receiver and held it to his ear.

'Lucía? Can you hear me?' Florin's voice echoed from afar.

Ortiz said nothing.

'Lucía, my love, can you not hear me?'

Ortiz passed the receiver to her while holding the battery pack.

'Jesús? Hello?'

'Lucía! Are you all right?

'The army are here, Jesús, trampling all over our house!'

Ortiz tried to snatch the phone from Lucía but she ducked away.

'Their minions are openly ignoring your diplomatic status . . .' she shouted as Ortiz switched off the telephone's power.

'You are under arrest!' he fumed. 'Both of you,' he shouted as Lucía was about to say something to her mother. He turned to one of his men and barked an order to guard the women before marching out of the room and to his jeep where he made a call over the radio.

Twenty minutes later the dull *thud-thud* of a helicopter's main rotor could be heard in the distance. The noise got louder as it drew closer. The bungalow shook as the army Huey hovered over its roof before settling on the front garden between the house and the edge of the cliffs.

Both pilots remained on board as the party approached. Ortiz and the corporal led the women firmly by the arm. With her free arm, Lucía held María Luz tight against her breast. She saw the crew's green helmets and dark glasses through the aircraft's perspex canopy and thought they made them look even more menacing.

She just had to keep calm, she thought: this man was a junior officer, she would demand her rights under the Constitution – martial law or state of siege notwithstanding – and wait for Jesús's response. She was certain that at that very moment he would be on to the Cuban and Mexican ambassadors.

Ortiz pushed the women onto a rear facing bench seat. One of his men sat across from them while the corporal stood next to Ortiz by the open right door. The fourth man had been ordered to remain behind and guard the house.

The shuddering increased with the engine noise as they lifted off the Florin's garden, tilting away over the cliff and west towards the ocean.

'Where are you taking us?' Lucía demanded as the helicopter gained height and flew away from the coast. The men did not reply. A minute later Ortiz sat opposite her and leaned forward.

'What about your own organisation?' he asked her. He did not shout and she had to concentrate to hear his words over the aircraft's din.

'What about it?' Lucía could feel the fear rising in her and hoped that it did not show. This was a man younger than herself. An officer in her country's army.

It was getting colder in the cabin, the air blowing turbulently through the open right door. She instinctively hugged María Luz closer in an effort to keep her warm.

'What can you tell me about it?' Ortiz

'Can you close that door?' she demanded. 'My daughter is getting cold.'

'Didn't you hear me?' Ortiz raised his voice.

'I'll say nothing until we reach our destination!' Lucía hoped she sounded sufficiently assertive.

'Who says we are going anywhere?'

Lucía realised that her face must have betrayed the terror caused by Ortiz's words, for she saw his expression slowly change from real anger into a sadistic smile. She tried deep breathing to stave off panic.

'Take the child, corporal,' ordered Ortiz, still smiling.

'No!' Lucía and Eva screamed almost in unison. Lucía tightened her hold on María Luz, wrapping both her arms around the frightened child whose face was buried in her mother's chest. The helicopter shook briefly as it levelled off and flew through scattered clouds.

'Please, let me have the child.' The corporal stood in front of Lucía, holding out his hands.

Eva Bamberg looked at Ortiz in horror and started to cry. 'Leave the baby alone,' she pleaded between sobs.

Ortiz looked at her as if he had only just noticed her presence. He stood up, slowly but purposefully leaned across to where Lucía's mother was sitting and, grabbing her by the top of her hair, pulled her to her feet.

Eva cried out in pain and Lucía screamed at the top of her voice, echoed by a frightened María Luz. Undeterred, Ortiz transferred his left hand to the back of Eva's neck and, holding on to the overhead rail with his right hand, thrust his weight behind his left arm in one clean, arcing movement of his body that flung Eva Bamberg through the aircraft's open door and down towards the ocean.

'You,' he bellowed, pointing a finger at a stunned Lucía, Eva's sudden violent death seemingly not worth any comment, "are now going to tell me everything I want to hear or that little bastard of yours is next through the fucking door!"

Lucía was overtaken by total terror and jumped to her feet, no longer in control of her actions. The corporal tried to restrain her and managed to wrench María Luz away from her mother's arms, but Lucía still continued her charge and attacked Ortiz, clawing at his face with both her hands and causing him to lose his footing and stumble towards the void. He barely managed to grab hold of the web netting by the door long enough for the young conscript to pull him back to safety.

The helicopter's pilot, seeing what was taking place behind him, spoke briefly to his colleague and then banked the helicopter hard to the right to set course for home. Lucía came up hard against Ortiz again, punching and kicking blindly and at the same time pushing him towards the open door once more.

The private, coming to the aid of his superior, tried to pull Lucía away from him. But at that moment the aircraft tilted, making her lose her footing and fall backwards towards the ocean with a terrified pleading look on her face that would haunt the unfortunate soldier, whose call-up for National Service had come at a most unfortunate time, for the rest of his brief life.

For a moment no one said anything. The co-pilot looked back once and all he could see was Ortiz standing there with a bleeding face, an evidently shocked conscript and the corporal on the back seat with a child in his arms.

'Chuck the bastard out,' Ortiz finally ordered.

'I can't, sir,' replied the corporal.

'I'll do it, then!' Ortiz stood up and took a step towards the NCO.

'We have orders, sir!' the corporal reminded him, tightening his grip on María Luz, 'Very specific orders from headquarters, sir!'

Ortiz wavered.

The conscript's and the pilot's stares were fixed on him. He muttered under his breath, then slowly moved to the rear-facing bench and took a seat by the door.

1980

33

Luis Vilanova rose at half-past five, thirty minutes earlier than usual, after a sleepless night. He left the bedroom quietly and walked towards the kitchen of his large apartment. He switched on his wife's new Italian coffee-maker and stared at it absent-mindedly as it clicked and hissed. The morning papers had not yet arrived and there was little point in turning on the radio. The news would be censored, manufactured by the State of which he was a part.

For a brief moment he recalled that day so many years ago when he had first arrived at the Military College, a proud, enthusiastic eighteen-year-old realising a dream. He had wanted a Horse Grenadier's uniform since childhood when his parents had taken him to see the ninth of July parade. But it was not to be. Vilanova was a better administrator than he was a fighter. Quartermaster Division, they decided. Mundane jobs in regimental headquarters during democratic interludes, ministerial assignments each time a military regime stepped in. Over the years Vilanova built up a reputation. Reliable, dependable, his superiors said. So he made it to Staff College and rose to Colonel. But nothing prepared him for what was to come.

He took his coffee and walked silently on the polished parquet floor towards his study, overlooking Avenida del Libertador. It was still dark but he could discern the shapes of the tall trees across the road in Palermo Park. Early-morning traffic from the affluent northern suburbs traced their multicoloured lights along the wide boulevard seven floors below. Beyond the woods and lakes, by the River Plate, the sound of jet engines announced the first departures of the day from the Aeroparque.

The myth of a New Argentina was starting to crumble. The post-World Cup euphoria had receded into a nebulous past. The country was in a mess and getting worse. Even the Junta was in disarray and General Videla was sure to emerge as President.

But the regime that had been cheered by the nation when it deposed the Perón tart had lost its way. It had turned to oppressing its own people with unprecedented brutality. Vilanova knew what went on at a dozen torture and detention centres. Proclamations made by Buenos Aires's military governor verged on insanity: 'We'll kill the subversives,' he said, 'then their collaborators, then their sympathisers, followed by the indifferent and finally those too timid to speak up!'

Word within the army was that the toll surpassed 20,000. The way they said it sounded more like a boast than an apology.

Perhaps, thought Vilanova, he should be thankful he had never been accepted by the Grenadiers: he might have been ordered to become a murderer. Instead, he'd been ordered to become a thief – and a very good thief, as it turned out.

Luis Vilanova had an office at the Ministry of Public Works and another at the Banco de la Nación. He processed dirty money for the generals and their friends and inevitably became a wealthy man himself.

The flat on Avenida del Libertador – Susana's ultimate dream, the symbol of having arrived – cost twenty times a colonel's annual salary. He'd paid for it in cash. No one had dared ask questions and as long as the Junta ruled no one ever would.

At first it had been the usual, just plain bribery. With all ministries effectively run by the military, nothing could happen without the Junta's approval. No public works, no planning consents. No wage settlements, mineral concessions, transport licences and, even worse, no payments for work already carried out.

The wheels of commerce needed oiling if existing contracts from the Perón era were to be honoured and avoid being investigated ad nauseam as suspect transactions from a discredited deposed regime – which they almost certainly would have been.

And the only acceptable lubricant was cash.

Then the greed escalated. The military themselves wanted their toys and the purchases would run into billions. Planes from the US and France, warships from Britain, anti-aircraft batteries from Switzerland. Guns, ammunition and bombs from wherever they were to be found. As each general or admiral established his links with foreign vendors and arms dealers they laid the foundation for their own personal enterprise. On payday, Luis Vilanova took care that everyone involved got his share.

The choice of materiel was less dependent on its suitability than on the hierarchical position of the sponsoring staff officer and his closeness to the Junta. Incompatible equipment was bought, overpaid for and thereafter left to one side to languish, temporarily forgotten or handed down to minions once the primary objective of earning 'commissions' had been achieved.

Vilanova made the remittances. To bank accounts in Uruguay for the smaller payments, to Miami and Toronto as they got bigger, Cayman and Geneva for the larger sums. By the end of 1980 money was haemorrhaging out of control, the goods and the thievery financed by foreign loans supported by government guarantees.

'Armed Forces Account' became a common designation at the Banco de la Nación, both in Argentina and abroad. By the time the eventual bill was rendered to the nation, the thieves would be long gone.

Vilanova was well rewarded for his efforts and a percentage from each deal was invariably set aside for him. But small commissions, when they emanated from so many sources, soon mounted up and, his wife's needs notwithstanding, Luis Vilanova quietly invested the bulk of his earnings far away and above board to lay a solid foundation for his future. To see Vilanova's real wealth you would have had to look in Spain.

He had seen the Argentine economic cycle before. Rags to riches and back to rags again. Last time round, in the 1960s, his father had been ruined. This time Vilanova planned to get out while things were on a high. He had a meticulous plan in place and ticked off each step along the line with precision becoming a top administrator.

He had a trump card in his pocket too. Luis's parents

had been born in Spain and though they had emigrated to Argentina they had still retained dual nationality. Though Argentine-born, Luis Vilanova was entitled to Spanish citizenship and, by extension, so were his wife and child. He felt that Argentina had cheated his family, robbed them of their dreams. Now he was about to cheat her back.

His parents had already gone ahead. With access to Luis's funds they had started buying orange groves in their native Valencia, carefully following their son's instructions. They were developing a brand and soon they might add their own transport. By the time Luis and his family got to Spain the Vilanova family would be well established in the very place they stemmed from.

Leaving the army at this juncture, however, was no easy feat. A serving officer – especially one in possession of so much sensitive knowledge – could not simply walk away. Quitting in the midst of a bloody war against subversion would be suspect at the very least. When coupled with Vilanova's crucial role in administering the generals' finances, resigning his commission would have been nigh on impossible.

On the personal front he had to consider Susana's wishes. She was Argentine through and through. Living *abroad* would be anathema to her. She would never leave her country, her friends or her showcase flat on Avenida del Libertador.

So Luis addressed both issues with one masterstroke. For months he complained about feeling tired. He made an effort to be late for work with alarming regularity, twice feigning illness and leaving early when staff officers were about.

On Friday next he had an appointment with a senior

medical examiner at the Hospital Militar. A serious heart problem would be diagnosed and confirmed by a cardiologist. Luis Vilanova would request and undoubtedly be granted early retirement. He'd be awarded a full pension. He would make an orderly handover to his successor and then, accompanied by his family, he would go on an open-ended visit to his parents in Valencia.

The apartment, he would promise his wife, would be neither let nor sold. It was their home and would be there, just as they would leave it, awaiting their return.

The doctors had agreed to share a hundred thousand dollars for their troubles. Luis regarded it as a cheap price. He might have paid considerably more had he known that General Videla would last less than a year, be succeeded briefly by General Viola and he in turn by General Galtieri who would come into office with ideas of his own about the right way to solve Argentina's political and economic problems. And in the process would return the nation to rags.

Luis Vilanova would never again set foot in Argentina. Susana would return for an occasional visit, but not for another fifteen years.

2004

34

As July loomed closer, Mercedes went around the flat packing up for the summer recess. Her own time at the University was at an end. She felt no sense of urgency in deciding what to do next.

She was still shaken by Rosa Uribe's death though she could not understand how someone she had known so briefly could have made such a profound impression on her.

Rosa's funeral had taken place at *La Almudena*, the cathedral of Santa María la Reál, close to the Royal Palace and not five hundred metres from the eastern boundaries of the Casa de Campo.

Between the cathedral and the former royal hunting ground, the Manzanares flowed unimpeded as the last remaining ice and snow melted down from the Guadarrama.

Inside the church, *Todo Madrid*, as Ramiro de la Serna would have put it, listened with moist eyes while Cardinal Paredes de Orfila delivered his eulogy.

'This was a child,' he told the congregation, 'whom I held in my arms at the baptismal font, in the crypt of this very church.'

The Prince and Princess of Asturias sat on the front row, next to Máximo Uribe and Rosa's distraught parents. Aunts and cousins, including Ramiro, sat behind them. Across the aisle, sporting suitably pained expressions, Spain's Foreign Minister was flanked by the Trade Minister and the Prime Minister's representative.

Victoria Pinto, next to her husband, was still shocked by the death of her dentist's wife and was somewhat baffled by the high-profile attendance. But she had been unable to extract from her unhelpful husband any inside information worth whispering to her friends.

'I'm married to the best-informed man in Spain,' she would often lament, 'yet I'm always the last to learn anything worth knowing.'

Max Uribe acknowledged Victoria's pained expression with an understanding smile and glared briefly at Pinto who could do nothing but avert his eyes.

'We gather here today,' the Cardinal continued, 'to bid a dear friend goodbye, to rejoice in the life of a dedicated servant of her King and Country, a very special woman who overcame personal pain and life's adversity without ever losing faith, a true Christian who always had time for the less fortunate.

'Today we all share with Máximo' – he looked kindly in the widower's direction as others craned their necks for a better view – 'the profound and palpable loss that leaves an unfillable void in the lives of those fortunate enough to have known Rosa.'

Hadley and Mercedes held hands four rows behind and

wondered how Pinto could have the nerve to be here at all. But in Pinto's world appearances were crucial and an absence could be easily misconstrued as an admission of guilt.

There was whispered speculation about Rosa's involvement with the government and Mercedes remembered that even as life slowly ebbed away from her she had whispered in despair, 'Fetch Pinto.'

Jack's children were due to spend a month in Spain with their dad. Both he and Mercedes were looking forward to having them along but had braced themselves for the inevitable judgement that their young minds would pass on a potential step-mum.

Remaining in Salamanca for the boys' visit had been dismissed as an option from the outset. A one-bedroom city-centre flat would not accommodate four people. Besides, grand old buildings and ancient monuments were not a child's idea of summer bliss.

Mercedes's parents had suggested that they should come to Xátiva. There was plenty of room in the house and the Vilanovas openly relished the prospect of seeing young smiling faces in Sant Feliu again.

For this first visit, however, Jack wanted time alone with Mercedes and his children so Susana Vilanova had obligingly found a house with a garden and a swimming pool that they could rent for the entire month. It was only forty minutes away, close to Grau beach near Gandía. From there they could visit the Vilanovas as often as they wished and Luis was looking forward to introducing the boys to the Argentine art of barbecuing while Mercedes in turn hoped to teach them how to ride.

Since the Porsche could barely accommodate Mercedes's

own clothing – which had actually increased in quantity during her time at Fonseca – she was packing all they would need for the summer and shipping it off to Sant Feliu.

She and Jack had also agreed to hire what he called a 'proper car with four seats' for the duration of the children's stay. Meanwhile, Mercedes would drive the Porsche to Valencia, passing through Madrid along the way to drop Jack at Barajas.

At long last Hadley had found time to go to Luxembourg, collect the mysterious last instalment of The Aztec's notes and, as the man himself had told him, 'write the final chapter'.

Because of flight schedules, he would not be able to make the trip in one day. Instead he planned to arrive in Luxembourg in the evening, do his banking the following morning and then catch a flight to Barcelona for the quick connection to Valencia.

The city of Luxembourg is home to just eighty thousand people – and one hundred and fifty banks. To a casual observer watching Hadley pay his taxi and walk up to the dark oak doors, Duhau & Cie.'s austere grey-stone frontage on Rue de Capucins would not have looked like that of a bank at all.

A small brass plate to the left of the doors, engraved with the firm's name but without stating the nature of its business, was the only adornment on that side, below a neat brass-encased doorbell. A similar plate to the right merely recorded the house number. Hadley wondered if he had come to the right place and double-checked the address.

He raised his left hand to the bell but before he could

press it a uniformed porter opened the door as if on cue and greeted him with a smile. Once inside, a young man in an immaculately cut suit welcomed Hadley to the bank in perfect, barely accented English.

Hadley admired the lobby's understated elegance and wondered how the man had guessed the appropriate language.

'I would like to access my safe deposit box,' he explained, trying to sound as if he did this every day. He removed a small card with a twelve-digit number from his wallet. His greeter nodded approvingly and guided him to a chair on one side of a Sheraton partners' desk.

'If I may?' he asked solicitously, extending his hand.

Hadley handed him the card as the man sat opposite him, opened a navy-leather box file and took out a blank form. He wrote the date and time on it and copied Hadley's numbers before passing it across the desk for him to sign.

Formalities completed, the banker rose to his feet and invited Hadley to follow him down a corridor before ushering him into a softly lit elevator. Once the door was shut the only evidence of motion came from the changing electronic display above it. When the amber numeral froze on minus three, the door slid open as silently as it had closed.

Though this was Hadley's first foray into the subterranean realm of banking he had seen enough films to realise that he was inside a vault. The plain grey walls and diffuse lighting bore no resemblance to the lobby's warmth, and the thick steel door that led into the austere anteroom would undoubtedly be locked shut at the end of each business day, turning this repository into an impregnable Aladdin's cave.

'And your key, if I may, sir?'

Hadley gave him the small key with its complex cuneiform stem. As the banker checked the number engraved into the key, Hadley realised that no names had been requested or proffered.

The banker's smile seemed to indicate to Hadley that everything was in order and his guide opened another door, this one marked simply 1015-1085. It led into a smaller room whose walls were covered in their entirety by unadorned, numbered steel doors of varying shapes and sizes. In the middle of the room stood a sterile, rectangular, grey metal table with one chair pushed up against each long side.

The young man inserted Hadley's key into box 1061, followed by his own key into a second slot alongside. He turned both keys and cracked open the door, wide enough to establish that the keys had worked but without quite exposing whatever was stored inside.

'If you press this bell when you are ready to leave, sir,' he told Hadley, 'I'll be close by.'

Hadley peered into the eye-level safe deposit box. There were three bags inside: two large identical black-leather upright cases of the top-opening variety and a slim folding briefcase, also in black leather.

Hadley removed the briefcase and placed it on the table before turning his attention to one of the larger cases. At first he tried to slide it out of the safe but the bag refused to budge. It felt as if it was bolted to the locker's floor and Hadley looked for some form of attachment to release.

When he could find none he tried to move the case again and realised it was much heavier than he had expected. He tried to move the second case but the result was the same.

Thrusting both arms into the safe to clasp one case, Hadley gripped its far end with both hands and pulled it out slowly. It was very heavy indeed and Hadley struggled to hold it in a bear hug and carry it to the table.

After pausing briefly for breath, he released both catches and opened the top flaps. He could hardly believe what he was seeing: the bag appeared to be filled entirely with gold coins. Hadley thrust a hand inside it and scooped up a handful of sovereigns: Queen Victorias and Edward VIIs, all in mint condition.

Hadley tried dipping his arm into the case: the bag appeared to be filled with coins as deep as his hand would go. He could only guess their number but it had to be in the thousands, he was sure. He closed the case and repeated the exercise with its twin. The contents were identical. Jack pulled up one of the chairs and sat down trying to recover from the shock.

After a few minutes he unzipped the smaller briefcase – the zipper went round three of its four sides – and laid it open on the table. He had expected to find the last instalment of The Aztec's notes. Instead it contained a collection of photographs and official-looking papers.

The first bundle of photos, wrapped in brown paper and tied neatly with yellow string, was made up of black-and-white photographs and fading sepia prints. Some showed men in uniform looking solemnly into the camera, others smiling groups of men and women in relaxed poses and apparently content. Slowly Hadley realised he was looking at Natalia Florin, her two young boys and the extended Radischev family during The Aztec's Moscow days.

The second item, a translucent paper envelope, contained

a dozen colour photographs. Every shot was of a strikingly attractive blonde woman and a small baby. Many showed the sea as the backdrop and a small garden with a white palisade at the end. *Chile*, thought Hadley. *Lucía and María Luz*.

There was also a sealed brown quarto envelope in this briefcase.

'I'll have to trust you Hadley: don't open it. Shred it, burn it, it's for the best. I thought about it carefully. Please promise me you'll do as I ask.'

'As you wish, Jesús.'

There were other papers, too. Florin's Mexican birth certificate and documents in Russian lettering that Hadley could not read let alone understand.

There was a bill of sale for the *Granma* motor yacht, dated 1956 in Veracruz and a 1939 receipt signed by the President of the Spanish Republic's government-in-Exile for a large quantity of gold.

It was pretty obvious to Hadley that he was in no position to remove the bags there and then. He certainly could not carry them without help and even then he would need to hire a car and drive all the way to Spain. Besides, Jesús had said nothing about wanting this gold in Spain.

Hadley closed both bags and was in the process of returning them to the safe when he had second thoughts. He reopened one of the cases and transferred a fistful of gold sovereigns into the smaller briefcase. With both large cases back in the safe he pressed the button that summoned the banker.

'How long have I got left on the safe's rental contract?' Hadley asked as the elevator stealthily went up.

'Until the thirty-first of December 2006, sir,' came the

immediate reply. Clearly the account's status had been checked before access had been granted. He thanked the banker for his service and told him he would be back again soon.

Hadley walked some fifty metres along Rue des Capucins, trying to fathom the significance of what he had found before he thought of hailing a taxi to take him back to his hotel. He had already checked out of his room but had left his suitcase in reception. He still had three hours to kill before his flight departed for Barcelona. He dialled Florin's number but there was no answer.

Hadley had no idea what a sovereign was worth. A hundred euros? What was he supposed to do with all those coins? Keep them? Were there strings attached? Another hideous mission? Didn't The Aztec understand? Hadley was done with soldiering a long time ago. He'd had enough of pointless fighting and wars. For all that had taken place over the last few months, Hadley had as little sympathy for Florin's popular crusades as he did for Pinto's machinations.

And what was he to do with the family photo album? It would certainly add value to his book. The photos were probably worth a great deal in their own right, as would be the foreign language documents once they were translated.

Then there was the brown envelope that he had promised to destroy. It was tempting not to, but he had given his word and the old man had looked visibly happier. Had he not trusted Hadley to do exactly as he promised, Florin could easily have withheld the key to the safe and left it at that. He would shred the envelope as promised, Hadley decided, and felt better for it.

Close to midday he gathered his overnight bag and took

a taxi to Luxembourg airport. As he passed the news-stand, Hadley bought a copy of the *Financial Times*. It was the previous day's edition, but it would do for the purpose. Later as they cruised towards Barcelona, he opened the paper and found what he wanted: the current London price for modern sovereigns was £69 per coin.

It was difficult to estimate how many coins were in each suitcase. He looked at one of the sample coins and tried to guess its size. 20mm in diameter? 2mm thick? He had no pocket calculator so he passed the time trying out some old-fashioned arithmetic. How big were the bags? He played with figures but was unable to believe the results. No wonder he could hardly lift the bags. Even a conservative estimate, allowing for the coins being loosely packed, made it close to a million euros' worth in each bag.

It was a huge amount and Hadley still couldn't fathom why he'd been given access to it. He remembered Florin's initial message to Pinto: *we'll share the remains between Spain and Cuba*.

Was this meant to be Pinto's half?

There was not even a note from Florin to explain anything. He would try calling him again from Barcelona.

Hadley disembarked and made his way from Terminal B to Terminal C from where the Air Nostrum shuttle would depart in forty minutes. On his way he redialled Florin's number but once again there was no reply not even an invitation to leave a recorded message.

He was replacing his phone in his pocket when a newspaper headline caught his eye. A man was holding an open copy of *La Vanguardia* in front of him and Hadley was able to read bold writing on its front page:

MUERE EN CUBA JESUS FLORIN

He froze and stared at the paper in disbelief. The reader noticed Hadley's stare and turned the paper (he had been looking at the sports pages) to glance at the front page himself.

'Jesús Florin is dead?' Hadley asked the stranger, stating the obvious.

The man nodded, as if surprised that anyone should be so concerned. He had heard of Florin — most people had — but only in connection with events from long ago. The man had assumed that The Aztec was already dead.

'Where did you get . . . ?' Hadley started to ask and the man nodded at the shop behind him.

Hadley bought a copy of *El País* and tried to read the leading article as he continued on his way to Terminal C.

FALLECE JESUS FLORIN
De nuestro corresponsal, La Habana, Jueves 3

Hadley found it hard to focus on the details as his own thoughts raced ahead.

Jesús Florin dies peacefully in his sleep . . . natural causes . . . aged 88 . . . two wives and three children predeceased him . . . soldier, statesman, philosopher, revolutionary . . .

According to his wishes, he will be cremated today at a private ceremony in Havana and his ashes scattered over the Gulf of Mexico.
Obituaries, p. 38

Hadley slowly regained his composure and managed to get down a drink shortly after take-off. He read the full obituary and realised that so much was missing. Nor had the writer had the knowledge to update recent events. Perhaps that was what Florin had meant by the final chapter.

'*You write it, Hadley, you know as much as I do.*'

Hadley looked out through the large window. It was a crystal-clear day and in the distance he could see the outline of the Balearic Islands, Mallorca with its high Tramontana range, Minorca and Ibiza on either side. Then he remembered the brown envelope.

Did his promise still hold true now that Florin was dead? Could Hadley, the historian, destroy a document that might have bearing on the truth?

'*It's for the best,*' Florin had said.

But The Aztec was gone. And the truth about The Aztec's life had been entrusted to Jack Hadley.

There was little doubt in his mind as he stood up and retrieved the little briefcase from the overhead compartment. If the contents were personal and with no historical value, he would destroy them as Jesús had asked. But if they impinged significantly on the completeness of The Aztec's biography, Hadley would be forced to take a view.

He peeled open the envelope's flap carefully and pulled out the contents.

There were two birth certificates stapled together. Both attested to the birth of a white female weighing 3.75 kilos at 11.25 pm on 20 June 1972.

The first document named the child as María Luz Florin del Valle, born at the Hospital Alemán in Valparaíso, Chile.

The second recorded the birth of Mercedes Susana Vilanova at the Hospital Militar in Buenos Aires, Argentina.

Hadley was stunned. The gold and its meaning suddenly paled into insignificance. *Oh, Jesús Florin!* Hadley cried out silently, *how can you place this burden on my shoulders? I'll be in Valencia in fifteen minutes. She'll greet me at the airport with that smile. Do I take this to my grave? How do I tell Mercedes that the people she believes to be her parents got her through the 1970s military trade in stolen babies? How can I ever tell her who her parents really were?*

'Don't open it. Shred it, burn it, it's for the best.'

Dear God. Hadley wished now that he had done as he'd been asked. He had seen her happy, he had chosen to be denied. Had he forgiven Vilanova. It had been The Aztec's ultimate act of love.

'*What now, silly boy?* Hadley could almost hear Jesús asking at his mischievous best.

At CNI headquarters Pinto looked at the unopened package on his desk. It was a small padded bag marked for his personal attention. It had been scanned and sniffed and pronounced safe by Security downstairs. He had been too absorbed by pressing matters earlier on but now, finding a moment's respite, he turned his attention to it and cut it open.

Four coins tipped out onto the desk with an alluring gleam and rattle and Pinto looked at them with growing interest. He looked inside the envelope and pulled out a folded sheet of paper. It was handwritten and read simply 'Your share'. It was signed 'JF'.

Pinto shook with excitement as he slid the coins into a neat line with his index finger: a 1933 American Double Eagle, a 1755 Russian twenty-rouble piece, a 1343 Edward III Double Florin and a 1907 twenty-dollar Liberty Ultra-High Relief.

Pinto did not have to look them up. He knew that he was staring at over ten million dollars. He replaced the coins in their envelope, put the envelope in his pocket, pushed his chair away from his desk and smiled the most earnest of all smiles.

EPILOGUE

(From *EL* País, Madrid, Friday 4 June 2004, page 38)

OBITUARIES

JESUS FLORIN 'THE AZTEC': 1916–2004

Soldier, revolutionary, committed socialist crusader
whose personal life was marred by tragedy.

Jesús Florin, better known as The Aztec, passed away in
his sleep at his home close to Havana on Wednesday night.

Jesús María Florin del Valle was born in Veracruz,
Mexico, on 12 March 1916. He was educated at Jesuit
schools in his state capital and later in Madrid, before
entering the University of Salamanca to read Humanities
in the autumn of 1934.

As the only child of landowner and political grandee

Emilio Florin del Valle and Doña Isabel de Guzmán y Sotomayor, Jesús might have been expected to return to Mexico after graduation and follow in his father's footsteps.

Instead, with the outbreak of the Civil War in July 1936, he travelled to La Mancha where he joined the newly formed International Brigades at Albacete and was commissioned into XI Brigade under its experienced Romanian commander Emilio Kléber.

XI Brigade, together with the Hungarian Lukács's XII, was deployed to the Casa de Campo on the western edge of Madrid and tasked with halting the Nationalist advance. On 29 October, Florin led the infantry counter-attack behind Pavel Arman's Red Army tanks. During the brutal Nationalist offensive that followed, his unit was sent to reinforce Mercer's Brigade and engaged in house-to-house fighting around the university area. Florin was later cited for his bravery and promoted to Captain. During this brief campaign at the Madrid front he met the Russian General Anatoly Radischev for the first time as well as Antonio Mercer, the man who would become his lifelong friend and mentor.

Removed from Madrid as the Legion pulled back, Florin was attached to Mercer's staff and spent time abroad, possibly in Moscow.

Back in Spain in February 1937, he rejoined the Mercer Division, fought in the battles of Brunete, Teruel and Ebro where he was wounded in action and was twice decorated, attaining the rank of Major. With the Republic's defeat in 1939 he made his way over the Pyrenees into France before moving to Russia.

In 1940, Florin joined the Red Army's 13th Guards and

was posted to the Western Front under General Radischev. When the latter was tasked by Stalin with the defence of Stalingrad, Florin joined his staff and fought with courage, determination and ferocity for the entire duration of the siege. His qualities were noted by the then political commissar Nikita Khrushchev and in March 1943, by then a Colonel, Florin stood alongside Radischev in Red Square when the latter was proclaimed a Hero of the Soviet Union.

In 1945 Jesús Florin married Natalia Radischeva, his commanding officer's niece, before returning to the Western Front until the end of the war. Back in Moscow he joined the newly created intelligence directorate working under Beria – who in 1954 would establish the KGB.

In 1947 Jesús's first son, Leonid, was born, followed by Yuri in 1949, but in 1952, caught up in a wave of paranoid Stalin purges, Florin and his family were exiled to Siberia and condemned to a slow death in the gulag. Stalin's death in 1953 came too late for Natalia who succumbed to pneumonia only days before Generals Mercer and Radischev approached Stalin's successor, Khrushchev, and secured their mutual friend's pardon and political reinstatement.

In 1954 Florin and his sons moved to Mexico City and for the next two years he focused his energies on bringing up the boys. Awarded an honorary degree, he was appointed Adjunct Professor of Political Science at Mexico's Autonomous University where he wrote many papers on Latin American issues and social injustice. It was during this period that he first came into contact with Cuban exiles.

His high profile attracted a new breed of Latin American middle-class socialists, including Ernesto 'Ché' Guevara,

Camilo Cienfuegos and Raúl Castro, who looked upon the hero of Madrid and Stalingrad with respect verging on awe.

In November 1956 the motor yacht *Granma* sailed from Veracruz to Cuba. It carried eighty-three Cuban exiles with Fidel Castro in command. There were only five foreigners on board: Guevara, Done, Guillén, Mejía and Florin. They took to the Sierra Maestra and waged guerrilla warfare for two years until the Batista government was brought down.

Over the next five years, following Fidel Castro's triumphal entrance into Havana on New Year's Day 1959, Florin worked on political ideology, but by 1964 the soldier in him cried out for action and he joined Ché Guevara in the fight for Congo-Kinshasa.

In 1965 Florin faced personal tragedy again as his younger boy, Yuri, barely nineteen, was killed in a CIA-sponsored operation in Bolivia successfully aimed at taking out Guevara. More tragedy was to come the following year when his elder son, Leonid, died in battle during an MPLA operation in Angola.

Little more was known or heard of Florin's life until 1970 when he was seen standing behind Salvador Allende on the balcony of the Moneda Palace, following the latter's democratic election to the presidency of Chile.

In 1971 Florin, then aged 55, married Lucía Bamberg, twenty-three years his junior, a lawyer, member of the Chilean Communist Party and advocate for the poorer rural communities. In 1972 Lucía gave birth to their daughter María Luz and the family moved to the outskirts of Viña del Mar for what was, forebodingly perhaps, the happiest year in Florin's life.

But the political situation in Chile, undermined by catastrophic economic failures and foreign intervention, became unstable and by 1973 virtually untenable. Seeking a solution, Florin flew to Cuba for a secret summit briefing with Cuban and Soviet leaders and during his absence, on 11 September, General Augusto Pinochet launched a bloody *coup d'état*.

Barred from returning to Chile by Castro himself, Florin watched impotently from a distance as left-wingers were rounded up and herded into jails, army barracks and football grounds. Thousands died in the first few days. It is believed that Lucía Florin and her daughter perished during the purges that followed. Their bodies were never found, though this was not unusual during the tragic decade of South America's *desaparecidos*.

In the late 1970s and throughout the 1980s, Florin travelled extensively in Africa, often visiting Angola and Mozambique, as well as Russia, dealing with political issues and, some believe, acting as treasurer for various left-wing liberation movements. But following the break-up of the Soviet Union he never left Cuba again.

His last years were spent quietly and modestly in his secluded bungalow near Havana where he is believed to have written his (thus far unpublished) memoirs. From time to time he played host to world luminaries such as Isabel Allende, Mikhail Gorbachev and Nelson Mandela.

Jesús Florin was a citizen of Mexico, Cuba and the Soviet Union. In 1988 Prime Minister Felipe Gonzáles offered him Spanish citizenship in recognition for his past services to our nation but Florin famously declined, saying that 'a man's heart can only be cut into so many pieces'.

He leaves no close family behind.

ACKNOWLEDGEMENTS

Many people have assisted me in making *The Aztec* possible. Robert Lambolle read my draft synopsis and made a number of constructive suggestions. At Random House, Alban Miles encouraged me to write it and Jason Arthur agreed to publish it before seeing the completed manuscript. Laurie Ip Fung Chun was a brilliantly perceptive editor and my friends Peter Guise and Lizzie Smith read and corrected as I wrote, as did my wife Vivienne late into the night.

The history of the Spanish Civil War has always fascinated me and Anthony Beevor's *The Battle for Spain* remains, to my mind, the definitive chronicle of the conflict. His account of the Spanish gold reserves' removal to Moscow gave me an idea. The rest – the errors, speculations or downright fantasies as told in *The Aztec*, are mine and mine alone.

ALSO AVAILABLE IN ARROW

The Clayton Account

Bill Vidal

Thomas Clayton is a City trader working the markets in London's Square Mile and living, financially, on borrowed time. But when he returns home to New York for his father's funeral to discover he has been left nearly $50 million in a numbered Swiss bank account, he's at a complete loss to explain how his professor father could have come by such a sum. Whatever the explanation, the mysterious windfall has come at exactly the right time.

So he travels to Zurich, secures the funds, and tells his wife to make an offer on her dream country mansion. What Tom doesn't know yet is that his father was being used as a 'ghost' to clean up dirty money by a New York laundry operation: really the money belongs to Carlos Morales, Medellín's biggest cocaine baron.

Tom's actions in Europe spark a murderous turf war in the Americas between the cartels of Medellín and Cali, involving a cast of bent lawyers, cops, undercover DEA – and transatlantic assassins who'll stop at nothing or no one to make Tom pay his debt . . .

arrow books

THE POWER OF READING

Visit the Random House website and get connected with
information on all our books and authors

EXTRACTS from our recently
published books and selected
backlis

COMPE
DRAWS
audiob

AUTHO
of our authors are on tour and
where you can meet them

LATEST NEWS on bestsellers,
awards and new publications

MINISITES with exclusive
special features dedicated to our
authors and their titles

READING GROUPS Reading
guides, special features and all

WATCH video clips of
interviews and readings with
our authors

RANDOM HOUSE INFORMATION
including advice for writers,
job vacancies and all your
general queries answered

Come home to Random House
www.rbooks.co.uk